A MURDER TO DIE FOR

STEVYN COLGAN

Unbound

This edition first published in 2018

Unbound
6th Floor Mutual House, 70 Conduit Street, London W1S 2GF

www.unbound.com

Text Design by Ellipsis, Glasgow

A CIP record for this book is available from the British Library

ISBN 978-1-78352-438-9 (trade pbk)
ISBN 978-1-78352-439-6 (ebook)
ISBN 978-1-78352-437-2 (limited edition)

Printed in Great Britain by Clays Ltd, St Ives Plc

1 3 5 7 9 8 6 4 2

For Michael 'Myghal' Colgan (1940–1991)
and the novels he never got to write.

Dear Reader,

The book you are holding came about in a rather different way to most others. It was funded directly by readers through a new website: Unbound. Unbound is the creation of three writers. We started the company because we believed there had to be a better deal for both writers and readers. On the Unbound website, authors share the ideas for the books they want to write directly with readers. If enough of you support the book by pledging for it in advance, we produce a beautifully bound special subscribers' edition and distribute a regular edition and ebook wherever books are sold, in shops and online.

This new way of publishing is actually a very old idea (Samuel Johnson funded his dictionary this way). We're just using the internet to build each writer a network of patrons. At the back of this book, you'll find the names of all the people who made it happen.

Publishing in this way means readers are no longer just passive consumers of the books they buy, and authors are free to write the books they really want. They get a much fairer return too – half the profits their books generate, rather than a tiny percentage of the cover price.

If you're not yet a subscriber, we hope that you'll want to join our publishing revolution and have your name listed in one of our books in the future. To get you started, here is a £5 discount on your first pledge. Just visit unbound.com, make your pledge and type **murder5** in the promo code box when you check out.

Thank you for your support,

Dan, Justin and John
Founders, Unbound

Agnes Crabbe – The Mysterious Mistress of Murder Mystery

By Colin Tossel, President, Nasely Historical Society
(Reproduced with kind permission from the Agnes Crabbe
Murder-Mystery Festival brochure 2014)

The fertile lowlands of South Herewardshire have, since Saxon times, provided generations of farmers with the finest dairy and beef herds and the plumpest of pigs. It is where the deliciously unique Herewardshire Hog, famed throughout the colonies for its rich, fatty bacon, was bred. And it is why the county became known during Regency times as 'the meat locker of England' and the heart-attack capital of the Empire. But while blessed with silty chocolate-coloured soil, lush green fields and clean, fresh streams, the county had little else of value to exploit; no coal or salt or metals to mine, no coastline to fish, no stone to quarry, and, with almost everyone in some way involved with the lucrative business of turning pasture into meat, there was little room for genius to flourish.

As the county's coffers swelled, a contented indolence settled over the uncommonly productive farms and villages. South Herewardshire became synonymous with unimaginative, gouty businessmen and solid, dependable workers who didn't seek to rise above their station because they enjoyed far better pay and conditions than their contemporaries elsewhere. The county produced no Brunels, no Austens, no Turners, no Wordsworths. The storytellers had no brave or bawdy tales to tell. The balladeers had no folk heroes, no rogues or wild rovers to sing about, and the county's most popular folk song – 'Go to Hell!' – describes the death by diet-induced stroke of a gluttonous murderer. South Herewardshire would have to wait until the end of the nineteenth century before anyone that could be regarded as historically significant appeared, and, even then, Agnes Crabbe would not achieve that fame until she had been dead for more than half a century.

Agnes Emily Gertrude Brock, the second and youngest child of a family of farmers from Nasely, came quietly and uneventfully into the world on 8 May 1895. She grew into a plain, shy girl with a penchant for daydreaming and, although she worked diligently, if unexceptionally, at school, she failed to display any notable talent or aptitude for any particular subject. At the age of eighteen, she seemed quietly content to be married off to a neighbouring pig-farmer called Daniel Crabbe, and everyone assumed that this unprepossessing young woman would live out the rest of her life as a respectable, hard-working, but otherwise unremarkable housewife and mother.

But war was about to change everything. Daniel was one of the first to sign up when the recruiters arrived in the village and, as was the fashion, so did most of his friends and family. However, just eleven months after taking the King's shilling, Daniel lay dead in Flanders' fields, along with Agnes's father and older brother, and most of the men from her village. The news brought great sorrow to Nasely and Agnes withdrew from village life, hiding herself away inside the little cottage that she had shared, for such a tragically short time, with her young husband. Meanwhile, her grief-stricken mother, robbed of both husband and son, took to her bed and refused all food and drink, and met her maker not long after.

As the months passed by, rumour and speculation began to grow. The fires of gossip were fuelled by the fact that Agnes never left her house, having almost everything delivered to her. The only person she ever admitted inside was her older brother's fiancée, Iris Gobbelin, another tragic young woman who had lost her lover to the Great War.

For the next two decades, Agnes's only contact with the outside world was through Iris. But Iris would never speak of her reclusive friend, which led to a proliferation of lurid tales about what went on inside the Crabbes' cottage.

Agnes's last link with the outside world was severed in 1936 when Iris was killed falling from a horse and, almost immediately, the rumours got sillier and the tall stories got taller. It was said that she lived in one room, surrounded by the debris of her tragic life. Meanwhile, other, more preposterous tales were concocted by village children involving witchcraft or child-stealing.

Agnes Crabbe died of cancer in 1944 at the age of just forty-nine and her story might have ended there but for an unusual bequest. As the world celebrated the start of the third millennium, a solicitors' office in the nearby market town of Bowcester found itself in possession of something quite unexpected and very special.

In 1943, knowing that she was near the end of her life, Agnes Crabbe had contacted a solicitor called Charles Tremens and gave into his care a heavy locked suitcase, a sealed envelope containing the key and instructions that neither were to be opened until on or after 1 January 2000. With no family or heirs to whom she could leave her modest estate, she requested that the solicitor sell all that she owned so that there would be sufficient funds to ensure that her wishes were carried out.

The opening of the suitcase caused a sensation. Mr Tremens's grandson Andrew, now a senior partner in the firm of Tremens, Mallord, Hacker and Budge, discovered that the case contained a number of handwritten and typed manuscripts: twenty-one complete novels – twenty of them detective fiction – and twenty-seven short stories. There were also the scripts for two plays and several volumes of poetry, as well as a substantial number of Agnes Crabbe's personal diaries that spanned the years between 1909 and 1943. A handwritten letter gave authority to Mr Tremens's firm to act as her proxy and to see that the manuscripts, none of which, she maintained, had been read by a living soul other than herself, were submitted for publication.

Mr Tremens duly submitted the work to a number of literary agents, all of whom quickly realised that here was something quite remarkable; a cache of original, unread detective novels from the golden age of crime fiction. A bidding war began, culminating in a six-figure book deal, and the first three titles – *Broken and Snared*, *The Beginning of Sorrows* and *The Dead Do Not Rise* – quickly became bestsellers. In the absence of living relatives, Tremens arranged for a proportion of the proceeds of sale to be paid to charities that supported war widows/widowers and their children.

Examination of the diaries revealed a very different Agnes Crabbe from the one portrayed in rumour. Far from being the tragic and lonely young widow that everyone had assumed she was, Agnes recorded that she was happy and content and had, in fact, always preferred her own company to that of other people. She expressed great sadness for the death of her husband but more for the life that he would never live than for her own loss.

She was not entirely sure that she had ever loved Daniel Crabbe but she had been very fond of him; they had grown up together in a small village, after all. However, his death had freed her from other people's expectations of her and the death of her mother had released her from all other obligations. Tragic circumstance had provided her with the time, the funds and the isolation to explore the world inside her own head. As she wrote in one of her diaries, 'Reality is at best a poorly constructed and inadequate substitute for the wonder room of my imagination.' She began to write in 1915 – not for publication but for her own pleasure – and she would continue to write almost until the day she died.

Her early works were poems that expressed her feelings about love and loss. But she soon migrated to writing short stories, each one a miniature murder mystery of the kind she so enjoyed reading. Then came the novels. By the age of thirty she had produced five books but had made no attempt to have them published. She was not hungry for recognition and the human contact that would inevitably ensue. She also knew that her prose was too scandalous, her murder scenarios too full of grim realism, and her middle-aged heroine, Miss Millicent Cutter, far too promiscuous for the repressed sensibilities of polite 1920s society.

By 1942, she had completed twenty novels and had begun her twenty-first when she became gravely ill and learned from her doctor – the first person, other than Iris, to speak to her at any length in decades – that she had a terminal illness. But she continued to write, grimly determined to finish the knowingly named *All Things Must Pass*. Once that was done, she bequeathed her life's work to future generations if, indeed, there were to be any, with the words: 'I hope that the combined wisdom of humanity will eventually bring us to a sense of our situation and that the dawning of the twenty-first century will see a world that has cured all men of the insanity of war.'

The books proved to be enormously popular and Miss Cutter soon became as much of a household name as Sherlock Holmes, Lord Peter Wimsey and Hercule Poirot. Literary reviewers held Crabbe's writing in high esteem and her strong female characters were celebrated by feminist writers. But, more importantly perhaps, her complex and ingenious plots quickly gained her a legion of fans, particularly among a certain kind of lady reader who revelled in Miss Cutter's razor-sharp intuition, frequent romances and sexual encounters with beefy farmhands and swarthy foreign agents. In the character of Miss Cutter, readers caught a glimpse of the kind of woman they wished they could be, living a life they wished they might have had. Crueller social commentators called the canon 'a curious coupling of Jackie and Wilkie Collins' but no one could argue that the formula didn't engage with the fans. The factors that had made Agnes Crabbe unprintable in her lifetime were now her strongest selling point. Within just a few years of their discovery, all of her books had enjoyed dozens of reprints and translations and the number of her fans worldwide was legion. For many readers of golden age detective fiction, the name Agnes Crabbe was spoken with passion and reverence, and the fact that she had been completely unknown until the millennium only added to people's fervour to elevate her to the ranks of the greats. The arrival of award-winning TV adaptations further cemented her popularity and the multi-award-winning series *The Miss Cutter Mysteries* quickly transformed actress Helen Greeley from a bit player into an international star.

Which is why, on or around the date of her birth every year, hundreds of her most devoted fans descend upon Nasely, the tiny

South Herewardshire village in which Agnes Crabbe lived out her entire life, to enjoy a weekend of readings, competitions, screenings, dramatic re-enactments, historical tours and talks by Crabbe scholars and other eminent people. From what started out as little more than a local book club, Nasely's annual Agnes Crabbe Murder-Mystery Festival has quickly grown to become one of the most popular literary festivals in Great Britain.

We do hope that you enjoy your visit.

Agnes Crabbe Bibliography
(year of writing)

The Miss Cutter Mysteries
Broken and Snared (1923)
The Beginning of Sorrows (1925)
The Dead Do Not Rise (1926)
Bite the Dust (1927)
Brood of Vipers (1928)
My Brother's Keeper (1929)
Wit's End (1930)
Absent in the Flesh (1930–1931)
Babel (1931) (Guest feat. Colonel Trayhorn Borwick)
Swords into Ploughshares (1932–1933)
Wallowing in the Mire (1934–1935? Suspected 'lost' manuscript)
Teeth Set on Edge (1940)
Lying Lips (1940)
A Wrathful Man (1941) (Guest feat. Colonel Trayhorn Borwick)
Alpha and Omega (1941–1942)
Ministry of Death (1942)
Punishment of the Sword (1942–1943)
All Things Must Pass (1942–1943)

The Den of Thieves Trilogy (Colonel Trayhorn Borwick)
Den of Thieves (1936)
Dire Straits (1937–1938)
Pearls Before Swine (1939–1940)

Other Fiction

A White Stone (1931)

Poetry Collections

A Thorn in the Flesh (1915–1918)
Remembrance of Former Things (1916–1933)
The Shadow of Your Wings (1936–1943)

Short Story Collections

A Multitude of Sins (1920–1930) –
includes the Miss Cutter story 'A Soft Answer'

Die by the Sword (1937–1942) –
includes the Miss Cutter story 'Sour Grapes'

Plays

Doubting Thomas (1933) – Featuring Colonel Trayhorn Borwick
Evil Company Corrupts (1936) – Featuring Miss Cutter

A warm drizzle began to fall just as the very last piece of festival bunting was being hung. Up and down the little High Street, stepladders were hastily folded and toolboxes were slammed shut as people made their way indoors out of the rain. Most of the work was done and what little remained could wait until morning. In the meantime, there were windows to decorate and costumes to press, props to be dusted off and cakes to be baked.

Over the course of a fortnight, the village of Nasely had been returned to how it would have looked in the 1920s. It wasn't such a difficult trick to pull off as most of the buildings dated from the nineteenth century, and their caramel-coloured stone walls, attractive sash windows and wrought-iron railings were already authentically vintage. The shops too were old-fashioned in style, and the street furniture was traditional and restrained. Wherever possible, unavoidable evidence of the twenty-first century had been hidden or disguised; the street was too narrow for anachronisms such as traffic lights or speed cameras but there were satellite dishes to obscure with hanging baskets and telephone junction boxes to hide behind street vendors' barrows. It was important that Nasely looked just right for the annual Agnes Crabbe Murder-Mystery Festival. The little village wasn't just the venue. It was the star.

The great crime-fiction author had lived her entire life in the village and had used it as the template for Little Hogley, the setting for many of her hugely popular novels. The two villages were identical; every one of her murder scenes had a counterpart in reality, making a visit to the festival a must for all true fans. As long as somebody had been bludgeoned, poisoned or in some other way done to bloody death at or near its literary doppelgänger, the most banal of locations would attract hordes of devotees in the days to come. They would flock to Chetwynd's Butcher's Shop in Sacker Street because it was where Claude Hindeshott had made his arsenic-laced game pies in *Absent in the Flesh*. They would pose for photographs outside the Gondolier Italian restaurant because it mirrored the location of the Staines family bakery in *Bite the Dust* (where husband and wife John and Rosina had engineered Sally Foddenam's grisly explosive end among the flour sacks). And they would queue for hours to visit the village's most sacred site: the picturesque little cottage at the corner of the High Street and Ormond Road in which the reclusive writer had penned all of her novels and where her much-loved lady detective, Miss Millicent Cutter, had made her fictional home. In recent years, the cottage had been converted into a museum and among its most popular attractions were Miss Cutter's sitting room and Agnes Crabbe's study. The sitting room, meticulously reconstructed from descriptions found in the books, was where Miss Cutter routinely scolded Inspector Raffo of the Knollshire Constabulary for his blundering. The study, meanwhile, had been somewhat imaginatively dressed and decorated to look nothing like it probably had done in Agnes Crabbe's lifetime. The museum would do a roaring trade over the weekend and so too would the happy shopkeepers who rubbed their hands with glee in anticipation of the hugely increased footfall that the festival would bring to their premises.

At the other end of the High Street the village's only pub, the curiously named Happy Onion, was also preparing for the busy weekend ahead. The saloon bar had been decorated with Agnes Crabbe memorabilia including framed book covers, a school report, prints of the only known photographs of her, a portrait of her tragic young husband, Daniel, in his Herewardshire Rifles regimental uniform, and several of the letters that had passed between him and his young bride before his death in the Great War. There were also autographed monochrome glossies of Helen Greeley, the glamorous star of *The Miss Cutter Mysteries* TV series and, standing incongruously next to the Gents, a shop manne-quin wearing one of her costumes from the show: a pleated 'flapper' dress and matching cloche hat, and the trademark double string of pearls with which Miss Cutter daringly lassoed guns, whipped villains across the face or scattered across the floor to make her enemies slip and tumble. Throughout the festival, the pub would be a bustling hive of activity but tonight it was almost empty, a fact that landlord Vic Sallow ascribed not to the rain but to the behaviour of one of his regulars. Savidge was having one of his bad days.

'Historical accuracy, my arse,' he growled. 'You don't see them taking down the TV aerials, do you? And no one says we should remove all the burglar alarms or paint out the yellow lines on the road. Oh no. Not if it inconveniences the cosy middle classes.' Savidge was a well-built man in his late forties, with a receding hairline of dark curly hair turning grey at the temples. His unshaven cheeks were ruddy with anger. 'As usual, it's people like me who get victimised. Working-class people with businesses to run who need our vehicles to earn a bloody living. And another thi—'

'Be sensible, man,' said Vic, deliberately cutting him off. He had known Savidge since he was a boy, and experience had shown that the best way to tackle one of his venomous lectures was to prevent him from getting a word in. 'There's only so much the festival organisers can do for authenticity. I mean, they can't stop jets flying overhead or people using their mobiles, can they?'

'If you can ever get a bloody signal,' grumbled Savidge. 'It's like a black hole around these parts.'

'But they can clear the High Street of vehicles,' continued Vic, ignoring him. 'And, anyway, it's not like they've sprung this on you, is it? They pedestrianise it every year.'

'That doesn't make it right. My burger van has had that pitch—'

'And besides, moving your van is more about health and safety than historical accuracy.'

'I didn't think his burgers were that bad, Vic,' said Frank Shunter, the only other person who had braved the Saloon Bar on festival's eve.

'Oh, ha ha,' said Savidge humourlessly, breaking off from a deep swig of his beer. The froth on his upper lip gave the impression that he was foaming at the mouth. 'Just what the world needs, a copper who thinks he's funny.'

'Ex-copper,' corrected Shunter, smiling at Savidge's irritation. During his thirty-year career with the Met in London, he'd been insulted and screamed at more times than he could remember and had grown a skin as thick and impenetrable as an armadillo's. Savidge's regular rants didn't bother him and he'd learned to tune them out. However, the burger man was having a particularly vociferous evening and even the beer, which would normally help

4

to bolster Shunter's stoicism, was ineffectual. He'd therefore resorted to attack as a form of defence by throwing the occasional barbed remark into the conversation and watching as Savidge's face got redder and redder. It was proving to be tremendously satisfying. He finished the dregs of his pint, wiped his neatly clipped grey moustache on the back of his hand and returned to reading his book.

'You know what it's like over Agnes Crabbe weekend,' continued Vic. 'The High Street will be heaving with Millies and someone would be knocked down for sure if we allowed vehicles through. And it's only for one weekend a year.'

'Yeah, the busiest weekend,' said Savidge. 'That's my point. I'll be the only mug not making any money. It's all right for you. The Onion is on the High Street but I have to—'

'Rubbish,' said Vic. 'You've got a great pitch over on the village green. You did all right there last year. I saw the queues.'

'There may have been queues but they didn't bloody buy anything,' moaned Savidge. 'All they did was complain. Is the beef organic? Is the coffee Fairtrade? They need shooting, the lot of them.'

'Probably not the best time to commit a homicide,' said Shunter. 'What with eight hundred murder-mystery fans descending on the village. You'd be caught for sure.'

'It would be worth it,' said Savidge.

'Or you could extend your range of products?' suggested Vic.

'It might mean less bloodshed,' added Shunter.

'Poxy festival,' snapped Savidge. He sank into a desultory silence and stared at his hands, clenched into fists on the bar.

Shunter shook his head in despair. He was only six years older than the burger van man but their outlooks on life were polar opposites. While Shunter had seen the very worst of humanity, he remained resolutely optimistic about life and the future. He knew that there were far more good people than bad, and that more acts of kindness were done every day than acts of evil or wickedness; they just didn't get reported in the increasingly sensationalist and fear-mongering tabloids. Savidge, meanwhile, believed everything he read and, as far as he was concerned, the world was going to hell in a handcart. He could find the negative in any situation and seemed to take perverse pleasure in believing that he was either cursed or being deliberately put upon all of the time. His almost constant frown had carved deep crevasses into his forehead.

'Another pint, gents?' said Vic, attempting to lighten the mood. 'Something different perhaps? The Cockering Brewery has put on a special edition ale for the festival called To Die For. I can give you an advance preview if you like. On the house.'

'Go on then,' said Shunter.

'Savidge? One for the road?'

'Do you want to get me nicked for drink driving?' said Savidge, pointedly. 'I've had two pints already and, as you well know, I have to move my van off the High Street because it's a sodding anachronism. It's like I said, it's us traders who—'

'G'night then,' said Vic firmly. Savidge glowered at him but took the hint. Vic Sallow had the curious build of a man who was simultaneously both short and large, like a fridge with limbs. His shoulders bulged and he didn't seem to have a neck. There was a lot of strength contained within his oddly shaped body. You didn't need a gym when you spent your day moving full firkins about. Savidge drained his glass, clonked it heavily on the bar and stormed out of the pub.

'Drive safely,' said Shunter, smiling.

'Thank Christ for that. That man is kryptonite for publicans,' said Vic, puffing out his cheeks. 'I should bar him.'

'He did have a bee in his bonnet tonight, didn't he?'

'Swarms, more like. He drives all my customers away. I reckon he needs stronger medication.'

'Ah, he's all bluster.'

'He's getting worse, I swear,' said Vic. 'One of these days he'll lose it completely, you wait and see.'

'In my experience, it's the quiet, introverted ones you have to watch out for,' said Shunter. He shut his book and placed it on the bar. Vic swivelled it around to read the title.

'*Dalí Plays Golf,*' said Vic. He tapped the author's name. 'Shirley Pomerance is a local girl, you know. Her family comes from over Tingwell way.'

'So I understand.'

'Any good?'

'No idea. She uses seven words when one would do, and all seven are words I didn't even know existed.'

'That bad, eh?'

'Bletchley Park would have struggled to decode it,' said Shunter. 'There should be some way of checking people's IQ at the till. I'm clearly not smart enough for them to have sold it to me.'

'I've heard people buy her books just so that they can look brainy,' said Vic.

'Only a masochist would buy them for fun.'

'She can't be that unreadable, surely? She's won awards.'

'I'll give you a taster,' said Shunter, riffling through the pages. 'Ah. Here we go. "Lavinia acquiesced her lubricious girlflesh to his dexterous phalanges, all the while assiduously palpating his tumescent boypole to priapic . . ."'

'Eh?'

'It's a sex scene.'

'If you say so,' said Vic. 'I think I'll stick to Agnes Crabbe.'

'As I should have done. At least her saucy bits are saucy,' said Shunter, sipping his pint. 'Shirley Pomerance's idea of foreplay is fingering a thesaurus.'

2

Two miles outside the village, a coach driver glanced nervously at his wing mirrors and pined for the wide open carriageways of the M13 motorway where he usually did most of his business. But this was the eve of the Agnes Crabbe Murder-Mystery Festival weekend and, for the next seventy-two hours at least, this would be his lot: ferrying fans to and from Nasely on some of the least coach-friendly roads in South Herewardshire. The contract was lucrative, to be sure, but the drive was horrible. There were only three roads into the village and all of them involved negotiating canals, low-hanging trees, narrow lanes and sharp corners. There was no street lighting either, and the light spring rain reduced his visibility still further. He cursed under his breath and prepared to tackle yet another humpback bridge.

Sitting behind him, and oblivious to his discomfort, three dozen middle-aged ladies hungrily devoured the novels of Agnes Crabbe, or discussed the novels of Agnes Crabbe, or listened to Agnes Crabbe audiobooks, or watched *The Miss Cutter Mysteries* on laptops and tablets, or leafed through the festival brochure and made their plans for the weekend. The atmosphere on the bus was fragrant with lavender and anticipation.

Esme Handibode swept her lifeless silver-grey hair back from her eyes and perched a pair of half-moon reading glasses upon the humpback bridge of her nose. She frowned at the brochure laid out on her friend's lap.

'I don't know why you're even considering going to the Helen Greeley talk, Molly. It'll be standing room only and you'll learn nothing, mark my words.'

Molly Wilderspin looked up into her friend's face and smiled weakly. 'Oh, but I hear that she's very nice.'

'Nice she may be,' said Mrs Handibode. 'But we only have two days. You must stick to events that add value to your visit, like the Andrew Tremens talk.'

'I'm definitely going to that one, Esme,' said Miss Wilderspin. Short, timid and thickly bespectacled, she was both physically and behaviourally the opposite of her friend, the taller and more bombastic Mrs Handibode. She turned to a different page in the brochure and tapped the photo of a middle-aged man with a very nice smile. 'It says here: "Andrew Tremens will make an announcement of major importance to all Crabbe fans." It's very intriguing.'

'I dislike that term immensely,' said Mrs Handibode.

'Intriguing?'

'Fan. You wouldn't call a Shakespearean scholar a fan, would you?'

'No, I suppose not.' Miss Wilderspin looked through the programme of events again, eyes lingering on the seductive black-and-white image of actress Helen Greeley who had agreed to open this year's festival.

'She is so brave,' said Miss Wilderspin. 'If I ever found myself in a situation like the one she was in last year, I'd go to pieces. She's like a real-life Miss Cutter, isn't she?'

'I very much doubt it,' huffed Mrs Handibode. 'I'd be surprised if she's even read any of the books.'

'Actually, I meant because of the way she dealt with that stalker,' said Miss Wilderspin. 'So brave. I'd have been too terrified to do anything.'

'You mark my words: her talk will be packed to the gunwales with star-struck spinsters making silly old fools of themselves and you'll learn nothing of any worth. Andrew Tremens, on the other hand, has had sole responsibility for the Crabbe archive since its discovery. He has an intimate acquaintance with her work and her diaries and he will have some fascinating insights to share.'

'There's a rumour going around that he's found some kind of manuscript. Maybe an unpublished story or—'

'You should know better than to listen to gossip. It's invariably nonsense.'

'I'm sure you're right, Esme,' said Miss Wilderspin, resignedly. 'But we could go to both talks, you know. They don't clash. Do you think we're very far away now? I tried looking at the satnav on my phone but there's no signal around here. I thought that only happened in films.'

'We'll be there very soon,' said Mrs Handibode, looking out of the window. The coach was gingerly inching its way over the bridge while the driver desperately tried not to scrape the bottom of his vehicle. 'This is the Dunksbury Road canal bridge, just outside Nasely. But do you know which bridge it corresponds to in the books?'

'Is it the Vallory Road canal bridge?' ventured Miss Wilderspin.

'Very good,' said Mrs Handibode, smiling.

'That's where Maynard Grader was murdered in *Swords into Ploughshares*, isn't it?'

'And where Mavis Frusty threw away the murder weapon in *Ministry of Death*. I've taught you well.'

'How exciting to actually be in the real Little Hogley!' Miss Wilderspin clapped her hands with glee. 'I can't wait to find other locations from the books.'

'You can pay a tour guide to show you around,' said Mrs Handibode. 'But I've been to Nasely several times before and I'm willing to show you around for free.'

'Well, I thought I might—'

'No one knows Agnes Crabbe and her books better than I do,' said Mrs Handibode. 'In fact, were I to believe in such things, I would say that it was entirely possible that I was her in a previous life.'

Miss Wilderspin considered pointing out that her friend's life had actually overlapped that of the great author's by two years but decided to bite her tongue. Esme Handibode was not a person who took kindly to being corrected, even in the face of unimpeachable logic. She considered herself to be the foremost expert on Agnes Crabbe and there was every good reason to think that she might be. She ran the Agnes Crabbe Fellowship, the largest of the many fan clubs and societies, and edited and published the quarterly *Agnes Crabbe Fellowship Journal* (circulation 27,910). She had amassed an enviable collection of first editions and memorabilia, and had even appeared on TV's *Mastermind*, although she had eventually lost in the semi-finals to a man who knew a ridiculous amount about Vincent motorcycles. Her knowledge of Agnes Crabbe was nothing less than encyclopaedic, and she threw herself into her studies with a single-mindedness that, if the gossip was true, had seriously affected her marriage. Certainly, no one had seen Mr and Mrs Handibode together in many months and their relationship was rumoured to be frosty at best.

Naturally, there were pretenders to her crown; people like

Denise Hatman-Temples, who ran the Agnes Crabbe Literary Society; Gaynor Nithercott of the Agnes Crabbe Book Club; Brenda Tradescant of the Millicent Cutter Appreciation Society; Elspeth Cranmer-Beamen of the Miss Cutter Mysteries Fan Club and many others who purported to know just as much as she did. But Esme Handibode was confident in her superiority; as far as she was concerned, no other Agnes Crabbe-related fan club could hold a candle to her Fellowship and she refused even to acknowledge claims to the contrary. Instead, she reserved the bulk of her ire for a journalist named Pamela Dallimore who, irritatingly, was the media's go-to person whenever they needed a perspective on Crabbe's life and works. Dallimore was chauffeured in luxury cars, or sent by air or rail in first-class comfort to Crabbe conventions and TV appearances all over the world, despite appearing to be quite vague about Crabbe and her books. The reality was that her entire reputation was based upon a bestselling biography that she'd written called *The Secret Queen of Crime* in which she had alleged that Crabbe was involved in a same-sex relationship with her best friend, Iris Gobbelin. The fact that Dallimore's claims were based upon specious or entirely apocryphal stories didn't seem to matter to the thousands who'd bought a copy.

But it mattered to Esme Handibode, and she had made it her business to publicly denounce the book at every opportunity. As far as she was concerned, Pamela Dallimore embodied everything that was wrong with the cult of celebrity in twenty-first-century society: the adoration of the banal; the elevation of the ignorant; the hunger for gossip and scandal; and the complete lack of value placed upon self-discipline, systematic research and hard-won expertise and knowledge. Mrs Handibode had dedicated fifteen years of her life to the study of Agnes Crabbe and her creations, but her thunder was continually stolen by a second-rate hack who just happened to have sold a lot of copies of a very bad book. Hate was not a word that Mrs Handibode used lightly and she rarely wished ill-will to anyone. But she had no qualms in admitting that she hated Pamela Dallimore with a passion and secretly wished that something very nasty would happen to the wretched woman.

3

The springs in Gaynor Nithercott's car seat squeaked and groaned as she sped along a dark tree-lined country lane, her ancient Mini Cooper's thin wheels unerringly finding every rut and pothole. But she was oblivious to everything except the words issuing from her car's ancient speaker. The audiobook of *Punishment of the Sword* was reaching its dramatic conclusion and Millicent Cutter had cornered her Belgian nemesis and occasional lover, Dr Florian Belfrage, among the dangerously grinding machinery of a windmill running at full tilt. While Belfrage flustered and ranted, Miss Cutter explained how she had unravelled his dastardly plot to steal the formula for Professor Hubert Foig's improved form of gunpowder. When Miss Nithercott's eyesight had become too poor for extended bouts of reading, she'd taken to audiobooks, and was now so addicted to them that she could recite large sections from memory. She joined in as the narration reached one of her favourite moments; when Belfrage realises that he and Miss Cutter have now become so opposed in their moral standpoints that they can never again be lovers.

The flames that had for so long warmed Belfrage's passions flared all at once and then died. His heart was instantly and for ever baked into a hard, unyielding mass; as insensitive as a fist, as impenetrable as iron, it would lie buried deep inside his chest – for ever still, for ever cold, for ever beyond repair. In that instant, he knew that he would never again be able to stoke those fires to life. He would be eternally invulnerable to Eros's darts.

A stabbing pain in Miss Nithercott's chest made her take a sudden deep breath and, for a moment, she wondered if she was suffering an empathetic response to Belfrage's heartbreak. But, she reassured herself, it was most probably indigestion caused by the jam sandwiches she'd snacked on half an hour ago. She'd eaten them far too quickly and the bread had been very heavy. She fumbled in her handbag for an antacid tablet.

Mrs Denise Hatman-Temples drove sedately along a road that ran parallel to the canal and wished that driving her little Peugeot didn't preclude her from shutting her eyes and letting her imagination roam more freely. She was listening to a radio drama-tisation of *Teeth Set on Edge*, the book in which Miss Cutter and Dr Belfrage finally ended the 'will they/won't they' speculation with a spirited lovemaking session atop Scafell Pike. Mrs Hatman-Temples's mental image of Miss Cutter looked nothing like Helen Greeley's high-cheekboned and glitzy portrayal for the TV series. It looked rather more like she herself had done in her thir-ties, a fantasy that was enhanced by Maggie Woodbead – the actress who played Miss Cutter in the BBC radio dramas – having a voice not dissimilar in tone to her own. The fact that the TV series portrayed the characters so very differently from the way they appeared in her mind's eye was one reason why she tended to stick to audio; as Agnes Crabbe herself had once said, 'Words have all the best pictures.'

He looked deeply into my eyes. His own were full of confusion.

'No, it's you who doesn't understand, Florian,' I said. 'Love has no foundation in logic. It is possible to love someone whose morals are not cut from the same cloth as one's own. In many ways, it is often the tension of opposition that excites; the fact that it is wrong makes it desirable.'

He straightened to his full height and, without another word, slowly buttoned his waistcoat and slid his sword stick back into its Malacca sheath. He took a deep breath and a wry smile crept across his full lips.

'So where does that leave matters, dear lady?' he said, his words forming a milky cloud on the frigid night air. 'Where does that leave . . . us?'

An old Mini suddenly came roaring out of the dark and, in the last second before it smashed into the side of her car, Mrs Hatman-Temples caught a glimpse of Miss Gaynor Nithercott slumped sideways in the driver's seat. The impact flipped the Peugeot on to its side and it tumbled over and over before plunging upside-down into the shallow waters of the canal. The Mini, meanwhile, careened away from the impact and crashed headlong into the substantial trunk of an ancient oak. The noise of the car horn, stuck on a continuous ear-splitting bleat, echoed across the flat landscape, and a mushroom-shaped cloud of radiator vapour rose above the wreckage and was lost among the high-arching branches above.

4

Somewhere in the middle distance, sirens wailed. Shunter found himself wondering whether they belonged to a police vehicle or an ambulance. Police sirens were very rare in this sleepy corner of rural South Herewardshire but ambulances weren't uncommon; no surprise really given the average age of the population. He twirled the corner of his moustache, a habit he often indulged in while thinking. Heavier rain had replaced the light drizzle and he didn't have an umbrella, but he was a patient man and he'd decided that it was worth waiting a few minutes to see if it eased off before walking home. Besides, Mrs Shunter was in a foul mood, which was what had driven him to the pub in the first place. Her unlikeable and flighty younger sister had just returned from a two-week holiday in Las Vegas at some temporary boy-friend's expense and had been boasting ever since about what a wonderful time she'd had. To rub salt into the wound, she'd also won over ten thousand pounds purely on games of chance. Mrs Shunter was, understandably, fuming at the injustice of it all.

Shunter had never been ambitious. While friends, colleagues and family had chased promotions, salary increases and bonuses, he'd been content to plod along in public service, happy with his policeman's lot. All he'd ever wanted to do was catch the bad guys and he had steadfastly rejected the idea of a higher pay grade as it would have meant less hands-on thief-taking and a lot more desk-bound admin. It had also meant living a respectable, if modest, life, but one that he'd found satisfying. However, while Mrs Shunter rarely complained, he knew that she secretly envied her sister's glamorous lifestyle and that visiting their friends' ever more extravagant houses made her feel too embarrassed to consider inviting anyone back to her humble suburban semi in west London. Shunter hated the obsessive and greedy keeping-up-with-the-Joneses nature of it all and had little time for people who considered wealth to be life's primary goal. But he also felt guilty about not having given Mrs Shunter a better life. She deserved better and, not for the first time, he wondered why she'd stayed with him for nearly thirty years.

It was why he had suggested that they move to the country upon his retirement where they could start afresh, away from the corrosive one-upmanship of London. It had meant using all of their savings but they'd been very lucky to find a pretty little cottage in picturesque and much-sought-after Nasely. And, for a while, things in the Shunter household had improved immensely. Mrs Shunter had become embroiled in a handful of local societies and they'd made some lovely new friends. But then her sister and her latest boyfriend – a Premiership footballer – had visited and remarked that the cottage reminded them of a 'pokey little holiday gîte in Clohars-Fouesnant' they had once stayed in and old wounds had been reopened. All of which meant that, rather than enjoying his retirement, Shunter now spent much of it looking for a lucrative second career so that he could afford to have the cottage upgraded to a standard that Mrs Shunter would be proud to show off. It had also led to him skulking in the pub and drinking far more beer than he had ever done before.

To lift his mood, he peered out from the pub doorway and up

and down the High Street. It was looking very good, he thought, authentically vintage. No one could say that the people of Nasely didn't put the effort in. This was his first Agnes Crabbe Murder-Mystery Festival, having only moved to the village ten months previously, and it had been interesting to watch its transformation this past week. The shop-window displays were now delightfully retro with the chemist's boasting adverts for Goddard's White Horse Oils and something called Cavanaugh's Wonder Remedy, and the newsagent's full of antique posters for Will's Gold Flake and *Titbits* magazine. A billboard outside the Masonic Hall advertised the Agnes Crabbe play *Evil Company Corrupts*, which was due to be performed on Sunday evening as a finale to the festival, and, diagonally opposite the pub, the Empire Hotel displayed a banner that read 'Welcome Millies!' Shunter frowned at the hotel, a 1960s Bauhaus, quite out of keeping with the rest of the village, and wondered how the place had ever got planning permission. Backhanders presumably. The current owners had tried to soften its stark outlines by adding rooftop crenellations, balconied windows and a portico over the front doors but the pretence at grand Victorian splendour hadn't worked at all. When the facade was up-lit at night it had the same effect as a person holding a torch under their chin; it highlighted the true horror of trying to merge two entirely uncomplementary architectural styles. And to make matters even worse, the hotel's white stuccoed walls had faded to a sickly yellowish colour that gave the building a distinctly jaundiced look. The wet pavement reflected the yellow light from the floodlit hotel and also from the fluted and filigreed cast-iron lampposts, expensively installed along the High Street in an effort to enhance the charm of the village.

Shunter had recently discovered that there were CCTV cameras hidden inside two of the lampposts; as faithfully antique as

Nasely might try to appear to be, evidence of the Modern Age was there to see if you scratched the surface. And was there anything that said twenty-first century more than public surveillance? Shunter wondered whether the cameras were ever misused by the staff that monitored them. After all, there was almost no crime in the village but there were plenty of pretty teenage girls around, thanks to the nearby boarding school at Harpax Grange. Big Brother may not be watching, but some pimply youth employed by the village council probably was. Were they watching him now, he wondered? Was the video definition of sufficient quality to identify him from this distance? He was suddenly very aware of his every move. How often had he adjusted his crotch or scratched his backside while forgetful of the cameras? He knew for sure that, during the winter, he'd fallen flat on his face after glissading on ice outside the library. Had he given the lads in the control room a good laugh?

A sudden noise drew his attention to a coach idling slowly up through the High Street towards him. He looked at his watch and saw that it was 10.30 p.m. Coaches and minibuses had been arriving all day, dropping off the faithful in time for the start of festivities in the morning. This one – a special service run by a local company that picked up from Bowcester railway station and from the surrounding villages of Spradbarrow, Tingwell, Panswick and Sherrinford – was probably the last of them, he mused. The vehicle pulled up in front of the village hall and, with a loud hiss, hunkered down on to its suspension like a camel kneeling. The passengers, all middle-aged ladies dressed in an assortment of drab colours, began reaching bags down from overhead racks and pulling on coats and jackets. The door opened and they disembarked noisily while glancing at pieces of paper and pointing in different directions. Sensing that beating a hasty retreat would spare him a good thirty minutes of questions regarding the whereabouts of their various accommodations, Shunter slid quietly back inside the pub.

'I thought you'd gone home,' said Vic. 'I was just closing up.'

'I would if I were you. Another coachload of Millies has just turned up,' said Shunter. 'And if they're anything like the bunch I met on the way here, they'll keep us pinned to the wall with questions for the next half hour. Can I hide in here for a few minutes?'

'Another one for the road then? On the house?' said Vic as he bolted the pub doors shut.

'Cheers, Vic. Maybe just a half.'

'They look so innocent, don't they?' said Vic, looking out of the window. 'But I'll tell you this, for a bunch of librarians, primary school teachers and Women's Institute types, they can't half put it away.'

'Really? They look more like the occasional glass of dry sherry with the vicar types.'

'Don't you believe it. I reckon this is their once-a-year chance to let their hair down. You'll see what I mean once they're all in costume tomorrow. It's like they dress up as someone else and it gives them permission to . . . Oh hang on . . . something's kicking off.'

As Vic had been talking he'd become aware of raised voices outside getting louder and angrier as the passengers gathered around the coach's luggage compartment. Two women were now facing off against each other and a crowd had formed around them.

'There are two Millies out there and—'

'I'm retired,' said Shunter, opening his book.

*

22

While the driver had been handing out the suitcases, the rusting catches on Mrs Handibode's ancient leather case had sprung open, spilling the contents on to the wet road. That it had happened at the feet of Miss Brenda Tradescant of the Millicent Cutter Appreciation Society was pure bad luck.

'What have we here then?' said Miss Tradescant, picking up a paperback and pointing at its lurid cover illustration. '*Love's Moist Promise*, Esme? And by someone called Simone Bedhead I see. There's a name that reeks of fine literature.'

'It's for research,' said Mrs Handibode, struggling to refill her case and desperately hoping that none of her other books had been spotted lurking among the neatly folded clothes. It was bad enough that the ghastly woman had seen just one of them.

'Research, eh?' said Miss Tradescant, reading the back-cover blurb with a derisory snort. '"Orphaned and alone, Chastity Fox uses her ample charms to travel halfway across eighteenth-century England in a quest to discover the truth about the death of her brother. But after an unplanned night of searing naked passion with a mysterious stranger known only as Captain Standish, Chastity races out of his bed and his life when she discovers a dark secret hidden inside a—"'

'If you don't mind!' snapped Mrs Handibode, snatching the book from her rival's hand.

'Esme, Esme, Esme,' tutted Miss Tradescant. 'I expected better of you.'

'It's not what you think.'

'Oh really?' said Miss Tradescant.

'Really. I am making a study with a view to writing an academic paper.'

'On what?' goaded Miss Tradescant. 'Terrible romance novels?'

'In a way, yes. Agnes Crabbe incorporated romantic fiction

into her murder mysteries in a way that no other golden age crime-fiction writer ever did. In order to assess how successful she was, one must compare and contrast. I am therefore studying the entire canon of romantic fiction from the sublime to—'

'There's no shame in admitting that you enjoy a dirty book, Esme,' said Miss Tradescant with a smile.

A ripple of nervous laughter ran through the assembled Crabbe fans. Watching two well-known aficionados squaring up to each other was a delicious and unexpected pre-festival treat. If it came to a fight, the two women were fairly equally matched. Both were tall, broad-shouldered and ferociously bosomed. They were dressed similarly in pastel cardigans and pleated skirts. The only obvious difference was that Miss Tradescant wore her grey-blonde hair up in a bun while Mrs Handibode's had apparently been cropped while she was wearing a crash helmet.

'As I said, it's for research. Nothing more,' said Mrs Handibode, firmly.

'Pull the other one! This is pure smut. Even the author's name is sleazy. Simone Bedhead, for goodness' sake!'

Mrs Handibode closed her suitcase and glared at Miss Tradescant. 'Well, you'd know all about sleaze with those revolting sex stories you write, wouldn't you? Slash fiction – isn't that what they call it? Such a vulgar term.'

There was a sharp intake of breath among the assembled fans.

'I prefer the term erotica,' growled Miss Tradescant. 'And I'm adding to the Miss Cutter canon with—'

'With poorly written filth? I don't think so,' snapped Mrs Handibode. 'I have dedicated fifteen years of my life to the study of Agnes Crabbe, the writer. To the quality of her writing, to her character development and plot devices. All you've done is sully her memory with your smutty stories.'

'At least I'm making my readers happy,' said Miss Tradescant indignantly. 'Can you say the same, Esme? Do you ever make anyone happy? Is Mr Handibode happy?'

Another audible mass inhalation from the audience.

'That was a cheap shot, Brenda, even for you,' said Mrs Handibode. 'And no, I'm not trying to make people happy. I'm trying to educate people. Any true Agnes Crabbe scholar would say that they are doing the same. Meanwhile, all you do is inflict cheap tawdry pornography upon us all. You've reduced Miss Cutter to nothing more than a promiscuous slattern.'

'She *was* promiscuous.'

'Not to the degree to which you paint her in your nasty little stories.'

'Which you have presumably read if you feel qualified enough to criticise me,' said Miss Tradescant, smiling venomously.

'As I said, I'm researching the history and breadth of romantic fiction from the sublime to the ridiculous. The very ridiculous in your case and—'

'Ladies, ladies. It's late and I have to get back to the depot some time tonight,' the coach driver wearily interrupted. 'So if you could all just make your way to your hotels and guest houses, please?'

'Come, Molly,' said Mrs Handibode. She threw her chin high, unfurled a large black umbrella and walked off through the drizzle towards the Empire Hotel with Miss Wilderspin trotting at her heels like a terrier.

'One of these days, someone's going to push you off your high horse, Esme Handibode!' shouted Miss Tradescant. 'And I, for one, want to be there to watch you fall!'

*

'Looks like the coast is clear now,' said Vic. 'Rain's easing off a bit too.'

'Best I get off home then,' said Shunter, slapping his copy of *Dalí Plays Golf* on the bar. 'Here, you can add Shirley Pomerance to the pub library. I'm admitting defeat.'

'G'night, Frank. Safe walk home.'

'G'night, Vic.'

As Shunter left the pub, the now empty coach drove past him, noisily clunking into a kerbside pothole and soaking his shoes and socks with rainwater. He cursed the pothole and then the coach driver as he pulled his jacket collar up to offer some protection from the elements. And as he set off on the short squelching walk home, he mused upon the nature of obsession. What compelled people to become fixated upon a particular author or series of books? he wondered. Perhaps it was something deep and primeval; a need to belong, to be part of a tribe. He'd read that loneliness had become an epidemic in the twenty-first century as families fragmented and people migrated to the cities in search of work. It was possible to feel completely alone and isolated within a large population because you were surrounded by millions of strangers. Finding people who shared your passions, whether they focused on a particular movie franchise, or a boy band, or a sports team, or even the novels of a murder-mystery writer, meant that you were once again part of a tribe, which was infinitely better than being alone. That said, tribalism had its dark side too. As an outside observer, Shunter had difficulty understanding why the members of the many and various Agnes Crabbe-related fan clubs and societies always seemed to be at odds with each other. Surely if they all liked her books they had more in common than they had differences? It made no sense.

The rain became heavier again and he quickened his pace,

thankful for the lack of hills. One reason why Nasely and the villages surrounding it were favourite retirement spots was the flatness of the countryside. It was perfect for the slower driver, the older car, the wheelchair user and the tipsy retired detective making his way home. It was not so good for mobile phone reception though, as there were lots of trees and scant high spots on which to erect transmitters. Nor were there any telecommunication masts, thanks to an older generation of influential not-in-my-backyard campaigners. It was a shame they hadn't been so vocal when the planning application for the Empire Hotel was first made public, he thought to himself.

He reached his cottage and, noting with some degree of relief that all the lights were off, opened the front door quietly and went inside.

5

Helen Greeley, jetlagged and impressively tipsy for ten in the morning, lifted the microphone to her mouth and then winced as a jarring shriek of feedback ripped through the peaceful stillness outside the Agnes Crabbe Cottage Museum. Below the platform on which she stood, the several hundred festival-goers who had come to watch the opening ceremony recoiled in horror. After the respectful minute of silence they'd just held for Denise Hatman-Temples and Gaynor Nithercott, the hideous blast of noise had come as a sudden and painfully unpleasant shock.

'Sorry,' said Greeley. 'But thank you all for that silent tribute to those poor ladies who died last night. So sad. Isn't it, though? And both were fan-club presidents too. It's a real tragedy. But I know that both Bernice and Gaynor wouldn't want us to be sad. No. They'd want us all to be happy. Well, not so sad anyway. They would want us to enjoy the festival just as they would have done if they were still alive and not dead. So that's what we're going to do, okay? We're going to have a great time. Aren't we? Yes?'

The audience cheered and applauded.

'It's Denise, not Bernice,' grumbled Esme Handibode.

'Yes, we are going to have a great festival!' said Greeley. 'So I now declare the thirteenth annual Agnes Crabbe Festival of Murder-Mystery . . . er, Festival officially open!'

She fired the ceremonial starting pistol into the air and grimaced at the sudden noise. This was the signal for the town band from nearby Bowcester to strike up with a stirring rendition of 'Jerusalem' to honour the fact that both of the crash victims had been very active within the Women's Institute. The crowd sang along lustily.

'"And did those feet in ancient time walk upon England's mountains green—"'

Standing deep inside the crowd and made anonymous by the fact that they were wearing almost exactly the same outfits as everyone else, Mrs Handibode and Miss Wilderspin applauded as the song came to an end. The crowd began to disperse and Mrs Handibode tutted loudly.

'Why people dote on her I have no idea. She is clearly what the unkinder corners of the media refer to as a bimbo. Pretty and stupid. And, I suspect, drunk.'

'She is very pretty, though, isn't she?' said Miss Wilderspin. 'And so brave.'

'So you keep saying,' said Mrs Handibode in mild irritation. 'But good looks butter no parsnips, Molly, brave or otherwise.'

'I do like your outfit,' said Miss Wilderspin, changing the subject. 'I can never wear green. It doesn't suit me at all.'

Esme Handibode glanced down at her lime-green summer dress, complete with golden tasselled hem. It was set off by a long string of pearls, a gold handbag and a green cloche hat decorated with silk daffodils.

'That's because of your blood pressure, Molly,' she said matter-of-factly. 'Green would clash horribly with the pinky purple colour in your cheeks.'

'And I'd look like a tennis ball. I have put on quite a few pounds in the last year or two.'

'But your outfit is nice,' said Mrs Handibode, appraising her rotund friend's cocktail dress. 'Though I'd have chosen a colour other than white. It can be a dirt magnet.'

'It was the only outfit in the fancy dress shop that fitted me,' said Miss Wilderspin.

'Then let's hope you don't get too grubby,' said Mrs Handibode. 'Now, here is my plan for today's—'

'Do you think we might have a look at the museum?' interrupted Miss Wilderspin. 'I mean, as we're right here outside. I've always wanted to visit.'

'Everyone does that on the first day and it will be a frightful crush,' said Mrs Handibode. 'Mark my words, we'll be better off leaving that until last thing tomorrow when it will be practically empty.'

'Oh but—'

'Now. I've designed an itinerary that will maximise the benefit we get from today,' said Mrs Handibode. 'We'll start at the western edge of the village at the Dunksbury Road canal bridge. As you rightly mentioned last night, there's a spot on the towpath there that equates to where the village blacksmith was murdered. Come along.'

'Yes, Esme,' said Miss Wilderspin with a silent sigh and a last longing look at Helen Greeley signing autographs outside Agnes Crabbe's cottage.

Frank Shunter mouthed 'good morning' to a brace of older ladies and wondered whether he'd already said hello to them today. It was so hard to tell. The streets were full of Millies, as the fans liked to call themselves, all dressed as Agnes Crabbe's detective heroine Millicent Cutter. Flapper-style summer dresses, cloche hats and strings of pearls proliferated, which made identification of individuals difficult unless there was something particularly striking about the wearer. So far this morning he'd seen a couple who were very tall and several who were excessively overweight. He'd also seen a pair of African-Caribbean Millies, a Japanese Milly, some wheelchair-using Millies and a Muslim Milly, who'd been wearing a hijab under her hat. Many were wearing wigs that mimicked Miss Cutter's fashionable short bob, and some of the younger fans, most of whom were boarders from Harpax Grange, had opted for a sexier look with shorter skirts. But, for the most part, the Millies were middle-aged Caucasian women in 1920s dress, pretty much indistinguishable from each other. Those few men he'd spotted were also mostly dressed as Millicent Cutter, although some had come dressed as Agnes Crabbe's other, less popular detective, Colonel Trayhorn Borwick. A handful were cosplaying as Miss Cutter's nemesis and on-off love interest, Dr Florian Belfrage, and rumour had it that their choice of outfit was a coded message that these were men on the lookout for a festival romance.

Overnight, the entire feel of the village had changed from sleepy rural retreat to bustling convention site. Shunter had come into the village to catch the opening ceremony but, despite being told how many attendees there were likely to be, he still hadn't been quite prepared for the size of the crowds. Sheer weight of numbers made it difficult to even walk along the High Street and he now understood why it had been so necessary to remove Savidge's burger van and any other vehicles. A morris side was performing outside the Masonic Hall, their clacking sticks, stomping feet and jingling bells almost drowning out the wheezing accordion music that accompanied them. Shunter watched them capering for a short while and tapped his foot to the tune, a curiously popular local folk song about divine retribution called 'Go to Hell!', and then pushed his way through the crowds towards the village hall to buy a ticket for an event at 12 p.m. A criminologist from Oxford was due to give a talk titled 'Homicide as a Spectator Sport', and he strangely felt compelled to go and watch. Based on the title alone, he was pretty sure that he was going to hate it.

It was Dan George, making an early start with his milk round, who discovered the body under the bridge. In recent months, Dan had come to believe that the visions of Armageddon that had once plagued his nights were behind him, but the sight of the blacksmith's corpse, sprawled in an ungainly posture, the mutilated chest opened up like a gory flower, resurrected those images of horror that had tormented him, befuddling a brain that was still attempting to recover from drumfire. The constant crash echoing inside his head became suddenly louder and louder still and he was unable to stop the tears rolling down his reddened cheeks. Bottles tumbled from his nerveless quivering fingers and shattered on the ground.

'Stretcher bearers!' he yelled, his voice reverberating among the arches. 'Stretcher bearers!'

Mrs Handibode was reading aloud from a well-thumbed and heavily annotated copy of *Swords into Ploughshares* in order to work out exactly where Agnes Crabbe must have been standing when she'd described the grisly murder by scythe of blacksmith Maynard Grader. One peculiar and particular aspect of Esme Handibode's obsession was the need to stand in places where the great writer had herself once stood, as if she could absorb some kind of echo of her past presence. Every year, the festival gave her the perfect opportunity to research the genesis of a particular novel and, this year, she had decided to work on Crabbe's most celebrated work. Even outside of Crabbe fandom, *Swords into Ploughshares* was considered by many to be one of the finest murder mysteries ever written. As Mrs Handibode moved about, looking at the scene from various angles and taking the occasional photograph, Molly Wilderspin lay supine on a blanket, portraying the unfortunate smithy.

'Can I get up now?' she said miserably. 'I think there's an ant in my ear. I'm worried I may be lying on a nest.'

'Yes, yes, please do,' said Mrs Handibode, distractedly scribbling a note in her paperback. 'I think we're done here.'

'In that case, I quite fancy that midday talk at the village hall,' said Miss Wilderspin, getting to her feet clumsily and frowning at some dirty marks on her white dress. 'It's by an Oxford professor and it's all about the psychology of crime fiction. If we head off now we'll only miss the first few minutes.'

'You wouldn't enjoy it,' said Mrs Handibode. 'No, we'll go on to Mountebank Farm next. That's where much of the novel was set. There are at least four locations on the site that I want to visit. There's the cottage where Primrose Pengelly has her breakdown after the birth of—'

'A farm? But I'm dressed in white,' said Miss Wilderspin. 'And it takes us even further out of the village. I would like to see some of the presentations, Esme. This is my first festival.'

'There are talks all weekend,' said Mrs Handibode. 'And we are going to the Andrew Tremens's talk at four, aren't we? That's the important one, mark my words. And there's a dance afterwards with a live jazz band, if you like that sort of thing.'

'But that's hours away. Surely we're not going to be traipsing around a farm for all that time?'

'Of course not.'

'Oh thank goodness.'

'No, we have Handcock's Alley and The Butts to visit too,' said Mrs Handibode with a smile. 'Now come along. You'll never be a proper Agnes Crabbe scholar if you don't put in the legwork, Molly. So many murder scenes, so little time! Chop chop!'

'Yes, Esme,' said Miss Wilderspin with a sigh of resignation. Her feet hurt terribly in her patent leather shoes and she had begun to think murderous chop-chop thoughts of her own.

6

Some people believed that Stingray Troy Phones Marina Savidge's anger management issues stemmed from his loutish adoptive father's insensitive decision to name him after his second favourite TV show and its primary characters. It had, after all, meant years of remorseless childhood bullying and even occasional insensitive sniggers from his teachers. Others suspected that his rage stemmed from a sense of abandonment; his birth mother had given him away and had never made any effort to contact him in later life, so it was entirely possible that this too was a contributory factor to his condition. However, the psychologists who had examined him as a child believed that his outbursts were rooted in something much deeper, some personality disorder or chemical imbalance of the brain that Mr and Mrs Savidge couldn't have known about when they had first adopted him. Mrs Savidge often said that he had arrived on their doorstep wearing nothing but a nappy and a scowl, and that even if they'd named him Harry Happiness it wouldn't have made any difference. He had rarely smiled as a baby and had grown into a stroppy boy, and then a resentful teenager, and finally an angry man whose patience was as thin as graphene. Medication helped to take the edge off his anger and, on the rare occasions he saw her, his adoptive mother nagged him to take it. She would also point out that, despite having similar psychological problems, and having endured an identical troubled childhood, his brother Thunderbirds Jeff Scott John Virgil Gordon Alan Parker Lady Penelope Savidge had grown up to become a jolly and gentle soul, a Christian missionary and a Church of England vicar to boot. Savidge would then remind his mother that it was self-medication with alcohol that had turned his brother into the man he was today and that the Reverend Thunderbirds's situation was nowhere near as idyllic as she chose to paint it.

Whether it was something the government had done (or not done) or despondency over the performance of the Nasely First XI, Savidge could always find something to get worked up about. His acquaintances had learned the hard way that there were certain dates when he was to be avoided at all costs, such as Halloween, when his extreme displeasure with Trick or Treating had caused more than one parent to complain to the police about a 'red-faced man' who had made their children watch as he'd eaten all of their sweets in front of them. It was also a good idea to give him a wide berth during local and general elections, and the one week when it was definitely in everyone's best interests to avoid him was during the run-up to the Agnes Crabbe Murder-Mystery Festival. This year the event was celebrating the author's one hundred and twentieth birthday, and was predicted to be the biggest to date. It was also anticipated that Savidge would achieve startling new levels of indignation.

Despite having been open for business for less than an hour, he was already snapping at his clientele. The problem wasn't a lack of customers; the queue for his van was substantial and he was one of only a handful of hot food stalls on the village green. The problem was that these were not his usual customers. The Saturday afternoon sports fans, or tipsy drinkers returning home from the Happy Onion that he met most evenings, weren't that fussy about what they put into their bodies, but his festival queue was formed of more discerning eaters. Possessed of medical issues ranging from irritable bowel syndrome and coeliac disease to Crohn's and diabetes, and living with a diversity of allergies that took in pretty much every ingredient he used, each customer had insisted upon asking long and involved questions before deciding whether to buy or, in most cases, not to buy his food. Did he have gluten-free buns? Was there a reduced-sugar ketchup option? Did he use vegetarian cheese on his veggie burgers? Could he guarantee a total absence of nuts? He'd been asked to provide the provenance for the beef and whether the eggs in his mayonnaise were free-range and, with each and every interrogation, Savidge's blood pressure had climbed a little higher and his replies had become considerably snippier. Meanwhile, the line of increasingly grumpy Miss Cutter look-alikes got longer and longer and, as the sun grew warmer, more irritated and inclined to drink a great deal more liquor.

Savidge reached into his pocket and took out a bottle of pills.

'When Aristotle said that "Probable impossibilities are to be preferred to improbable possibilities", he was, of course, articulating the idea that we may create worlds that don't exist, but the denizens of those worlds must abide by the rules set by their creator if that world is to have integrity. For example, as readers, we can accept that Gandalf can do magic within the worlds of Middle-earth. But were he to do something jarringly out of place such as buying a sports car, or joining a reggae band, perhaps . . .'

The audience tittered and guffawed at such ludicrous ideas. The speaker continued.

'Middle-earth has its own reality and, consequently, if one of

Tolkien's characters were to do something that is quite possible in our world but highly improbable within the context of his world, our suspension of disbelief would collapse and it would destroy the character's illusion of reality. And we can see the same effect in crime fiction. As Agnes Crabbe herself once said: "Great novelists persuade you to believe their lies." Even the most outrageous plot device can be accepted by the reader as long as it follows the rules that the author has established. Let's take the classic country house murder-mystery, for example. By that I mean stories like Agatha Christie's *And Then There Were None* or Agnes Crabbe's *Brood of Vipers*. Both feature a "closed circle of suspects": a group of people isolated from the outside world while a murder investigation takes place. It's a situation that almost never occurs in the real world. It's fantasy. It's *Cluedo* for grown-ups. But it's now such a staple of detective fiction that we don't question its veracity. We accept it and, by doing so, it has become a common trope. And why not? It's fun to guess whodunnit, which is why we prefer detective fiction to real life; the lie is preferable to the truth because the truth isn't entertaining or intriguing enough. Ask any policeman and he'll tell you that the real business of murder investigation is dull by comparison because the rules by which the game is played are the rules of our mundane reality.'

Shunter frowned and twirled his moustache. He understood what the speaker was trying to say, that the mechanics of investigating serious crime were unglamorous, often repetitive, and not at all like the exciting investigative journeys of someone like Inspector Wexford or Holmes and Watson. But saying that it was 'dull' because it wasn't 'fun' or 'intriguing' enough seemed to him to devalue the death of a human being. He had particularly taken umbrage at the speaker referring to it as a 'game', something that it most certainly was not. Every killing was a tragedy for all concerned, even for the perpetrator most of the time, and it galled him to hear the speaker treat the subject so lightly. She had also insisted on using the word 'murder' throughout her talk when, in the real world, very few people plotted the death of another with malice aforethought. Homicide was usually the result of a brutal, unplanned act of violence, not a meticulously researched and organised campaign involving poisons, mechanisms, traps or misdirection. Homicide was pushing a knife into someone's guts during a momentary fit of rage and then leaving them to bleed out while you panicked and ran away and, as such, it was a world apart from the average murder-mystery plot.

As the speaker began detailing a list of her top ten most entertaining murders, Shunter apologised to the sour-faced Milly sitting next to him, stood up and shuffled crab-like along to the end of the row of chairs and towards the door. As he'd anticipated, the talk had only made him grumpy.

Outside, the pretty little High Street was awash with spring warmth. All evidence of the overnight rain had gone and red kites soared high above in a Wedgwood sky. Flies and wasps buzzed busily by and Miss Cutter clones of all shapes and sizes, ethnicities and ages trotted between venues for talks and screenings or followed tour guides around in little fan-club groups. Idly, Shunter wondered what the collective noun would be for a group of lady detectives. A *sleuth*, perhaps. Or a *murder*? He eventually settled upon a *gaggle*, because they reminded him of geese as they waddled about, selfie sticks raised high in the air like long necks as they photographed themselves at locations they recognised from the books.

Outside Mrs Scattergood's Olde Fashioned Sweete Shoppe, the site of Smitheram's Grocery in *The Dead Do Not Rise*, he spotted a brace of bewildered-looking police officers and he felt some genuine sympathy for them. They would have been bussed in from Bowcester – the village was too small and too law-abiding to warrant its own bobby – and they would undoubtedly be pressed men. No young cop would voluntarily give up the excitement of everyday police work for a weekend of lost property enquiries and being treated as a glorified information bureau by a village full of middle-aged ladies. And what young coppers they were, he noted. Shunter remembered an old saying that went something like, 'You know that you're getting old when the police officers start to look young.' These two looked like children who'd been in the dressing-up box and Shunter suddenly felt very old indeed. He caught sight of himself reflected in the shop window and scowled. His hair had turned grey in his thirties and his waist had got lost somewhere in his forties. His jowly face, even when relaxed, looked like an old bulldog whose bone had been confiscated and the scowl was doing him no favours at all. Also mirrored in the glass were the many Millies behind him and Shunter suddenly realised that, dressed in nondescript dark trousers and a short-sleeved polo shirt, he was the person who stood out from the crowd.

Somewhere in the distance, the staccato piano theme to *The Miss Cutter Mysteries* was being played on a bad PA system, probably by a busker. It clashed with the maudlin accordion accompanying the morris dancers and the irritatingly upbeat carnival music coming from the village green. The sounds of the mechanical organ carried with it the smell of delicious and unhealthy fatty foods and Shunter's stomach growled in counterpoint. He made his way through the bustling gaggles towards the green and Savidge's van. He might be a pain in the arse at times but the angriest man in the village grilled a damned fine burger.

*

Savidge's day was going from bad to worse. The queue for his van was getting longer and his customers ever more quarrelsome and irascible. Many were hungover, having celebrated their arrival in Nasely by drinking long into the night at the hotel bar. Others had made an early start and swigged from wine glasses and hip flasks as they waited in line. Having just fielded a volley of questions about the safety of eating genetically modified onions, which he didn't actually use, Savidge now found himself passively watching as two fierce-looking ladies argued over the definition of free-range chicken. As the discussion raged on he reached for his medicine bottle and frowned. He had already reached the limit of his daily dosage and it was barely midday. He could feel his temper rising up inside, like the contents of a saucepan preparing to boil over. He closed his eyes and mentally ran through a relaxation exercise that he'd once been taught on an anger management course: *Inhale deeply for four seconds . . . One. Two. Three. Four. Then exhale for eight seconds . . . Feel the air moving in and out of your lungs.* His meditation was rudely interrupted by a loud rapping on the burger van's metal counter.

'You there! Young man! Wake up!' snapped a fearsome-looking virago brandishing a walking stick. 'I asked you a question! Does it still count as free-range if the chickens are fenced in?'

'What?' said Savidge.

'Yes. And what if the chickens have names?' slurred her companion.

Savidge growled dangerously.

Shunter walked past stalls selling local farm produce, jams, cakes and handicrafts. He waved and nodded to the villagers who were manning them, some in character as Miss Cutter, others in striped blazers and boaters in an attempt to recreate the Roaring

Twenties and looking like podgy extras from *The Great Gatsby*. A noisy traction engine was powering the mechanical pipe organ and there was a display of vintage farm machinery that nobody seemed very interested in. He said hello to a team of fire officers from Bowcester who, as part of their community outreach programme, had parked an engine on the green. Small children swarmed all over it wearing outsized yellow helmets and pressing buttons and swivelling levers that perhaps they shouldn't. He had a go on the tombola and won a bottle of terrible wine, which he immediately donated back to the prize table, and then joined the end of a disappointingly long queue for the burger van. He watched as Savidge fielded question after question and felt some sympathy for the man. Some of the Millies were really quite demanding and a few were downright rude, barking questions in that special imperious way that only older people who have been used to the good life can. A large number of them were obviously tipsy and several were very drunk indeed. An irritating cloud of midges was drawn to the line of warm bodies and added to everyone's grumpiness. As the minutes dragged by, Shunter began to realise that the queue was barely moving and, at its current speed, he'd be waiting at least half an hour for his food. With a resigned sigh, he walked away, beating the midges from the air in front of him, a move misinterpreted by Savidge as Shunter pretending to slap someone. He replied by miming wringing someone's neck. Shunter smiled wanly. Perhaps he'd avoid going to the Onion that evening if Savidge was having a particularly bad day. Even he had limits of patience.

Ever since her spat with Esme Handibode the night before, something had been gnawing at the back of Brenda Tradescant's mind. It concerned the book that had spilled out of the infernal woman's suitcase and the several other tacky romance novels that she'd hastily and unsuccessfully tried to conceal among her clothes. More specifically, it concerned the books' author, Simone Bedhead. Miss Tradescant knew a *nom de plume* when she saw one.

Erotic fiction had become a huge amateur industry in recent years and had spawned a few superstars such as E. L. James, the pseudonymous author of *Fifty Shades of Grey*, and 'Rocky Flintstone', whose books were the subject of the hugely popular *My Dad Wrote a Porno* podcasts. Miss Tradescant spent a great deal of her spare time surfing chat rooms and trawling through blogs and forums to find and read work by other writers, hoping to discover the magic formula that would offer her the same kind of success. She also wrote a great many erotic stories herself, mostly about Millicent Cutter, and did so under the name of 'Mademoiselle Bellefrage', a play upon the name of Miss Cutter's mortal enemy and *amour interdit*. Miss Tradescant knew that her bank manager fiancé would be horrified if he ever got to read the filthier kind of stories that she revelled in writing. He had no inkling of her baser literary passions or, indeed, of her somewhat promiscuous and regretful past, and that was the way she intended things to stay. 'Mlle Bellefrage' allowed her private life and her writer's life to be held away from each other at arm's length.

That Simone Bedhead was a pen-name, she had no doubt. The French-sounding Simone was a dead giveaway and, while Bedhead was a legitimate surname, a cursory Internet search had revealed it to be uncommonly rare. This made her suspect that the author of *Love's Moist Promise* and four other equally terrible books was, most probably, using it as a saucy pen-name. After all, 'bed head' was another name for a headboard, and it was also descriptive of the kind of hairstyle you'd have after a night of wild passion.

'Do you want another tea, dear?'

Miss Tradescant's train of thought was broken by the appearance of Mrs Ann Moore, proprietor of the delightfully named 'Moore Tea, Vicar?' café in which she sat. The café was bustling with Millies because it famously doubled as Crowfoot's Tea Rooms in *Broken and Snared*, in which Miss Rummage had been murdered with a strychnine-laced Bath bun. Mrs Moore was a kindly lady with a penchant for opal rings, ripe gossip and gimmicks. An oversized plaster bun decorated with raisins stood on the counter alongside an equally large bottle marked 'poison'.

'No thank you,' said Miss Tradescant.

'Doing the crossword, are you?' asked Mrs Moore, peering at the newspaper on the table. After completing the Sudoku, Miss Tradescant had doodled 'Simone Bedhead' several times in the page margins. 'What's the clue?'

'It's not a clue. It's more of a puzzle really,' said Miss Tradescant. 'Simone Bedhead is the author of several quite awful books and I am convinced that the name is an alias.'

'Looks like an anagram to me,' said Mrs Moore. 'I can see a Mona there straight away. And an Enid.'

Mrs Moore bustled off to talk to some other customers and Miss Tradescant found herself pondering upon her suggestion. Moving the letters around she quickly identified the surnames Meades, Shand, Mason, Bond, Haines, Dean and Osman and forenames including Denise, Niamh, Sinead, Damon, Aiden – there were plenty of men who wrote erotic fiction too – and even a Desdemona. But then her heart skipped a beat as the name Esme appeared. A sudden, incredible thought struck her and she quickly scribbled the name down again and began crossing off letters, one by one. As she drew a line through the final letter E, her heart began to race. There it was in black and white in front of her. Simone Bedhead was a letter-for-letter anagram of Esme Handibode.

The revelation quite took her breath away.

7

Savidge didn't start the fight, at least not directly. The first sputtering fuse had actually been lit by a sozzled member of the late Denise Hatman-Temples's Agnes Crabbe Literary Society, who had suggested to an equally intoxicated member of Gaynor Nithercott's Agnes Crabbe Book Club that the latter was responsible for the death of the former.

'Why was she still driving?' snapped the lady from the Agnes Crabbe Literary Society. 'She was nearly blind, for goodness' sake.'

'Her eyesight was obviously good enough for the DVLA,' said the lady from the Agnes Crabbe Book Club.

'Then how could she possibly not have seen the car in front of her?' said Society.

'It was dark. And raining. Maybe your dithery Hatman-Temples woman hadn't turned her lights on,' countered Book Club.

'Oh, now you're just clutching at straws. She was clearly a menace to other road users.'

'You can't say that. That's libel, that is.'

'You can't libel the dead,' said Society. 'Any fool knows that. It would be slander. At least know the difference between torts before you make silly accusations.'

46

'Silly accusations? It was you who said that Miss Nithercott caused the accident,' said Book Club. 'I've a good mind to report you to the police.'

'Fine with me,' said Society. 'I'm sure a proper investigation will prove that your Nithercott woman killed Mrs Hatman-Temples as surely as if she'd plunged a dagger into her heart.'

'You take that back!'

'No.'

'Take it back, you old sow!'

'I will not!'

It was at this moment that Savidge chose unwisely to intervene. 'Ladies! Ladies!' he said from the serving hatch of his van. 'Can't you go somewhere else and argue? You're upsetting my customers.'

'We *are* your customers!' said Society.

'Not if you don't buy anything, you're not,' snarled Savidge.

'She started it with her baseless allegations,' said Book Club.

'I don't care,' said Savidge.

'Baseless my foot!' blustered Society. 'It was—'

'Look, I don't give a toss who started what!' said Savidge, his face red with frustration. 'Just go away and take your silly bloody argument with you.'

'Hardly a silly argument!' snapped Society.

'Of course it's silly,' said Savidge. 'All this fighting between fan clubs is ridiculous. You're all the bloody same.'

The ladies bristled.

'We most certainly are not the same!'

'Most definitely! For a start, the Agnes Crabbe Literary Society has over—'

'Yes you are,' snapped Savidge. 'You're all obsessed. For fuck's sake, she was only a writer.'

Savidge ducked as a string of pearls whipped towards his face like a striking cobra. A venomous-looking crowd suddenly surged forward and, from somewhere within the melee, a selfie stick was thrown. Savidge deflected it with his burger flipper and it cartwheeled through the air before connecting heavily with the head of a tall, muscular and quite obviously male Miss Cutter. The man replaced his cloche hat and wig, picked up the selfie stick and glowered. Sensing that withdrawal was his best tactical option, Savidge shut the van's serving hatch and locked all of the doors. Outside, a small army of gin-soaked and angry Millies slapped and thumped the side of the vehicle and beat at the hatch with their walking sticks. Rumours ran through the crowds like Chinese whispers, becoming more insulting with each retelling.

'. . . said she was only a writer. Only a writer!'

'. . . had the audacity to suggest that she was a terrible writer . . .'

'. . . claimed that her stories are dreadful and that she couldn't write for toffee . . .'

'. . . said she was a talentless hack . . .'

Muscling his way through the mob, and a good six inches taller than everyone around him, the beefy drag artist reached the van and peered angrily inside. He began hammering on the passenger window with a sizeable fist, and many of the enraged and inebriated Millies joined in with the beat, drumming on the side of the van.

'What did you do that for?' he shouted through a badly applied lipstick sneer. He pointed to a red mark on his forehead. 'Come out here and apologise!'

'Not happening,' shouted Savidge, having decided that discretion was the better part of valour.

'Come out here, you coward!'

The drag artist grabbed the door handle of the van and began repeatedly pulling at it. The vehicle began to rock from side to side. Seeing this, the Millies added their weight to his efforts and the van began to sway more violently.

'Come out here and apologise, you little shit!' yelled the drag artist. 'Be a man!'

'You first, mate!' Savidge shouted back.

The taunting made the big man double his efforts. By now he'd been joined by even more drunken Millies, who had heard that the burger man had apparently stated that Agnes Crabbe was the worst writer who had ever lived.

Savidge was confident that the big cross-dresser couldn't get the door open but he could still feel the panic and anger rising inside him. He closed his eyes, took a deep breath and tried once again to focus on his anger management exercises. The rocking of the van was becoming more and more pronounced, and he began to wonder if there was even a remote possibility that it could tip over. Suddenly, the fridge door whipped open, spilling cans and soft drinks bottles on to the floor. Utensils and bags of bread rolls began toppling from shelves and, more worryingly, the hot oil in the deep-fat fryer began to splash about. Savidge looked over his shoulder and realised that, even if tipping the van over wasn't possible, he still had a problem.

'Okay, I get the point! I'm sorry!' he shouted at the crowds outside. 'Can you stop now, please? There's hot oil back there!'

His begrudged apology was lost in the din of their massed rage. Fuelled by a liquid diet of gin and Pimm's, and exhibiting exactly the kind of partisan-inspired violence that set football fans at each other's throats, the militant Millies continued to attack the van of the man who had, apparently, dared to say that Agnes Crabbe's novels were only fit for use as toilet paper. Meanwhile, several small fights had broken out between members of rival fan clubs who had seized the opportunity of the crush to settle old scores. Heavy handbags were swung, wrinkled faces were slapped and varicose shins were kicked. Inside the van, Savidge bounced off the walls as he tried to make his way into the kitchen area to turn off the appliances. But he was too late. The nearside wheels lifted from the grass and, as the vehicle crashed back down, the sudden lurch sent a small wave of cooking oil sloshing from the fryer on to the hot plate where it burst into flames. Savidge searched desperately for a fire extinguisher and it was his misfortune that the first one he found was the wrong one. As he squeezed the trigger he was treated to a near perfect demonstration of why you should never use water on an oil fire. The fryer erupted and, all of a sudden, the whole interior of the van seemed to be ablaze. Having thrown himself back into the driver's compartment, and caught his groin painfully on the gearstick in doing so, he scrabbled desperately for the door handle and launched himself into the open air just as the cans of fizzy drinks, which had been sitting in the middle of the burning floor, began to explode. The van was rocking no longer – at the first suggestion of a fire, the mob of Millies had disappeared back into the large crowd that had gathered to watch – and as cans and bottles began to burst with a sound like shotgun fire, the crowd pulled back further still. Toes were trodden upon and ribs were elbowed and several more fights broke out as old rivalries and unsettled scores added energy to the violence. By the time that the two young police officers arrived at the scene, the fire was very fierce and very high and the local fire officers who, handily, had an engine parked just fifty yards away, were gearing up to tackle it. Their job wasn't made any easier by the scrum of at least eighty Crabbe fans who were attempting to knock seven bells out of each other. One of the police officers strode into the crowd.

'You will stop fighting immediately and disperse!' he shouted. 'I repeat. You will stop fighting immediately and disperse!'

No one stopped fighting immediately and no one dispersed.

Savidge had got a good distance clear of his burning van but he hadn't managed to avoid the irate female impersonator who still seemed intent on his pound of flesh. Having chased his quarry down and rugby tackled him to the ground, the big man was now sitting astride the burger man's chest, his knees painfully pinning his prisoner's arms down crucifixion-style and his crotch pushing insistently against his chin. Savidge wriggled violently and howled in frustration.

'Apologise!' snarled the drag artist.

'Get . . . off . . . me . . . you . . . freak!' shouted Savidge. The drag artist dug his knees deeper into Savidge's fleshy biceps and watched the man's anger rise several notches, as did the tone and timbre of his agonised yelps. Starved of blood, Savidge's hands began to turn a ghastly white.

'Say you're sorry first!'

'Fuck you! Fuck all of you and Agnes fucking Crabbe and her stupid fucking books!' screamed Savidge. His face was dangerously purple and fat veins stood out at his temples. His nose started to gush with blood and he began to thrash about wildly. The big drag artist rode him like a bucking bronco, bearing down even harder and grabbing his prisoner's wrists in an effort to keep him under control. Savidge frothed and gurgled, blood spurting from his nostrils like a geyser and somewhere deep inside his brain something went 'click'. Pinned to the wet grass by eighteen stones of female impersonator and desperately gasping for breath, he glared at the bulging gusset that filled his field of vision and sank his teeth into the man's plump scrotum. The drag artist screamed and seemed to launch five feet vertically into the air and, in a second, Savidge was up on his feet and running, blind and deaf to the agonised yells of his victim and to everything else except the pounding of hot blood in his ears and his own desperate need to get as far away as possible from people dressed as Millicent Cutter.

As he dodged and weaved between the Millies, his oxygen-starved brain barely registered any details of his surrounding; all he saw was a blur of people all dressed the same. Miss Cutters. Cutters here. Cutters there. Cutter after Cutter after Cutter. A group of them was making its way towards the Empire Hotel and blocked his path. At its centre was a woman he recognised immediately from posters in the pub and from the television. The name Greeley surfaced briefly in his head but then vanished. All he knew for certain was that this was Cutter Prime. The Alpha Cutter. The Queen of the Colony. For a moment their eyes met, but then he swerved to the left, giving her entourage a wide berth, and he ran on, blood still spraying from his nose and spattering the dresses of outraged festival-goers as he passed by them. Tall Cutters, short Cutters, fat, thin and bespectacled Cutters, young sexy Cutters, black, brown and pasty-white Goth Cutters . . . his crazed vision accentuated their features as if he was seeing them through a fisheye lens and his sense of reality began to slip quickly away. His mind conflated the sights before his eyes with every post-apocalypse film he'd ever seen. He ran past the pub and along the Coxeter Road as fast as his legs would carry him.

Shunter had bought himself a bacon butty at the Moore Tea, Vicar? café but had neglected to buy a drink with which to wash it down. Or, to be more accurate, he had elected to take the sandwich away rather than eat in. Mrs Moore knew that he was an ex-police officer and always insisted on sharing the local gossip with him, but he wasn't in the mood today to hear about Mr Hemerton's late-night lady visitors or Mr and Mrs Farmery's penchant for rubber goods. Therefore, he'd bid her a good morning and, despite his best intentions, had found himself being drawn towards the Happy Onion. There was nothing on offer in the festival programme that took his fancy at that particular moment and, while he enjoyed Agnes Crabbe's books, he had no time for the fawning sycophancy that pervaded most of the live events. The next one that he wanted to see was solicitor Andrew Tremens's talk at 4 p.m. and so, as he had a few hours to kill, a pint or two of To Die For seemed a reasonably good way to spend them.

From somewhere towards the village centre there suddenly came a curious strangulated wail, like an animal in pain, and Shunter stopped and looked towards the eerie sound. There was a sudden commotion among the crowds of Millies as a bloodied Savidge, plum-faced and screaming 'Cutters! Cutters!' at the top of his lungs, barged his way through them. He was moving so fast that he was already out of sight before Shunter had decided whether he should see if the man was okay or not.

Helen Greeley thanked the members of the Festival Committee for their kindness in seeing her to her hotel but insisted that she was fine getting to her room by herself. She had, admittedly, been slightly rattled by the sudden appearance of the bloody man who had been screaming in the High Street, but he had obviously not been interested in her and her anxieties had quickly subsided. She stepped into the lift and waved to the fans that had gathered in the foyer for yet another impromptu signing session. But as the doors slid shut and she was finally alone, her expensive smile faded, she exhaled deeply and her shoulders dropped. It had been a long morning. She felt as if she weighed several tons.

She quickly checked all of the smaller rooms in her suite and then made a more detailed inspection of the bedroom and lounge, checking inside wardrobes, behind curtains and under the bed. Satisfied that she was alone, she kicked off her shoes and made straight for the mini-bar. She was still jetlagged after flying back from a personal appearance at a convention in California two days before, and the opening ceremony, followed by two hours of meets and greets, had left her exhausted. The fact that her break-fast had consisted solely of gin probably hadn't helped either. The morning had seemed to go on for ever, what with the long queue of fans thrusting DVDs, books and posters under her nose for her to sign, and being asked question after question after question about Agnes Crabbe and Millicent Cutter that she didn't have the knowledge to answer. The fact that her agent wasn't on hand to act as a buffer hadn't helped; Portia Furstinhinde was fiercely protective of her clients and didn't suffer fools gladly. But she had been selected for jury duty and hadn't been able to get out of it. The choice, therefore, had been left with Greeley as to whether or not she wanted to attend the festival alone and, despite Portia's advice to the contrary, she had decided to do so. She didn't relish the idea but, as demanding as these gigs were, she felt obliged to attend. After all, her fans had made her the star that she was and she was not about to forget that. Besides, she told herself, it would also be good for her to build up her self-reliance. Memories of 'the incident', as she chose to call it, were still fresh in her mind and she'd suffered nightmares and panic attacks ever since. Despite her bold outward appearance, the events of the past year had shaken her confidence badly.

She dismissed the collection of tiny bottles in the mini-bar and went to her suitcase, producing a large bottle of gin and a bottle of tonic. She carried them into her bedroom and walked out on to her balcony. It had a lovely view of the hotel's landscaped gardens and the canal beyond but she had no time for such things. What she needed was sleep. She shut the net curtains but left the French windows open to allow a breeze into the room. She stripped off her Miss Cutter costume and, lying on the comfortable bed in her underwear, she poured herself a very large gin and a very small tonic and finished off the glass in two gulps before reaching over to her bedside table drawer for the bottle of sleeping pills she knew were in there. But then she decided against it. The tablets wouldn't mix well with the amount of gin she'd drunk in the past few hours, and she had an event to attend at 6.30 p.m. She didn't want to oversleep or make herself ill. She shut the drawer and reached for her earplugs and sleep mask instead.

Savidge slowed to a trot and caught his breath. His head pounded and his nose was still bleeding profusely. 'Cutters,' he panted. 'Cutters.'

The air seemed to suddenly disappear from his lungs and blackness edged his vision. His heart was beating so loudly that the sound drowned out everything else. He felt his legs go weak as nausea washed over him. He was barely conscious as his body slammed into the tarmac of the road and was therefore mercifully oblivious to the pain that the impact would have caused him. His head clonked noisily off a kerbstone and the last thing he saw before he passed out was a crowd of Miss Cutter look-alikes ambling towards him, their gnarled hands outstretched.

'Cutters . . .' he gurgled.

In the First Aid Tent, there was some confusion about how to treat the female impersonator's injury. The volunteers, a huddle of barely pubescent St John Ambulance cadets, were doing little more than giggling among themselves and it was only due to the appearance of one of the village's oldest residents that anything was being done at all. Ninety-four-year-old Mrs Joan Gawkrodger, who'd popped in to get a sticking plaster after pricking herself on a brooch pin, had been an ambulance driver during the war and a career midwife. She certainly wasn't shocked by the sight of a bloodied groin.

'So when was your monthly due, my dear?' she said as she attempted to pull a pair of surgical gloves over hands made claw-like by osteoarthritis.

'I'm not a girl. And I'm in agony.'

'Yes, I used to get frightful cramps myself when I was your age too,' said Mrs Gawkrodger. 'And no, you're not a girl any more. You are a woman now. The Scourge of Eve has—'

'No, you don't understand. My name is Baxter Pole, I'm thirty-eight and I'm a man,' said the patient. 'And I'm in quite a lot of pain.'

Mrs Gawkrodger groped in her handbag and located her

spectacles. She clumsily manoeuvred them on to her nose and the lenses magnified her eyes to alarming proportions. 'Good grief, so you are. How on earth can you be menstruating then?'

'I'm not menstruating,' snapped Pole. 'And most of the blood is someone else's.'

'You mean another woman has—'

'It's from a nosebleed.'

'I don't know . . . boys turning into girls and girls turning into boys,' muttered Mrs Gawkrodger, desperately trying to get a grip on the situation. 'I suppose there are bound to be some side effects. I mean to say, it's not natural, is it? Removing this and opening that and—'

'I haven't had a sex change and I'm not having a period,' said Pole in exasperation. 'I've been bitten on my . . . down there.'

The cadets giggled some more.

'Bitten? Bitten by what?' said Mrs Gawkrodger. 'A horsefly? A mosquito? Don't say a dog?'

'A burger van man, if you must know.'

'I see,' said Mrs Gawkrodger, who didn't. She fell back upon practicalities. 'Well, I suppose we'd better have a look then. Hitch your skirts up, there's a brave . . . er . . .'

The damage wasn't nearly as bad as the amount of blood made it seem. Savidge's nose had supplied most of it, and his bite had barely broken the skin but, even so, Mrs Gawkrodger found herself wondering how to treat such an injury. A sticking plaster seemed obvious but she wasn't so far removed from the memory of male genitalia to know that removing said plaster would be painful in the extreme, especially when it involved an unshaved scrotum. She therefore decided upon a gauze pad and began unrolling a length of bandage with which to hold it in place. She left Pole to clean his own testicles with a sterile wipe rather than take on the job herself.

'How can you have lived in Nasely your whole life and know so little about Agnes Crabbe?' asked Mrs Handibode with a little too much disdain.

'She died long before I was even born,' said Vic defensively. 'And no one really knew anything about her until her books were published, did they? All we ever heard as kids were daft rumours and gossip.'

'People can be so unkind,' said Miss Wilderspin.

Mrs Handibode and Miss Wilderspin had made good time visiting the places on their itinerary and were now half an hour ahead of schedule. Mrs Handibode had therefore suggested that they take a refreshment break in the pub. They found themselves a table and while Miss Wilderspin excitedly soaked up the atmosphere of the bustling bar with its olde worlde charm and Agnes Crabbe memorabilia, Mrs Handibode reproached the landlord.

'My dad told me that she was a witch and ate babies,' continued Vic. 'And my Aunt Meg said she was like that Miss Haversham in *Great Expectations*.'

'Miss Haversham wasn't a cannibal!' said Mrs Handibode.

'No, I mean pining away in her cottage, grieving for her lost love.' Vic pointed to the framed photograph of Daniel Crabbe in his army uniform.

'What nonsense,' said Mrs Handibode. 'She was a perfectly happy young woman, if her personal diaries are to be believed. And she'd hardly lie to herself, would she?'

'Just repeating what I was told,' said Vic, emptying the glass washer.

'And anyway, theirs wasn't some great love affair,' said Mrs

Handibode. 'As was normal back then, her marriage was more to do with her father's wishes than her own.'

'But it is true that she never left the house after he died, isn't it? Which you'll admit is a bit weird. I mean, she was only in her early twenties. It wasn't too late for her to start again.'

'She didn't want to start again. She craved solitude, as people of genius so often do. In *A Writer's Diary* Virginia Woolf wrote that "lonely silence is inseparable from the creative impulse". Seclusion freed Agnes from the distractions of everyday life and allowed her to write.'

'Yes, but that doesn't answer my original question,' Vic persisted. 'Why write books if you don't want anyone else to read them?'

'Actually, she would have loved to see her work in print,' said Mrs Handibode. 'But Agnes knew that Miss Cutter's promiscuity would have been seen as scandalous. Her stories were much too racy and she would have felt the sharp point of the critics' pencil if she'd tried to get them published, mark my words.'

'That's why she insisted that they only be submitted to a publisher after her death,' added Miss Wilderspin.

'Not quite, Molly,' said Mrs Handibode. 'Her express instructions were that the suitcase into which she'd placed her writings must not be opened until the first day of the new millennium. I think, like many who lived through the two wars, she maintained a kind of *fin de siècle* optimism; that the twenty-first century would see the dawn of a new golden age of peace and tolerance. She would be so disappointed in us.'

'You really do know your Agnes Crabbe, don't you?' said Vic.

'I've often said that I could have been her in a previous life,' said Mrs Handibode proudly.

'So this talk this afternoon, what's that all about?' asked Vic.

'Andrew Tremens is the grandson of the solicitor with whom Agnes left her manuscripts,' said Mrs Handibode. 'He was the person who opened the suitcase and discovered what it contained. And, consequently, in the absence of living family, he is trustee for her corpus of work. He knows almost as much about Agnes Crabbe as I do.'

'So if he says he has something new and important to tell the world it'll be something good then?' said Vic.

'You can be sure of it.'

'I do hope the rumours are true,' said Miss Wilderspin.

'Now then, we mustn't fall prey to silly speculation,' said Mrs Handibode.

'Rumours?' asked Vic.

'Some people are saying that Andrew Tremens's announcement is about the discovery of a lost manuscript,' said Miss Wilderspin. 'Wouldn't it be amazing if that were true?'

'I guess it would be.'

'It's very unlikely,' said Mrs Handibode.

'But there is a gap in her writing,' said Miss Wilderspin. 'She wrote at least one book a year, often two, but there is nothing for 1934 or 1935. And that's right in the middle of her most productive period.'

'We shall see,' said Mrs Handibode.

'Excuse me for butting in, but I couldn't help overhearing,' said Frank Shunter. Seated at an adjacent table, the conversation had piqued his interest. 'Are you saying that there may be an unpublished Agnes Crabbe novel?'

'Yes,' said Miss Wilderspin. 'Exciting, isn't it?'

'The evidence is quite circumstantial, I'm afraid,' said Mrs Handibode sniffily. 'The theory is based on conjecture and wishful thinking. You'd know all about it if you subscribed to my journal.'

'But the diary entries . . .' said Miss Wilderspin.

'Diary entries?' asked Shunter.

'Agnes kept very detailed diaries and she often recorded ideas for her stories in them,' explained Mrs Handibode. 'And there are a number of plot devices and character studies in her 1934 diary that don't correspond to any of her known books.'

'Yes, and then, in an entry from July 1935 she left the cryptic note: "Loaned WITM to IG",' said Miss Wilderspin excitedly. 'And her diary pages for July eighth to twelfth were torn out.'

'And this has been interpreted by some people as meaning that she loaned a manuscript to someone to read,' said Mrs Handibode. 'Presumably Iris Gobbelin, her brother's widow and closest friend, judging by the initials.'

'Ah, the girl who Agnes Crabbe might have had a relationship with?' asked Vic.

'Absolute rot,' said Mrs Handibode. 'There is no evidence of any such relationship.'

'But didn't I read—'

'What you read was a figment of Pamela Dallimore's puerile imagination,' sighed Mrs Handibode. 'That stupid woman and her wretched so-called biography have done a great deal of harm to the serious study of Agnes Crabbe and her works. I could strangle her some days.'

'IG could be Iris Gobbelin,' said Miss Wilderspin, returning to the subject under discussion. 'And WITM could stand for *Wallowing in the Mire*.'

'You know, of course, that all of her book titles are based on biblical quotes?' said Mrs Handibode.

'Indeed,' lied Shunter, who hadn't noticed.

'But there's no persuasive evidence that WITM is even a book title,' continued Mrs Handibode. 'It might stand for . . . oh I don't know . . . Williams' Invigorating Tonic Medicine, for all we know.'

'Interesting,' said Shunter, twirling his moustache. 'I'm sorry, I should introduce myself. I'm Detective Sergea— Sorry. Old habits. Frank Shunter.'

'You're a policeman?' said Miss Wilderspin.

'Retired,' said Shunter. 'I moved to the village last year. This is my first Agnes Crabbe Festival.'

'Agnes Crabbe Murder-Mystery Festival,' corrected Mrs Handibode.

'So, this possible new manuscript,' said Shunter. 'Will it be—'

The remainder of his sentence was lost behind the sound of a loud 'Aha!' as Brenda Tradescant and a small group of her supporters from the Millicent Cutter Appreciation Society entered the pub and marched purposefully towards Esme Handibode.

'There you are!' barked Tradescant. 'I have a bone to pick with—'

She stopped suddenly and the two women stared at each other aghast. Quite by accident they had both chosen to wear lime green and, while the cut of each dress was slightly different from the other, the colour was identical. Miss Tradescant quickly regained her composure and thrust a tablet into her rival's face.

'Your dirty little secret is out, Esme,' she said triumphantly, showing the tablet to Shunter and Miss Wilderspin. On the screen was the lurid cover of a book called *Her Tender Wound* by Simone Bedhead.

'Pay her no heed,' said Mrs Handibode. She turned to Miss Tradescant. 'If you don't mind, we were having a private conversation.'

'Really? And during this conversation did you happen to mention what a massive hypocrite you are, Esme? Or should I call you Simone?'

'Oh!' said Miss Wilderspin.

'That's quite enough!' snapped Mrs Handibode.

'Enough? I've barely started,' said Miss Tradescant. 'Do you deny that you wrote this book?'

'What? Yes, I most certainly do deny it!'

'So it's a complete coincidence that you had several Simone Bedhead books in your suitcase? Don't pretend you didn't, because I saw you try to hide them.'

'I don't deny it. As I said, I have them for research purposes and—'

'And I suppose that it's also a complete coincidence that Simone Bedhead, author of such literary gems as *Love's Moist Promise* and *Gushing with Passion* is a perfect anagram of Esme Handibode?'

'Oh!' said Miss Wilderspin again.

'Don't listen to her ridiculous nonsense, Molly,' said Mrs Handibode. 'Of course it's not a coincidence. It's why I've been reading the books, you old fool. I'm looking for clues as to who the real writer is and why they've chosen to target me.'

'What?' said Miss Tradescant, caught off-guard.

'As you say, it's unlikely to be a coincidence. Someone is out to defame me.'

'What rubbish! You wrote these books. Admit it.'

'I will do no such thing. This is nothing but a clumsy attempt to undermine my authority. Probably by a member of some inferior rival society. It might even be one of your lot, for all I know.'

'My lot?' Miss Tradescant looked around her small coterie of followers and they all shook their heads vigorously in denial.

'Or you yourself,' said Mrs Handibode. 'I wouldn't put it past you for one minute. And if you are responsible, you should know that I have reported this nasty business to the police.'

'You're accusing me?' snapped Miss Tradescant.

'It's the sort of crass muck you revel in. And this is precisely the kind of petty and pathetic form of attack I'd expect from someone like you. You've always been jealous of my standing in the Agnes Crabbe community.'

'Don't you dare try to turn this around on me! You are Simone Bedhead! Admit it!'

'I admit no such thing. That is libel and I have a witness. He's an ex-policeman too.'

'Whoa now, ladies,' said Shunter. 'I'm sure we can sort this all out quite civilly if we just—'

'You haven't heard the last of this!' said Miss Tradescant. 'I am going to expose you to the world for the charlatan you are!'

And with that she stormed out of the pub.

Things had not gone to plan at the First Aid station. Mrs Gawk-rodger had made a decent enough job of bandaging up Baxter Pole's groin, despite her lack of dexterity, but had then dropped the unused end of the roll of bandage, which had bounced away across the floor, unravelling as it went.

'I'll just get a pair of scissors to cut off the excess,' she said. 'Someone might trip over it otherwise.'

Pole, who was feeling much better now that the painkillers had kicked in and the throbbing in his groin had subsided to a dull ache, grunted in reply. In the background, Mrs Gawkrodger clumsily clattered among the first aid boxes.

'Ah, here we go,' she said triumphantly as she walked back towards him and caught her leg on the very same length of bandage that she'd been concerned about as a tripping hazard. As she fell, losing her false teeth in the process, the bandage was pulled taut and tightened abruptly around her patient's genitals. Pole yelled and leapt off the medical table, desperately tearing at the bandages that were strangling his manhood, while Mrs Gawkrodger, her hip quite broken and in a great deal of pain, gummily called for help and then passed out. The cadets crowded in on her, delighted to finally have a patient they weren't too embarrassed to deal with.

'This is a fucking madhouse,' said Pole as he removed the last of the dressing and limped painfully out of the First Aid station. Outside, he took several deep breaths and glared at the Millies who pointed at his bloodstained dress. He promised himself that if he ever saw the burger van man again, he would teach him a lesson that he would never forget.

Savidge woke up in a brightly lit room. He had no idea where he was or how he'd come to be wherever he was. He was in a bed with white sheets – that much he could see without lifting his head – and a plain white curtain enclosed him on three sides. The ceiling was composed of white tiles with a complex and seemingly random pattern of decorative holes punched into them and his bed was made of grey painted tubular metal. Above his head he could see a curious collection of wires, tubes, knobs and switches. He realised that he must be in a hospital of some kind, presumably Bowcester General. Did that mean he was ill? He became aware of a throbbing ache in his head and, reaching a hand up to touch it, he found it swathed in bandages. Whether the injury had happened by accident or been inflicted by someone, he had no idea. Everything was a blank. Through a gap in the curtain he could see a poster that explained the dangers of deep vein thrombosis and, just above it, a clock showed that it was nearly three o'clock. Was that a.m. or p.m.? How long had he been unconscious?

The curtain swished open and a female voice from somewhere near his feet said, 'Hello there.' Savidge attempted to lift his head off the pillow but it made his temples throb so painfully that he was forced to lie back down again.

'Just lie still,' said the voice. 'You've had a nasty knock on the head. It's a good job someone phoned for an ambulance as you were losing a lot of blood. Head wounds are like that. And you'd had a heavy nosebleed.'

Savidge squinted at the clock, suddenly aware of its loud ticking. Like a bomb. A time bomb. He attempted to lift his head again but the world began to darken all around him and the sudden image of a hundred predatory Miss Cutters closing in, their twisted claws reaching for his throat, popped into his mind. Fear washed over him like a wave as he lapsed into unconsciousness again.

As the clock of St Probyn's struck the half hour after three, a buzz of excitement began to grow among the Agnes Crabbe fans who had started to gather outside the village hall. Some were looking distinctly the worse for wear, with torn dresses, dishevelled wigs and broken handbag straps, all evidence of the scuffle on the green. A few even had visible cuts and bruises. Shunter watched from the pub window and sighed.

'Doors open at quarter to,' he said, downing the dregs of yet another enjoyable but unintended pint. 'I suppose I'd better get over there and join the queue if I want to get a seat.'

'Have fun,' said Vic.

Towards the front of the queue, Esme Handibode and Molly Wilderspin stood in stony silence. Several times, Miss Wilderspin had considered opening a conversation but had then thought better of it. Her friend had been monosyllabic since the confrontation in the pub, which was very uncharacteristic of her, and had been giving off clear and unmistakeable signals of wanting to be left alone. There was an intensity behind her taut face and expressionless gaze; not so much a powder keg about to explode as someone pondering exactly how much explosive to buy at the powder-keg shop in order to inflict the maximum possible carnage. And her mood surely hadn't been improved by the discovery that Pamela Dallimore, the person she disapproved of more than anyone else in the world, was manning the door to the venue. Yet again the wretched woman had been given a major part to play in an Agnes Crabbe-related event: the revealing of possibly the most important news story in over a decade, if the hyperbole of the festival brochure was to be believed. Every so often, their eyes would meet by accident. There was nothing but hatred to be seen in either pair.

'I should have known that fraud would wheedle herself into the limelight somehow,' growled Mrs Handibode. 'And she hasn't even bothered to get the costume right. Where are her pearls? Miss Cutter would never go out without her pearls.'

'Oh, Esme,' said Miss Wilderspin. 'I've been so worried about you. You've hardly said a word for ages! Not since . . . well, you know . . .'

'I am livid, Molly, livid. You don't believe Tradescant's ridiculous accusations, do you?'

'Of course not. I know that you didn't write those books.'

'Thank you. That means a great deal to me. As if I'd ever sink so low as to write that kind of smut.'

'How long have you known about the anagram?' asked Miss Wilderspin.

'It was pointed out to me six weeks ago by one of my subscribers. And I've been trying to discover who this terrible Simone Bedhead is ever since. She has proven to be surprisingly elusive. Self-publishing may have given writers a great deal more freedom but it's also given them anonymity. The owners of the websites that host her mucky stories have been of no help what-soever. I ordered some physical printed copies of her beastly books in the hope that they might provide some clue. But they didn't.'

'And have you really told the police?'

'I have. But there's little they can do until I have some hard evidence. Unfortunately, an anagram of my name, as unlikely as it sounds, could genuinely be a coincidence. And I've received no threats or demands and my career has suffered no harm as the result of her, or his, actions. Until today, that is. That harridan Tradescant will tell everyone she knows, mark my words. She has a nasty streak running through her.' Mrs Handibode began searching through her handbag.

'I think it's probably just a prank that's gone a little too far,' Miss Wilderspin said, trying to sound reassuring. 'There may be no malice in it.'

'You always see the best in people, Molly, and I commend you for it. But I'm sure you understand that I cannot let them get away scot-free,' said Mrs Handibode, continuing to rummage in her bag. 'This could undermine my authority as a serious scholar. Perhaps I should talk to Andrew Tremens? He'd understand my situation. Blast. How annoying.'

'What's annoying?'

'I can't seem to find my—'

'Doors open in nine minutes, ladies,' shouted Pamela Dalli-more suddenly, eliciting a chorus of excited noises from the assembled Millies.

'How she has the gall to stand there masquerading as some kind of expert amazes me,' said Mrs Handibode. 'She's a lazy, attention-seeking idiot.'

'Shhh! She'll hear you,' said Miss Wilderspin.

'So what if she does? I've said the same to her face. It's obscene that she gets all the acclaim when all she did was write a very bad book. It makes my blood boil.'

'Hear hear,' said a voice from the queue behind.

'She's a disgrace,' said another.

'Stupid woman,' said a third.

Molly Wilderspin looked towards Mrs Dallimore and it was quite obvious from the furious expression on her face that she had overheard the comments too.

'Listen, I need to quickly go and do something before the talk starts,' said Mrs Handibode. 'Hold my place for me, Molly.'

'Yes, of course, Esme.'

Mrs Handibode walked past the front of the queue and favoured Pamela Dallimore with a joyless smile before disappearing from sight down Handcock's Alley, the narrow lane between the village hall and the library. Miss Wilderspin wondered where she was going and what was so urgent that she was willing to risk missing the start of the event.

'Seven minutes, ladies,' said Mrs Dallimore through gritted teeth.

'Ooooooh!' went the crowd.

'And gents,' said Shunter, quietly. He was, as far as he could see, one of only a handful of men to have joined the queue. Admittedly, most of the others were in drag, but there were at least two Dr Belfrage look-alikes. Although, looking again, he realised that one of them did have a suspiciously fulsome chest. Cross-dressing worked both ways, of course.

Several minutes passed by ponderously slowly. Miss Wilderspin looked anxiously around for Mrs Handibode but she was still nowhere in sight.

'Hurry up, Esme, or you'll miss it,' she said to herself.

Suddenly, there was a screech of brakes. A white van emerged from Handcock's Alley and skidded to a halt to avoid hitting a group of tipsy Millies tottering towards the rear of the queue. The driver, dressed as Miss Cutter but undoubtedly a man if his five o'clock shadow was anything to go by, glared out of the window and shook a gloved fist at the women he had narrowly avoided mowing down. The gaggle of inebriated Millies wobbled unsteadily towards the pavement cackling with laughter and waving apologies. The van then drove off at speed down the Sherrinford Road, tooting its horn to clear the way ahead.

'Well, we nearly had a real homicide to investigate there, didn't we, ladies?' shouted a visibly shaken Mrs Dallimore. 'But it won't stop the countdown! Two minutes!'

'Oooooh!'

Time seemed to stand still as people glanced excitedly at their watches and mobile phones. One particularly geriatric Milly fainted to the ground and had to be revived by her companions using their festival programmes as fans.

'One minute!'

An intense ripple of expectation ran through the crowd as the final few seconds passed by. Pamela Dallimore counted them down.

'Ten. Nine. Eight. Seven. Six . . .'

'Oh, where are you, Esme?' said Molly Wilderspin, looking frantically around for her friend.

'. . . Three. Two. One . . .'

As the church clock struck the quarter hour before four, Mrs Dallimore unlocked the double doors and threw them open. The crowd surged into the hall, and the screaming began.

10

Detective Inspector Brian Blount stared at his computer screen and tried to remember whether it was 'stationary' or 'stationery' that he had to type if he wanted to order some headed notepaper from police stores. The spellchecker offered no help at all. Just like him, it could spell both words correctly but it was annoyingly vague regarding their proper use. Blount had a similar blind spot for the words 'affect' and 'effect', and no matter how many times he learned the difference the information never seemed to stick. Resignedly, he looked up the answer in an online dictionary. He couldn't ask his staff. That would mean admitting that he didn't know something that they probably did, and that would never do.

Sudden whooping sounds from the main CID office next door broke his concentration. He stood up and, to the casual observer, he might have looked something like a wading bird unfolding its long legs and neck. Blount was unusually tall, just over six feet six, and skeletally thin. His two young nephews had been known to use him as a unit of measurement; one 'Uncle Brian' equated to two metres and the use of the term made estimations of height and length much easier for them to visualise. He opened his office door and ducked his head under the lintel.

'What's all the noise?' he asked.

'There's been a murder!' said Detective Sergeant Clifford Jaine, smiling.

Blount paled. 'What? Where? In Bowcester?'

'Nope.'

'Thank goodness for that. You had me worr—'

'In Nasely!' said Jaine, excitedly. 'Smack bang in the middle of the murder-mystery festival!'

'Are you sure it's not just some old spinster who's got a bit overexcited and popped her clogs?'

'No. It's a proper homicide. A nasty one too, judging by the info coming in.'

'The control room has sent a car over there with a couple of uniformed officers to preserve the scene,' added Detective Sergeant Nicola Banton.

'Isn't it great?' said a beaming Jaine. 'They had one in Uttercombe five years ago and it was a licence to print money for the investigation team!'

'Only if the overtime is authorised,' said Blount.

'Yeah, but DCI Chatterjee is on holiday in India, isn't he?' said Jaine. 'That means that you'll be the senior investigating officer for the case.'

'Yes. I suppose I will be,' said Blount, uncertainly. His brain frantically tried to recall operational procedures for homicides. He knew that he had a binder in his office that explained it all, but he wasn't about to refer to it while anyone was watching. He stroked his angular chin and looked at the excited chubby face of Clifford Jaine. The man was a competent detective, if a little childish and cheeky at times. Scruffy, untidy and overly fond of practical jokes and risqué humour, he was the polar opposite of the altogether more smart and sensible Nicola Banton. She was neat, methodical, and she enjoyed a good joke too but, unlike her colleague, was much better at gauging when it was appropriate. She was also an expert researcher and analyst and was tipped for promotion in the not-too-distant future. Annoyingly for Blount, both of his detective sergeants were better educated than he was and, he feared, were considerably more intelligent.

'A murder mystery at a murder-mystery festival, eh?' said Banton. 'It sounds like the plot of a bad TV detective series.'

'So what do we do first?' asked Jaine.

'Surely our priority is to identify witnesses and preserve any forensics,' said Banton.

'Yes. Exactly that,' said Blount, thankful for the reminder. 'You said that there's a patrol car en route. Are there no officers on scene?'

'No,' said Banton. 'There were two officers covering the festival, but they're downstairs in the custody suite.'

'They got duffed up by some old dears,' said Jaine. 'Apparently there was a fire and then a set-to between rival Agnes Crabbe fan clubs and—'

'What? No, never mind. Get over there now,' snapped Blount. 'Quickly, before the fans trample all over the crime scene.'

Jaine and Banton rushed out of the door and Blount stalked back into his office, pleased with how decisive he'd appeared to be. He reached down the operations manual for serious crime from a high shelf. The realisation had suddenly struck him that here was a golden opportunity to make his name. There hadn't been a homicide on Bowcester Division for well over ten years and, now that there had been, fate had decreed that he was to be the senior investigating officer. Finally, he had a case of sufficient gravitas to prove his worth, maybe even to get him a promotion into senior management and a cosy desk job managing budgets and resources, rather than having to deal with the visceral complexities of investigating crimes. And surely any homicide that happened in the middle of a bustling murder-mystery festival was bound to be a trouble-free investigation? After all, there were probably dozens of witnesses and, with them all being crime fiction fans, they'd probably have an unusually sharp eye for detail and would supply excellent descriptions of any suspects. As long as he followed procedure and didn't make any poor decisions, it was a dead cert that he'd be credited with solving the case and promotion would surely follow. He took a deep breath and smiled. This, he realised, was his moment to shine. He blew the dust off the operations manual and began to read.

In Nasely, Blount's worst fears about the crime scene were already becoming reality. The body of a woman lay on her back on the wooden floor of the village hall. Her face, or what was left of it, was a thing of bloody ruin that had been pulped and smashed as if by some kind of heavy object. She was, unsurprisingly, dressed as Millicent Cutter and had lost so much blood that the casual observer might have assumed her dress to be bright red even though the clean parts showed that it was green. A long, sinuous scarlet river ran away from the body and under the rows of empty chairs, pooling around a knot hole in a floorboard where, presumably, it was now dripping down into the foundations. Several Millies had already trodden in it and there were bloody size-five footprints all over the floor. A macabre element had been added to the grisly scene in the form of a large kitchen knife that protruded from between the victim's ribs. To add an extra level of mystery to the situation, there was no sign of Andrew Tremens – unless he was the victim. It was quite conceivable that the solicitor might have, as part of his event, got into drag. But, whichever theory you subscribed to – disappearance or death – it was certain that whatever Tremens had planned to reveal to the world had gone with him. Nothing had been left behind.

Having got over the initial shock, a number of Millies had taken it upon themselves to start examining the crime scene to look for clues. Some sported magnifying glasses and notebooks; a decade of reading Agnes Crabbe books, and several decades more of reading crime fiction in general, had instilled in them the notion that they could investigate any murder just as thoroughly as Campion, Barnaby or Wimsey could. They'd simply never had this kind of an opportunity before. Others were taking photographs and members of the various fan clubs had formed into small huddles to discuss possible scenarios.

'What if the killer hid inside a cupboard, slipped out, killed the victim and then sneaked back inside and only came out again when the crowds had filled the place? They could have hidden among all the confusion. Of course, they'd have to have been dressed as Miss Cutter to blend in . . .'

'Ooh, then they could be among us right now! How exciting!'

'Maybe Andrew Tremens was really a woman but had been living as a man. Or maybe he'd had a sex change? Either way, maybe it's his body . . .'

'The victim had a terminal illness and wanted to give us all a really good mystery to solve as her dying wish . . .'

'You do realise that the village hall occupies the same position on the High Street as the Little Hogley spiritualist church in *The Dead Do Not Rise*? Could that be significant?'

'So exciting!'

In the absence of police officers, Pamela Dallimore had tried her level best to keep people away from the body but with limited success; no one took her very seriously and every time she shooed one lady away, two more would pop up to peer at the gruesome scene like some embrocation-scented hydra.

'Ladies! Please keep back. You're contaminating the crime scene!' she shouted, having heard police officers say that on the TV.

'Do we know who it is?' asked a thickly bespectacled Milly.

'No formal identification has been made yet,' said Mrs Dallimore, falling back on TV police jargon once more.

'It looks like Esme Handibode to me,' said the Milly.

'It must have been a frenzied attack,' said another, sporting a brooch shaped like a skull. 'I take it that you counted the number of stab wounds?'

'Would you please stand back?' said Mrs Dallimore. 'The police are on their way.'

'Of course, seven is a very significant number, you know,' said brooch lady. 'In Hinduism there are seven chakras and there are seven sacraments in Catholicism.'

'Yes, I—'

'Muslim devotees walk seven times around the Ka'ba in Mecca,' said the informative Milly. 'And Buddha is often seen sitting within the seven petals of the lotus flower. Oh, and the Jewish Menorah has seven branches. It seems to me that there is a ritualistic flavour to this murder.'

'Look, you need to—'

'Did you know that the number seven appears throughout the Bible and is mentioned fifty-five times in the Book of Revelation alone?'

'But she's been stabbed eight times,' said Mrs Dallimore.

'Oh,' said the number-obsessed Milly, standing over the body and counting the stab wounds again. 'Ah yes. Silly me. I didn't include the one that the knife is poking out from. However, eight is considered a lucky number in China and the equivalent of our Lucky Seven, of course, and there's—'

'Wasn't very lucky for her, was it?' snapped Mrs Dallimore. 'Now would you mind moving along?'

'You did spot the pearls clutched in her fist, I assume?' said a Milly with shocking green eyeshadow.

'I did.'

'And there's a trail of pearls to the back door of the hall, look,' said Eyeshadow. 'Perhaps she threw them on the floor to try to make her attacker slip and fall over, like Miss Cutter does in the books?'

'No, that can't be right,' said another Milly with her broken arm in a cast. 'The victim is still wearing hers so they must belong to her attacker.'

'Oh yes! So she is. Then she must have grabbed at them during the attack,' said Eyeshadow. 'So her attacker may have been dressed as Miss Cutter too.'

'That's a significant clue.'

'I think the victim looks more like Brenda Tradescant.'

'The murderer could be someone in this room!'

'I thought that too.'

'Oh yes!'

'Isn't it exciting!'

'I've been waiting for the call all my life!'

'Me too! I can't wait to get started.'

'Excuse me,' said Molly Wilderspin. She sidled up to Pamela Dallimore, trying to avoid looking at the victim's mutilated face. 'But is that—'

'I think so, yes,' said Mrs Dallimore.

'Oh dear,' said Miss Wilderspin.

*

The arrival of the first police car, announcing its presence with flashing blue lights and sirens, caused further ripples of excitement throughout the Millicent hordes. The two uniformed officers on board immediately began ushering everyone out of the hall while setting up a crime-scene-tape perimeter around the building. Ten minutes later, CID officers Jaine and Banton arrived, closely followed by the police photographer and a forensics officer in a blue plastic boiler suit who began poring over the body and its immediate environs. A quite unnecessary but nevertheless legally required confirmation of death was issued by a local GP, although it was done at a distance as the unfortunate Dr Meissen hadn't seen anything quite so gory since his days as a hospital intern in the seventies and the crime scene made him feel quite bilious. Once all of the inquisitive Millies had been marshalled outside and the hall declared out of bounds, Jaine and Banton emerged from the building to look for witnesses.

'Who found the body?' asked Banton.

She was treated to a loud chorus of Miss Cutters all claiming that they'd been the first through the door.

'Look, you can't all have found the body,' she shouted. 'I just need to speak to whoever saw it first.' She was treated to another vocal barrage.

'They all went in at once when the doors were opened,' explained Shunter.

'And you are?'

'Frank Shunter. Retired DS. I live here in the village.'

'Nicola Banton, also a DS. Come inside for a minute. I might get more sense out of you than from this lot.'

Shunter ducked under the police tape and accompanied the detective back inside the hall. The warm, iron-rich scent of fresh arterial blood still hung in the air. It was something that he had hoped never to smell again. The irritating buzz of opportunistic flies, quick to catch the scent of death, broke the silence.

'I'm sorry I couldn't do more to preserve the scene,' said Shunter. 'I was some way back in the queue and the crowds meant that I couldn't get near it.'

'What's done is done. Mrs Dallimore did her best,' explained Banton, nodding her head towards the journalist who was sitting on a nearby chair looking shell-shocked and sipping at a cup of tea. 'Listen, as you're a local, I don't suppose you can confirm who the victim is, could you? We have a handbag and some personal effects that suggest that she's a Miss Brenda Tradescant, a local lady from over near Sherrinford. Mrs Dallimore also thinks that it's her. But someone else has suggested that it might be a Mrs Esme Handibode.'

'I can have a look,' said Shunter. 'But I hardly know either of them. I only met them today and then only briefly.'

'Perhaps the clothes then? To be honest, the face isn't going to help you.'

'You do realise that there are several hundred ladies in the village right now that are all dressed alike, don't you?'

'Yes, but we have to ask in case either of them were wearing something distinctive,' said Banton. 'We've also heard from Mrs Dallimore that Mrs Handibode and Miss Tradescant were involved in some kind of a fight earlier.'

'I heard it was a blazing row,' chipped in Mrs Dallimore. 'I understand that things got very heated. Apparently that old fraud Handibode has been moonlighting by writing—'

'Actually, I was there,' interrupted Shunter. 'And it was more of a spat. It certainly wasn't serious enough to lead to something like this.'

'You don't know Esme Handibode,' said Mrs Dallimore. 'She's

a spiteful woman. Hard as nails. She's made herself a lot of enemies over the years, Brenda Tradescant among them.'

'Sergeant Banton, could you come over here?' said the forensics officer. He held up a folded and bloodstained piece of paper
with a pair of forceps.

'Want me to wait outside?' asked Shunter.

'Not unless you want to,' said Banton, walking across to the
crime scene and snapping on a pair of surgical gloves. 'I guess
you've seen this kind of thing before.'

'Too often,' said Shunter, following her. 'I worked eighteen
years in homicide.'

'This is my first,' said Banton. 'It's all I can do not to throw
up.'

'No one could blame you,' said Shunter, grimacing at the
body. 'That's a nasty one. And, for what it's worth, I have no idea
who it is. It could be either of the ladies you mentioned. Or any
other woman of that build who's wearing a green dress.'

'Now then, what have we here?' said Banton. She took the
forceps carefully from the forensics officer. The bloodstained
paper bore a single bleak sentence written in thick black marker
pen:

Pay up or else.

'My my,' she said, showing it to Shunter. 'This adds a whole
new twist to things.'

The front door opened and the hall was momentarily filled
with the noise of several hundred Millies discussing the murder.
DS Clifford Jaine emerged from the crowd and slammed the
door shut behind him. 'That was a complete waste of time,' he
said. 'No one saw or heard anything prior to the doors opening.

But they've all got a bloody theory about whodunnit of course. Who's this then?'

'Frank Shunter,' said Shunter, extending a hand. 'Retired DS. Ex-Met.'

'London, eh? Probably seen more homicides than we've had hot dinners,' said Jaine.

'A few,' said Shunter, modestly.

'First one we've had in donkey's years. It's my first anyway.'

'We have two names,' said Banton. 'We have a Miss Brenda Tradescant and a Mrs Esme Handibode. Both ladies fit the description of the victim.'

'That's something to go on then,' said Jaine. 'I can put out a public appeal for both of them to contact us.'

'There's more. Mrs Dallimore says that there was a quarrel between them earlier.'

'So whoever this is, the other might be the suspect? Excellent. But which is which?'

'It seems most likely that the victim is Miss Tradescant,' said Banton. 'Her handbag was found next to the body. We have her driving licence, credit cards, her phone . . .'

'Must be her then,' said Jaine.

'Unless the victim stole the bag from Miss Tradescant,' said Shunter. 'Or the perpetrator left it behind in a panic.'

'Good point,' said Jaine.

'About this quarrel earlier,' said Banton. 'As a matter of inter-est, what was it about?'

'Miss Tradescant accused Mrs Handibode of having written some trashy novels,' explained Shunter. 'The exchange got a bit heated, but that's all.'

'But they were from rival fan clubs,' said Banton. 'And they take their fan-clubbing very seriously around here.'

'Well, that particular fan got seriously clubbed, didn't she?' said Jaine, looking closely at what remained of the victim's head.

Banton frowned at her colleague. 'Have a bit of respect, Cliff.'

'You're not suggesting that she's the victim of some kind of turf war, are you?' said Shunter.

'Stranger things have happened,' said Jaine.

'Maybe in London or LA, but not in Nasely,' said Shunter. 'The most heated this lot ever gets is over the correct pronunciation of "scone".'

'I dunno. There was a fight between fans on the green earlier and two uniformed officers got hurt,' said Jaine. 'Of course, there could be a much simpler explanation than fan-club rivalry.' He nodded towards the note in Banton's hand.

'You mean blackmail?' said Banton.

'Or a gambling debt that got out of hand,' said Jaine. 'She didn't pay up, so they sent some heavies around.'

'I guess it might be as simple as that,' said Banton.

'Except that the pearls don't make sense then,' said Shunter.

'The pearls?' said Jaine.

'She's wearing a string of pearls but her hand is clutching another broken string of pearls,' said Shunter. He bent to look more closely at her clenched fist. 'Cadaveric spasm, I presume.'

'Eh?'

'It's too early for rigor mortis to have set in, but her hand is locked around those pearls. There is a condition called cadaveric spasm or instantaneous rigor. It's not terribly common but I've seen it a few times. At the moment of death, most people go limp, but occasionally a person can suffer sudden muscular stiffening. If that's what's happened in this case, it's likely that she was grabbing those pearls at the exact time she died.'

'So she might have snatched them off the killer?' said Jaine.

'And loan sharks don't usually wear pearls,' said Banton. 'Which means that the suspect was possibly dressed as Miss Cutter.'

'Great. There's only about eight hundred of them in the village right now,' said Jaine.

'It does add some weight to the Handibode theory, I guess.'

'There's also the question of what the victim was doing in here before the doors were opened,' said Shunter.

'What do you mean?' asked Jaine.

'This afternoon's event was supposed to be one of the festival highlights. Andrew Tremens was going to reveal some big news; the most popular theory was that a previously unknown and unpublished Agnes Crabbe novel had been found. The place was locked down tight and surrounded by secrecy to avoid spoilers. So the victim, whoever she is, was either part of Tremens's event, or she was a fan and should have been queuing outside with the rest of us. If it's the latter, how did she get in here?'

'She could have broken in,' said Jaine.

'Or Tremens let her in,' said Banton.

'Why would he do that?'

'That's the other big unanswered question of course,' said Shunter. 'Where is Andrew Tremens?'

'Look, all I'm asking you to do is to carry on with business as usual,' explained Blount. 'The last thing we want is panic and a mass exodus of potential witnesses.'

'A mass exodus? After a murder?' said Mr Stendish, Leader of the Village Council. 'You don't know Agnes Crabbe fans.'

DI Blount had arrived in Nasely to take over the investigation and, as one of his first actions, had summoned the three members of the Festival Committee to meet him at the library where he was doing his best to convince them to carry on with events as if nothing had happened. The committee was having none of it.

'I wouldn't be at all surprised if visitor numbers increase,' added Stendish.

'Glen's right. They've never been so happy,' said a sharp-suited woman in a beret. Miss Imogen Olivia Clark was Head of Arts and Culture for Bowcester Borough Council.

'Our problem is that we're struggling to fill seats,' said Glen Stendish. 'All of this afternoon's scheduled events were sold out but no one has bothered to turn up to any of them so far. Everyone is hanging around outside the village hall like flies around a . . . well, you know . . . like bees around a honeypot.'

'Can't you issue a statement or something to make them

disperse?' asked Miss Clark. 'I mean, just look at them. They're like ghouls.'

She pointed out of the window to the village hall next door where a large crowd was rubbernecking outside the police-tape perimeter in the hope of catching a glimpse of the activity within. Many were huddling in small fan-club groups, discussing possible theories. Others were actively interviewing potential witnesses and recording their findings in notebooks and on their mobile phones. Local newspaper and radio reporters, who had expected to turn in the usual sedate coverage of the event, couldn't believe their luck and wandered among the crowds getting vox pops and interviews before the nationals arrived. Rumour had it that several outside broadcast vans were en route.

'I have speakers due to take the stage tomorrow who are threatening to go home if we can't guarantee them bums on seats,' said Miss Clark. 'So if you want us to carry on with business as usual, you need to get people away from the murder scene and back to the scheduled events.'

'The one saving grace we did have was Helen Greeley's talk this evening,' interjected Mr Horningtop, Community Projects. 'She's always a big draw. But the village hall is the only space large enough to accommodate everyone who bought a ticket.'

'We can't use the Masonic Hall because it's too small and, anyway, it's being set up for a dance at 8 p.m.,' said Miss Clark. 'You can see our dilemma, Inspector.'

'So if you can see your way clear to letting us have the village hall back for this evening that will help us immensely,' said Mr Stendish.

'But it's a crime scene!' said Blount. 'Don't you realise what that means?'

'Yes, but—'

'I can't release the hall until all of the forensic work is done,' said Blount. 'You can't disturb a crime scene. You'll just have to do the best you can with what you have.'

'We're trying to,' said Mr Horningtop. 'And we're keen to cooperate with you, but if we can't put on the events that people have paid to see, then some of them are bound to leave the festival and go home. Which is what you're telling us you don't want to happen.'

'It doesn't help that you've commandeered the library for your incident room,' said Mr Stendish. 'That's another venue we can't use now.'

'I'll see what I can do,' muttered Blount.

The committee seemed less than satisfied with this answer but they realised that it was all that they were going to get and left. Blount watched them walk off through the crowds and wondered why people seemed to be going out of their way to make his investigation more difficult. He was sure that he had, in his hands, the makings of a career-defining case and, with selection interviews for promotion to chief inspector just three months away, it couldn't be timelier. But this wasn't turning out to be the simple open-and-shut case he'd hoped for.

He ran over the facts in his head once again. A homicide had taken place on the first day of one of the UK's largest murder-mystery festivals where almost everyone – the victim, all of the witnesses and, very possibly, the offender – was dressed as the fictional detective Miss Millicent Cutter. The victim hadn't yet been officially identified, and the witnesses he'd banked on were all frustratingly unreliable and given to wild flights of fancy. And, to add to his troubles, it was a gift of a story for any reporter to cover; a murder to die for, you might say. With so many microphones and cameras coming into the area, Blount knew that his leadership would be under the microscope. He could not afford to have anything go wrong. And yet, so far, nothing was going right.

'We need to make some progress on this case,' he barked. 'Do we have a positive ID on the victim yet?'

'Not yet. The general consensus is that it's probably Brenda Tradescant,' said Jaine. 'But it might also be a lady called Esme Handibode. Apparently, neither lady has been seen since just before the body was discovered. I've issued a media statement that we want to speak to both of them as a matter of some urgency.'

'So one is the victim and the other might have done a runner?' said Blount.

'Maybe,' said Jaine. 'We found Tradescant's handbag next to the body, so she's one or the other. Mrs Dallimore was pretty sure that she's the victim but couldn't confirm it though. And nor could DS Shunter.'

'Who?'

'Mrs Dallimore?' said Jaine. 'She was on the door when the fans were let in. She's been acting as the Festival Committee's Agnes Crabbe expert because she wrote a biogra—'

'Yes, yes, I know that,' said Blount who, in fact, didn't. 'Who is DS Shunter?'

'Local bloke. Retired. Used to be in the Met,' explained Jaine. 'He lives in the village now.'

'Why was there an unauthorised DS at our crime scene?' said Blount. His voice had noticeably risen by several keys.

'Retired DS,' corrected Banton. 'He was queuing up to see the talk along with everyone else. And it's not like he was just some random member of the public that we let in. He's one of us, after all.'

'No, he isn't,' said Blount. 'Retired. That's the operative term. He used to be a police officer. But he isn't any more and he had no right to be at our crime scene. A closed crime scene.'

'But he specialised in homicide,' said Jaine. 'So we thought his input might be helpful.'

'And he did point out some very useful features of the crime scene,' added Banton.

'So you'll just let any unauthorised person trample all over our crime scene just because they say that they're an ex-homicide detective, will you?' snapped Blount.

'But—' began Jaine.

'Don't be so naive. These city cops all say that they were homicide detectives to show off,' said Blount. 'He was probably traffic or admin or something. So how much does this Shunter know?'

'As much as anyone does at this time, guv,' said Jaine.

'Which is not very much,' said Banton.

'Good. Let's keep it that way. From now on, he's not to be allowed back in there. Closed crime scene means closed. Author-ised personnel only. Do I make myself clear?'

'Guv?'

'City cops like him think we're all country bumpkins and vil-lage idiots,' said Blount. 'If we give him an inch, he'll muscle in and try to take over just to "show us how it's done". They can't help themselves. Look at Quisty.'

'DCI Quisty from Uttercombe?' said Banton.

'Yes, Quisty,' said Blount. 'Just because he had a bit of success in Birmingham, he thinks he can just transfer into this force and then presume to tell us all how to do our jobs.'

'A bit of success?' said Banton incredulously. 'He solved a series of cold cases that everybody claimed were unsolvable. And he caught that guy they called "the invisible man" who committed all of those seemingly impossible burglaries. He's a bloody genius.'

'He's like some kind of Sherlock Holmes, he is,' said Jaine.

'No detective is as good as he appears to be,' said Blount. 'He just got lucky. Or he's bent.'

'You don't really think that, do you?' said Banton.

'All I know is that he turned up at HQ, brown-nosed the Chief Constable and baffled her with his city bullshit, and suddenly he made Chief Inspector instead of me even though I had more service as a DI,' said Blount, bitterly. 'Trust me, city cops all think that they're better than us. But this is my case. It's not Quisty's, and it's not this Shunter bloke's either. He is not to set foot in the village hall and you will not share information with him. Do I make myself clear?'

'Yes, guv,' Banton and Jaine replied in unison.

'Good. Now, do we know what the victim was doing in the hall?'

'No,' said Banton. 'She might have been part of the event. But only Andrew Tremens knows that and he's vanished.'

'So who was the last person to see Andrew Tremens?'

'Mrs Dallimore I think,' said Jaine.

'And where is she now?'

'She was here,' said Jaine. 'She went back to her bed and breakfast quarter of an hour ago. To get changed, I think.'

'Then go and get her,' said Blount. 'And where is Shunter now?'

'I think he went to the pub.'

'Right. Go and get Dallimore. I'll be back shortly,' said Blount and he left.

'What was that all about?' said Jaine.

'Rampant male insecurity?' said Banton.

*

In his hospital bed, Savidge napped fitfully, twitching like a dreaming dog. His limbs jerked spasmodically, his face was red and his lip curled back into an occasional snarl. He muttered angry gibberish in which the only comprehensible word was 'Cutter'. In his confused half-sleeping fantasies, he was a highly trained combat specialist being hunted down by his ruthless arch-enemy and her army of zombie look-alikes. There were hundreds of them, possibly thousands, stumbling and shambling after him like in a scene from every shoot-'em-up video game he'd ever played. Every turn, every potential hiding place, revealed yet more Cutters whose only aim was to either kill him or drag him before their leader. He strafed them with machine-gun fire. He lobbed grenades at them. Blood spurted in fountains, heads exploded like dropped watermelons and severed limbs flew about like obscene fleshy boomerangs. But still they came. Relentless. Untiring. The wrong side of fifty. His way was suddenly blocked by a barricade of burning fast-food vans and a wall of murder-mystery novels stacked vertiginously high. Tall flames licked up the wall and crisped the leaves. Hot black embers of burning prose filled the air like dirty snowflakes, their edges glowing a bright orange. Bottles and cans of fizzy drink exploded noisily inside the burning vehicles and, at the very summit of the high wall, stood the Queen of the Cutters. She looked remarkably like Helen Greeley and she was laughing demoniacally. There was no way to get to her and there was no chance of breaking through the wall. He was trapped and the Cutter hordes would soon be upon him. Savidge took a grenade from his belt and pulled the pin with his teeth. At least he'd take some of the cloche-hatted bitches with him . . .

He woke up with a start. His head didn't hurt quite so much and some of the dizziness seemed to have gone. He was now aware, however, of pains elsewhere. He sat up slowly and saw that his knees were bloodied and bandaged and so were his elbows. He tried to gather his chaotic thoughts but clarity was hard to find. A bullied childhood, an abusive father figure, a naturally combative nature and many years of trying to suppress his anger had all conspired to leave him teetering on the edge of a nervous breakdown. But now the destruction of his van, his fight with the big man in drag and a good hard blow to the head had kicked him over, and his imagination had responded by constructing a mostly imaginary world to explain all of the terrible things that seemed to be happening to him. Elements of all the action films he'd ever seen merged and blended together. He was James Bond, he was John Rambo, he was someone dangerous played by a gravel-voiced Liam Neeson. He was a secret agent, a special forces commando, a lone wolf in a dystopian world ruled by Miss Cutter and her army of doppelgängers. They were alien body-snatchers, or evil clones, or androids, or mind-slaves or something like that, and they were all hell-bent on capturing or killing him. But he would not give them the satisfaction. Twice they had tried to kill him – first with fire and then between the powerful thighs of a murderous transvestite – and twice they had failed. They would try again, of that he had no doubt, unless he stopped them first. But there were too many of them for him to fight alone. He needed to take out their leader, the evil master-mind – or was it mistressmind? – who controlled them. '*Kill the head and the body will die,*' someone wise had once said. Savidge didn't know who had said it, but he did know where the 'head' was hiding, and without her guidance, her army would be direc-tionless and impotent.

He swung his legs off the bed and, finding his clothes in a locker, he considered getting dressed. Escape was imperative. It was time to take the fight to Millicent Cutter herself. But after a bit of a lie-down maybe. He was still feeling a little too dizzy to save the world.

Shunter sat in the Happy Onion and nursed his pint, wondering if he could have done more at the crime scene and concluding that the answer was probably no. All of the authority and power that went with the job of being a cop had been handed in, along with his warrant card, over eighteen months ago. But that didn't mean that he'd lost the urge to do the right thing.

He'd left the police service for a number of reasons. Firstly, because he'd felt like some kind of lumbering dinosaur alongside the younger, more progressive cops with their tablets, mobiles and other technological aids. He didn't even understand his own smartphone. Secondly, because cases were regularly being thrown out of court, not for lack of evidence, but because pettifogging lawyers picked holes in police adherence to ridiculously complex rules and regulations. Plainly guilty villains were walking free, while police officers were being made to look like the bad guys because they'd incorrectly labelled an exhibit or hadn't used the correct forms. And thirdly, it was his frustration with budget cuts, staff shortages and the political point-scoring that went on at command level. As soon as he'd completed his thirty years' service, he'd jumped at the offer to retire rather than stay on for an extra few frustrating years. But none of that meant that he no longer felt the need to fight injustice. It was Shunter's personal belief that any good and decent society had to be built upon a solid bedrock of justice. Truth formed the foundations; fairness, integrity, compassion and respect the building blocks. The structure was further shored up by good manners, professionalism and empathy. It was patently obvious to him that an erosion of these values was responsible for all the troubles of the world. Greedy expenses-claiming politicians and bent bankers had no part to play in his ideal democratic society. Nor did postcode-lottery NHS treatments, a so-called free press controlled by a handful of right-wing billionaires, and huge multinational companies employing staff at slave-labour rates while refusing to pay millions in business taxes. Shunter understood the nature of good and evil and felt morally obliged to fight bad people on behalf of those who couldn't fight for themselves. During his career, he'd surrendered any prospects he might have had for promotion to do just that.

He sipped at his pint and tumbled the curious events of the day over in his head in an attempt to make some sense of things.

'Penny for them?' said Vic.

'I was just thinking . . . three deaths and a missing person. Possibly several missing persons,' said Shunter. 'And all leading lights in the Agnes Crabbe industry.'

'You're not suggesting that there's a connection between the murder and the car crash last night, are you?' said Vic.

'No. Probably just coincidence. Shit just happens sometimes. But, whichever way you look at it, it's been a hell of a start to the festival, Vic.'

'Excuse me. Mr Shunter?'

Molly Wilderspin had appeared at the bar. She looked tense and her whole body was trembling. Shunter offered her his bar stool, which she accepted gratefully.

'You look like you could do with a stiffener,' he said. 'Brandy?'

'Perhaps a small one, thank you,' said Miss Wilderspin. Vic poured her a Hennessy and she took a sip of the proffered glass, her hands shaking so badly that the glass tap-tap-tapped against her teeth.

'I've never seen a dead body before,' she said. 'Well, not a . . . you know . . . with all that blood and . . . oh dear.'

'No need to apologise,' said Shunter. 'It must have been a shock. It's been a shock for everyone. I'm sorry, but I didn't catch your name earlier.'

'Wilderspin. Molly Wilderspin.'

'So how can I help you, Mrs Wilderspin?'

'Miss. And it's my friend Esme,' said Molly. 'I'm terribly worried that she's gone and done something silly.'

12

Pamela Dallimore fumed quietly as she changed out of her Miss Cutter outfit and into something far more suitable for what she had in mind. Bitchy comments, like those she'd overheard coming from the queue outside the hall, were nothing new. They followed her wherever she went and she had to concede, there was some justification for them. She hadn't read all of Agnes Crabbe's books – she had read very few, in fact – and she wasn't the expert on the author that the media seemed to believe she was. She was a journalist, not some obsessive fan, and the Agnes Crabbe biography had been just one of her many projects. Her career had been built upon a string of similar populist books of little merit and dubious accuracy. And if she was being completely honest, she would have to admit that the whole murder-mystery genre struck her as incredibly silly. Remote country houses, hidden passages and deadly poisons being administered in various unlikely ways? It was all complete nonsense. But *The Secret Queen of Crime* had been, by far, her bestselling book to date and it was the gift that just kept on giving. She was constantly in demand to appear at conventions and on TV shows all over the world, and the kudos of being Agnes Crabbe's biographer kept her bank balance nicely in the black. If people chose to believe that she was the fount of all knowledge, more fool them. But, for some reason this year, the snide remarks and the bitter asides had really got to her and she wondered why.

She pulled on a pair of heavy walking boots and began lacing them, all the while fulminating on the sneering arrogance of the most fanatical Millies. She had never been concerned by people calling her a fraud; she had never claimed to be an expert in the subjects she wrote about. And it was hardly her fault if the media was daft enough to assume that she was. However, there was a big difference between being labelled a charlatan and being called stupid. She prided herself on her intelligence and, now that she came to think about it, she realised that it was the taunts and comments about her intellect that had ruffled her feathers. She was a shrewd woman, a clever and Oxford-educated woman, and she did not take kindly to being called stupid and ignorant. She had therefore come up with a plan to prove to all of the ridiculous simpering Crabbe fans that she was smarter than the lot of them. She would solve the murder herself.

She certainly had several advantages. Firstly, the Millies might have a century of crime-fiction knowledge to guide them, but they probably knew little about twenty-first-century crime investigation. Theirs was a world of ratiocination and immaculate deduction, while hers had DNA profiling, fingerprint scanners and CCTV. She was also an experienced investigative journalist and had the Internet at her fingertips – when she could get a Wi-Fi signal – and two decades' worth of contacts that she'd cultivated within a wide range of organisations including the police. Plus, she had written a string of books about notorious crimes and how the killers had been caught, so her knowledge of such things was enviable. But above all else, she had youth on her side; Mrs Dallimore was in her early forties and she was fitter and stronger than most of her detractors. She was convinced that she could discover more about the murder than any Agnes Crabbe fan ever could. And what a joy it would be to actually catch the murderer or, at least, to be instrumental in their capture. That would force the haughty, supercilious Milly hordes to shut their mouths and give her a little more respect.

There was a knock at her door. She looked through the security peephole and saw DS Jaine, unshaven, wild-haired and his pot belly accentuated by the fisheye lens. He was standing outside her room scratching some part of himself thankfully below her field of vision. She opened the door.

'Mrs Dallimore? If you don't mind, DI Blount would like to speak to you in the Incident Room,' said Jaine.

Mrs Dallimore smiled. Perhaps her worth had already been spotted.

'What do you mean by silly?' asked Shunter.

Miss Wilderspin sipped her brandy shakily.

'I don't think for a minute that Esme was involved in that horrible business at the village hall,' she said. 'But she has disappeared and I'm very worried about her. There are all sorts of rumours flying around and I'm sure that some of them will get back to the police.'

'I see,' said Shunter. 'Look . . . have you considered that she might be the—'

'The victim? No, that's not her in the hall,' said Miss Wilderspin firmly. 'I don't know who it is but I know Esme very well and that isn't her.'

'Could it be Brenda Tradescant?'

'I'm not sure. I only met her for the first time yesterday evening.'

'You need to tell the police that,' said Shunter.

'I know. And I will,' said Miss Wilderspin. 'But I wanted to ask your advice first. You see, just before we were let inside the hall, Esme told me that she had to go and do something.'

'What sort of something?'

'I don't know. But she was very cross about being accused of writing those books and she mentioned taking legal advice from Andrew Tremens. Then she went down Handcock's Alley and she didn't come back.'

'So you think that she went to see him and may have stumbled upon the crime?'

'I think it's possible. They have known each other for years and . . . oh, I don't know what to think. I didn't want to bother you but you're the only policeman I know.'

'Retired policeman,' said Shunter. 'And, to be honest, there's probably not much that I can do. As I said, you need to speak to the non-retired police officers.'

'Mr Shunter?'

Shunter turned to find himself face to chest with a very tall, very thin man. His black hair was receding and his nose was long and beak-like. He held a warrant card out in front of him, gripped between a knotty twig-like finger and thumb. 'Detective Inspector Brian Blount, Bowcester, CID,' he said simply.

'Ah! Speak of the devil,' said Shunter. 'I've just been advising Miss Wilderspin here to come and talk to you. Her friend is missing.'

'Most unfortunate,' said Blount, without interest. He folded his long body on to a vacant bar stool. 'I understand that you were of some use earlier today thanks to your past policing experience. I just wanted to come and thank you in person for that.'

'You're welcome. Not that I could do much,' said Shunter.

'But I'm happy to help in any way I can. Have any more leads emerged?'

'I'm afraid I'm not at liberty to share that kind of information. I'm sure you understand,' said Blount. He smiled unconvincingly and stood up, narrowly avoiding cracking his head on a low beam. 'Rest assured we know what we're doing and we're following several promising lines of enquiry. So thank you again for your assistance. Much appreciated. And I'm sure you understand that the biggest help you can be to us from now on is to stay out of our way and to tell others to do the same. You can leave it to us country coppers now. Good afternoon.'

As the tall detective left the pub, Shunter scratched his head. 'Am I being paranoid or was he sneering as he left?'

'Sounded to me like he was warning you off,' said Vic. 'Perhaps he's worried that you'll solve the crime and rob him of his glory.'

'Then he's an idiot,' said Shunter. 'I'm retired. And anyway, it's not a bloody competition. It doesn't matter who nails the murderer as long as he's caught.'

'Or she,' said Miss Wilderspin, miserably.

'I'm sure your friend is innocent,' said Shunter. 'She didn't seem like the murderous type to me.'

'I don't know what to think any more,' said Miss Wilderspin.

The library was a hive of activity. The building stood next door to the murder scene and Blount had established his Incident Room in the children's reading area because it had the best Wi-Fi and phone signal strength. Several desks had been arranged in a square horseshoe and Nicola Banton was feverishly tapping away on a keyboard, searching databases and cross-referencing the known facts. Bookshelves had been cleared for the storage of exhibits and statements, and box files sat incongruously among the boy wizards, cats in hats and very hungry caterpillars. A magnetic whiteboard on castors stood facing the desks covered with photographs of the crime scene, a map of the village, a portrait of Andrew Tremens taken from his company website and a rather grumpy and washed-out photograph of Brenda Tradescant scanned from her driving licence. The year of expiry slashed across her throat like a human 'use by' date.

Mrs Dallimore glanced at the whiteboard and seemed suddenly a little unsteady on her feet. 'That poor woman,' she said. 'I couldn't stand her, but still, what a dreadful way to go.'

'Mrs Dallimore?' said Blount, entering the library and extending a hand. 'DI Brian Blount. Thank you for coming in.'

'Glad to be involved. I have some thoughts on the crime.'

'I'm sure you do,' said Blount. 'We were wondering if you can shed any light on why Miss Tradescant, if that's who the victim is, might have been in the hall before the doors were opened?'

'What? Oh. I have no idea,' said Mrs Dallimore.

'You don't know of any reason why she might have been in there?'

'No I don't. No one was allowed in the hall; only Andrew and members of the Festival Committee. And even they weren't allowed in after three o'clock in case they ruined his big surprise.'

'And do you know what the big surprise was going to be?'

'Not a clue. Andrew was playing his cards very close to his chest. That's why everyone was kept out.'

'So no one else was involved?'

'No one, as far as I know. It was a one-man show.'

'How secure was the hall?' asked Banton.

'All the doors and windows were locked and I was on the front door,' explained Mrs Dallimore. 'It makes me quite ill to think of what was going on in there when I was standing just outside . . .'

'Yes, quite. So when was the last time you saw Mr Tremens?'

'That would have been around three. We locked up and then I went off to get some food. I came back to the hall at half past three to man the doors. I checked all around the outside when I got there and the place was still locked up tight. And it stayed that way until I opened the doors at three forty-five. I suppose Andrew could have let someone in between three and three thirty, but it seems very unlikely.'

'And who has keys to the building?'

'The caretaker, Mr Cuckolde. And I had a set for the opening. I still have them, in fact.' She jangled a small set of keys on a ring.

'I can track the caretaker down and find out how many keys there are and who has them,' said Banton.

'One last thing, Mrs Dallimore,' said Blount. 'We've had reports of a van leaving the scene just before you opened the doors. Were any deliveries being made to the rear of the hall this afternoon?'

'Not that I know of. I did see a white van in the car park behind the hall when I did my walk around. It was parked down near the canal towpath so I didn't think anything of it. There are often cars parked there because it's free, and people use it when they go for walks along the canal. And I saw it drive away, of course. It nearly knocked down a couple of ladies.'

'And you don't know who was driving the van or have a registration number or anything useful like that?'

'No, sorry. I only saw it from the side, like most of us did. The driver seemed to be a man dressed as Miss Cutter, if that helps.'

'Yes, well. Thank you for your time,' said Blount and he walked away.

'Is that it?' said Mrs Dallimore, somewhat deflated. 'I have some ideas you might be interested in.'

'Thank you for popping by,' added Blount over his shoulder.

Mrs Dallimore frowned. Not even the police took her seriously.

'I really think that you should reconsider,' said the doctor. 'You've had a nasty knock on the head and it's clear to me that you are suffering the after-effects of a concussion. You can't even remember the ambulance journey here. I can't discharge you in your condition.'

'Then I'll discharge myself,' said Savidge. He had been in the process of walking out of the hospital when he'd been spotted and stopped. 'I can do that, can't I?'

'I would strongly advise against it.'

'But time is of the essence!'

'Er . . . look, while you are within your rights to discharge yourself—'

'We must act while we have the advantage of surprise,' said Savidge. 'Where do I sign?'

'What?'

'We must strike while the viper is in the nest!'

'I'll get the forms,' said the doctor, with a sigh.

Twenty minutes later Savidge was on a bus and heading towards Nasely. As the vehicle trundled through a pretty landscape marred only by the malodorous stench from local pig farms, he removed the bandages from his knees and elbows, and idly wondered where he might be able to get his hands on a gun. It was time for humanity to retaliate against Miss Cutter and her murderous army of drones.

*

Pamela Dallimore left the library and decided to buy herself some sandwiches for the day ahead. The Moore Tea, Vicar? café was as busy as ever with fan-club groups huddled around every table. Every snatch of conversation she overheard related to the murder and it seemed that the most popular theories currently under discussion revolved around Andrew Tremens. Mrs Moore was moving from table to table and suggesting that he had, for reasons unknown, murdered Brenda Tradescant. However, she was forced to concede that the trail of pearls, starting with the victim's clutched fist and ending at the canal towpath, cast some doubt on the idea. Tremens was unlikely to be wearing pearls unless, of course, he'd disguised himself as Miss Cutter; it was very much part of the fictional detective's ensemble as she always wore a double string given to her by her beloved 'Aunt Pie' – Dr Phyllis Ida Edwin – a brilliant detective in her own right and Miss Cutter's inspiration.

'He would know that no Miss Cutter costume is complete without the pearls,' said Mrs Moore, looking pointedly at Mrs Dallimore. 'It's only people who don't care that much about authenticity and accuracy who would fail to include them as part of their outfit.'

'And dressing up as Miss Cutter would be the perfect way to escape unnoticed with so many of us about,' said a Milly dressed all in red. 'But why would he then make his escape via the rear of the building when he could have simply hidden in plain sight by joining the crowds as they swarmed in through the door? After all, who would spot one more Milly in a village full of Millies?'

'That's a good point,' admitted Mrs Moore.

'Perhaps the pearls belonged to a female accomplice?' suggested a Milly in an extraordinary floral hat. 'Esme Handibode perhaps? After all, she has disappeared. And she and Andrew Tremens are acquaintances.'

'And it's common knowledge that she's had several tiffs with Brenda Tradescant at the festival already,' added Mrs Moore. 'I'm not joking. Full-on cat fights, I heard.'

There were also any number of other theories being discussed, some wilder than others.

'It's clear to me that Andrew Tremens's grandfather was having an affair with Agnes Crabbe's mother and a letter has been found that proves that he . . .'

'Eight knife wounds! Don't you see? Eight is a number steeped in lore and mysticism! The Greeks thought it was an all-powerful number. There were eight survivors on Noah's Ark from which all of humanity sprang. And Christ's number is 888, the opposition to the Devil's 666 and . . .'

'I heard that Esme Handibode's marriage is in trouble. Perhaps she and Tremens were caught *in flagrante delicto* . . .?'

'It's alphabetical. Andrew Tremens, initials A.T.; Brenda Tradescant, initials B.T. The next person at risk will have the initials C.T. It's obvious. I would put a guard on Claire Timmins from the Agnes Crabbe Society and Colin Tossel who runs the Nasely Historical Society if I were you . . .'

'Andrew Tremens and Esme Handibode have eloped together . . .'

'It's a clever conspiracy by the publishers of a rival author . . .'

'Agnes Crabbe is still alive and . . .'

'It's aliens.'

Mrs Dallimore took it all in as she bought her provisions. Whatever theory you subscribed to, the fact remained that the trail of pearls stopped near the canal where the mysterious white van had been parked. And most people, including Blount and his staff, seemed to have decided that the van was how the murderer had got away. But Mrs Dallimore wasn't so sure. It seemed too obvious. To begin with, there had been no attempt to sneak the vehicle away from the scene. Therefore, she reasoned, it was either an innocent driver or the van was a deliberate and carefully staged red herring. Either way, it meant that the murderer could have actually made their getaway on foot via the towpath, or on the canal itself in some kind of boat, while the van was causing a distraction. It was unlikely that they'd waded or swum across the canal because the open fields beyond led on to miles of flat grazing land in all directions. There were no hiding places, especially from the police helicopter. And she'd seen no sign of a boat on her walk around the building earlier. Therefore, she concluded, the most likely explanation was that they'd used the towpath on foot. The question was, in which direction? The logical choice was west towards Dunksbury Locks where there were ample escape routes on to several major roads and where they might have a getaway car parked. Eastwards was a much less likely route as, once beyond the village, the canal moved away from the road making a clean escape problematic. It was also peppered with popular fishing spots, a boat works and a reed bed known as The Rushes where a community of canal people lived, many of them so-called New Age Travellers who had stopped travelling. These places were likely to supply too many pairs of inquisitive eyes for any murderer or kidnapper to risk walking past.

Mrs Dallimore left the café and walked the short distance across the High Street and down Handcock's Alley. She arrived at the canal and considered her options. If everyone believed that the least likely escape route was on foot travelling east, then the perpetrator or perpetrators would know that too. What if they had deliberately gone that way to throw their pursuers off the scent? It was so often the case in fictional cop and spy dramas that the villain did exactly the opposite of what the authorities would expect. And if, as some believed, Tremens and his accomplice, or kidnapper, were dressed as Miss Cutter, they'd probably attract very little attention whichever way they went. The sight of several groups of Millies already combing the westbound towpath for anything that might have been overlooked by the police decided her. Eastwards it was. It wasn't yet 5 p.m. and she had a good two hours of daylight to play with; two hours to find the evidence she needed to show the naysayers that she was more than just a hack author.

She set off at a good pace, baggy shorts flapping against her thin bony knees and her stout walking boots clumping on the path as her eagle eyes scanned the ground for any form of clue. And then, quite to her surprise, she found one.

13

The arrival of a hearse to collect the victim's body raised the excitement among the festival-goers to a whole new level. Blount supervised the removal and then faced the inevitable barrage of questions. There were more cameras and microphones than ever and he grimaced inwardly at the thought of the national and possibly international exposure that his detective work would soon receive as the result.

'Do we know who the victim is yet?' asked a reporter from the *Bowcester Mercury.*

'Is it true that the killer was dressed as Miss Cutter?' asked a lady from the BBC.

'Do we know what Andrew Tremens was going to reveal?' asked Miss Joscha Ambrose-Leigh, editor of *ACDC*, the *Agnes Crabbe Detective Club* magazine.

'I'm not at liberty to answer any questions at this time,' said Blount. 'There will be a short press conference at five fifteen in front of the library. I'd be obliged if you could give us space to conduct our investigation. Thank you.' He made his way next door to his Incident Room feeling quite pleased with his performance. He'd exhibited just the right balance of authority and reassurance, he felt.

His staff was hard at work. Banton was on the phone chasing

up results from the police laboratory at Coxeter and Jaine was interviewing the caretaker of the village hall who had quickly been eliminated from enquiries as he'd been part of the morris-dancing side performing outside the Masonic Hall at the time of the incident. Mr Cuckolde had also revealed that, other than his own set of keys and the set that he'd loaned to Mrs Dallimore, there was a third set that had been specially cut for Andrew Tremens to use. They had not yet been found. A detailed examination of the hall had revealed no signs of forced entry, which suggested that Andrew Tremens had let the killer in. Or had given his keys to a third party. Or was the killer himself. The latter was a theory that the investigation team had heard many times from the constant flow of Millies who had been coming into the library throughout the day to make witness statements and to share their theories. There were so many of them that additional CID officers from Bowcester – DC James and DC Carr – had been seconded to the investigation. They sat to one side of the main operations area, wearily listening to the fans' ever more extravagant hypotheses and making a record of them all.

'It was Miss Tradescant's partner dressed as Miss Cutter. What better way to anonymously kill off your fiancée, eh?'

'Andrew Tremens was going to reveal some dark secret – like maybe Agnes was a child molester or something – and Brenda tried to stop him and they got into a fight . . .'

'I heard that the victim could be Esme Handibode. If so it could have been her husband that did for her. I've heard that they're estranged these days . . .'

'Tremens wrote this supposedly new Agnes Crabbe novel himself. Or maybe Brenda worked on it with him – she was a writer, you know – and Esme found out so the two of them killed her . . .'

'They never found Lord Lucan . . .'

Blount sat himself down behind the librarian's desk, having taken advantage of his rank to bag the biggest and most comfortable chair, and attempted to purge from his mind the slew of theories he'd heard. He fretted at a jagged fingernail. Things were not going well. He'd looked forward to an early arrest or, at the very least, a definite suspect, a strong motive and some credible witnesses with which to work. But, at the moment, he had nothing. If he continued to have nothing for too long there was a good chance that HQ would take the case away from him and assign it to a more senior and experienced investigator. His heart sank as he realised that the most likely person to inherit the case would probably be DCI Gavin Quisty; the man that his own team had called a genius and 'like Sherlock Holmes'. Although Quisty had only been a DI for half the time that Blount had, his sharp intellect and greater range of experience had landed him the promotion to Detective Chief Inspector that Blount had set his heart on. Admittedly he had been the better candidate, but this was scant comfort to Blount and he was damned if he would let his first homicide case get passed to his rival. Or, for that matter, let some show-off ex-London detective like Shunter get a toehold on the investigation. He needed to up his game.

He stood, his balding head colliding with a cardboard mobile of witches and black cats that hung from the ceiling, and paced the room, his long legs allowing him to do so in just a few strides. He needed a suspect and he needed one fast. Hopefully the forensics people would return some results soon and a post-mortem would reveal exactly how the victim had died. Massive head trauma was the most obvious cause of death but then there was the matter of the eight stab wounds to the chest. Had she been stabbed and then bludgeoned, maybe in a clumsy attempt to disguise her identity? If so, why would the killer then leave personal effects with the body, including identifying documents like the victim's driving licence? Alternatively, she could have been bludgeoned first and then stabbed, but what would be the point of that? She'd have quite clearly been dead before any knife was used. And eight stab wounds smacked of a deranged killer. Blount hoped that there was no ritualistic or cultish element involved, as several Millies had suggested. That would be a definite cause for a handover to a senior officer, maybe even to some specialist from New Scotland Yard.

'Guv, we have some fingerprint results back for the knife,' said Banton, finishing her call.

'At last,' said Blount, excitedly.

'It's an odd result, though. Most of the fingerprints were too smudged to be of any use but we did get a hit on a partial. It belongs to Brenda Tradescant.'

'So now we're saying that she smashed her own face in and then stabbed herself eight times?' snipped Blount.

'I didn't say anything of the sort,' said Banton, irked by the DI's sarcasm. 'I'm just reporting the facts. The print is hers. We have her on file. She got convicted several times during the eighties for obstruction, breach of the peace, assault on police, that sort of thing. She used to be an active anti-nuclear campaigner. Greenham Common, CND, etc.'

'There are definitely no other prints?' asked Blount.

'Nothing usable.'

'Maybe Tradescant is the murderer rather than the victim?' said Jaine.

'Maybes are no good to me,' said Blount. 'I have a press conference coming up. Is that all we have?'

'Forensics is a dead end, I'm afraid, until the body has had its fingerprints taken at the mortuary,' explained Banton.

'What? Why haven't they done it yet?'

'It's the weekend so there's only a skeleton staff on and—'

'Skeleton staff! Ha!' said Jaine.

'Then hurry them up!' said Blount. He bit at his jagged nail again. It tore across the quick and began to bleed.

Frank Shunter and Molly Wilderspin threaded their way through the stew of excitable Millies and ducked down Handcock's Alley, a name that brought a wry smile to Shunter's lips. Local tradition was that the alley had once been a favourite haunt of boatmen and barge operators who would enjoy a 'thruppenny upright' or a 'below job' with the prostitutes who operated out of the Happy Union pub. As much a brothel as it was an alehouse back in the sixteenth and seventeenth centuries, the pub was notorious across the county and its cheeky name had been quite deliberate. But then, in 1766, a puritanical priest called Sleight had famously climbed the tall post that supported the pub's hanging sign and defaced it. The resultant 'Happy Onion' so amused the locals that they had adopted it and, in time, so had the licensee who had quickly come to realise that you can't fight public preference. The pub had kept the name ever since.

Handcock's Alley led from the High Street to the village hall car park and the canal. It also provided an access point into a confused jumble of cottages called The Butts, a name that added yet another delicious layer of double entendre to this part of the village. Several Millies were in the alley. One was leaning over the police-incident tape and trying to peer into the hall through a side window. Two others were comparing notes.

'How long would it take to remove the whole pane and replace it? More than five minutes?'

'Not if the putty had been removed first.'

'It's double-glazed, dear.'

'Oh. Maybe the killer didn't get in that way.'

'Unless he was a window fitter . . .'

'So, you said that she might have gone to see Andrew Tremens for legal advice?' Shunter asked Miss Wilderspin.

'Yes. But the more I think about it the more it seems unlikely,' she replied. 'After all, he was just about to host a big event and he would have been very busy organising things.'

'But, given the mood she was in, would she have considered that?'

'She was very distracted just before she walked off. She kept rummaging in her bag, like she was looking for something. Perhaps she left something behind when we were exploring The Butts? Oh, but that wouldn't explain why she's gone missing.'

'Unless she walked into something that was happening at the rear of the building,' suggested Shunter. 'The timings are right for her to have caught people leaving.'

'Oh dear.'

'I'll tell you what, why don't we go and have a nose around? I'm not entirely sure what that pompous stick insect of a DI's problem is but we won't be hampering his investigation if we're just looking for a lost umbrella or something, will we?'

'Really? That would be very kind of you.'

'Truth be known, I could do with a break from the hustle and bustle. Reminds me too much of London. So, let's retrace your route from earlier.'

'Then we start at The Butts,' said Miss Wilderspin.

*

Blount could feel the panic rising in his chest. He had just lied to his Chief Superintendent and, now that he'd had a minute or two to reflect on his actions, he was cursing himself for his own stupidity. There had been no need to lie. He was being methodical and he hadn't deviated from established procedures or force policies. He was faced with a tricky and complex case and, understandably, it would take a little time to unravel the truth. He'd only been on the case for an hour or so, for goodness' sake. He had done nothing wrong, and he had nothing to be ashamed of. So why then, when his boss had called him for an update, had he said that he had a suspect and was prepared to name them at the press conference? He had no such thing. He hadn't even officially identified the victim yet. He should have said that the investigation was proceeding along approved guidelines and that more evidence was bound to surface soon and left it at that. But he hadn't because he knew that his Chief Superintendent would be under pressure from the Chief Constable to get results and that she would be under pressure from local politicians who, in turn, would have the Home Secretary breathing down their necks. And so, insecure and desperate to keep the case, he had lied. He turned to Nicola Banton and asked anxiously, 'Anything?'

'Not really,' said Banton. 'The search teams have completed a grid-by-grid search along the towpath and the helicopter has done the length of the canal from Oxford to Bowcester and all of the countryside around it. Nothing to report.'

'What about the van? There must be something about the van surely? It was seen by at least fifty witnesses.'

'At least fifty drunk or unreliable witnesses. We have several partial registration numbers, most of which disagree with each other, so we have nothing to circulate. And there was nothing to distinguish it from any other box van. There are thousands of them on the roads.'

'But it was being driven by someone dressed as a woman.'

'Women do drive vans these days, guv.'

'You know what I mean,' said Blount. 'I mean a man dressed as a woman.'

'Most of the men in Nasely right now are dressed as women,' said Banton. 'I've circulated that fact too, but hats and wigs can be removed. Without more information, we're stymied. Are you sure you want to run a press conference so soon? I mean—'

'Just . . . keep digging. Find me something I can tell the public,' said Blount and he headed towards the toilets.

Mrs Dallimore had barely begun her walk when something had caught her eye. Partially hidden in the long grass that skirted the towpath was a battered and well-thumbed paperback copy of Agnes Crabbe's *Swords into Ploughshares*. It was barely a hundred yards from where the suspicious van had been parked, which suggested that any police officer who had passed this way had either missed it or assumed it to be simply litter left behind by some irresponsible river dweller or festival visitor. Mrs Dallimore had discovered that it was something much more interesting. She flicked through the pages, seeing the handwritten notes crammed into every header, footer and margin, and wondered which obsessive fan it belonged to. But then, inside the front cover, she found a printed sticker bearing the name of Esme Handibode and an address in Oxford. The discovery had made her smile. So, the old battleaxe had been on the towpath some time during the day, had she? And just a short distance away from where the white van had been parked too. That, in itself, didn't prove anything but the thought that this information might implicate the bombastic old cow in the murder was a very pleasant one indeed.

She wondered whether she should tell Blount about her find; it was only a short walk back to the library after all. But then she remembered how readily he had dismissed her insights. He would laugh at her, she was sure. Besides, she couldn't actually be certain that what she'd found was evidence anyway. No, she would tell the police about the book upon her return by which time, with a bit of luck, her detective skills would have turfed up something more concrete and credible. She considered taking the book with her but then decided against it. It wouldn't help her in her investigations and she didn't fancy being accused at a later date of removing or tampering with evidence. And if a police officer found it in the meantime, all the better. Mrs Dallimore wiped the book clean of her fingerprints and put it back in the grass in a position where it was very likely to be seen by anyone walking past. She felt no guilt; Esme Handibode had it coming.

As the bus hissed to a stop, Savidge slid off his seat, ducked below window height and peered over the sill. As he'd expected, there were Cutters patrolling the streets around the Empire Hotel, although not as many as he'd anticipated. More surprisingly, there seemed to be a lot of police activity around the village hall. The Cutters didn't seem at all perturbed by this and many had gathered outside of the taped-off area. Did this mean that the police service was in cahoots with their mistress? If so, no one could be trusted and he would have to be doubly careful. He moved in a curious crouched waddle to the other side of the bus and, hunkering down behind a seat, he peered out of the open door. There were fewer Cutters on this side of the bus.

'Are you getting off or what?' snapped the driver. 'We have to at least appear to try to stick to a timetable, you know.'

Savidge glared at the man and jumped off the bus. He hit the ground running and sprinted towards some industrial-sized wheelie bins standing by the side of the hotel in Bowler's Lane.

'Bloody loony,' said the driver, shaking his head. The doors closed and the bus spun slowly around and headed back up the Coxeter Road, the driver grumbling audibly about the closure of the High Street and his awkward change of route.

Savidge considered his next move. He could hardly organise an assault on the Queen of the Cutters without being armed in some way but, short of burgling one of the local farms where there might be a shotgun, he could see no easy way to get his hands on a firearm. But did he need one? After all, it wasn't the weapon that mattered but the skill and the resolve of the person handling it. In the right hands, the most innocuous and harmless item could become a deadly weapon. Scenes from several Jackie Chan films inserted themselves into the confused narrative in his mind as he took his Swiss Army knife out of his pocket and unfolded several of the blades. One by one, he felt them with his thumb and wondered whether the fish hook disgorger, the saw or the largest of the flat blades would be the most effective. None of them were particularly threatening but all of them could do some damage if he decided to use them. He folded the knife shut, put it back in his pocket and peered out from behind the bins at the bustling High Street. The world had become a dark and sinister place peppered with threats and traps to snare the unwary soldier and he would need all of his wits, or those that remained to him at least, to avoid falling victim. For just a moment there were no Cutters in sight. Seizing his opportunity, he dashed down the alleyway.

The hotel's rear gardens were bordered by tall square-trimmed privet hedges but there was a metal gate set into one that allowed access to and from the lane. Savidge gingerly stepped inside and, after surveying the area for enemies, made a swift dash to a substantial sycamore and hid behind it. As he caught his breath, he scanned the rear of the building, quickly identifying the biggest and most expensive room – the second-floor Victoria Suite. He was sure that that was where she would have made her nest. Her nest? Or her command centre? Either way, she would surely not have settled for anything less than the best. Savidge knew the interior layout of the building well. Before his burger van days, he'd worked as a handyman at the hotel until his lack of anger management had got the better of him. His overenthusiastic and explosive campaign against the moles that were ruining the lawns had been mostly successful, but his spectacular final assault had toppled an ancient oak and blown out all of the windows in the conservatory and he'd consequently been asked to collect his cards. He frowned at the fragment of memory and tried to reconcile it with his current mission. Why had he been working at a hotel? Had he been undercover? And why did the fresh and prominent molehills that dotted the lawn seem to be mocking him? He dismissed all such negative thoughts. There was work to be done.

Looking around once again to make sure that he was unobserved, he moved stealthily to the hotel's back wall, scrabbled atop the box-shaped heating-oil tank and began to climb an old cast-iron wastepipe.

Shunter and Miss Wilderspin had spent a good half an hour wandering among the maze of alleyways that threaded their way through and around The Butts. They emerged next to the canal with nothing to show for their efforts except Miss Wilderspin's sore feet.

'That just leaves the towpath then,' said Shunter. 'And I'm pretty sure that the police will have combed it in both directions already. Still, I don't suppose it will do any harm to have a look with fresh eyes. Any preference for which way we go?'

'None,' said Miss Wilderspin. 'But I don't think I'll be able to walk very far in these shoes.'

Shunter took a coin out of his pocket. 'Okay then. Heads we go towards The Rushes, tails we go towards Dunksbury Locks.' He flipped the coin and went to catch it but it bounced off his wedding ring, wheeled along on its edge and plopped into the canal. A paddling of mallards immediately surrounded the disturbed water looking for food.

'Make a wish,' said Miss Wilderspin.

'I wish I hadn't used a two-pound coin,' said Shunter. He looked up and down the towpath and saw several groups of Millies searching the grass to the west. 'My guts are telling me to go east, towards the reed beds.'

Mrs Dallimore's perseverance had been rewarded once again. She was now over a mile from the village and had come across a small industrial complex where narrowboats, barges and pleasure cruisers had once been refitted, repaired and redecorated. Back in the fifties, when a holiday on the water had been de rigueur among the upper middle classes, the boat works had done a brisk trade, but it had long since fallen into picturesque dilapidation. Mrs Dallimore strolled past former dry docks that, thanks to decades of rainwater collection, were now filled with a soupy green swamp of algae, Canadian pondweed and pennywort that buzzed and twitched with life. Plump moorhens dabbled on the surface, hoovering up fat tadpoles and getting their heads pointillistically decorated with duckweed. Dragonflies fizzed through the air, grasshoppers fiddled noisily and tall cow parsley waved in the whispering breeze. The site consisted of three large boat sheds, their corrugated roofs bronzed and pitted with rust, and a number of smaller and older ivy-covered outbuildings; the original Victorian boat works that had existed before the larger sheds had been added. Their walls were warped and leaning and the gutters sprouted miniature roof gardens. The grass surrounding the works had been left to grow to waist height but a fresh path had been recently trampled through it towards the nearest shed.

Mrs Dallimore decided to follow the path, noting as she did so that the building had lost some of its wooden cladding and that she could see into and even through the structure. Her heart skipped a beat as she suddenly spotted a white box van parked behind the building.

She squatted down behind a stack of rusting oil drums, her heart hammering in her chest and a cold sweat prickling her forehead. Following a possible trail in search of clues was one thing; confronting a possible murderer was quite another. Up until this moment she'd got a genuine buzz from playing detective. But now the huge gulf between real life and the silliness of fictional murder-mystery descended upon her and she became very scared. With shaking hands, she fumbled in her baggy shorts for her mobile phone and discovered that she still had no signal.

'I thought that only happened in films,' she mumbled as it dawned upon her that she was well and truly on her own. Another quarter of a mile 'up river' she would find plenty of canal folk at The Rushes. But here there was no one and she hadn't told anyone where she was going. She could die out here and no one would ever know.

There was only one sensible course of action: she had to go back the way she had come until she got a phone signal and could dial 999.

It grew suddenly dark and she looked up, expecting to see that the lowering sun had dipped below the trees. Instead there was a balaclava, a pair of staring, bloodshot eyes and gloved hands reaching for her throat.

14

Blount furiously paced the Incident Room, all the while juggling words and phrases in his head as he tried to think of a way to save face. His press conference was imminent and he needed to say the right things to reassure his bosses that he was on the case while not making any false allegations that could come back to haunt him. Damage limitation was the name of the game.

'Still no ID on the victim?' he snapped.

'Not yet,' said Banton. 'I managed to get someone to the mortuary but fingerprints had to be taken by hand because of the cadaveric spasm. It takes a lot longer than scanning. But we should get a result soon.'

'I need something now.'

'You could postpone the press conference.'

'I can't,' said Blount. 'I've already told the . . . er . . . what about those reports of a man running around screaming and covered in blood earlier?'

'We looked into it,' said Jaine. 'He's a local bloke called Savidge. He was involved in that fracas on the village green when his burger van caught fire.'

'And that was hours before the murder so the blood, wherever it came from, isn't anything to do with our case,' added Banton. 'You could mention that we've circulated details of the ring.'

'Ring? What ring?' said Blount.

'The one that the victim was wearing,' said Banton. 'It's quite distinctive and someone might recognise it. There's a photo of it in your briefing notes.'

Blount looked at his watch. 'A ring won't keep them happy. I need names. I'll just have to say that the victim is the Tradescant woman. We have her handbag next to the body and lots of the Millies have said that it's her.'

'Yes, but only based on her build and the colour of her dress. There's been no proper confirmation of identity.'

'It must be her.'

'But what about the fingerprints on the knife?' said Banton. 'I thought you were considering her as a suspect?'

'There could be a perfectly obvious reason for that,' said Blount. 'Maybe she was trying to pull it out of her chest at the moment she died? The point is that we have more evidence to suggest that she's the victim, rather than the murderer.'

'Only circumstantial,' said Banton.

'Admittedly, yes. Which is why I am not going to accuse some-one of being a killer without more evidence. I could get sued for slander,' said Blount. 'But there's no harm in saying that we think she's the victim.'

'There is if we do it before we've told her family. If her fiancé sees it on the *Six O'Clock News* before we've told him . . .'

'Then tell him now.'

'Without a confirmed ID? Are you sure?' asked Banton.

Blount ran a finger around inside his sweat-dampened collar. His hangnail caught on the material and he winced. 'Do you think it's Tradescant?' he asked.

'It's either her or Handibode, I reckon,' said Jaine.

'What about you?' asked Blount.

'It's possible,' said Banton. 'But we can't be sure and—'

'We all know it's probably her,' said Blount, sucking his finger. It was really sore. 'Tell her fiancé.'

Savidge cautiously climbed from the wastepipe across to one of the balconies of the Victoria Suite and, gratifyingly, found that the French windows were open. He peered inside. The room was large, ornate and tastefully decorated with striped and patterned wallpapers, ebullient swags and drapes, and a small crystal chandelier. A slightly incongruous and very large widescreen TV dominated one wall. There was a small dining table and two chairs, a quality leather sofa and matching recliner, and a well-stocked mini-bar. Several open doors led off from the suite's main room. Savidge crept silently in from the balcony, barely noticing the depth of plush in the carpet that helpfully absorbed any sound his boots made. The first door hid a creamy-coloured bathroom with a sunken marble bath and jacuzzi. The second room was a walk-in wardrobe with a dressing table and a mirror with naked bulbs set all around it like he'd seen actors use in theatres. There was a suitcase in there and several outfits that had been hung up. All of them were Miss Cutter uniforms, he noted. The door to the final room was partially closed. Savidge put his eye to the crack and could see another set of French windows and a sumptuously draped dark wood four-poster bed. And asleep and snoring gently on top of the plump duvet was his arch-enemy, the criminal genius Miss Millicent Cutter.

'Ladies and gentlemen, welcome to this afternoon's press conference. I am Detective Inspector Brian Blount, the officer in charge of the investigation into this terrible crime that has shocked everyone with its brutality, and which has soured what should have been a joyous celebration of the one hundred and twentieth birthday of our local heroine, Agnes Crabbe.'

Outside the library, an eager audience of Crabbe fans and reporters with cameras and microphones had gathered. There was an audible murmur of expectation among the Millies.

'Shortly before four o'clock this afternoon, the body of a woman was discovered at Nasely village hall. The victim had suffered fatal injuries inflicted by person or persons unknown. The crime would have happened some time between three and three forty-five p.m. We believe the deceased to be Miss Brenda Tradescant, president of the Millicent Cutter Appreciation Society.'

The crowd began to murmur more loudly at this news. One member of the Millicent Cutter Appreciation Society uttered a long wailing 'Noooo!' and fainted.

'At this time, we are anxious to trace the whereabouts of the solicitor Mr Andrew Tremens and Mrs Esme Handibode of the Agnes Crabbe Fellowship. We need to speak to both of them as a matter of some urgency.'

Louder murmurs and exclamations of surprise.

'We are also keen to interview the driver of a white Transit-style box van seen leaving the vicinity of the village hall at around three forty-five p.m. He was an unshaven white male in his late forties or early fifties and wearing a plum-coloured dress, matching hat and black driving gloves. He was, we presume, dressed as Miss Millicent Cutter, the fictional detective. We would greatly appreciate it if anyone with information that may be pertinent to our investigation could please come forward, especially as the event was so recent. Now, I will take a few questions but do bear in mind that this is a freshly opened investigation and I may not have the answers you want. Nor will I be able to give out any information that may prejudice or compromise any of our lines of enquiry.'

'Are Mr Tremens and Mrs Handibode considered to be suspects?' asked a reporter from the *Mirror*.

'We would appreciate being able to speak to them as soon as possible.'

'Is it true that both of them have been abducted in mysterious circumstances?' asked a man from *Aliens Are Here!* magazine.

'All we know at present is that we don't know where they are.'

'So we can't rule out extraterrestrial involvement?' said the reporter whose press pass declared his name to be Ray Dalekcat. His tinfoil hat caught and reflected the light from the photographers' flashguns.

'Er . . .'

'Do we know of any motive for the killing?' asked a man from the *South Herewardshire Bugle*.

'It's too early to say.'

'There have been three deaths in less than twenty-four hours, all prominent figures in Agnes Crabbe fandom,' stated Miss Ambrose-Leigh of the *Agnes Crabbe Detective Club* magazine. 'Is there some connection?'

'One is a homicide and the other two were the result of an unrelated road traffic collision,' said Blount. 'It's hard to imagine any kind of link between the events.'

'But you haven't ruled it out?'

'It's not a line of enquiry that we're following at this time.'

'Do we know what Mr Tremens was going to reveal in his talk?' asked a lady from the Agnes Crabbe Book Club, hopefully.

'No. And that's all I can tell you at the present time. There will be further updates as new evidence emerges. Thank you.'

Blount stepped back inside the library and closed the doors behind him. Nicola Banton was waiting for him.

'I thought that went rather well,' said Blount.

'We have a problem,' said Banton. Her face was grave.

'Oh, for goodness' sake, what now?'

'It's the victim,' said Banton. 'She isn't Brenda Tradescant.'

I5

Miss Wilderspin stooped to pick up a paperback that was lying in the thick grass that bordered the towpath. 'This is Esme's,' she said.

'Are you sure?' asked Shunter.

'Positive.' Miss Wilderspin opened the book to show Shunter the name label inside. 'This must have been what she went back to find. She wouldn't have wanted to lose it. There's years of work in here.'

'But I didn't think that you'd walked this far with her,' said Shunter. He looked back along the towpath. 'We're a good hundred yards from The Butts and Handcock's Alley.'

'No, we didn't come this far. She must have walked along here on her own for some reason. Oh dear.'

'Something isn't right here,' said Shunter.

'Perhaps she did it deliberately, like leaving a trail of breadcrumbs?'

'People who are scared rarely think that clearly. Besides, I can't see her throwing it away if it contains years of her work. I think it's more likely that she dropped it by accident and didn't realise, or someone else left it here. But that still begs the question of why she walked this way and when. And also why she didn't notice that she'd dropped it. Maybe she was in a hurry. Or she was distracted.'

'Oh dear,' said Miss Wilderspin again.

'And, as much as it galls me to do so, we have to tell Blount about this. Have you got a phone signal?'

Miss Wilderspin checked. 'No.'

'Incredible,' said Shunter, checking his own phone. 'I thought that only happened in films. We can send photos back from Pluto but we can't make a phone call to a building ten minutes' walk away. Well, we can't leave it here. There might be finger-prints other than ours and Esme's on the cover. I don't suppose you have a carrier bag with you?'

'Of course,' said Miss Wilderspin, rummaging in her handbag. 'They charge five pence for them these days, you know.'

'Perfect.' Shunter put the book into the bag. 'Besides, you really are in some discomfort, aren't you?'

'I'm sorry,' said Miss Wilderspin, looking down at her patent leather shoes. 'I hadn't anticipated doing quite so much walking and I'm paying the price now. I really don't think I can go any further today.'

'Let's head back then. We'll drop this in at the library en route.'

Miss Wilderspin took a last look up the towpath and sighed. 'Poor Esme.'

'Chin up,' said Shunter. 'She'll probably turn up overnight with a completely understandable reason for her disappearance.'

'I do hope so,' she replied.

Pamela Dallimore felt the bag being whipped off her head and squinted in readiness for the light but it didn't come. Wherever she had been brought was almost as dark as the inside of the bag had been. It had been a short terrifying walk from where she'd been captured to where she now sat. She'd stumbled several times, having been blindfolded, but she knew that she must be somewhere inside one of the big wooden boat sheds. A formless shape lumbered away from her and by the time she was able to make out its human outline, it had climbed a short ladder and exited through a hatch in the ceiling. There was the sound of locks being thrown.

As her eyes adjusted to the gloom she could see that she was inside the shell of a boat, a long-disused barge by the looks of it. The smells of mould and musty old timber came to her now; the bag had screened much of it out. Dim light streamed through a handful of thin cracks that had developed in the curved hull as old wood had dried and shrunk. Dust motes danced in the beams and something scuttled around in the dark empty spaces furthest away from her where the walls curved inwards to form the prow. Her hands were bound behind her back with what felt like a large cable tie and her legs had been immobilised with her own belt. Her long bootlaces and her hanky had been used to make a gag. The old vessel creaked and complained as she shuffled herself around in a circle to examine every part of her prison. There was no one else with her in the belly of the boat, that much was clear. But she was not completely alone. Apart from the noises being made by what she assumed were mice or rats, she could hear footsteps on the creaking deck above her head. Her captor was still on board. Her heart fluttered as she realised that they may be the same person who had committed the murder at the village hall. Pamela Dallimore was a strong woman, but it took all of her willpower not to burst into tears.

'So we don't know who it is?'

'No, guv,' said Nicola Banton. 'It's definitely a woman but it's not Brenda Tradescant.'

Blount had returned to his agitated pacing and his face looked pale and drawn.

'And there's no possibility of error?'

'None,' said Banton. 'Tradescant's prints are on file. The victim's aren't, whoever she is.'

'Ah! So, if Tradescant isn't dead then she must be the murderer, as we suspected earlier,' said Blount. 'The handbag belonged to her, not the victim. She must have dropped it in her haste to escape.'

'That's possible,' said Jaine.

'So do we now have enough evidence to circulate her as wanted?' asked Blount.

'As a possible suspect, yes,' said Banton. 'But you've just announced to the world that she's dead.'

'And we just informed her partner,' said Jaine.

'What?' said Blount.

'You told me to send someone around to tell her fiancé that she'd been murdered, so I contacted a bereavement counselling officer and—'

'Then send someone around to tell him the good news that she's alive!' snapped Blount.

'It's not strictly good news if we then have to tell him that she's a murder suspect, is it?' said Banton.

'Can't either of you come up with any positive ideas instead of just attacking mine?' barked Blount. He mopped at his brow. 'Just let me think for a minute. We still have an unidentified victim, don't we? And two missing persons and/or possible suspects in the form of Andrew Tremens and the Handibode woman, yes?'

'Yes,' said Jaine.

'So, could the victim be Handibode?'

'It's possible,' said Banton. 'All we know is that, whoever it is, they don't have a police record or we'd have got a hit on the fingerprints—'

'Then do DNA or dental records!' said Blount in exasperation. He ran his hand through his thinning hair. 'Talk to a psychic. Hold a séance. Just do something!'

'And do I circulate Tradescant as the murderer now?' asked Jaine.

'Yes! And—'

The front door of the library swung open and Frank Shunter and Molly Wilderspin entered.

'Oh, for fuck's sake! What now?' hissed Blount.

'We thought this might be of interest,' said Shunter. He tipped the paperback out of the carrier bag and on to a table. 'We found this on the towpath. It belongs to Esme Handibode.'

'Interesting,' said Banton. 'Where exactly was it?'

'I'll show you,' said Shunter, walking towards the map of the village on the display board.

'No no no!' said Blount, interposing himself between Shunter and the board. 'This is an official police Incident Room and only authorised personnel are allowed inside. Are you authorised personnel? No, you're not.'

'I'm just pointing at a map,' said Shunter.

'Not in here you're not! You are not part of this investigation and this area contains confidential information for police eyes only. You're not a policeman any more, Mr Shunter, and I thought I'd made it perfectly clear that you can best help us by staying out of our way.'

'Yes you did. But if I can't point at your map, how can I show you where I found the book?'

For a moment, Blount looked lost for an answer. 'You are investigating my homicide,' he said accusingly.

'No, I'm being public-spirited,' said Shunter. 'I was helping this lady, Miss Wilderspin, to find her friend Mrs Handibode, who seems to have gone missing.'

'And I've said that we want to speak to Mrs Handibode as a matter of some urgency,' said Blount. 'I made a public appeal and—'

'Exactly. So by trying to find her, I'm actually doing just what you asked the public to do with your appeal, aren't I? None of which affect your resources or your investigation, and, as it happens, led to us discovering something that may turn out to be evidence. Evidence, incidentally, that your people apparently missed.'

'Oh, so now my people are incompetent.'

'That's not what I said and you know it.'

'The flatfoot bumpkins unable to solve their own cases so the big London detective has to help them out, I suppose,' Blount said with a sneer.

'Your words, not mine. So tell me, as a matter of interest, what should I have done, eh? Kept the book to myself and not told you? Is that what you want?'

'What I want is for you to go and enjoy the festival and leave us alone to get on with our job!'

'Fine with me.'

'Good.'

Blount glowered as Shunter and Miss Wilderspin walked out of the front door.

Banton filled the awkward silence. 'So do you want the book tested for fingerpr—'

'Yes!' snapped Blount. 'And find out where he found it!' He stormed off to fume privately in the toilets.

Banton smiled.

'He does seem to have a chip on his shoulder,' said Molly Wilderspin.

'A chip? That's a full hundredweight sack of sodding King Edwards he's carrying there,' said Shunter. 'I've never met anyone so uptight. He looks like he might explode any minute.'

Back once again in the Happy Onion, Shunter was spitting vitriol into what he had decided would definitely be his last To Die For of the day.

'Okay, so some city cops might look down their noses at the constabularies. I accept that. There are snobs in every profession,' he explained. 'But equally there are plenty of rural officers who believe that all city cops are dodgy wide-boys with an inflated sense of their own importance. And it's all nonsense. Cops are cops wherever they work, and different environments mean different kinds of policing are needed. None are any more or any less valid than any other. Blount is accusing me of exactly the kind of bigotry that he exhibits.'

'Oh dear,' said Miss Wilderspin.

'I'm sorry. Rant over,' said Shunter. 'And I suppose I ought to be heading home.'

'Are you not coming to the Helen Greeley talk?'

'Not really my thing. Besides, I don't have a ticket.'

'I do, but I'm not sure if I'll get in now. They've had to change to a smaller venue and it's oversubscribed.'

'Then I'll wish you good luck and a good evening. And, if you want to pick up the search again tomorrow, I'll meet you here at ten.'

'Really? You're very kind,' said Miss Wilderspin.

'To be honest, this isn't about you now. Or your friend,' said Shunter. 'This is about pissing off Blount. Enjoy the Greeley talk.'

'I will. Goodnight, Mr Shunter.'

'Call me Frank. Goodnight, Molly.'

'New girlfriend?' said Vic, once she'd gone.

'Hardly,' said Shunter. 'I'm just being the Good Samaritan. I think she might play for the other side anyway. She seems besotted with Helen Greeley.'

'I'm a bit besotted myself,' said Vic, looking at one of the posters on his pub wall. 'Fine-looking woman.'

'Bloody hell, what a day,' said Shunter. 'I moved to the country to get away from this kind of madness. Tell me it's not always like this?'

'It really isn't,' said Vic, laughing. 'Festival weekend is always as busy as hell but there's never any trouble. I expect it's just a blip.'

'Hmm. It's been my experience that trouble has a tendency to snowball.' Shunter stood up and stretched his back. 'And, after all, there's still a killer out there somewhere.'

'Thanks for that comforting thought,' said Vic.

'Sleep well,' said Shunter, grinning.

Stepping outside, he watched as a police officer patrolled the crime-scene perimeter, occasionally asking a tipsy Miss Cutter look-alike to move back whenever he found them pushing too enthusiastically against the tape. He glanced back over his shoulder and saw Banton and Jaine moving around inside the library and felt a small pang of envy. There was no denying that he missed the buzz of an incident room. But he quickly shrugged it off. He was too old for all that now. And if being a detective these days meant working for people like Blount, he was glad to be out of it.

He walked up the High Street whistling the theme tune from *The Sweeney*.

16

Helen Greeley rolled on to her side and resumed her dainty snoring. The earplugs and soft quilted sleep mask had made it easy to block out the world and, to ensure that she woke in time for her talk, she'd set the alarm on her phone and tucked it under her pillow. She was something of a heavy sleeper, but the angry vibration would be more than adequate to wake her. Or would have been if Savidge hadn't spotted it poking out from under her pillow and carefully removed it. Not knowing her pass code to turn it off, he'd thrown it out of the French windows and into the garden two floors below. He'd also unplugged the hotel phone, just in case.

At the hotel's reception desk things were getting fractious. The Festival Committee had turned up at 5.30 p.m. to see if Ms Greeley needed anything from them before her evening event. However, the hotel manager, acceding to the note on the actor's door saying 'Do not disturb', had insisted that he would not allow anyone to knock on her door. As the minutes ticked by and the clock reached 6 p.m., relationships between the two parties had become ever more strained.

'But she's onstage in half an hour,' explained Mr Stendish.

'I appreciate that but she has indicated that she doesn't want to be disturbed,' said the hotel manager. 'And, as our first duty is to the welfare and needs of our guests, we are obliged to respect her wishes. I wouldn't want to suggest that we favour some guests more than others, but Ms Greeley is a major star and the most famous guest we've ever had staying here. A poor review from her could be catastrophic.'

'But she might be ill.'

'That seems most unlikely.'

'Or had a fall,' said Miss Clark.

'With all due respect, she is not some frail pensioner,' said the manager.

'Maybe she's taken an overdose?' said Mr Horningtop.

Miss Clark frowned. 'She's not a drug addict, Geoff.'

'She does like a drink though.'

'A "Do not disturb" sign generally means that someone wishes to sleep or is . . . how shall we say . . . otherwise occupied?' said the manager. 'Nothing sinister about that, surely?'

'I wouldn't be so sure the way things have been happening around here this past twenty-four hours,' muttered Mr Horningtop.

'I think that you might have read too many Agnes Crabbe books,' said the manager with a cynical smile. 'I'm sorry but I'm not going to go against her wishes.'

'But she'll miss her appearance,' said Mr Stendish. 'People have paid to see her talk.'

'I can't help that. Ms Greeley's wishes come first.' The manager mopped his brow. 'Dear oh dear, what an upsetting day this has been for everyone. The late Miss Tradescant was a guest here as well you know. Such a tragedy. I don't suppose anyone will settle her bill.'

'Miss Tradescant? But she's not dead,' said Mr Stendish.

'But they said at the police press conference . . .'

'Yes, I know, but the body isn't hers after all. They just announced it. They're now saying that she may actually be the murderer.'

'A murderer? Staying in my hotel?' said the manager, looking startled. 'That would be most unfortunate.'

'For your reputation or for your other guests?' said Mr Horningtop snidely.

'Oh god. You don't think she'd harm anyone here, do you?'

'I would have thought that harming people is what murderers do best,' said Mr Horningtop. 'And when was the last time anyone saw Helen Greeley?' He arched his substantial eyebrows meaningfully.

The manager paled and dialled the number of Helen Greeley's room on his phone. 'Well, in light of this new information, perhaps I ought to just check on her,' he said. He waited patiently, biting his lower lip. 'It's engaged.'

'Or off the hook,' said Miss Clark.

'Perhaps we could just go and knock on her door,' said the manager, nervously. 'As a courtesy. In case she's feeling poorly or something.'

Shunter smiled as he watched a group of very drunk Millies fall flat on their backsides after attempting a high-kicking cancan chorus line to the music provided by a street busker. As they got to their feet, dusting themselves down and roaring with laughter, they reminded him of a happy Beryl Cook painting, all chubby legs and big grins. Their antics would give the lads in the CCTV control room a giggle, he thought. And, all of a sudden, he was struck with an idea. Had Blount and his team considered CCTV? After all, they weren't from the village and maybe didn't realise that a couple of cameras had been recently installed. The system wasn't linked to any police control room and the fact that the cameras were unobtrusively incorporated into the vintage design of the street lamps made it even less likely that Blount's people would have noticed them. Shunter turned around and walked towards the control room, located in a flat above the Moore Tea, Vicar? café.

Helen Greeley woke to the alarming sensation of a hand being clamped over her mouth. She scrabbled to take the sleep mask off and found herself looking at a man with a bandaged head who was mouthing silent words at her. In his other hand he held a knife. Not a very big knife, it had to be said, but a blade nonetheless and it was inches from her face. She began to hyperventilate. It was happening again. Her worst nightmare was happening all over again. The man folded and pocketed the knife with one hand while keeping the other over her mouth. He put his finger to his lips to tell her to be quiet and reached out towards her. Greeley closed her eyes in terror but then felt the earplug being pulled gently from out of her left ear.

'Can you hear me now?' said the man. His clothes were stained rusty brown with dried blood.

Greeley nodded.

'Good. I'm going to take my hand away from your mouth. If you scream or shout, I will be forced to take drastic action. So please be quiet.'

The man slowly removed his hand and she bit her lower lip, desperately trying to subdue her instinct to scream. Memories of the previous year came flooding back . . . of the crazed fan who'd got a job as a security guard and then used his access to get close to her, to break into her house and keep her prisoner at gunpoint.

He'd made her act out some of the most dramatic scenes from the TV series with him, and had told her that they were meant to be together for ever. She'd used her charm and the man's obvious obsession with her to trick him into selecting a dress for her to wear from her walk-in wardrobe and had then managed to lock him inside while she ran for help and called 999. In her nightmares, she could still hear his frenzied screams and the sound of the bullets splintering the sturdy oak door as he tried fruitlessly to escape. He had used the last bullet on himself. The story had generated acres of newsprint and had done her career no harm at all, but it had given her a year of terrifying flashbacks and a dependence on the bottle that was sailing worryingly close to alcoholism. And now the nightmare had returned and become all too real.

'That's good,' said the man. 'Very good. Keep quiet like that and we'll get on just fine. And you might want to put some clothes on.'

Greeley suddenly realised that she was wearing nothing but some expensive and quite revealing underwear and grabbed a pillow to cover herself with. She saw, to her dismay, that her mobile phone was not underneath it.

'Wait . . . I know you,' she said shakily. 'I saw you earlier. You were in the street. Oh god, you were covered in blood . . . what . . . what do you want?'

'What do I want . . .?' said the man and, just for a second, he didn't look as if he knew the answer either.

'Yes. What do you want?'

'I ask the questions. You'll get nothing from me except my name, rank and serial number. Get dressed. We need to get moving.'

'Okay,' said Greeley. After the initial shock of finding what appeared to be some kind of middle-aged commando in her hotel suite, she had started to calm herself a little. This strangely befuddled and bloody man wasn't anything like the cold, calculating monster who had stalked her before; he had been armed with a pistol and was quite obviously organised and dangerous, while this man seemed to be just as nervous as she was, maybe more so, and only seemed to possess a Swiss Army knife. From his breath, she could tell that he wasn't drunk and she was pretty sure he wasn't high on drugs either. He seemed more confused than anything else and, what's more, he'd apparently been in her room before she'd woken up and had done her no harm, even though she was practically naked. With no false modesty, she knew that she was an attractive woman – an attractive, famous and wealthy woman – and men wanted her. But this one hadn't taken advantage of her. This wasn't some rabid fan who intended her harm. He was more like an escapee from a psychiatric hospital living out some odd soldier fantasy. The realisation of this gave her an unexpected boost of courage. Or perhaps it was the gin.

'Could you get me a dress from the walk-in wardrobe?' she said.

'What's wrong with those clothes on the floor?' asked the man.

Greeley frowned. It had been too much to hope that the same trick would work twice. She stood and wriggled herself into her discarded Miss Cutter outfit.

'So what are they?' she said.

'Eh?'

'Your name, rank and serial number.'

'Why do you want to know?' asked the man suspiciously.

'I don't. But it's all you offered.'

He pondered on the question. 'Stingray. My name is . . . I mean my codename . . . is Stingray.'

'And what do you want, Stingray?' She was feeling quite calm, she realised. Undoubtedly the pre-nap drinks were helping, but there was something else at work here, some other factor she couldn't yet identify.

'I need to take you to my command post. To be held there until I get orders from above regarding your transfer to a more secure facility.'

'Can't you just guard me here?' said Greeley. 'I'm sure it's more comfortable than your command post, wherever that is. We have a huge TV with lots of channels. And I can get room service to send up some food if you like. It's really good here.'

'No phone calls. Now get dressed.'

'I am dressed.'

'I mean get a coat on and some sensible shoes.'

'Listen, I'm sure you believe that you're on some kind of mission but—'

'Please get dressed,' said the man. He produced his penknife again and opened the longest blade with as much menace as he could muster. He began pulling the sheets off the bed.

The Incident Room was filled with the delicious aroma of roast pork. Clifford Jaine had popped over to the village green to get something to eat and had returned with a substantial portion of hog roast for the investigation team to share. He'd also bought several cups of lukewarm grey liquid that might optimistically be called tea.

'It's still chaotic over there,' he said, picking a piece of meat out from between his teeth. 'There's a fire investigation team climbing all over that burnt-out burger van. I asked about the driver, the one who went a bit bonkers, and they told me that he got taken off to hospital. Anything new happening around here?'

'A very angry phone call from Miss Tradescant's partner,' said Banton. 'I fielded it to the guv'nor.'

'Seems only fair,' said Jaine. 'It was his call to tell him she was dead.'

'I tried warning him.'

'I was just thinking on the walk back, why did Tradescant bother to smash her victim's face in? To make identification harder?'

'Maybe,' said Banton. 'And leaving her handbag behind threw us off the scent for a while. Well, it threw Blount off anyway.'

'This case is a friggin' mess. Glad it's not my reputation resting on solving it. Where is the guv'nor anyway? He's missing out on the pig.'

'I think he's having a sulk in the loo.'

Blount sat on the toilet and pondered his next move. Or, rather, he squatted on the tiny, child-sized lavatory with his knees around his ears, and pondered his next move. Perhaps using the children's section of the library hadn't been such a good idea after all. But he needed somewhere quiet to think, somewhere without distractions, and the lavatory had become his sanctuary. The whiteboard in the Incident Room was a constant reminder of how little he'd achieved since assuming leadership of the investigation. He missed the peace and quiet and generally administrative work of his office at Bowcester.

Telling a barefaced lie to his superiors had been stupid. But to then make such a public error of judgement over announcing the identity of the victim had been a whole new level of stupid. Unsurprisingly, Miss Tradescant's fiancé had been very angry and very vocal on the subject of legal action and, as things stood, Blount couldn't see any easy way to row himself out of trouble.

Time was against him because most crimes of this kind were solved within the first forty-eight hours and, if they weren't, they tended to drag on for weeks and months as the trail got colder and new evidence became harder to find. The first few hours were critical because potential witnesses would soon begin to forget vital details and forensic evidence could be lost or contaminated. Plus, of course, the culprit, or culprits, could be putting distance between themselves and Nasely. If he couldn't crack this case in the next twenty-four hours, his prospects for promotion were bleak. However, if he did discover and arrest the killer, his mistakes so far might be overlooked.

He flushed the toilet to make it look as if he'd used it for its proper purpose and walked back into the Incident Room.

'There's some pork left,' said Jaine.

'I'm not hungry.'

'Bad tummy? You were gone for ages.'

'No,' said Blount, frowning. 'Any developments?'

'Well, there's some good news. Well, sort of good news,' said Banton. 'And there's some maybe not-so-good news.'

'What's the good news? I could do with some.'

'I think we can be pretty sure that the deceased isn't Esme Handibode.'

'And that's good news, is it?'

'We're still awaiting confirmation by way of dental records but lots of people who know her well have assured us that she doesn't ever wear jewellery,' explained Banton. 'So she would never have worn a fancy ring like the one we found on the body.'

'So we can tick one more spinster in fancy dress off our list of possible murder victims and only several hundred more to go,' said Blount. 'If that's the good news, I'm dreading the bad.'

'I've checked Mrs Handibode's paperback for fingerprints and it looks like it had been wiped clean before Mr Shunter and Miss Wilderspin handled it.'

'Wiped clean? That's suspicious, surely? I bet Shunter wiped the book clean just so that we couldn't get anything useful from it.'

'Why would he do that and then hand it in with his prints on it?' said Banton.

'Hmf,' huffed Blount, stumped for an obvious answer.

'The other news is that HQ has sent through the results of the autopsies on the two ladies who died in the car crash last night.'

'What? Why?' A sudden terrible thought struck him. 'Oh dear god, please don't tell me that their deaths are related to this investigation. I don't think I could bear it.'

'There's no problem with Mrs Hatman-Temples,' said Banton. 'She died of her injuries, no question.'

'But . . .'

'But Miss Nithercott was already dead at the time of the accident. And there's evidence that she was poisoned.'

'Poisoned? What do you mean poisoned?'

'Taxine,' explained Banton. 'Deadly stuff. You find it in yew trees; almost every single part of the tree is loaded with it. Except the berries, that is. Well, they're not actually berries. They're little red fleshy cups called arils with a seed at the centre and—'

'I don't want a bloody botany lesson,' said Blount. 'What has any of this got to do with me?'

'The arils taste a bit like grapes,' Banton continued. 'You can eat them. And make jam. And Nithercott had the remains of jam sandwiches in her stomach. Yew-berry jam sandwiches.'

'But you said that the berries aren't poisonous.'

'They're not. But the seeds are. And the toxin isn't neutralised by cooking. So if the jam was made with whole arils, seeds and all, it would be loaded with taxine.'

'Who would be stupid enough to make jam with poisonous berries?' said Blount.

'Someone who wanted to do for Miss Nithercott?' offered Jaine.

'Exactly. Which is why HQ sent the analysis to us, I guess, in case it's relevant,' said Banton. 'After all, this is a murder-mystery festival and Agatha Christie used taxine in *A Pocketful of Rye*. She put it in some bloke's marmalade.'

'Marmalade?' Blount shook his head in dismay.

'Of course, it may just have been an unfortunate accident,' said Banton.

'I remember reading about some old duffer who cooked daffodil bulbs thinking they were onions,' said Jaine. 'They're poisonous too.'

'Full of lycorine,' said Banton. 'Not fatal generally, but if you're old or infirm or have a heart condition they could kill you. Taxine is a lot nastier.'

'Bloody hell,' said Jaine.

'Welcome to the world of murder mystery,' said Banton, smiling. 'And you have to admit that it is kind of ironic, isn't it?'

'What is?'

'Poisoned jam,' said Banton. 'And with her being a leading light in the Women's Institute. You know, "Jam and Jerusalem".'

'This is real life, not some ridiculous bloody detective novel,' said Blount angrily. 'Can you imagine what all those Millies will think if they start hearing about daffodils and poisoned jam? I want this idea nipped in the bud. Now.'

'You mean the berry,' said Jaine.

'Or the aril,' said Banton.

'Shut up! Get someone to search her car. And get on to the

local police where she lives to search her house. Find that jam. I want it eliminated from our enquiries. Find me something I can work with!'

'Yes, guv,' said Jaine.

'My life is turning into a bloody Agnes Crabbe novel,' said Blount. All of a sudden, he realised that he genuinely needed the toilet and excused himself, grabbing Esme Handibode's annotated copy of *Swords into Ploughshares* as he left.

'That's the third time in less than an hour,' said Banton.

'He must have the runs,' said Jaine. 'Mind you, if I were him, I'd be shitting myself too.'

Toilets were very much on Pamela Dallimore's mind as well, and she cursed herself for having drunk so much tea earlier in the day. As the hours had slowly crept by, her bladder had become more insistent, but her captor had left her with no facilities to make use of. As desperation had kicked in, she'd attempted to call for help – even her kidnapper would be a welcome sight if he was willing to offer her a comfort break – but her muffled shouts for assistance had gone unheeded. And now, as desperation turned to pain, she began to realise that she'd just have to let nature take its course. As she did so, she pondered on the irony that, despite being at least twenty years younger than most of her rivals, she was the one who'd look like she had a weak bladder when they found her. If they ever found her. She felt utterly wretched.

Inside the toilet cubicle, Blount did his business and tried to think calmly. The last thing he needed were more deaths to investigate. Just the one was proving intractable. He opened Esme Handibode's dog-eared paperback distractedly and began to read.

It was appearing increasingly likely that both Brenda Tradescant and Esme Handibode were involved, in some way, with both the homicide and Tremens's disappearance. He wondered if, perhaps, Mrs Handibode's notes would give him some insight into the kind of woman she was and whether she might be capable of brutally killing someone. However, he soon found himself being drawn into Agnes Crabbe's prose instead.

The thunderous roar of a shotgun interrupted the tranquillity of the early winter's evening. Roosting birds hurriedly quit their temporary sanctuaries, complaining bitterly at being so crudely disturbed and evicted. The force of the shot punched a jagged hole in the chest of the police constable's tunic as it propelled him backwards off his rattling bicycle.

'Oh great. A dead cop on page one,' Blount said to himself. 'Just what I need to cheer me up.'

The constable lay still, the front wheel of his bicycle continuing to rotate as it rested on its side on the grass verge. It made a ticking sound that became slower and slower and then stopped, as if marking the passage of the man's life from this realm to the next. Blood mingled with the early dew and the autumnal coloured carpet of fallen leaves. A second shot barked and the constable's body jerked in response, only to resume its previous inanimate state. Upon the face of the constable's shattered service watch the hands stopped at seven o'clock and moved no more . . .

'Good grief.' Blount skipped forward a handful of pages.

At police headquarters, Superintendent Curtis Godolphin busied himself setting up an Incident Room from where he would conduct the inquiry. Extra telephones had to be installed, and typists and uniformed officers for house-to-house enquiries were seconded from other duties.

'Sergeant, I want a pro-forma prepared, and every person between the ages of ten and eighty living in the parish to fill one out,' said Godolphin.

Sergeant Angwin dutifully made notes in his pocketbook.

'I want their names and addresses and don't forget the married women's surnames prior to marriage,' continued Godolphin. 'I want their date and place of birth, and a personal description. I want it to include where they were between 1800 hrs on Wednesday and 0700 hrs on Thursday and to include the names of anyone who can verify that. Did they see the constable between those times? And, if so, where? Also a description of anyone they saw and did not know by name. Oh, and make sure the woodentops note those people who are away at work or whatever, then get a team back in the evening to sort them out. Use the Voters' List to mark off who has been seen. Have you got all that?'

'Yes, sir,' said Angwin.

So, things hadn't been so very different back in Agnes Crabbe's day, he mused. A homicide investigation was logical and methodical and built upon step-by-step procedures. The only real difference was that they'd used paper pro-formas back in the 1930s, whereas he was able to put all of his data directly on to a computer using tablets and smartphones. But investigation still came down to asking questions and slowly but surely eliminating people from enquiries. And, yes, there was still that frisson of rivalry between the CID and the 'woodentops' – the uniform branch – over eighty years after Crabbe had written those words.

Blount's eye was drawn to the scrawl of pencilled notes clustered in the margins of the book. Mrs Handibode's jottings were extensive: historical details, character traits, weather conditions, the names of real locations in and around Nasely that had inspired the fiction . . . she had been very thorough. He ran his thumb along the edge of the pages, genuinely amazed that anyone could devote so much time and effort to studying and analysing a murder-mystery novel, when his eyes alighted on a word as the yellowed pages flickered past. He stopped and quickly worked his way back through the book and there the word was, clearly written and in capital letters. TAXINE. And below that, a set of notes about how a person might introduce it into the body of another. 'Yew-berry jam' was one of the options listed. Blount quickly cleaned himself up, pulled on his trousers, washed his hands and walked triumphantly into the Incident Room.

'Upgrade our alert on Esme Handibode,' said Blount. 'She is now officially a murder suspect.'

'She is?' said Jaine.

'I believe that she may have killed one of the drivers in that crash,' said Blount, waving the paperback in the air. 'And the silly cow has literally confessed to doing so in her own handwriting. So, what are the odds that she was responsible for today's incident too?'

17

Shunter was amazed by the expertise displayed by the young lad who operated the CCTV system, particularly as every other indication seemed to suggest that he was barely sentient. Certainly, he couldn't string three words together without interposing some kind of animal grunt. It had also surprised Shunter how easily he had managed to persuade the lad to let him have a look at the CCTV recordings. After all, he wasn't a cop any more. Maybe it was his air of authority, honed over thirty years. Or maybe it was the fact that Shunter had half-jokingly suggested that it would be easy for an unprofessional operator to misuse the system to leer at schoolgirls from Harpax Grange and they'd be bound to get the sack if someone, say, a police officer, or even an ex-police officer, suggested checking the video archive.

There were only two cameras. Camera One was sited in a lamppost at the western end of the High Street and gave a clear view of the shops, Crabbe Cottage and the Masonic Hall. Camera Two was at the eastern end of the street by the Masonic Hall and took in the pub, hotel, library and village hall. While the smart money was on the suspect escaping by van, there was always a chance that they had escaped on foot using the crowds to hide in plain sight. If they had, one of the cameras would surely have picked them up. Shunter had therefore decided to look for evidence to support either theory by requesting video footage starting at around 3.45 p.m. when the body had been discovered. As he watched Mrs Dallimore open the doors for the Millies to flood inside, he spotted himself among the crowd. Or a figure that he assumed to be him; the CCTV footage wasn't of the highest resolution. He was at least spared the screaming as there was no sound to accompany the video. It was soon obvious that there was no one trying to make their escape; the human traffic was all one way as the Millies attempted to push inside to view the crime scene.

'Damn. We'll have to start working back from here,' said Shunter. 'Can we put the video into reverse and run it at double speed?'

'Yuurr,' said the operator.

The Millies began emerging backwards from the hall at a comical pace and started queuing up. Mrs Dallimore closed the doors and took up her position outside. A few minutes later the white van reversed along Sherrinford Road and into Handcock's Alley, stopping only to have an altercation with a group of Millies. To Shunter's frustration, the angle was all wrong to read the number plate and it was impossible to see the driver; Camera One was too far away and only the passenger window was visible from Camera Two. The van disappeared out of sight behind the hall and the number of fans standing in line began to dwindle. He then saw Esme Handibode walk backwards out of Handcock's Alley and rejoin the front of the ever-shortening queue. Then, at a little after 1530 hrs, Mrs Dallimore suddenly left her post by the front door and walked backwards around the building before making off down the High Street. Another ten minutes passed by with nothing more exciting to watch than a few Millies walking about. But then Shunter spotted the white van as it reversed out of Handcock's Alley and into the High Street. The time stamp said 1513 hrs.

'Whoa, stop there,' said Shunter. 'Can you run it forward to just before the van turns into the alley, please?'

The video stopped and started to play at normal speed and in the right direction. As the crowd of Millies moved out of the way to allow the van to turn into Handcock's Alley, the CCTV operator froze the picture, providing a blurry view from Camera Two of the driver – a man in a dress and hat and wearing gloves.

'Now, who, I wonder, is that?' said Shunter.

'Doesn't it strike you as a bit premature?' said Banton. 'I mean, declaring Handibode a murder suspect based on a jam recipe? Damned if I'd have done it.'

'And especially after making such a balls-up with Miss Tradescant,' said Jaine. 'But it's his call. And you must admit, it is a hell of a coincidence . . . someone dies from eating poisoned yewberry jam and Handibode just happens to mention it in her notes.'

'Yeah, but the jam wasn't part of our murder investigation, was it?' said Banton. 'Now it is, and we have three deaths to investigate. And that concerns me.'

'More overtime,' said Jaine, smiling.

'Yes, but saying that she's responsible for the car crash – which is dubious – is one thing. Saying that she must therefore also be responsible for bludgeoning and stabbing our victim to death is a massive leap.'

'That's our guv'nor,' said Jaine. 'He can't see a shark without jumping it.'

*

Blount's pacing habit had brought him to the back of the library and to the crime-fiction section. The stars of the golden age of murder mystery shone down on him: Agatha Christie, G. K. Chesterton, Ronald Knox, Margery Allingham, Michael Innes, Dorothy L. Sayers, Ngaio Marsh and Josephine Tey among them. The Sherlock Holmes books of Conan Doyle were there too and one entire bookcase was taken up with Agnes Crabbe books and DVDs. If ever there was a good place to inspire someone who was trying to work out how a murder had been committed, and by whom, this was it, he guessed. He sat down, took a deep breath and once again opened Esme Handibode's copy of *Swords into Ploughshares*. He began scanning through her handwritten notes and tried not to get distracted by the novel itself.

'Let me get this right. You expect me to clamber over the railings of a second-floor balcony and climb down to the ground on a home-made rope with my legs tied together?' said Helen Greeley.

'Yes,' said Savidge. He had used a pair of tights to secure her ankles and had then proceeded to cut her bed sheets into strips before knotting them together to make a rope. He had then tied one end to the balcony railings and thrown the remaining length to the gardens below to create an escape route. 'If I don't tie you up, you'll run away as soon as you reach the ground.'

'But I can't climb without using my legs,' said Greeley. 'I don't have the upper body strength.'

'I suppose I could tie the rope around you and lower you down. Or you can abseil.'

'I fucking can't.'

'You can,' said Savidge, waggling his penknife.

'Do you intend to stab me if I don't do as you say?' asked Greeley.

Savidge thought about this.

'I might,' he said unconvincingly.

'I am not abseiling down the outside of a hotel or trusting you to lower me down on a sodding rope made from torn bed-sheets,' said Greeley firmly. 'You'll just have to stab me and be done with it. But I don't believe that you will. You don't look the stabby type.'

Savidge saw the resolute look on his captive's face and knew that she was right. He didn't believe he was going to stab her either. What was wrong with him? He had a licence to kill, didn't he? Or did he? He closed his eyes and tried to focus on his mission. Why was everything so hazy?

There was a sudden loud knock at the door.

'Ms Greeley?' said a voice. 'This is the manager. Are you all right in there?'

Savidge placed the point of the penknife against her breast bone and whispered, 'Not a sound!'

There was another knock.

'Ms Greeley? There's been some concern expressed about you not turning up for your talk. Can you please just let us know that all is well?'

'Don't answer,' said Savidge.

'But . . .'

'Just a "yes" will do and then we'll go away,' said the manager. 'Otherwise, I will have to come into the room to check for myself.'

'I'll have to say something,' said Greeley.

'Tell them you don't want to be disturbed,' whispered Savidge. 'Say you're ill.'

'Look, if I call out, they will be in here in seconds and you'll be off to prison,' Greeley whispered back. 'You and I both know that you're not going to stab me so why don't you—ow!'

Savidge hadn't realised quite how sharp the knife was. As Greeley had been speaking she had accidentally pushed against the point and it broke her skin. A bead of wine-red blood appeared and ran down into her cleavage. Horrified, Savidge pulled the knife away and was about to apologise when Greeley took a deep breath.

'I'm fine!' she shouted. 'But I have a tummy bug!'

'I'm sorry . . .' said Savidge, transfixed by the trickle of blood.

'Do you want me to call a doctor?' asked the manager.

'No, it's nothing serious,' Greeley said loudly. 'I just don't want to get too far from a loo. Don't come in. It's not very nice in here right now. I'm going to try to sleep it off.'

'Are you sure?'

'I'm sure. Please send my apologies to the Festival Committee.'

'Actually, they're here with me,' called the manager. 'They were concerned too.'

There was a muffled chorus of voices all saying hello from behind the door.

'Can we reschedule for tomorrow?' shouted Greeley. 'I'm very sorry for any inconvenience.'

There was another muffled chorus of approving noises.

'Well, as long as you're sure,' said the manager. 'We'll leave you in peace then.'

'Thank you, Mr Gilderdale. I'll speak to the committee tomorrow. When I'm free.'

Outside the door, Mr Stendish felt satisfied that they'd done all they could. 'Well, that's that then,' he said. 'We'll just have to shuffle Sunday's programme.'

The manager scratched his head. 'But my name is Jaycocks,' he said.

*

'Well, how long ago did he die?' barked Godolphin impatiently.

'First of all, there are two shotgun wounds, fired, I would say, from quite close range, some ten yards,' said Dr Angus MacDonald. 'I base that on how the shot is concentrated. You'll note that there's not a lot of spread. As to the time, well, given the conditions, I would say fourteen to sixteen hours ago. Early yesterday evening, I'd imagine. Oh, and if it helps at all, he didn't suffer. Death was instantaneous. I doubt I will find his heart at the post-mortem. The two shots have played havoc with his insides.'

Blount had once again succumbed to the lure of Agnes Crabbe's prose and had discovered that, despite his best intentions, he had quickly developed the need to know who had killed the constable in Chapter One. Flicking ahead to the final few pages had revealed the answer, but it was strangely unsatisfactory without knowing the why and the how. So he now found himself dipping randomly into the book in an effort to piece together the whole plot. It said something about his own procedure-driven nature that he was finding it difficult to concentrate on his own case until this fictional one was resolved in his mind. Finally, after some twenty-five minutes, he was satisfied. But he'd also discovered some curious Handibode-penned notes along the way.

Most of them related to the plot, a murder mystery involving a shell-shocked ex-soldier turned farmer who was slowly but surely killing off the surviving members of the platoon who had left him for dead in No Man's Land during the Great War. But written on a mostly blank page at the end of a chapter he'd spotted what appeared to be a random assortment of words and phrases all listed under the heading of 'ANDREW T – SECRET':

Evidence of MC
Marr Harry?
S&B.
Falk.
Crib p.103?

At first, he'd assumed 'Evidence of MC' to mean the facts that
Millicent Cutter had strung together to solve the crime. But most
of the words and phrases seemed to have no bearing on the plot
of the book. There was indeed a crib mentioned on page 103, but
why Mrs Handibode had made a note of this, he had no idea.
'S&B' could mean anything and 'Falk' sounded like a name but
there was no one in the book called Falk. 'Marr Harry' might also
be a name, or maybe it was an abbreviation of 'Married Harry'?
But the names Marr and Harry also didn't appear in *Swords into
Ploughshares* either. And then there was that cryptic heading –
'ANDREW T – SECRET'. Blount assumed it referred to Andrew
Tremens and wondered if Mrs Handibode's notes had anything
to do with the solicitor's important announcement. If it did, then
it might be important to decode what the notes meant. Maybe
Banton could figure them out? Of course, he couldn't admit to
her that he didn't know, so maybe he'd set her a challenge and
make her think that it was some kind of test that he had already
passed. He headed back to the Incident Room.

'Is that the best resolution you can get?' asked Shunter.

'Yuurr,' said the CCTV operator.

On the screen was a pixelated image of the man driving the
van. His hair was cut in a fashionable 1920s bob so it was
undoubtedly a wig. His stubbled face, though indistinct and plastered with badly applied make-up, had a familiarity to it.

'I assume that there's no way to enhance the image to make it sharper?'

'Nuuur. The CIA might have . . . you know . . . errrm . . . software like that but we're still . . . like . . . running on Windows 98 here.'

'Can you do me a printout of it?'

'Yuurrr.'

'Thanks,' said Shunter. 'You might just have helped catch a murderer.'

'Sick,' said the operator.

Shunter walked back down the stairs from the control room and considered what to do next. The right thing to do was to give the printout to Blount, but he wouldn't be thanked for doing so. He wouldn't even put it past the man to have him arrested for interfering with his precious investigation. With hindsight, he realised that he should have got the CCTV operator to email the photo to the Incident Room. But he hadn't, and he could hardly expect the operator to lie on his behalf. He would have to take it to Blount himself and face the consequences, whatever they turned out to be.

He ran the gauntlet of several inappropriately saucy drunks as he ambled across the road towards the library. There were nowhere near as many Millies on the streets now as most of them would be getting ready for the dance at 8 p.m. Others, meanwhile, would be back in their hotels and guest houses busily updating blogs, forums and newsfeeds with spurious theories, largely inaccurate descriptions of the day's events and endless photographs. The main social media platforms were already abuzz with speculation and #AgnesCrabbe was trending on Twitter. Most of it was nonsense, human memory being notoriously fallible and prone to exaggeration and outside influences, and the various descriptions of events clashed and disagreed with each other. But interest was high and, among the Crabbe fan community, it seemed that a good story was always much more entertaining than the truth. The one noticeably missing voice was Pamela Dallimore's and a number of commentators had pointed out her absence.

He arrived at the library and steeled himself for the inevitably fractious meeting with Blount. The DI was a microcosm of every bad manager that Shunter had ever encountered during his career. But public safety and the needs of the community came before personal feelings. He had to do the right thing. He looked once again at the photograph and suddenly realised who the van driver reminded him of. He looked quite like Savidge.

'Perhaps calling you Mr Gilderdale was a coded message?' suggested Mr Stendish. The Festival Committee had regrouped in the hotel lobby along with the manager. 'In *A Wrathful Man*, there's a moment where Miss Cutter sends a message to Colonel Borwick in the form of an acrostic.'

'A what?' said Mr Jaycocks.

'A sentence where the first letter of each word spells out a hidden message,' explained Mr Stendish. 'In that instance it was "Craneflies always swarm towards late evening." C.A.S.T.L.E, you see. It told Borwick that she was imprisoned in Heversedge Castle.'

'"Thank you, Mr Gilderdale" would be a very short acrostic,' noted Miss Clark. 'And "TYMG" would be nonsensical.'

'It may be simpler than that,' said Mr Horningtop as he typed an enquiry into a search engine on his smartphone. 'I don't profess to know as much about Agnes Crabbe's books as some of them do round here, but I do know that in one of the stories there's a character called Gilderdale. Ah, here we go. Oh. Oh dear.'

'What?' said the manager.

'I think we need to call the police,' said Mr Horningtop, looking at the result of his search.

'Guv, there's a call for you. Transferred from HQ.'

Blount took the phone from Clifford Jaine. 'DI Blount. What? If I must, I suppose. Put her through.'

As Blount took the call, Jaine looked around the Incident Room. 'I bet it was much more exciting back in the day,' he said. 'There would have been loads of people in here bustling about, indexing everything on cards, taking paper statements. I've seen photos.'

'Computers have simplified the process,' said Banton.

'You'll never replace a copper's hunch with a machine,' said Jaine.

'No, no, I do not, madam!' said Blount suddenly. He jabbed angrily at the red button on the phone, wishing for the old days when you could slam the receiver down on to the cradle to make a point. 'Incredible. HQ gets a call from some spinster claiming that Helen Greeley has been kidnapped or is being held hostage in her hotel room, and they pass it on to me! Can you believe that? Like we haven't got enough on our plate already.'

'Think we should check it out, guv?' asked Jaine.

'What? No, of course not! It's just another one of their silly bloody conspiracy theories. I've been hearing them all day. Nazis. Aliens. Nazi aliens. Illuminati. The Mafia. Cross-dressing solicitors. You would not countenance the tripe I've had to listen to. Just because she didn't turn up for her talk this evening doesn't mean she's been kidnapped.'

'She didn't turn up for her talk?' said Banton. 'That's a bit unusual, isn't it? I mean, to drop out of a gig without an explanation.'

'Is it? She was probably having a hissy fit. These pop stars and so-called celebrities have them all the time. And who says that there isn't an explanation? Just because the caller isn't aware of it . . .'

'She was held hostage by some nutter fan a while back,' said Jaine. 'It would be really bad luck if it's happened to her again.'

'Don't you think that if she'd genuinely gone missing someone might have told us? Her agent or someone?' said Blount.

'I suppose so,' said Banton.

'You suppose right. And even if it were true, it's nothing to do with us. We have quite enough to be getting on with. The woodentops can deal with it. We have a murderer to catch and I'm damned if I'm going to give any credence to . . . Oh Jesus Christ. That's all I need.'

Shunter had appeared at the door of the library.

Savidge was in a state of extreme confusion. As the chemistry of his brain had finally begun to stabilise, the imaginary world of spies and espionage and zombies and commandos that he had constructed had started to dissolve away, leaving behind the stark realisation that he had done something very, very stupid. He had taken a world-famous actress hostage in her hotel room and he had stabbed her. Well, maybe 'stabbed' was a somewhat exaggerated description of what had happened but, nevertheless, it was more than enough for a charge of GBH to be added to his tally of offences. He suddenly found himself in a very tricky situation of his own making.

'So what happens now?' said Greeley.

'Be quiet. I'm thinking,' said Savidge.

'Well, can we have a drink while you think?' she said, reaching for the gin.

To Shunter's surprise, any initial frostiness from Blount had thawed immediately upon the production of the photograph. There had been no snide comments, no accusations of interfering: Blount had taken one look at the photo, shaken him by the hand and then asked DS Jaine to show him to the door before reaching for his phone and excitedly barking orders into it. The name Savidge featured a great deal.

'Is he all right?' asked Shunter. 'I expected to get my head bitten off.'

' 'Well . . . I shouldn't really say but . . .'

'Ah yes. I'm outside the circle of trust.'

'Look, you know the score,' said Jaine, quietly. 'We've been struggling to get anywhere with this case and this is the first concrete lead we've had. Any suspect is going to give Blount a hard-on.'

'There's a mental image I could have done without. But look, can you do me a favour? I only said that it *looked* like Savidge. The photo is very blurry and he has a generic kind of face. There isn't much distinctive about him. So please, bear that in mind and don't go in all guns blazing when you catch up with him.'

'Duly noted. Your best bet now is to stay well away from here. Get out while the going's good.'

'I don't need telling twice,' said Shunter. 'Just go easy on Savidge. He's probably not the man you're after. I can't really call the guy a friend and he's very difficult to get on with, but I've never known him to be violent and I really can't see him murdering anyone.'

'I'll do what I can,' said Jaine.

At the Empire Hotel, Miss Clark returned the phone to the receptionist. 'Well, he was very rude,' she said.

'He didn't take you seriously?' asked Mr Jaycocks.

'Not at all. Perhaps I forgot to tell them something pertinent?'

'I think it's more that DI Blount is a complete arse,' said Mr Horningtop.

'Tell me again why you think Ms Greeley is being held captive?' said Mr Jaycocks.

Mr Horningtop tapped his smartphone. 'It says here on this website that in *My Brother's Keeper* there is a character called Honoria Gilderdale who discovers that she has a long-lost older brother whose reappearance threatens her inheritance. So she invites him to her house, drugs him and then locks him away in an attic room for years, denying to all and sundry that he even exists. It's a storyline that Ms Greeley would be very familiar with because *My Brother's Keeper* was dramatised in her last TV series. It's the episode that won her a BAFTA.'

'So you think that she's being held against her will in her suite?' said Miss Clark. 'And that's why she used the name Gilderdale . . . as a form of code?'

'Yes. And may I remind you all that she used the words "when I'm free", which suggests to me that she isn't free now?'

'Oh god,' said Mr Jaycocks.

'She was kidnapped before, by that security guard,' said Mr Stendish. 'It couldn't be him again, could it?'

'I thought he shot himself?' said Mr Horningtop.

'Oh god,' said Mr Jaycocks again, imagining the tabloid headlines.

'So what are we going to do about it?' said Miss Clark. 'If the police have made it clear that they're not at all interested . . .'

'Then we need to provide them with hard evidence,' said Mr Stendish.

'But how? We can't force our way into her room,' said Mr Jaycocks. 'It would be a monstrous breach of privacy if we're wrong.'

'Plus, her captor might panic and hurt her,' said Miss Clark. 'I've heard that happens sometimes.'

'We need the help of an expert in kidnapping,' said Mr Horningtop.

'Then you're in luck,' said Miss Clark. 'The village is full of them.'

'The Millies?' said Mr Jaycocks.

'Let's face it, they've probably read more kidnap plots than any Scotland Yard detective ever has,' said Miss Clark. 'And, besides, they're all we have.'

18

Helen Greeley had poured herself another gin and tonic and was feeling strangely relaxed, considering her position. She perched on the edge of her bed, watching the man she only knew as 'Stingray' pace up and down. He reminded her, in a curious way, of a polar bear that she'd once seen in a distressing online video. The poor beast had been driven insane by captivity in some Eastern European zoo. And, just like the bear, all of the wild savagery and power you'd expect to see had somehow been stripped from this man and replaced by a kind of tragic acceptance of circumstances. Besides, he wasn't a bad-looking chap, she thought, and, despite his earlier threats, he didn't give off that aura of danger you got when face to face with truly evil people. It occurred to her that what she was currently feeling was more like sympathy for the man than fear for her own safety. She was intrigued.

'I've had my share of experience with lunatic fans and you don't strike me as the stalker type,' she said. She tipped her drink down her throat in one. 'These days I can spot a psycho a mile off, and the fact is that when you first came into my room I was half naked on the bed and you behaved yourself. I'd have woken up if you'd tried to cop a feel, so I know that you didn't. That tells me that this isn't sexual and you don't want to harm me. I'm right, aren't I? Oh, be a darling and get another bottle, will you?

There's one in my luggage. This one's empty and my legs are tied together.'

Savidge harrumphed and walked to the dressing room. His faculties had now fully returned and he was under no illusions as to just how much trouble he was in. He was then struck with a sudden idea. He returned to the bedroom with the fresh bottle and poured her a quadruple measure of gin and topped it up with tonic. Perhaps if he got her plastered enough she'd forget the whole incident. Or at least be hazy enough about the details to make his role in it less incriminating.

'Ta. Bottoms up.' She downed half of the glass in one slug, apparently oblivious to its potency. 'Look, it's not all doom and gloom. There's no reason why we can't sort this mess out and go our separate ways, is there? I mean to say, the worst thing that's happened to me today is a little prick with a knife.' She burst out laughing.

Savidge raised an eyebrow.

'Unfortunate choice of words,' she said. 'Blame the booze. The lovely, lovely booze. So tell me, Mr Codename Stingray, what do you want from me? Money? Some signed books or DVDs? A set visit when we film the next series? Most things are doable. Can we negotiate?'

Savidge considered her words. As things stood, he was likely to be facing charges of criminal trespass, possibly aggravated burglary, GBH, unlawful imprisonment . . . the list was long and so would be his sentence. Even if he managed to persuade the court that he'd been suffering with a short-term psychological illness, he'd still be looking at an indefinite stay at some high-security clinic for tests and observation, which was no better than a prison sentence and would probably involve a lot more injections. Perhaps, if she was a woman of her word, she really might let him off in return for her release. After all, he'd done her no real physical harm except for that one small incident with the knife, which even she was now admitting was an accident. Trusting her was a big risk, he knew. But what choice did he have?

'Yes,' he said finally. 'We can negotiate.'

'Excellent,' said Greeley. 'Let's toast that with a little drinkie. And, as a show of goodwill, can you untie my legs now? I'm so pissed they barely work anyway.'

Shunter left the library and strolled along the still busy High Street. Loud blasts of music and mutterings of 'one-two, one-two' were coming from the Masonic Hall as the people running the evening dance set up their equipment and tested the sound levels. Millies of all shapes and sizes were already flooding towards it. The hotel, meanwhile, also seemed to have a large crowd gathered in the foyer and a number of people were visible in the breakfast room. Some Agnes Crabbe-related fan event, no doubt. He then spotted Miss Wilderspin hobbling painfully along the street towards him.

'Hello again,' he said. 'No room at the talk?'

'I got in. But Helen Greeley didn't show up.'

'And with everything that's happened today, I suppose people are already suggesting that she's been abducted or kidnapped?' said Shunter, with a knowing smile.

Miss Wilderspin nodded.

'She's probably just being a diva,' said Shunter. 'There will be a logical reason for her not turning up, just wait and see. There's no reason for people to get melodramatic.'

'Such an upsetting day,' said Miss Wilderspin. 'I think I'll go back to my hotel room and read. I doubt that I'll sleep very much tonight.'

'Good idea. I'm off home myself. See you in the morning if you feel up to it.'

'Thank you. I'll wear some sensible shoes this time,' said Miss Wilderspin. She smiled wanly and set off towards the Empire Hotel. Shunter watched her go and then yawned. It was only early evening but he'd had a long day, a lot of fresh air and way too much beer. He turned left at the pub and walked up the Coxeter Road towards his cottage.

'. . . and that's why we suspect that there may be someone keeping her hostage inside her room,' said Mr Stendish above the murmur of voices in the breakfast room.

The Festival Committee had sought out the heads of the various Agnes Crabbe fan clubs in the hope that their combined knowledge of criminal investigation might help them with their difficult situation. It was somewhat ominous to discover that, of them all, only Penny Berrycloth of the Cutter Crime Club, Claire Timmins of the Agnes Crabbe Society, Lindsay Packering of the Crabbe and Cutter Club, Elspeth Cranmer-Beamen of the Miss Cutter Mysteries Fan Club and Anthea Pollwery from the Agnes Crabbe Detective Club were available. All of the other fan-club presidents were either dead, murdered or had gone missing in the past twenty-four hours. Mrs Dallimore was AWOL too. Even those who didn't normally put any credence in conspiracy theories were beginning to waver. Therefore, in the absence of any better ideas, the committee had widened the invitation to include anyone who might be interested in contributing ideas, a decision they were now regretting as the room was packed full of Millies all clamouring to put forward their theories and offer advice before heading off to the dance.

'If there have been no demands, then surely it's not a hostage situation,' said Miss Penny Berrycloth. 'Are you sure it's not a stalker?'

'But he's dead,' said Mrs Timmins. 'He shot himself.'

'It doesn't have to be the same stalker,' said Miss Berrycloth. 'Helen Greeley has thousands of fans. There is bound to be a percentage of wrong 'uns among them.'

'It could be a woman stalker insane with jealousy,' lisped Mrs Pollwery, who'd been in such a rush to attend that she hadn't put her dentures in.

'If you're saying that Ms Greeley is using the plot of *My Brother's Keeper* to send us a coded message, perhaps we should think about the plot of the book?' suggested Miss Berrycloth.

'Good idea,' said Miss Clark. 'What did Miss Cutter do in the story? How did she solve the crime?'

'The first thing she did was to make sure that it really was Cedric Gilderdale locked in the attic room before calling Inspector Raffo,' said Mrs Timmins

'There's a wonderful scene where she charms Honoria's guard dogs before climbing the wisteria,' added Mrs Pollwery. 'She sings to them. *Go to sleep, my ba-by . . .*'

'We need to know what's happening in Ms Greeley's room,' said Miss Berrycloth.

'*My ba-by, my ba-by, my ba-hey-beee,*' crooned Mrs Pollwery.

'Tell me . . . which side of the building is her suite?' asked Miss Berrycloth. 'Front or back? And what floor?'

'The Victoria Suite enjoys wonderful second-floor balcony views of the gardens and canal,' said Mr Jaycocks with consummate professionalism.

'I see. And the garden . . . does it have any mature trees?'

'Several. Why?'

'And could you see into Ms Greeley's suite from the top of one of them?'

'I imagine so. That's if anyone wanted to.'

'I'd want to!' shouted an undeniably male voice from somewhere among the Millies.

'I imagine there's no shortage of people who'd want to,' said Mr Horningtop. 'I'm amazed the trees aren't full of paparazzi already.'

'What are you thinking?' asked Mrs Timmins.

'I'm thinking of reconnaissance,' said Miss Berrycloth. 'Now, has anyone got a pair of binoculars I could borrow? And a long ladder?'

'So what you're saying is that you weren't responsible for your actions?' asked an increasingly squiffy Helen Greeley. 'That you suffered a kind of temporary insanity?'

'Insanity is a bit strong, but yes, I suppose I did,' said Savidge. 'It's been happening to me since I was a kid. Something, usually a stressful situation, sets me off and suddenly it's like I'm no longer in control of myself. I worried for years that I was schizophrenic. But, apparently, it's just some sort of chemical imbalance in a part of my brain. And the fact that there's never been any stability in my life just makes me more prone to attacks.'

'Can't they give you anything for it?'

'They do, but the tablets make me so sleepy. You can't afford to be half asleep all the time when you're self-employed.'

'I can relate to that,' said Greeley. 'Same with acting. My doctor prescribes me pills for my anxiety but you have to be a trouper in this job, no matter how crappy you feel. If I take the tablets, I get lethargic and I don't give a damn. That's no good to me. If I lose my edge, they'll just go and give the part to some younger, prettier cow. It's a bitch-eat-bitch world, trust me. Another drink?'

'Not for me.'

'This does the same job as the tablets and tastes a damned sight better,' said Greeley as she poured herself another triple.

'I know. I have a brother who controls his rages by staying too drunk to do any harm.'

'He has the same condition as you?'

'Yes. He's a vicar. The booze works for him because being permanently pissed isn't that much of a workplace issue in his job. But it is for me.'

'So what do you do, Mr Self-employed Stingray? I mean, apart from holding TV stars hostage.'

'I have a burger van. Or I had a burger van. It got destroyed today.'

'Oh god, was that the fire on the green earlier?'

'That was the start of everything going wrong,' said Savidge. 'Not that anyone will have any sympathy. They'll just say "claim on the insurance", like it's that simple. But first there will be a big investigation involving the police and the fire brigade. And then the insurance company will want their pound of flesh. Then, if they do agree to pay out – and that's a big if – I'll have to get a new van, have it kitted out, apply for permits and pay for safety checks. Then I'll have to restock. And all of this when I'm earning no money, of course. I now have to start from scratch and, on top of it all, I've done this to you.'

'I think your day has been considerably crappier than mine,' said Greeley. 'Go on, have a drink.'

'I've never harmed anyone. Except in self-defence, that is. I want you to know that,' said Savidge. 'That thing with the knife was an accident. You do know that you could just walk out of here now, right?'

'I could. But I won't.'

'Why not?'

'Because it's my fucking room.'

'Maybe I will have a drink after all.'

'Good boy,' said Helen Greeley, lifting her glass in a toast. '*Cin-cin!*'

'Can you see anything at all?' asked Mr Jaycocks. Above him, in the branches of a substantial horse chestnut, Miss Berrycloth peered through her binoculars.

'I see some movement,' she said. 'There's someone in the bedroom with her, but I can't tell who. The net curtains are closed. The two of them seem to be having a drink together.'

'That doesn't sound like a hostage situation,' said Miss Clark.

The members of the Festival Committee stood at the base of the tree. They'd been joined by the fan-club presidents, all keen to find out what was happening in Helen Greeley's suite.

'That's odd,' said Miss Berrycloth. 'There's a rope or something tied to the balcony railings that goes down to the ground.'

'Maybe that's how the kidnapper got in?' lisped Mrs Pollwery.

'Maybe that's how the kidnapper intends to get out,' said Mrs Timmins.

'We should stop him.'

The two women sneaked away together.

'Very nice,' said Savidge.

'No it isn't, and you know it isn't,' said Greeley. She had stumbled from the walk-in wardrobe dressed in another of her Miss Cutter outfits. It was certainly less flattering than the previous one, and Savidge thought that it made her look older, but he didn't dare say so. He swigged his gin and tonic. He was starting to feel the effects of the alcohol himself now; his extensive blood loss earlier in the day was undoubtedly helping to accelerate his intoxication.

'We have a new costume designer and this is what she's expecting me to wear for the next series,' said Greeley. 'And without wanting to sound self-pitying, you know as well as I do that it does nothing for my figure. Where are my curves? Where are my tits for god's sake?'

'You look okay to me,' said Savidge.

'It's for authenticity, she says. The flatter chest was fashionable in the olden days, she says. But the costume is doing me no favours. I look like a tube of toothpaste. I hate it and I know that the fans will hate it and, before you know it, the tabloids will be saying I'm too old and they'll replace me with someone younger.'

'You'll be fine.'

'I wish I had your confidence. My topless scenes worry me more and more every year. Everything is sagging. All I see in my immediate future is obscurity or playing the mum of a younger starlet in some poxy soap.'

'You look fine,' repeated Savidge. 'Honest.'

'I look like a man in drag.' Greeley took a deep swig from her glass. 'You'd look more feminine in this dress than I do.' She suddenly laughed.

'What?'

A cheeky grin spread across her face. 'Do you realise that you're probably one of the few men in Nasely who isn't in drag today?'

'Health and safety,' said Savidge. 'Can't have loose wigs and hats falling on to the hot plate. Can't have pearls dangling in the deep fat fryer.'

'Go on, dress up for me,' said Greeley. 'You'd look great as Miss Cutter.'

'Not my thing.'

'Oh, go on, do it for me. There are several spare costumes in there and you're just about slim enough to get into one of the looser summer frocks. The pleats allow for some expansion.'

'No, I'm fine really.'

'I'll tell you what. You dress up for me and I promise that you'll walk away from here and nothing will ever be said about what's happened today. How's that?'

'That's blackmail.'

Helen Greeley fingered the small wound on her chest and exaggeratedly winced in pain. Savidge made a grumpy noise and stomped into the walk-in wardrobe. Greeley poured them both another drink.

'I've never met a burger van man before,' she said, slurring her words. 'But I reckon we have similar lives in some ways. We constantly have to look for work because there's no steady wage. We have no regular colleagues to share a drink with. And we don't get invited to any office parties. I mean, don't get me wrong, I do get invited to parties – a lot of parties – but not with anyone I have any kind of meaningful relationship with. Showbiz parties are all about posing and pouting and hiding behind a facade. What I miss are the sorts of office parties where you can let your hair down and snog some bloke from accounts in the stationery cupboard and regret it in the morning; a party where we all get shit-faced and photocopy our arses. A real party with real people. Everyone thinks that the showbiz life is glamour and glitz but it's all very shallow. And we have pressures that lots of other professions don't have. The fans. The paparazzi. And worst of all is getting older. How old would you say I am, Stingray? Be honest.'

'That's unfair,' said Savidge from within the wardrobe. 'Anything I say will be wrong.'

'I promise you I won't be cross.'

'Thirty-six?'

'Not bad. I'm forty.'

'Well, you don't look it.'

'I shouldn't do with the amount I've bloody spent. But that's the point I'm making. You can't beat the clock. All those thousands of pounds on lifts and tweaks and tucks and plumps and all I look is four years younger than I actually am? Fuck you, Father Time. There are thousands of twenty-something wannabes out there with perfect hair and straight white teeth and perky breasts all waiting for the day that some casting director says "too dowdy" to me. And it's going to happen, Stingray. It's going to happen soon. And it's so bloody frustrating as I'm a better actor now than I've ever been. I just won a fucking BAFTA.'

'Age doesn't matter,' said Savidge.

'Maybe not to a doctor, or a pilot, or a chef, but it matters to actresses. Age is our biggest enemy.'

'Helen Mirren, Judi Dench . . . they do all right.'

'Yes, but they are wise and magnificent and glamorous,' said Greeley. 'There are loads of roles for mature women like that. But you try to find decent roles for the slightly-over-the-hill-pushing-forty actress like me. As soon as you leave your thirties, your parts dry up. Oh! Ha ha! I could have phrased that better, couldn't I? Ha! The point is that decent roles are as rare as hens' teeth. Too old to get the sexy roles; too young to play the matriarch. I'm sliding towards that pit of despair, my wilderness years, playing mine host in some godforsaken gastropub in the Cotswolds. Or fucking commercials! Oh god, I could end up as the mum in some perfect nuclear family advertising cook-in-the-fucking-bag chicken.'

'We all have to do whatever pays the bills,' said Savidge, walking into the bedroom. Helen Greeley took one look at him and collapsed with laughter on the bed.

'You look fantastic, darling!' she said.

'I look ridiculous,' said Savidge. He was wearing a red cocktail dress that bulged and creaked. He hadn't been able to get the zipper done up at the back. The outfit was set off by a double string of pearls, a hat like a velveteen bucket and Savidge's own Dr Marten's boots. Seeing his hostage collapsed and insensible with laughter, he began pacing again. He stopped suddenly and sniffed the air.

'Can you smell something burning?' he asked.

Having decided that the best way to ensure that Ms Greeley's kidnapper couldn't escape via the balcony was to remove the means, Mrs Pollwery and Mrs Timmins had set to work on the makeshift rope. However, five minutes of pulling, swinging and hanging on it had been fruitless; Savidge's knots were good and the wrought-iron railings to which the rope was tied were solid. They had therefore hit upon a very different idea. Finding a can of paraffin next to the heating-oil tank, they'd soaked the end of the rope, set it alight and run away.

'I can definitely smell something burning,' said Savidge as he moved around the room, sniffing.

'Must be you. You're smoking hot in that dress,' said Greeley in paroxysms of giggles.

'I'm serious. Maybe it's just a bonfire or something.'

He stepped out on to the balcony. Thick black smoke was rising in a column from somewhere in the gardens below. He peered over the railings and a wave of hot air hit him in the face.

'They've set fire to the rope!' he yelled.

'What? Who has?'

'I don't know but the rope is on fire!'

Savidge wrestled with the knot that anchored the bed sheets to the railings but he'd tied it too well and the exertions of the ladies below had tightened it still further. He rushed back into the bedroom, retrieved his penknife and then began sawing through the material. In just a few seconds, he had severed it and the burning rope fell away to his left and draped itself over the top of the heating-oil tank, which immediately bloomed with flame. He swore and rushed back inside, locking the French windows. He stared wild-eyed at Helen Greeley.

'Come on,' he said.

Miss Berrycloth had found herself a comfortable place to sit by straddling the crotch of two fat branches. She focused on the French windows of Greeley's bedroom. There was definitely another person in the room with the actress and, up until now, she'd naturally assumed it to be a man. But now the person had come out on to the balcony and, to her surprise, she saw that it was a tall woman in a red dress. It was then that she noticed the fire.

Fed by the paraffin, the flames had quickly begun to climb the knotted sheets and, within seconds, had engulfed half of the length of the rope. Pleased with their handiwork and unnoticed by Miss Berrycloth, the two amateur arsonists had rejoined the group under the horse chestnut to watch the results of their actions.

As flames suddenly appeared on the top of the heating-oil tank, the Millies ran away in panic. Many of them had been present during the burger van fire earlier in the day and that had been frightening enough. The idea that an entire tank of paraffin was now in danger of going up was even more terrifying. Around where pieces of the burning rope had fallen, small bushes had caught fire. It had been an unusually warm month and, despite the rain of the previous evening, everything was once again bone dry.

'Someone hold the ladder. I'm coming down!' shouted Miss Berrycloth but, just as she was placing her foot on the top rung, the ladder was knocked to the ground, leaving her stranded in the tree. She clutched at a branch for dear life and shouted for assistance.

'But where are we going?' said Greeley, suddenly a lot more sober and pulling on her shoes.

'Away from here,' said Savidge. 'I think it's probably just spillage around the filler cap that's caught fire but I don't want to be in this room if that tank blows. Come on.'

He grabbed her hand, flipped the lock on the suite's outer door and led her along the hotel corridor towards the lifts.

'Will someone please put the ladder back!' yelled Miss Penny Berrycloth, sitting high in the boughs of the old tree. Below her, all was chaos and panic. The carefully shaped screen of bushes hiding the unsightly heating-oil tank was now ablaze, creating an even more effective barrier than usual. Certainly, Mr Jaycocks and Mr Horningtop, who had had the sense to grab the fire extinguishers from the lobby, couldn't get close enough to use them on the tank. Somewhere in the distance, sirens could be heard. Mr Jaycocks hoped that someone had been organised enough to call the fire brigade.

Suddenly, a small explosion erupted near the oil tank.

Helen Greeley heard the explosion and took decisive action. She pulled off a shoe and used the heel to smash the glass on the red fire-alarm box on the wall by the lift. A loud electronic siren began to wail with ear-shattering volume.

'What did you do that for?' shouted Savidge as they both jumped through the opening doors of the lift.

'It's an . . . emergency, isn't . . . it?' said Greeley. She had developed hiccups. 'Wait . . . aren't we supposed . . . to not use the lifts during a . . . fire?'

'To hell with that,' said Savidge. 'We need to get out of here fast.'

Up and down the hotel corridors, people shuffled about in confusion. Thankfully, the majority of the Empire's guests were Crabbe fans who were at the dance but, even so, there were still a few in their rooms, and in other people's rooms where perhaps they shouldn't be, and now all of them crowded into the halls and stairwells in an effort to get out as quickly as possible. Among the evacuees were reporters and camera crews who immediately spotted the potential of the situation and jumped straight into professional mode, despite being in their bathrobes and pyjamas. And, unnoticed and anonymous among the crowds, Savidge and Greeley ran too.

'I think it was only a jerry can that exploded,' said Mr Horningtop. 'But it's made things a lot worse. The fire is spreading.' He pointed at what was left of the can that the two arsonist Millies had used to set fire to the rope. At the sound of the explosion, he and Mr Jaycocks had instinctively thrown themselves to the ground. That they'd chosen a flower bed that had been horse-manured only that morning was unfortunate.

'There may be more explosions,' said Mr Jaycocks. 'We store all the old paraffin and cooking-oil cans under the tank.'

'That doesn't seem like a very safe way to do th—'

As if on cue, another loud report signalled the destruction of a second can.

'We're too close and the fire is too big. We need to leave this to the professionals,' said Mr Horningtop. But Mr Jaycocks didn't hear him. He was already on his feet and running.

From high above their heads, in the branches of a tall tree, came a tremulous cry for help that went unheard.

'Where are we going?' huffed Greeley. The screams and secondary explosions behind them had lent an extra boost of energy to their feet and they had got as far away from the hotel as they could.

Savidge stopped to catch his breath. 'I don't know. But we can't just keep running. They'll have dogs and helicopters out looking for us shortly,' he gasped.

'Why would they be looking for us?' asked Greeley.

'That rope didn't catch fire by accident. They're after me.'

'I don't understand. Who is after you?'

'Someone who knew that I was up in your room. They deliber-ately cut off my escape route.' Savidge's eyes had suddenly become fierce, the pupils dilated. Even through her alcoholic fug, Greeley could see that he was slipping back into another manic episode. She grabbed his face between her hands and stared into his eyes.

'We're going to be all right, Stingray,' she said soothingly. 'Come on. I have an idea.'

*

The Masonic Hall dance was in full swing. As Greeley and Savidge entered the main room, they were treated to the once-seen-never-forgotten sight of several hundred older ladies dressed as Miss Cutter and dancing the Charleston frenetically to the sounds of a five-piece jazz band. The music was so loud that no one had heard the explosions.

'We just need to hang out in here for a while and then leave with everyone else,' said Greeley. 'It's the perfect hideout.'

'I don't like it,' said Savidge. 'Someone is bound to spot you. You're famous.'

'You'd be surprised. In costume and in semi-darkness I look no different from all the other Millies in here.'

Savidge looked around. Greeley was right; she blended in perfectly with the crowds as, indeed, did he. There was a fancy-dress competition at 11 p.m. and a few of the craftier party-goers had turned up dressed as subsidiary characters, such as Colonel Trayhorn Borwick or Miss Cutter's beloved Aunt Pie or her good friend from the Knollshire Constabulary, Inspector Raffo. They were banking upon the fact that the fewer entrants there were in those categories, the better the chances of winning. But most had simply not bothered to change and were wearing the same outfits they'd been wearing all day. The room was full of Miss Cutters.

'Besides, I'm even more disguised than usual in the new outfit,' shouted Greeley above the music. 'It hides two of my most distinguishing features. Come on, dance with me.'

'I don't really . . .'

'Half an hour ago you didn't do drag but look at you now. Come on, move your feet. Do you want to attract attention?'

Begrudgingly, Savidge began to dance.

'Shit,' he said suddenly. 'I left my wallet and all of my money in your room.'

'Ah. Me too,' said Greeley. 'I don't have a penny on me. And you threw away my phone.'

'Mine went up with the van.'

'So where do we go when we leave here? We can't go back to the hotel.'

'You can.'

'Not if there's been a fire. Where do you live?' asked Greeley.

'Over Bowcester way. But I don't know how I'll get there with no money. Anyway, you're famous. People will be queuing up to offer you a bed for the night.'

'Yes, and they'll be mostly rabid fans and obsessives,' said Greeley. 'We could go to the police, I suppose.' She saw the panic in his face. 'Or not.'

'Look, don't take this the wrong way but I do know of somewhere we can go,' said Savidge. 'It's a houseboat. It's not really mine and I don't exactly have permission to use it, but it would do for the night. It has a couple of bedrooms.'

'That sounds perfect,' said Greeley.

'Least I could do.'

'No, the least you could do is tell me your real name. I can't keep calling you Stingray.'

'It is my name.'

'Fuck off!'

'No, really. It's Stingray Troy Phones Marina Savidge.'

'Jesus. How on earth did you get a name like that?'

'An arsehole of an adoptive father who was a Gerry Anderson fan,' said Savidge. 'All of us boys got stupid bloody names.'

'No wonder you're so pissed off all the time.'

The song changed and suddenly everyone was doing the Lindy Hop. The music was loud but not quite loud enough to mask the sound of the hotel's oil tank exploding.

19

Frank Shunter dozed in his favourite armchair. In the distance there was a loud, deep, resonant boom. Mrs Shunter felt it through her feet.

'Sounds like they're setting off some mighty big fireworks,' she said.

Her husband grunted once, shifted position and began to snore.

Mrs Shunter tutted.

In the Incident Room, just a few buildings away from the hotel, the sound of the first exploding paraffin can made everyone jump.

'What the hell was that?' said Banton.

'It sounded like a gunshot,' said Jaine. 'It came from the hotel.'

There was a second loud bang and then the sound of a howling fire alarm. All of a sudden, there were people running past the front doors of the library.

'Wait . . . you don't think this is anything to do with that hostage phone call you took, do you?' said Banton.

'No,' said Blount firmly. 'That was just some Milly with an overactive imagination.'

'Those did sound like gunshots, guv,' said Jaine.

'But there's a fire alarm going off,' said Blount.

'Yeah, but there's no such thing as a gun alarm, is there?' said Jaine. 'It could be someone hitting the alarm in panic.'

'It might be worth checking out, guv,' said Banton.

'I am absolutely certain that there's no—'

A much louder explosion shook the whole building. Books toppled from the library shelves and Miss Tradescant's photograph slid from the whiteboard.

Blount's face drained of all colour.

In the months to come, the health-and-safety inquiry team would have much to say about the improper storage of flammables at the Empire Hotel in Nasely. Firstly, there was the fact that underneath the concrete base upon which the oil tank once stood was an area that had been used to store empty cooking-oil drums and containers used for other noxious liquids such as paraffin, methylated spirits, cleaning fluids and diesel for the emergency generator. Secondly, the flat top of the tank had been used as a storage area for things like old carpet tiles and bits of timber. The explosion had been caused by a combination of burning material both above and below the tank, which had very quickly raised temperatures to dangerous levels. By the time the fire brigade had arrived, it had been too late to do anything other than help evacuate the hotel. Had they pumped water into the fire, the superheated steam would have speeded up the reaction. Thankfully, the tank had only been half full when it had reached ignition point, but the large amount of vapour in the void above the oil level had been sufficiently explosive to launch the entire tank thirty feet into the air and to send fragments of shrapnel even higher and further. The searing shock wave had blown off most of the upper branches of the ancient horse chestnut and all of the hair and clothes off Miss Penny Berrycloth, who had been caught in the blast and thrown over the gardens to a mercifully soft landing in the canal, suffering a number of serious but thankfully not life-threatening injuries. The blast also took down approximately 60 per cent of the rear wall of the hotel, seriously injuring five guests and causing extensive burns to a reporter from the *Daily Mail* who'd been masturbating in the shower and hadn't heard the fire alarm. The authors of the inquiry report expressed the opinion that they were amazed that no one had been killed.

Three fire engines had forced their way through the garden hedges at the rear of the hotel and had set up on the mole-ravaged lawns where they played water over the smouldering and exposed rooms. Their work was hampered by small explosions every few minutes as the remaining cans burst under internal pressure. A cherry picker was busy rescuing people from the flat roof where they had fled upon finding the stairwells full of other panicking guests. A police helicopter chuntered noisily overhead.

Miss Berrycloth had been fished out of the canal and lay, wretched, depilated and naked, under a rough blanket on a stretcher, her left leg shattered in two places, her right arm in three, and covered in second-degree burns. She had been lucky to survive, but her indomitable spirit refused to be subdued and, as she was being lifted into the ambulance, she was still shouting about Helen Greeley being held prisoner in her room.

Most of the festival-goers had now drifted out of the dance and into the street to see what was going on. A monstrous pall of dirty black smoke hung over the hotel, illuminated by flashing blue lights. Emergency vehicles were parked ten deep by the building's incongruous fake portico and dozens of police officers roamed about looking busy and purposeful. And everywhere there were reporters and camera crews in their onesies, or in jackets thrown over their nightwear, getting in everyone's way, asking for opinions and thanking their lucky stars that they'd been right there, on scene, when whatever had happened had happened. They did pieces to camera describing, not always accurately, the events of the weekend so far: the horrific murder of a so-far unidentified woman at the village hall; the possibly sinister deaths of two other women in a car crash; the disappearance of a prominent solicitor and several leading lights in the world of Agnes Crabbe fandom; the possible abduction of TV star Helen Greeley; and now, what appeared to be a terrorist attack on the hotel that had seriously injured a handful of festival-goers, including Miss Penny Berrycloth, yet another important fan-club figure. Conspiracy theories abounded. Chief Superintendent Edwin Nuton-Atkinson, commander of Bowcester Division, had turned out to try to explain to the reporters why his officers had failed to prevent any of these events from happening. As he spoke, he jumped whenever another oil can exploded. For many of the Millies, the lure of the strobing blue lights and cameras was too much and they were drawn towards them like sharks to a wounded seal.

In the confusion, no one noticed as two of the Miss Cutter look-alikes headed out of the village towards the small group of houseboats moored on the canal near the Dunksbury Road bridge.

For Mrs Dallimore, sitting all alone in the pitch black of the old boat's hull, the night brought different terrors. Some distance from the village and shielded within the boat, she had barely heard the explosions. All she could hear was the scuttling of rodents, accompanied by the spooky noises of other night creatures, the sounds magnified by the eerie silence. Her wrists were chafing painfully and one hand had pins and needles, but it hadn't deterred her from making every effort to slip free of the cable tie. It had definitely jumped a couple of ratchet marks since she'd begun to force it and it felt looser. It was scant reward for several hours of excruciatingly painful effort but it was a start. Too scared to sleep but too tired not to, she had dozed spasmodically, waking to the sound of a screaming fox here or a creaking timber there. And between shallow naps, she'd continued the torturous work of defeating the cable tie that bound her wrists, rubbing it against the wooden bulkhead, pulling, tugging and twisting. Fear, and the realisation that she would soon need the toilet again, had loaned her a strength and a determination she hadn't realised she possessed.

20

Shunter ate a hearty breakfast while watching the TV with ever-increasing disbelief. All of the news channels were leading with the overnight events in Nasely.

'You're not seriously going back into the village today, are you?' asked Mrs Shunter.

'Of course,' said Shunter, matter-of-factly. He stood up and placed his breakfast dishes in the dishwasher.

'And you're just going to ignore the fact that there's been a murder, are you? And god knows how many explosions,' said Mrs Shunter.

'Of course. That's the British way. Can't let the buggers ruin our daily routine, can we? They'll think they've won.'

'But what about the danger?'

'I'll be fine, dear.' Shunter pecked his wife on the cheek. 'Half of the South Herewardshire Constabulary is on scene. Plus, lord knows how many Scotland Yard specialists they've pulled in, everything from Anti-Terrorist Branch to kidnapping experts, I'd have thought. Today the village is likely to be the safest place in Britain. You are, as always, welcome to join me of course.'

'Not likely,' said Mrs Shunter.

'Then I will see you at teatime.'

'I hate to think what this business will do to the house prices.'

'Ah, but think about all those friends we left behind with their posh houses and their boring corporate lives,' said Shunter. 'They don't get to see excitement like this on their doorstep, do they? I bet they'll be on the phone later, asking to visit. Do tell them what they can do.'

He popped a panama hat on his head as the forecast was sunny. Plus, he felt, it added a slight air of jaunty theatricality to his appearance that might help him to blend in better with the murder-mystery fans. He set off on the ten-minute walk into the village.

Savidge was woken by a bright shaft of sunlight that broke through a crack in the curtains and crept across his eyelids. He squinted and fumbled with closing the curtain before rolling over and trying to get comfortable again. He became aware of a warm body pressed against his leg and with it came remembrance of the evening before.

He and Greeley had arrived at the houseboat, scared, hungry and thirsty. The first thing he'd done, after forcing the lock on the cabin doors, was rummage in the galley cupboards for something to eat and drink. All he'd found were some packet soups and some teabags but the kettle worked and so they did, at least, enjoy a hot meal of sorts. However, thoughts of the delicious goodies on offer from room service back at the hotel had made the meal seem even more frugal. After the meal, Savidge removed the last of his hospital dressings and took a shower to clear the dried blood from around his injuries.

'So who does this boat belong to?' she'd asked him when he'd finished.

'A mate of mine,' he'd explained. 'He's away travelling at the moment. I'm pretty sure he won't mind me using it, as long as I fix the lock. Is it okay?'

'It's great,' said Greeley. 'I've never slept on the river before.'

'But not as comfortable as your hotel suite,' said Savidge.

'After that explosion, I'd be surprised if I still have a hotel suite. Or a hotel for that matter. Besides, this is much better.'

'How?'

'Listen, I had a really nasty experience last year when a man, a very disturbed man who I trusted to protect me, broke into my home and threatened me with a gun.'

'Shit. I had no idea.'

'When it happened, I was already going through a bad patch as I'd just got divorced and Terry was being a complete bastard, selling private photos and stories of our sex life to the tabloids,' said Greeley. 'Two people I really trusted screwed me over. It's made me suspicious of everyone. So I don't like being alone any more, especially in strange places, and it's really hard for me to find people I can be alone with and truly feel safe. But I feel safe here with you. Does that make any sense?'

'Not really,' said Savidge, miserably. 'I must have terrified you.'

'To begin with, yes, you did. But then, and I don't really understand why, I realised that I was safe with you. You seemed to be just as scared as I was and, despite plenty of opportunities, you didn't try to harm or molest me. I knew that you weren't a threat and, in some weird way, I also knew that I could trust you. I'll warn you now, the feeling may wear off and I may end up running screaming to the police. But, right now, at this moment, I feel safer and more comfortable here, on this boat with you, than at the hotel.'

'But anywhere must feel safer after the fire and those explosions.'

'That's not really what I meant. I don't suppose there's any booze on board?'

'None that I've found. We did better than I expected with the packet soups.'

'Probably best we get some sleep then,' said Greeley. 'Just one more thing . . .'

'Go on.'

'Can we sleep in the same room?'

'But there's only the one bed.'

'It's big enough for two. But listen, no funny business, okay? I just don't want to be alone.'

'I wouldn't do anything. Especially as you've had so much to drink.'

'I know,' said Greeley, smiling.

And so they'd slept together, deeply and chastely, back to back in the warm bed, exhausted by the events of the day.

Savidge rolled gently out of bed so as not to wake her and tiptoed to the toilet.

The atmosphere in the High Street was, understandably, very different from when Shunter had last seen it. Crime-scene tape surrounded the Empire Hotel, closing off Bowler's Lane, and there seemed to be police officers everywhere, strolling about in pairs or sitting in marked cars drinking tea and keeping a suspicious eye on the many groups of Millies nosing around. The events of the night had refreshed the Crabbe fans' levels of excitement and intrigue, and now, to add to the murder, they had the explosions and the apparent kidnapping of Helen Greeley to discuss, to build theories about and to argue over. There had already been several fan-club tussles. One was still in full swing as Shunter arrived in the High Street. A reporter from Sky News had asked Mrs Lindsay Packering for her theory about what had happened. Unfortunately, he'd asked her within earshot of several other fan-club leaders.

'It's quite clear to us in the Crabbe and Cutter Club that what we have here is a conspiracy to stop Andrew Tremens revealing whatever he was going to reveal,' she explained to the camera. 'Firstly, he is kidnapped, and then there is an attempt to assassinate Helen Greeley who is, presumably, some part of it and—'

'What utter drivel!' lisped Mrs Anthea Pollwery, pushing herself into the foreground and adjusting her hair. 'The Agnes Crabbe Detective Club boasts two private detectives and an ex-military policewoman among our ranks and it is our considered opinion that some relative or close friend of the man who stalked Ms Greeley last year is exacting revenge for his death and—'

'That's just ridiculous,' snapped Mrs Packering.

'It makes more sense than your stupid assassination theory,' said Mrs Pollwery.

"You're both wrong,' exclaimed Miss Joscha Ambrose-Leigh from *ACDC* magazine. 'We have heard that a gas leak was deliberately created to incapacitate Ms Greeley so that she could be kidnapped and held for ransom. It's just unfortunate that a spark ignited the gas.'

'Nonsense! There's been no ransom demand!' said Miss Gloria Febland of the Trayhorn Borwick Appreciation Society.

'That's the silliest thing I've heard all day!'

'You're all wrong! It's—'

Shunter strolled past the arguing Millies and glanced at his watch. It was nearly 10 a.m. so he walked to the Happy Onion to see if Molly Wilderspin had turned up. She was waiting by the door and was dressed in an unflattering grey fleece, matching trousers and white trainers; her leisurewear made her look even more spherical than her Miss Cutter costume had done. Her face, despite its usual ruddy complexion, was drawn, and dark hollows sat under her eyes. She looked as if she hadn't slept a wink.

'I was already anticipating a rough night because I was so worried about Esme,' she explained. 'Yesterday they were suggesting she might be the victim but today, it seems, they're saying that she's a possible murder suspect along with Brenda Tradescant. Isn't it awful? Esme wouldn't harm a fly.'

'Really?' said Shunter, raising an eyebrow. 'She strikes me as someone who could dish out a damned good thrashing if she was cross enough and felt that the person deserved it.'

'That may be true,' conceded Miss Wilderspin with a sad smile. 'But she could never kill anyone in cold blood. And definitely not in any premeditated way. Anyway, I tried to sleep, but then there were all those bangs and then a fire alarm went off and I came out of my room to see what was going on. Then there was a huge explosion and the whole building shook and everyone panicked and I got swept along with the crowd. We all ended up standing around outside in our night clothes for hours and the police wouldn't let us back in. Thankfully, it wasn't a cold night and there was no rain, but by the time they found a place for me in some kind person's spare bedroom it was gone four a.m. and I was wide awake. I think that I finally dropped off around six.'

'You needn't have come out this morning.'

'I'd like to keep busy today, if I can. It stops me worrying too much.'

'Then let's get some sandwiches and hit the road,' said Shunter, looking at the greasy cloud hanging over the hotel. 'It will be good to get out of the village. It's bedlam here.'

21

'Morning, Brian. Though I can't say it's a good morning, if I'm being honest,' said Chief Superintendent Nuton-Atkinson, a tall, big-bellied man with a shaved head and a moustache like a yard-brush. He yawned, showing off a tongue stained the colour of sandstone by strong coffee.

'No, I suppose not,' said Blount, stifling a yawn in response and wishing that he hadn't been summoned to appear at Bowces-ter Police Station quite so early. He hadn't slept for more than an hour himself.

'This is a bad business, Brian,' said Nuton-Atkinson. 'This is a good borough. A quiet borough. People come to live here because it's supposed to be one of the safest places in the UK. And now this. The Chief isn't at all happy. And now we have all of these Scotland Yard types running about all over the place showing us up.'

'Yes, but—'

'Let's be honest, Brian, we look like chumps. Incompetent chumps. And it's not like the old days when you could obfuscate and keep a story under wraps. You know the Chief. She's the modern type. University educated. Believes in transparency, accountability, all that sort of thing. She wants us to tell the news outlets what happened. No bullshit. No waffle. So I have to make

196

sure that we have a story that keeps her and the public happy. Not lies, you understand. Lies get rumbled. But a version of events where we don't look like complete oafs.'

'I understand,' said Blount.

'Good,' said Nuton-Atkinson. 'We need to show that the South Herewardshire Constabulary isn't staffed with halfwits and dunderheads. There isn't much we can do about that business at the hotel because the anti-terrorist lot have already taken over. But we can still nail this murder and earn some Brownie Points. So, I want you to tell me everything about the inquiry so far. Start at the beginning. Leave nothing out. But let's get some more coffee first. I need something strong to keep me awake. I was up for most of the night.'

Mrs Dallimore had woken in the faint light of dawn, and the little sleep she'd had, and her urgent bladder, had given her renewed strength and energy. She'd immediately begun working on the cable tie once more, pulling and stretching and ignoring the pain in her wrists. It slipped another ratchet mark and, all of a sudden, her hands were free.

After removing her gag and freeing her legs, she'd spent the next half hour quietly exploring the limits of her prison. She had no idea what time it was – she wore no watch and her captor had taken her mobile phone – nor whether her gaoler was still on the upper deck. There had been no recurrence of the sound of boots above, however, and this gave her the courage to start testing the strength of the walls. The boat's hull was firm despite its apparent age but, here and there, she found areas of rotten wood that crumbled under her probing fingers. None of the holes she'd so far managed to make were big enough for her to get through but they did allow her to see exactly where she was.

As she'd assumed, her vessel was inside one of the large tin-roofed sheds she'd seen from the towpath. Her boat was one of three that, presumably, had been brought in for repair but, for whatever reason, had sat here gathering dust, rust and woodworm ever since. There was an old red tractor that looked to be in good condition and lots of machines scattered about: winches, lathes and others the function of which she could barely guess. The only exit from her cell was the hatch that she'd seen her gaoler climb through the evening before, but that was locked. Or stuck maybe; a gentle, silent push was all she'd risked for fear that it would fly open or creak noisily and alert whoever it was that had taken her prisoner. But it hadn't budged. And so she'd returned to her exploration of the barge's interior, testing the wood with her hands and feet and hoping to find a way to break out.

The canal looked serene. Swans glided across the surface of the sluggish brown waters and looked snobbishly down their bills at other less-impressive waterfowl. Beyond the far bank, the fields of freshly cut grass, recently harvested for winter silage, were salt and peppered with the white and grey of lesser black-backed gulls dibbing for worms.

This stretch of canal, known as the Oxbow Deviation, had been built during the Victorian era to provide affluent boating enthusiasts with a scenic route through the flat landscape. The county boasted no large rivers and the nearest canals, like the Grand Union and the Oxford, were busy commercial routes, wholly unsuited to pleasure boating. And so the rich farmers and landowners of South Herewardshire had created their own, cutting a meandering waterway through the beautiful countryside that began near Scroobys Lift Bridge on the Oxford Canal and then wound its way past some of the county's prettiest villages. It ended at Dunksbury Locks just a few miles east of Bowcester, where it joined a spur of the Gloucester and Sharpness Canal.

Shunter breathed in deeply. The smells of the countryside, carried on the warm morning breeze, were intoxicating and he reflected upon his good decision to move to this part of the country. It was hard to believe that only yesterday, and just a few minutes' walk from where he stood, a woman had been brutally murdered.

He was, he realised, almost certainly wasting his time; Blount would undoubtedly have sent some officers along the towpaths to look for clues. But then he reminded himself that they hadn't found Mrs Handibode's book, so there was a possibility that they might have missed other clues too. With his experienced eye, he might yet spot something that the average street cop would miss. But, whatever happened, at least he was doing a good deed by keeping Miss Wilderspin busy and distracted from her worries. And, besides, it was a nice day for a walk.

'So how did you get involved in Agnes Crabbe fandom?' he asked.

'It was all rather serendipitous really,' said Miss Wilderspin. 'I was a big fan of the *Miss Cutter Mysteries* TV series and that made me start reading the books. And, just because it sounded like something fun to do, I looked into joining a fan club and discovered that the Agnes Crabbe Fellowship is based in a house in Oxford just half a mile away from where I live.'

'Mrs Handibode's house?'

'Hers and her husband's,' said Molly. 'Although he has nothing to do with the Fellowship. He doesn't really care for Agnes Crabbe or her books. Anyway, I went to a meeting there and I thoroughly enjoyed it, although I'll admit that I didn't take to Esme at first.'

'She's not the warmest of individuals.'

'I know that she can come across as joyless and even a bit rude, but that's just her way. She feels very close to Agnes Crabbe and she is passionate about her studies. A bit obsessive, maybe, but she's not a bad person.'

'So, in summary, what you're saying is that we have several possible suspects for the murder but none of them are in custody,' said Chief Superintendent Nuton-Atkinson.

'Yes, sir. I know how that sounds but—' said Blount.

'And you have no idea which one is most likely?'

'We have Tradescant's fingerprints on the murder weapon and Savidge was seen driving a van away from the murder scene just after it happened. He was also spotted covered in blood earlier in the day. So both are possible suspects.'

'Do they have any previous convictions?'

'Both have minor convictions for public order offences. And Savidge's father is a proper villain. He's been inside for robbery, assault, burglary . . . and he's still active in fencing stolen goods around Hoddenford way, even though he's a pensioner now.'

'How is that relevant?'

'Like father like son?' said Blount unconvincingly.

'Hmm. And this Handibode woman? What about her?'

'She might have made the poisoned jam.'

'Poisoned jam?'

'It's implicated in the fatal car crash the night before the murder. But that might be unconnected,' said Blount, painfully aware of how ridiculous his story sounded and, more importantly, how incompetent he appeared to be. 'She is missing, though. Which is a bit suspicious.'

'Yes. Well, returning to the village hall murder,' said Nuton-Atkinson. 'What do we know about the victim?'

'Fingerprints were taken from the body yesterday; they had to be done the old-fashioned way with ink and paper. They came back as no trace on the database.'

'So we still don't know who she is?'

'No, sir.'

'And the solicitor, Tremens, he's still missing?'

'Yes, sir.'

'But he's not the victim.'

'No, sir, it's definitely a woman.'

'And Helen Greeley, the TV star, is missing too?'

'Possibly,' said Blount.

'That woman who was up in the tree spying on her room . . . she says that someone was keeping Greeley hostage.'

'So I understand.'

'And they found this chap Savidge's clothes and wallet in Greeley's hotel room.'

'Yes, sir. It's possible that he's involved in her disappearance too.'

'But I thought the person seen in the room was another woman.'

'Probably Savidge dressed as a woman. He was dressed as a woman when he was seen driving the van too.'

'But we don't know where he is either?'

'No, sir.'

'Bloody hell, Brian. That's an awful lot of don't know,' said Nuton-Atkinson, rubbing his bald pate.

'I'm doing the best I can with the resources I have,' said Blount. 'We've made some progress and if you look at my report you'll see that everything has been done by the book. It's just been—'

'People are saying that I should assign a more senior investigating officer,' interrupted Nuton-Atkinson. 'Are they right?'

Blount felt his stomach drop to the floor. 'No, sir. Please. Not yet. Just give me a few more hours,' he pleaded. 'We're so close to a breakthrough. I know we are. Don't let all our good work go to waste.'

'I'm meeting the Chief Constable at two o'clock,' said Nuton-Atkinson. 'That gives you three hours to pull your case together. We've known each other a long time, Brian, ever since we were woodentops on the beat together, and that's why I'm giving you this chance. But three hours is the best I can do. Don't let me down.'

'Yes, sir. Thank you, sir.'

'I can't have us looking like a bunch of provincial thickos. Those Scotland Yard yobbos already think that they're better than we are and they'll take over at the drop of a hat. So, if you still have nothing in three hours' time, I will have no choice but to suggest assigning a more senior officer to head up the case. And you know who the Chief will choose, don't you?'

'Yes, sir,' said Blount miserably.

'Three hours, Brian.'

'I suppose I should just go back to the hotel and tell everyone we're all right,' said Greeley. 'I didn't like the sound of that explosion last night. I hope no one got hurt.'

'You must go. They check to make sure all guests are accounted for after a fire,' said Savidge. 'They'll think you're dead or missing.'

'Yes, I suppose you're right,' said Greeley.

'Or abducted,' said Savidge. 'And I bet you they try to pin the blame on me.'

'Surely not?'

'They'll have found my wallet in your room by now and they'll have put two and two together and made five. You wait and see. Especially after what happened to you with that stalker last year.'

'No, but . . . oh shit.'

'What?'

'I just remembered. Last night, when the hotel manager knocked on the door, before I knew you better, I tried to send him a coded message.'

'Coded message?'

'I mentioned a character from an Agnes Crabbe story who was kept prisoner against his will. I thought that they might realise that I was in the same situation.'

'Do you think that's why someone set fire to the rope?'

'I don't know. Maybe,' said Greeley. 'I'm so sorry. I was scared at the time and—'

'It's okay,' said Savidge, shrugging resignedly. 'There's no point me acting all outraged. I deserve everything that happens to me. I should just go and hand myself in. Straighten things out.'

'No. You weren't in your right mind yesterday,' said Greeley. 'I'll go back to the hotel and explain what happened. Well, a version that will keep everyone happy anyway.'

'You don't have to do that.'

'Yes I do. You wait here until I've cleared things up. It's going to be madness there after the explosions and I don't want to trigger another of your episodes. Just chill out and try not to worry. Do your relaxation exercises or something. Everything will be fine. I'll bring lunch back with me.'

*

Mrs Dallimore pushed against the rotten wood of a plank at knee level and was almost in tears of joy as her walking boot passed through it as easily as if it were made of polystyrene. She withdrew her foot and pushed again at the wood all round the hole she'd made and, very soon, she had made a space big enough to cautiously push her head through. There was no one in sight. She pulled her head back inside and began working on making the hole bigger. It wouldn't take long and she'd then be able to climb out. What she did then would be dictated by events. The only thing she knew for sure was that she needed to get away and find help.

Helen Greeley's unexpected arrival at the Empire Hotel had quickly become a much bigger event than she'd anticipated. She was shocked by the extent of damage that the hotel had suffered. From the front it looked no different, except for the surfeit of police vehicles parked outside, but the rear was a very different story. Half of the building had collapsed into the gardens and two fire engines were still on site, wetting down the smouldering fires. The building was completely cordoned off, which meant that returning to her suite – which was miraculously intact – was out of the question. She had also been surprised by the level of media attention; her supposed disappearance had become a major story on the morning news with intense speculation of kidnap or her death among the rubble. But before she could say a word to a reporter, a police officer had chaperoned her swiftly through the TV crews and their torrents of questions, towards the Incident Room at the library. Her subsequent cross-examination by the commander of Bowcester Fire Station and an exhausted DI Blount was yet another thing that she hadn't anticipated and she found herself having to think on her feet.

'So, what you're saying is that you met this man, Savidge, and you invited him to your room,' said Blount. 'What for?'

'Do I have to spell it out for you?' said Greeley. 'Because I'm under no obligation to do so. We're all adults here and, unless we've suddenly regressed to the Victorian era overnight, I am allowed to have male guests in my room, surely?'

'Yes, indeed. We're a very modern, accommodating and discreet hotel,' said Mr Jaycocks who had also attended the Incident Room to make a statement regarding the overnight drama.

'So why was there a rope hanging from the balcony?' asked Blount.

'Because I'm an actor, darling. A child of the theatre,' said Greeley. 'Have you no romance in your soul, Inspector? "With love's light wings did I o'erperch these walls, for stony limits cannot hold love out."'

'So it was some kind of Romeo and Juliet role-play thing?' said the fire chief.

'Very good!'

The fire chief blushed.

'He climbed up to my balcony. It was just a bit of silly fun,' said Greeley. 'And there was no damage done, I assure you.'

'No damage done!' said Mr Jaycocks. 'There's talk of condemning the place.'

'I'll happily admit that we ruined a few sheets and I'm more than happy to compensate the hotel for those,' said Greeley. 'But if you're saying that I'm responsible for the explosion, that's quite an accusation and I will—'

'I'm sure he's not alleging anything like that,' said the fire chief.

'Yes, but . . .' stuttered the hotel manager.

'Mr Jaycocks, if I may continue,' said Blount. 'Now then, Ms Greeley, tell me about the coded message.'

'Coded message?' said Greeley, innocently. 'What coded message?'

'Mr Jaycocks here tells us that you referred to him as Mr Gilderdale.'

'I did? I'm sorry. I stay in so many hotels and I'm afraid that they all tend to blur and merge into each other in my head. I do apologise if I got the name wrong.'

'So you're saying that you weren't giving a coded message?' asked Blount.

'What on earth for?'

'We thought you were referencing a character called Gilderdale in an Agnes Crabbe novel who's being kept prisoner—'

'Oh, you mean *My Brother's Keeper*,' said Greeley. 'That was a wonderful story to film.'

'Yes. That one,' said Mr Jaycocks, still stinging from the news that Ms Greeley apparently hadn't bothered to remember his name.

'Oh dear me, no,' said Greeley. 'The name must have been stuck in my head. It is a favourite episode of mine. I got a BAFTA for it, you know.'

'So I understand,' said Mr Jaycocks, snippily.

'Sometimes I think that you murder-mystery fans see secret messages and clues in everything,' said Greeley, smiling. 'I hope that I didn't cause you any worry.'

'We thought you were being held hostage,' said Mr Jaycocks.

'Really?'

'You didn't turn up for your talk and people were concerned for your safety.'

'And I faked a tummy bug, didn't I? That was awful of me. But I was feeling jetlagged and a bit sad and lonely and I met a nice man and that doesn't happen to me very often and, well, you know how it is.' She stood up and prepared to leave. 'It looks as if this has all been a ghastly misunderstanding.'

'Just one last thing,' said Blount. 'Perhaps you'd tell us where Mr Savidge is now? I assume you left the hotel together last night.'

'We did, during the fire alarm,' said Greeley. 'But I have no idea where he is this morning.'

'You're quite sure about that?'

'Of course.'

'And you do realise that you would be obstructing a police investigation if you did know where he was but refused to tell me? You could even be accused of harbouring a wanted criminal.'

'Wanted? What on earth for? I told you, I invited him into my room. There wasn't a kidnap or a—'

Blount held up the photograph of the van driver that Shunter had obtained from the CCTV footage. 'Do you recognise this man?'

'It's a bit blurry.'

'Is it Mr Savidge?'

'I suppose it could be him if he didn't shave for a day or two,' said Greeley. 'But then he has one of those faces. Really quite good-looking in a nondescript sort of way.'

'That was taken a short while before the murder took place at the village hall,' said Blount. 'And he was seen making his escape from there shortly afterwards. Still feel like keeping his whereabouts from us?'

'Oh god,' said Greeley, sitting down hard.

Mrs Dallimore slowly eased herself feet first through the hole she'd made in the hull and dropped the remaining six inches to the ground. Her heart pounding, she hugged the side of the vessel and looked around for signs that anyone had seen her. The nearest door was on the far side of the shed and no more than fifty yards away but it seemed like a million miles. Her legs and body were trembling. It was possible, she calculated, to get to the door and stay mostly hidden if she made a series of quick dashes between the machinery and the other boats. The only risk of being seen would come in the short sprints between places of concealment. Steeling herself, she took a couple of deep breaths and then dashed to the adjacent narrowboat. She caught her breath and listened. There were no sounds of pursuit, no raised voices. 'Brave heart, Pamela,' she said quietly to herself. 'You can do this.'

Suddenly, from the other side of the hull she was leaning on, came a sound; a muffled, mumbling and altogether human sound. Mrs Dallimore peered through a porthole into the gloomy interior. And there, looking back at her, were two faces that she knew all too well.

Those of Esme Handibode and Brenda Tradescant.

22

At Bowcester Divisional HQ, the news that a possible murderer was hiding on a houseboat was greeted with excitement by Sergeant Jack Stough, ex-Paratroop Regiment and now head of the South Herewardshire Constabulary Tactical Response Unit. Despite it being Sunday, he came rushing into work, thankful for the chance to drive his beloved TRV. The tactical response vehicle had been purchased some years ago when atrocities on both sides of the Atlantic had led to increased spending on anti-terrorism resources. But, barring the obligatory six-monthly training exercises he set for his team, the bullet-proof Range Rover had never seen active service. He whistled happily as he loaded it up with weapons from the armoury, contacted his small team and instructed them to meet him at St Probyn's churchyard in Nasely at 11.45 a.m.

Neither Jaine nor Banton had managed more than a few hours of sleep overnight. They looked exhausted, haggard and sleepy-eyed, but positively chipper compared to Blount. He was unshaven, dishevelled and the deep black hollows under his eyes made him look even more skeletal than usual. He had been chain-drinking cups of strong black coffee since his return from HQ and he tapped his fingers impatiently on the librarian's desk. Why did everything take so long?

'Some news, guv,' said Banton.

'At last,' said Blount, yawning. 'Please tell me something good.'

'We have an email from Thames Valley Police. They've searched Miss Nithercott's home in Amersham and they've found several pots of yew-berry jam in her fridge.'

'Which means she made it herself.'

'Or someone else made it for her. I'll ask the local scenes-of-crime guys to fingerprint the jars as a matter of urgency, just to be sure. If Handibode made it, her prints might be on the jars. We may get lucky.'

'Chance would be a fine thing. What about the houseboat? Any movement?'

'We have spotters on it. If Savidge tries to leave, we'll know.'

'Good.' Blount was perking up. 'I'm briefing the tactical response unit in half an hour. We'll soon have some answers once we have the sod in custody. Get some more coffee in, will you?'

Helen Greeley listened to the police officers talking about 'tactical response units' and was overwhelmed with guilt. She'd stayed at the library in the absence of anywhere else to go.

'Do you want a tea or a coffee?' asked Banton.

'You don't have anything stronger, I suppose?' said Greeley.

'I'm afraid not.'

'You will be gentle with him, won't you?'

'We'll do things by the book,' said Banton.

'Kid gloves,' added Blount, with an unconvincing smile.

Frank Shunter and Miss Wilderspin had been walking for more than half an hour and were now over a mile from the village.

They had stopped occasionally to give her sore feet a rest; despite her change of footwear, her blisters from the day before were still very painful. Shunter was endeavouring to lift her spirits.

'There are so many common plot devices that are simply non-sense,' he explained. 'Take the whole "good cop, bad cop" business. No one does that. It breaks the rules of evidence. You lean on a prisoner, that's called duress and that will see your case slung out of court.'

'Real life is rather dull and unglamorous compared to fiction, isn't it?' said Miss Wilderspin.

'It's a world away from murder-mystery novels to be sure,' Shunter agreed. 'Which is why I like to read them, I guess. They're all set in a nicer, lovelier world; a world without domestic violence, carjacking or teenage prostitutes. It's nonsense – pure escapism. That's the appeal. And, besides, I like figuring out the whodunnits. It's good mental exercise. How are the feet now?'

'Sore. But I can go on for a little while yet,' said Miss Wilderspin.

Shunter scanned the path ahead. About a half a mile away, he could just make out some large structures. 'Looks like a small industrial estate or something up ahead. We can stop for lunch there. Maybe there'll be a phone signal and, if your feet are still bad, we can call a cab to take us back to the village if you like. This is starting to look like a dead end anyway.'

At St Probyn's churchyard, DI Blount laid out a map of the village on the bonnet of the TRV, much to the annoyance of Sergeant Stough, who had lovingly polished it at least once a fortnight for the past ten years.

'The canal runs parallel to the High Street behind the hotel, the village hall and my Incident Room, which is at the library here,' he explained, pointing out the various buildings. 'If we follow it westwards, past the church here and out of the village, you come to the Dunksbury Road bridge. After that the canal widens and there are five houseboats moored there. The one we're interested in is painted green and is called *The Sweating Boatman*.'

'What do we know about the target?' asked Stough.

'I'm not sure I want him thought of as a target,' said Blount.

'All right, the suspect then.'

'He has a few minor convictions. Nothing serious. He has some anger issues.'

'Some anger issues?' said Stough incredulously. 'Didn't he smash some old bird's face into chutney and then attack her corpse with a carving knife? He sounds completely mental.'

'But he is still only a suspect at this time,' reiterated Blount. 'And he has medication to keep his anger under control.'

'Well, it doesn't work, does it? Is he armed?'

'Not as far as we know.'

'Hmm. Just because there's been no sighting of firearms so far doesn't mean he isn't tooled up,' said Stough. 'And being a nutter means that he'll be unpredictable. Oh, just one more thing . . . Didn't you circulate some woman as the murder suspect a short while back? What's happened to her?'

'Brenda Tradescant? We believe that she is involved somehow. And so, perhaps, is another woman called Esme Handibode. Between you and me, it's a very confused picture, which is why, and I cannot stress this enough, we must take this man alive and preferably unhurt,' said Blount. 'He'll know what's what. There is also a possibility that he has hostages stashed somewhere nearby. Their safety is our other major concern.'

'He doesn't have any on the boat?'

'Our informant didn't mention any. Just be careful, please.'

'Don't worry. My lads have taken part in dozens of simulated exercises.'

'Simulated?'

'They scored very highly,' Stough boasted.

Back in the Incident Room, Helen Greeley drank her coffee and tried to suppress her feelings of self-reproach. She reminded herself that she had nothing to feel guilty about. She knew very little about the man who had, after all, broken into her hotel room and kept her captive for several hours. Who knew what else he might be capable of, especially when his condition flared up? He'd told her that he was at war and had used phrases like 'command post' and 'armed assault' and seemed to believe every word of his self-constructed fantasy. But then she'd remember how fragile he was, how confused and vulnerable he'd been once the mania had passed, and how they'd spent the night together and he'd done her no harm. The guilt came flooding back and she felt like the worst person on the planet.

'I hope I haven't done the wrong thing,' she said.

'Of course you haven't,' said Banton. 'Look, if he's done nothing wrong he has nothing to fear, does he?'

'I suppose not,' said Greeley. 'But I feel awful. Like I've kicked a puppy.'

A laptop pinged and Banton checked her emails. 'Oh shit. This is really going to stir things up.'

'What?' said Greeley.

'I just found out who the victim is,' said Banton.

Mrs Dallimore had spent five fruitless minutes trying to force open the porthole on the narrowboat but was now resigned to the fact that it wouldn't open while locked from the inside. There was no way for the ladies inside to open it as they were gagged and bound, just like she had been. There was always the option of breaking the glass, but even if she could, the window was too small to allow her in or to let the two ladies out. Besides which, the noise might attract their captor or captors. The boat's hull was much newer and firmer than the one she'd been incarcerated inside so she wouldn't be able to break through the wood either. And even if she did find some way of climbing on to the upper deck to search for a hatch, she had no way of knowing whether she'd be spotted or whether she'd be able to access the area where Mrs Handibode and Miss Tradescant were being held. She therefore reluctantly decided that her best plan was to escape and to return with help. She performed an elaborate mime of running away and telephoning but couldn't be sure that her small audience understood. So she resorted to breathing on the glass and writing WILL GET HELP in the condensation. Judging by Mrs Handibode's agitation and red face, she guessed that maybe it wasn't her preferred choice of plan, but there was nothing else for it. She mouthed 'Sorry' at the captives, looked cautiously around and then made a dash to her next island of concealment behind the red tractor. She was now very close to the door and freedom. Her spirits sank as she saw the sturdy padlock fitted to the latch.

On board *The Sweating Boatman*, Savidge busied himself making up the bed and covering up all signs of overnight occupancy. He looked out of the window at the towpath and the trees and bushes beyond it and, once again, found himself wondering about Helen Greeley. She seemed to be genuine and she had said that she would clear things up. So why, then, had he just caught a glimpse of someone dressed in black ducking down among some gorse bushes? He stood back from the window, knowing that the darkness of the interior would hide him from view. But it didn't stop him from being able to see the give-away black-and-white chequered hatband that the person was wearing. His heart sank. The police were on to him. Greeley must have told them where he was.

He crept stealthily through the vessel, peering out of each window in turn, and spotted at least two other police officers taking up positions among the trees and bushes beyond the tow-path. One looked like he was holding some sort of rifle. Savidge had no medication with him to help calm his nerves and panic began to overwhelm him. A trickle of blood escaped his left nostril and he wiped it away with his hand. He pulled on the only clothes he had – the Miss Cutter costume and his boots – and looked out of the windows on the canal side of the boat. The far bank led off on to flat fields and there was nowhere for a cop to hide. He therefore reasoned that they were only watching him from the mooring side of the canal. Putting his wig and hat on his head, and adjusting his string of pearls, he gingerly slid open one of the canal-side windows and climbed through.

Shielded from the police officers' view by the vessel's super-structure, he gently lowered himself down the side but then choked as his string of pearls caught on the window latch. The string snapped and the pearls scattered noisily on to the floor of the cabin while the remainder plopped into the water. Terrified that the noise would alert the officers, Savidge clung motionless to the side of the boat for what seemed like an eternity before deciding to move again. He lowered himself down into the water. It was cold enough to momentarily take his breath away but he recovered his composure quickly and continued inching his way down until his booted feet met the silty mud of the canal floor.

He then slowly moved hand over hand down the length of the boat until he reached the prow. Ducking under the muddy water, he swam to the next boat and then surfaced quietly. There were four narrowboats moored nose to stern, and Savidge moved smoothly and silently between them, putting distance between himself and the police officers who were watching *The Sweating Boatman*.

As he reached the last of the narrowboats, he let go of the hull and performed a lazy half-walk half-breaststroke across the canal to the opposite bank, staying low in the water with his nose just above the surface and expecting a shower of bullets to come zinging towards him at any moment. But they didn't. His confidence began to grow as he reached the far side and, hidden from police eyes by the bridge, climbed quietly up on to the towpath. Taking a deep breath, he stood up, wrung out the hem of his dress to reduce any telltale dripping and emptied his boots of water. He walked slowly up the steps that led to the Dunksbury Road bridge. If anyone had spotted him, they gave no indication. But even if they had, presumably they would imagine him to be just another silly Milly out for a stroll; the other houseboats were being rented out to festival attendees, after all. He crossed the bridge and, from his elevated position, he could now see four armed police officers hidden among shrubbery, their guns trained on *The Sweating Boatman*. His heart skipped a beat as one of the marksmen suddenly looked in his direction. But then the officer placed his finger to his lips in a 'be quiet' gesture and, incredibly, winked at him before returning his concentration to the boat. Savidge walked back towards the village, shivering with cold but feeling reasonably safe from detection for the moment. Emboldened by his disguise, he was even able to walk confidently and anonymously past St Probyn's Church and the Crabbe Cottage Museum, outside of which sat the TRV.

Inside the vehicle Blount and Sergeant Stough were waiting for news of his capture.

'I hope you know what you're doing,' said Blount.

'This will be a cinch,' said Stough. He lifted the radio to his lips. 'All units prepare for mobilisation. On my mark . . .'

The festival weekend hadn't proven to be quite as much fun as Baxter Pole had hoped it would be. A keen Agnes Crabbe fan and murder-mystery reader, he'd entered into the spirit of the festival by turning up dressed as Miss Cutter, despite being six feet two and a regular prop forward for his local team in Bridport. But then there had been that incident on the village green and *that* bite. He still wasn't able to wear underwear and his dress, although he had scrubbed it repeatedly in the sink at his guest house, still bore the stains that had resulted from Savidge's nose-bleed. But at least he hadn't been one of the poor sods who'd been staying in the Empire Hotel. And there were still some great events scheduled for today, including a very special dramatisation of Agnes Crabbe's play *Evil Company Corrupts* at the Masonic Hall later that evening. For one extraordinary performance only, the Bowcester and District Amateur Dramatics Society was going to be joined onstage by not one but two famous Miss Cutters: Maggie Woodbead, who played her in the radio dramas, was making an appearance as Lady Creckerton, and Helen Greeley had agreed to cameo as Miss Cutter's beloved Aunt Pie, who speaks to her in a dream at the beginning of Act II. Greeley had also agreed to reschedule her cancelled talk from the previous evening to follow the performance. Tickets for the play had sold out instantly, leaving many disappointed, but there were plenty of other events going on to keep the fans happy. And so, Pole had decided to write Saturday off, to put everything behind him and to try to enjoy the remainder of the festival despite his tender scrotum.

A secondary school orchestra was in the street outside the Crabbe Cottage Museum playing a short concert of TV detective-show music, and the air was filled with the harrowing tones of a child using a French horn to murder the theme from *Van der Valk*. Savidge stopped for a moment to watch them and to consider his next move. There were, he noted, police officers everywhere. That was a complication, especially if his description had been circulated. Perhaps Helen Greeley was, at this very moment, briefing the police? If he was being honest with himself, he couldn't have blamed her if she was. Perhaps it might be better to surrender on his own terms rather than to run away and always be looking over his shoulder? Presumably they already considered him dangerous; certainly enough to warrant the use of armed police. He looked back at the armoured TRV and considered what to do. Just then, there was the loud report of a gun being fired.

'TRU 1, go!' barked Stough into his radio.

PC Gurveer Singh Khalsa, call sign TRU 1, took aim and fired. There was a loud crash as the CS gas projectile broke through one of the houseboat's windows. Smoke began to billow out from inside *The Sweating Boatman*.

'TRU 2, hold position and cover. TRU 3 and TRU 4, take him out,' ordered Stough.

'Down! Take him down!' snapped Blount. 'I need him alive!'

'TRU 3 and 4, take him down,' said Stough, disappointed.

PC Malcolm Purefound (TRU 3) and PC Abioye Oduwole (TRU 4) acknowledged their orders and ran towards the boat and jumped on board. Purefound wrenched open the cabin doors and, just as he had done during the many simulated exercises that Sergeant Stough had put him through, he lobbed a second gas grenade inside before pulling a gas mask down over his face. Shouting a muffled 'This is the police! We are armed!', he ducked inside the door and, almost immediately, his boots found the fat pearls that had spilled from Savidge's broken necklace and he fell heavily on to his back, the mask jumping off his face. As the gas began to stab painfully into his eyeballs, Purefound staggered to his feet, drew his riot baton and flailed blindly around himself. Swearing profusely, he made his way towards the largest blurry light source in the hope that it was the door that led to outside and the fresh air. Suddenly, a figure emerged from the shadows and Purefound instinctively lashed out. As the sweeping baton caught PC Oduwole squarely on the side of the face, his gas mask was knocked aside and his eyes too began to burn.

Baxter Pole nodded hello to his fellow Crabbe fans as he walked along the High Street taking in the sights and sounds. Sunday was even sunnier and warmer than the Saturday had been and, despite the overpowering smell of burnt oil and the police activity going on at the hotel, things had settled back to near normality. A few Millies were still hanging around the murder scene, hoping to catch a glimpse of what was going on inside the hall, but their interest was starting to wane. The only visitors to the place all morning had been a team of specialist cleaners; the police had finished with the building and it was being prepared for use by the public again.

Arriving outside the Crabbe Cottage Museum, Pole stopped to

watch some schoolchildren playing an erratic version of the theme from *Midsomer Murders*. And as he watched he became aware that the Milly standing next to him was dripping. He shuffled sideways to avoid contact between his shoes and what he assumed to be the result of some unfortunate bladder weakness but then noticed the woman's dark hairy calves. And Dr Martens. He looked up into the face of the wet Milly and their eyes met.

'You!' he yelled.

'Fuck!' said Savidge. He turned and ran, but he was no match for the cross-dressing and extremely fit rugby player who soon caught up with him and grabbed his arm. In desperation, Savidge swung a fist in his direction but Pole ducked and tackled Savidge around the waist, lifting him into the air and throwing him on to the bonnet of a parked Range Rover. But not just any Range Rover.

'Now will you apologise, you little shit?' roared Baxter Pole, putting Savidge into a headlock.

'Okay, okay, I apologise!' said Savidge. 'I fucking apologise, all right?'

'There, was that so hard?' said Pole, releasing him. 'Jesus Christ, man! All you had to do was say sorry. It could have saved us both . . . what the fuck?'

Pole and Savidge found themselves suddenly looking at two men, one very tall and thin and wearing a smile so wide that his head looked as if it might split in half, and one in police uniform and trembling with barely controlled rage. In his hand, he held a taser gun. Sergeant Stough glared at the dented bonnet of his precious Tactical Response Vehicle in horror. The taser shook in his hands.

'Put your hands on your heads, both of you, and kneel on the ground,' he said through gritted teeth.

*

Things had become even more chaotic aboard the houseboat. The two officers, eyes streaming as if someone had rubbed chilli powder and raw onions into them, stumbled blindly about, lashing out with their batons to try to keep themselves safe from the murderer they knew to be on board. Suddenly two more dark shapes appeared in Purefound's peripheral vision and he turned to face them, baton raised. 'It's us! Police!' shouted one of the dark shapes. Thankful for their arrival, the blinded officer stepped backwards, skidded on the pearls once again and fell on to his back, knocking himself unconscious on the corner of a cupboard.

'On the fucking ground!' shouted Stough.

'What? Why?' said Pole.

'Do as he says,' said Savidge, dropping to his knees. He winced. They were still painful from his fall the day before.

'I know my rights,' said Pole. 'What am I supposed to have d—'

He jerked as the taser barbs dug into his chest and delivered 1,200 volts to his nervous system.

'Take it easy, Sergeant,' said an increasingly worried Blount. 'Dents can be fixed.'

Begrudgingly, Sergeant Stough switched off the current.

'Hello, Mr Savidge,' said Blount.

Savidge looked up into the face of a tall cadaverous man holding out a police warrant card for him to see.

'Do I know you?' he asked.

'I don't suppose you do. But you will get to know me very well. I'm Detective Inspector Brian Blount. And I'm arresting you on suspicion of homicide in Nasely Village Hall yesterday afternoon. You do not have to say anything but it may harm your—'

'What? No. Listen, I don't know what . . .' began Savidge, but

Blount's mobile phone began to ring and he snatched it to his ear, indicating with his other hand for Savidge to be quiet. As the police officer listened, his eyes widened and his smile melted into a frown. With the reply that he'd be at Bowcester Police Station with his prisoner in a short while, he hung up.

'Good news?' said Stough.

'Not really,' said Blount.

23

Mrs Dallimore had decided that desperate times required desperate action. The padlock on the shed door looked to be fairly new and pretty robust. However, the wood around it was old and cracked and she suspected that it wouldn't survive a concerted assault. The problem was the noise that she'd generate. While she hadn't seen or heard any evidence of her captors being in the shed, other than the person who'd first imprisoned her in the boat, any loud noise would be bound to attract their attention. She either had to somehow be very quiet or she had to break the door down very quickly and escape at speed.

Frank Shunter and Molly Wilderspin had arrived at the cluster of buildings, which had turned out to be an abandoned dry dock and boat works. There was still no signal on either of their phones so it seemed that they would have to go on a little further until they reached The Rushes and the small community that lived there. But Miss Wilderspin was in need of another short rest so they sat on the edge of the towpath and ate their sandwiches while she paddled her sore feet in the cool water. Shunter looked at his useless phone.

'Not a single bar,' he said.

'I guess it doesn't just happen in films,' said Miss Wilderspin.

'I hope you haven't minded me asking so many questions. It's just that I've never had this much access to a policeman before. I've had it in my head for some time to write a crime novel, you see, and I'd like it to be accurate.'

'Have you written anything before?'

'Yes, but just silly stuff that I regret writing now. So, you were saying, there's no central library of dental records?'

'Of course not,' said Shunter, smiling. 'Whenever you hear the words "identified by dental records", it means that the cops already have a good idea of who the person is and have contacted the person's dentist to confirm it. You can't just check people's teeth like fingerprints and get a match. That would mean a huge change in the law requiring everyone, whether convicted or other-wise, to be on some kind of dental database. I can't see people agreeing to that.'

'Well, today has been an eye-opener. I can see that if I ever do write that murder mystery I'll have to come up with a very good plot to counter all the dull realism.'

'Or just make stuff up like everyone else does. That's wha—'

Shunter stopped as the sound of a loud diesel engine growling into life suddenly disturbed the tranquillity.

'It's coming from that shed over there,' said Miss Wilderspin. 'I thought the place looked deserted.'

'Me too,' said Shunter. 'But maybe it's worth looki—'

With a sudden crash, a red tractor came hurtling through the wall of the nearest wooden shed and thundered across the field of uncut grass towards them.

Mrs Dallimore had been brought up on a farm and she knew enough about tractors to know, having checked the machine over, that it would probably still be functional, provided it had some fuel in the tank. It was 1970s technology, solid and dependable, and she'd seen such machines start up after decades of neglect. Removing the fuel cap and having a smell inside had reassured her that there was some fuel in there and, thankful that it was an older model with a starter button rather than a key, she steeled her nerves, climbed into the seat and pressed the starter. The old engine turned over noisily but didn't fire. She looked around her, waiting for the inevitable cries of alarm and for the sight of her mysterious captors running towards her. She saw and heard nothing but the threat of detection spurred her on and she tried the engine again, to no avail. This time, she heard a voice. It was distant but it sounded like a man's. The words were indistinct, but they were shouted and they sounded angry. In blind panic, she jabbed repeatedly at the starter and the engine ground into noisy life. She revved the accelerator, creating plumes of black diesel smoke, then rammed the tractor into first gear and let out the clutch. With frightening power and speed, the vehicle lurched into violent life and charged towards the door, smashing straight through the wooden shingles. The tractor leapt and bounced as it raced across the uncut grass on under-inflated tyres, and Mrs Dallimore leapt and bounced with it as she tried desperately to stay in her seat and clung to the steering wheel for dear life.

Shunter pulled Miss Wilderspin to her wet feet and the two of them ran down the towpath as the out-of-control tractor roared past them and plunged into the canal, turning almost a complete somersault and throwing the driver against the far bank before landing upside down in the shallow water. Its wheels continued to spin uselessly, flinging mud about like a muck-spreader. The engine sputtered and died and a slick of diesel created a riot of rainbow colours across the surface of the canal. A woman's body floated lazily past, face down in the water.

'She might just be unconscious,' said Shunter, hurriedly stripping off his shoes and emptying his trouser pockets. He jumped into the oily water and began wading towards the still figure.

Behind the sheds, and unnoticed by anyone, a figure wearing a balaclava finished sloshing boat fuel around in the last of the boat sheds and then threw a burning wad of newspaper through a window of each. As the fires began to take, the arsonist sped away in a white van, down the dirt track that led to The Rushes.

24

Baxter Pole grimaced as the taxi hit a pothole on the road to Bowcester train station. He'd been questioned by the police, shot with a taser and informed that he would be invoiced for the damage to the bonnet of the Tactical Response Vehicle. The alternative was arrest and being charged with wilful criminal damage. He'd taken the easier option; he was keen to get away from Nasely as soon as possible. The taxi hit another pothole and he used a cupped hand to lift his aching genitals off the car seat.

He swore to himself that he would never ever go anywhere near an Agnes Crabbe-related event again.

'The date is Sunday the tenth of May. This recorded interview is taking place at Bowcester Police Station and is being conducted by me, Detective Inspector Brian Blount attached to the aforementioned station. Also present are Detective Sergeant Clifford Jaine and Mr Rory Bithersea acting for the accused as duty solicitor. The time is now thirteen-oh-five hours. Will you please state your name for the record?'

'Savidge.'

'Your full name, please.'

'Stingray Troy Phones Marina Savidge.'

Jaine snorted.

227

'Sorry,' said Savidge. 'I'm nervous. I've never been interrogated by police before.'

'We prefer the term "interviewed", Mr Savidge,' said Blount. 'I understood that you had been arrested before?'

'Is that relevant to this case?' said Mr Bithersea.

'I was merely expressing my surprise that Mr Savidge seemed unfamiliar with police interviews,' said Blount.

'I've only ever been arrested for minor stuff like breach of the peace or being drunk,' said Savidge. 'Oh, and common assault. But that bouncer had it coming. He was—'

Mr Bithersea interrupted him by laying a hand on his arm. 'Mr Savidge, you probably don't want to provide Inspector Blount with the rope he would like to hang you with, do you?'

'I'm just making the point that I've always admitted to things I've done wrong,' said Savidge. 'That's why I've never been interrogated before.'

'Interviewed,' corrected Blount.

'So who am I supposed to have murdered?' said Savidge. 'Because whoever it was, I didn't do it. And I didn't do Helen Greeley any harm either. Not on purpose.'

'We'll come on to that in a moment,' said Blount. 'Firstly, I need to tell you that a recording will be made of this interview, and you and your solicitor will be entitled to a copy of it. I am also obliged to remind you that you are still under caution. Do you understand what that means?'

'Yes.'

'Very well. We'll start with this then, shall we? What can you tell me about this?' Blount laid a clear plastic bag on the table. It contained a bloodstained shirt. 'We found this in Helen Greeley's suite at the Empire Hotel.'

'Well, you would have,' said Savidge. 'I left it there.'

'You admit it's yours?'

'Yes, of course.'

'Mr Savidge identifies exhibit SS/1 as belonging to him,' said Blount, for the benefit of the microphone. 'So, what can you tell me about it?'

'I bought it at Primark.'

'What can you tell me about the stains?' said Blount, pointedly.

'It's blood,' said Savidge.

Mr Bithersea shook his head.

'Mr Savidge identifies reddish-brown stains on exhibit SS/1 as blood,' said Blount, the faintest of smiles on his lips. This was going to be easier than he thought. 'And how did this blood get on your shirt, Mr Savidge?'

'Can I remind you that you really don't have to answer that?' said Mr Bithersea.

'It's okay. I had a nosebleed,' said Savidge. 'There was an incident. I got into a . . . situation and my nose started gushing. It does that sometimes when I'm stressed out.'

'What sort of a situation?' asked Blount.

'A fight. It was with the same bloke I was fighting with when you nicked me. That big bloke in a dress.'

'You mean Mr Pole?'

'I never knew his name.'

'Two fights with the same man and you don't know who he is?'

'Not a clue. Actually, some of the blood might be his. I did bite him hard.' Having decided that his best option was to get everything out into the open, Savidge was keen to volunteer as much information as possible. Holding anything back would just return to haunt him in the future, he reasoned. Mr Bithersea looked appalled at his client's apparent desire to incriminate himself.

'You bit him? Bit him where?' asked Blount.

'On the village green,' said Savidge.

'Very funny. Whereabouts on his person did you bite him?'

'Do I have to say?'

'It would help to clarify matters.'

'Well, if you must know, on the ball bag.'

Jaine snorted again.

'On the . . .?'

'On his ball bag. His scrotum,' Savidge explained. 'The bastard was straddling me and I thought he was going to suffocate me with his thighs, so I bit him as hard as I could. I felt it was justified in the circumstances.'

'Is any of this relevant to the accusations being made against my client?' asked Mr Bithersea. He looked at Savidge's damp dress and hat ensemble. 'What Mr Savidge does for pleasure in his own time is quite—'

'You've got completely the wrong picture,' said Savidge. 'I told you, I was in a fight. During the fight, he pinned me down. I couldn't breathe. So I bit the only part of him that I could reach.'

'And what time would this have been?' said Blount.

'Around lunch time,' said Savidge. 'Around one or one thirty maybe? It's all a bit of a blur. All I know is that I ran away from the village and woke up in Bowcester General.'

'The hospital?'

'Yeah, apparently I fainted. Probably because of the nosebleed. That's why I have all these cuts and bruises on my knees and elbows. And, as I fell, I hit my head and was unconscious for a bit. So they tell me.'

'What time is my client alleged to have committed the offence for which he has been detained?' asked the solicitor, checking his notes.

'With respect, Mr Bithersea, it's my job to ask the questions and your job to advise your client,' said Blount.

'Very well, you ask him then,' said Mr Bithersea.

'I will in due course,' said Blount, visibly irritated.

'Only I do believe that the answer is very germane and will save us all a lot of time,' said Mr Bithersea.

'We'll get there in a minute,' said Blount.

'Suit yourself,' said Mr Bithersea. 'I'm on the clock. And on a Sunday too.'

Blount returned to his questioning. 'So, you went to the hospital. Can anyone verify that?'

'Look, my brief has a point,' said Savidge. 'When was I supposed to have killed someone?'

'You tell me.'

'I don't know because I didn't do it. That's why I'm asking. I don't even know who I'm supposed to have killed.'

'Okay. We'll play your game. It would have been some time between 3.15 p.m. and 3.45 p.m. yesterday.'

'Then it couldn't have been me. I didn't leave the hospital until at least 4.45 p.m.'

'And there we have it,' said Mr Bithersea with a satisfied smile.

'I'm sure the hospital can confirm it,' said Savidge. 'They have records, don't they?'

'I imagine that the appropriate course of action now would be to terminate this interview while you confirm what my client has said, don't you?' said Mr Bithersea.

'Interview terminated at 1317 hours,' snapped Blount, jabbing at the recorder's stop button. He stormed out of the interview room and was surprised to find his Chief Superintendent waiting for him outside.

'Any luck?' said Nuton-Atkinson.

'He's claiming he has an alibi,' said Blount.

'Damn,' said Nuton-Atkinson. 'Listen, I just spoke to DS Banton and she's brought me up-to-date with the identity of the victim. Bad business.'

'Yes, sir, but—'

'There will be no way of keeping this quiet now, Brian. Shirley Pomerance is . . . was . . . a national treasure.'

'Yes, sir,' said Blount, gloomily.

'An award-winning author.'

'Yes, sir.'

'You realise that I have no choice now.'

'Please . . . no,' said Blount, his heart sinking.

'Sorry, Brian. Chief Constable's orders. She wants a more senior eye on the ball.'

'Not Quisty, sir.'

'Quisty.'

It had taken Shunter five minutes of fast-paced walking to reach The Rushes and thankfully, despite the New Age hippy vibe of the place, the phone signal and Wi-Fi were excellent. The emergency services had responded with an ambulance and a police car from Bowcester, but it had still taken nearly ten minutes for the first emergency vehicle to arrive, by which time Mrs Dallimore, though still unconscious, was breathing normally.

'And you have no idea what she was doing out here?' asked the first police officer on scene.

'No, but I suspect she was doing some snooping around in relation to yesterday's homicide in Nasely,' said Shunter. 'Searching those boat sheds, probably. One thing's for sure, she wanted to get out of there quickly enough.'

'You mean the ones that are on fire?' asked the officer.

He pointed to the cloud of thick grey smoke that was rising above the sheds.

Nicola Banton dialled a phone number and mused upon what she'd found out in the last few hours. Firstly, there had been the identity of the victim. In the hope that a public appeal might help to identify the body, she had circulated a description of the distinctive ring that the victim was wearing on her little finger. A jeweller from Sherrinford had immediately recognised it as one in which he'd reset a diamond for the famous author Shirley Pomerance two years previously. Armed with this knowledge, it had been a simple process to confirm her identity from her dental records. But the ring had revealed something else that Banton hadn't expected. The day before, at Blount's request, she'd run searches on the names 'Falk' and 'Marr Harry' that had been among the notes in Mrs Handibode's copy of *Swords into Plough-shares*. The latter hadn't turned up anything of particular interest but the former had started a trail that had ended with a marriage certificate from 1939 detailing the union of one Millicent Falk from nearby Tingwell to Henry Welter, a jeweller from Sherrinford. And now a jeweller from present-day Sherrinford had identified the ring on Pomerance's finger. Sherrinford was a small town, certainly much smaller than nearby Coxeter or Bowcester with their bustling shopping centres and High Street jewellery retailers. Would Sherrinford have more than one jeweller's shop, she wondered? In which case was it possible that Mr Welter, the Sherrinford jeweller who had married Millicent Falk in 1939, might be the same man as – or a close relative to – the jeweller who had identified the ring? It was too fascinating a coincidence not to investigate further.

'Good afternoon,' said a voice on the phone. 'Welter and

Dickentrice, jewellers. Peter Dickentrice speaking. How may I help you?'

'We're going to have to let him go,' said the custody officer. 'His story checks out. He was discharged from the hospital at 4.42 p.m.'

'But we can't let him go! Look!' said Blount. He showed the custody officer two photographs side by side: the CCTV image of the van driver and the photo of Savidge taken upon his arrival at Bowcester Police Station.

'I can't deny that there is a likeness,' said the officer. 'Even the dresses are similar. But your man has a cast-iron alibi. I've spoken to the hospital and he was definitely there at the time of your murder.'

'Couldn't they have made a mistake with the time?'

'It's not very likely, is it? And there is no other evidence, not even forensics, that puts him at the scene. I'm sorry, but his solicitor is pushing for bail pending further investigation and, if I were you, I'd go with it. If you don't, he could request unconditional release and we'd be hard pushed to deny it.'

'But it's him! Unless he has an identical twin,' said Blount.

'Oh right. An evil twin,' said the officer, sarcastically.

Blount frowned.

'But even if that were true, it would still mean that you have the wrong guy locked up,' the officer continued.

'Okay, okay. Bail him,' said Blount begrudgingly.

The fires in the boat sheds had been impossible to control. Once the old dry wood had caught alight there was no stopping them. Fuel on board the boats and in cans stored in the sheds had added to the conflagration too. The exhausted fire crews, many of which had been up all night dealing with the hotel fire, had decided that their best option was to let the fire consume itself while pumping water from the canal on to the grass around the perimeter to prevent it spreading. All three of the sheds were fiercely ablaze and one had already collapsed. With a noisy crash, the second shed's rusty tin roof fell to the ground, taking down an entire wall of blackened wooden cladding as it did so.

'Let's hope there was no one inside,' said Shunter.

Miss Wilderspin nodded and watched as the twisted metal skeleton of the third shed folded in upon itself, sending a shower of sparks up into the sky. She had recovered some of her energy and vitality but the incident with the tractor had left her very shaken.

'I keep wondering what Mrs Dallimore was doing in there,' she said.

'I assume that she was following a lead of some kind. She is a journalist after all,' said Shunter. He looked at the tractor, which was being fitted with chains so that a crane could lift it out of the canal. 'Though why she felt the need to break out of the place quite so dramatically I can only guess.'

'You think that she was escaping from the place?' said Miss Wilderspin.

'I do,' said Shunter. 'Her actions smacked of desperation. Maybe she spotted the fire and panicked? Maybe she was locked inside?'

'Locked inside by accident? Or on purpose?'

'Three fires in three separate boat sheds? I think we can rule out accidents.'

Blount returned to his Incident Room in a huff and rudely ignored the reporters who had gathered outside following the revelation that the dead woman was award-winning author Shirley Pomerance. He was surprised to find the library's front door locked and it did nothing to improve his mood. Nicola Banton let him in.

'We had to lock it,' she explained. 'The media people have gone nuts since they found out who the victim is. Anyway, I don't know how relevant this is but while you've been out I've found some interesting bits and pieces regarding those notes in Mrs Handibode's book that you asked me to research.'

Blount nodded but didn't seem to be hearing a word. Banton decided to carry on regardless. 'I looked at the surname "Falk" and I found a record of a Millicent Falk who married a jeweller and . . . what?'

Blount had raised his hand for her to stop. 'This isn't my case any more,' he said. 'Save it for Quisty.'

In the darkness of the box van's interior, Esme Handibode's head bumped against the wall and she cursed the driver. Opposite her, Brenda Tradescant looked to be asleep but it was hard to tell in the gloom.

Mrs Handibode wished that she could telepathically transmit a message to the other woman saying, 'This is all your fault.' But she couldn't, so she made do with a frown and the best sneer she could muster despite the handicap of her gag.

The white van drove on deeper into the flat countryside.

25

Detective Chief Inspector Gavin Quisty arrived at the Incident Room without warning at 3 p.m. trailed, as always, by his staff officer Detective Sergeant Kim Woon. It was rare to see one of them without the other and there had been suggestions that the two were romantically involved. They had both vehemently denied the rumours, saying that they had no time for the complexity and constraints of a relationship. However, they had no problem admitting that this hadn't stopped them from having a great deal of sex with each other.

Quisty was the golden boy of the South Herewardshire Constabulary CID and he was often asked why, after a glittering career with the West Midlands Police in Birmingham, he had transferred to such a small county force. His answer was always uncompromising: 'I'm going to be Chief Constable one day,' he would say. 'A small constabulary means less competition when it comes to promotion. Besides, I need to understand how county forces work in comparison to larger city forces. Different courses require different horses.' Tall, good-looking and intimidatingly intelligent, he seemed more than capable of achieving his goal, and was already, at the age of just thirty-two, one of the youngest Detective Chief Inspectors in the UK.

'I assume that you're Nicola Banton,' he said with a dashing smile and a firm handshake. 'May I call you Nicola?'

'Please do,' said Banton, trying hard not to blush.

'Excellent. Gavin Quisty. I think we can dispense with all of that "sir" or "guv" nonsense while we're working on the same team. And this is Kim Woon.'

'Nice to meet you both. I've heard a lot about you,' said Banton.

'Statistically, some of it is bound to be true,' said Quisty with a wink. He was dressed in a royal-blue three-piece suit, complete with pocket watch and chain. His brogues were mirror-shiny and he sported a lemon-coloured cravat and pocket handkerchief. His hair was dark but thinning and swept back like a crest. Facially, he was not dissimilar to Blount, high-cheekboned and angular, but somehow he wore his sharp features much better on his skull. 'Now, we've had a kind of briefing at Bowcester,' he continued. 'But it would be much more useful to get the full story from you excellent people who have been working at the coalface. Is it possible to arrange a meeting for everyone involved in the case? Say, for four o'clock?'

'I should think so,' said Banton.

'Thank you, Nicola. Now, is DI Blount about?' said Quisty. 'I'd like to say hello and reassure him that he is still very much an important part of this investigation.'

'I think he might be in the little boys' room,' said Banton. 'Coffee?'

'Lovely,' said Woon.

'I'd prefer tea. Earl Grey if you have it,' said Quisty.

Miss Wilderspin had elected to go to the hospital and wait for Mrs Dallimore to wake up in case she had any useful information to share. Shunter, meanwhile, had travelled in a police car to

Bowcester Police Station to make a witness statement before being dropped back home so that he could change into some dry clothes. The sight of her supposedly retired husband getting out of a marked police car in wet clothing that stank of diesel was not something that Mrs Shunter could let pass without comment and she did so at length, accusing him of 'hanging around with the boys' instead of looking for meaningful work. She was right, of course. He had no legitimate excuse for getting involved. He apologised, kissed her affectionately on the cheek and promised her that he would return to the job-hunting first thing on Monday morning. In the meantime, he headed back into the village to see the end of the festival.

'Consider this . . . plates don't make sense without gravity.'

For a long, uncomfortable moment there was silence around the table. Blount crossed his arms and rolled his eyes. Jaine looked at Banton and she gave a tiny shrug. Woon smiled, revealing an endearing gap between her top front teeth. She'd heard this speech before.

'It's something I heard that astronaut chap, Commander Chris Hadfield, say,' said Quisty. 'And it got me thinking.'

'Oh good,' muttered Blount.

'Imagine that you're a starship captain and you're meeting an alien race for the first time,' said Quisty. 'And maybe they look completely different to us, like a blob or something. You invite the alien captain on board to say hello and you lay on a banquet of Earth foods. So the aliens come aboard and they see us humans all trying to eat our dinner off plates and the food just keeps drifting away. Wouldn't they think, "What are those flat things they keep trying to put their food on? They make no sense." And they'd be right. Plates don't make sense without gravity.'

'Ah I see,' said Jaine.

'Of course plates make sense,' said Blount, snippily. 'They're just harder to use in space.'

'But that's exactly my point,' said Quisty. 'Plates make sense to you but that's only because you know that they are a part of our eating tradition and that we evolved on a world where the food doesn't just float into our mouths. You have all the facts so things make sense. But the aliens don't, so to them, plates don't make sense. They'd need to be given the missing facts in order to understand what's going on.'

There were unconvincing nods of understanding around the table. Blount folded his arms tighter and tried to sink even more deeply into his hard plastic seat. To his chagrin, Quisty had commandeered the big comfortable librarian's chair.

'It's the same story with chopsticks,' added Woon. 'Why would any culture develop such an awkward eating utensil when spoons are so much easier to use? You need additional facts to understand the context in which chopsticks were invented.'

'Are you Chinese then?' asked Blount. Woon did have something of a Far Eastern look about her; a look that was accentuated by her short black bob and straight fringe.

'Cornish, actually,' said Woon. 'But my grandmother came from Hong Kong.'

'Now there's a story of cosmic connections,' said Quisty. 'Woon is a Cornish surname. And also a Chinese surname. Kim's grandparents bonded over the fact that they had the same family name despite coming from vastly separated cultures.'

'Wow,' said Banton.

'Hmf,' said Blount.

'So why were chopsticks invented?' asked Jaine.

'No one really knows, to be honest. But probably because they were kinder to people's highly decorative porcelain or lacquered tableware,' explained Woon. 'Spoons would scrape the patterns off.'

'Interesting,' said Banton.

'But bugger all to do with the Shirley Pomerance murder,' said Blount. 'This is all a waste of time.'

'Brian, Brian, Brian. It has *everything* to do with it,' said Quisty. 'This murder doesn't make sense at the moment because the facts you have so far uncovered – and excellent facts they are too, by the way – don't connect with each other. We need to find the facts in between, the facts that help us to make sense of what's happened. We have a victim but we have no motive and no clear perpetrator. There appears to be no obvious reason why any of the people on our current list of suspects would kill Shirley Pomerance.'

'Have you read any of her books?' said Blount, simultaneously managing to somehow smile and sneer.

'A literary critic too? You are a man of many talents,' said Quisty, smiling in return. 'But, joking aside, there is a reason why someone murdered Shirley Pomerance. Find that reason and it will connect us to our killer. As Lord Peter Wimsey says in *Busman's Honeymoon*, "Once you've got the How, the Why drives it home." The answer always lies in the connections – we need to identify the gaps in our knowledge and then work out how to fill them. And we'll do that by exploring new avenues of thought and by accessing new sources of information that maybe we didn't realise existed.'

Blount harrumphed.

'In fact, Nicola here was telling me earlier that she's found some very interesting connections already,' said Quisty.

'DI Blount asked me to look into some notes he found that

Mrs Handibode had scribbled in a book,' said Banton.

'Well spotted, Brian!' said Quisty.

Blount harrumphed again.

'I found out, firstly, that a person called Millicent Falk married a jeweller in 1939 called Henry Welter who ran a shop in Sherrinford. And the ring that identified the victim as Shirley Pomerance came from a jeweller's shop in Sherrinford called Welter and Dickentrice.'

'You see? Connections,' said Quisty.

'Coincidence,' said Blount, secretly rather pleased with himself for making something of the notes.

'Coincidences can be very revealing, Brian. Go on, Nicola.'

'It is the same jeweller's,' said Banton. 'I phoned the current owner, a Mr Peter Dickentrice, and he said that the shop was owned solely by the Welter family right up until 1986 when the last of the Welters retired. He's been running the business ever since. He fixed Miss Pomerance's ring and told me that it was originally made by Henry Welter for his wife-to-be, Millicent Falk. It was her wedding ring. Sad story, really. He was killed during the Second World War and she had to learn to be a jeweller herself to keep the business in the family.'

'You see?' said Quisty. 'We have a ring made for someone called Millicent, an oh-so-pertinent name when you consider when and where our murder happened, and—'

'Why is it?' said Blount. 'There are probably hundreds of Millicents among the fans outside.'

'Actually, there aren't,' said Banton. 'Millicent isn't a common name at all. Milly, yes, but not Millicent. It was popular with the Victorians but then it tailed off in the early twentieth century. It wasn't even in the top one hundred most popular names around the time that Millicent Falk would've been born and I could only find about five hundred birth records nationwide in the census data. The name has only had a revival in the last decade, partly because of Agnes Crabbe's books.'

'It's still not relevant.'

'Don't be so dismissive, Brian. Try to think laterally. The more facts we have, the more connections we make and the more we understand. We're trying to construct a lattice, a web, a circuit diagram of causal events. If we add everything we know, plus anything that seems to have a connection, no matter how flimsy or insubstantial or coincidental it seems, the web will get richer. New connections will form spontaneously and new insights will appear. It's as if we're growing a mind, a brain, from scratch. And that, my dear colleagues, is why we call it intelligence.'

Blount's eyes rolled so high that all you could see were the whites.

'Mr Welter made a ring for the love of his life, a lady called Millicent Falk,' said Quisty. 'It must have been very precious to her. Especially after she then lost him in the war.'

'So?' said Blount.

'So, what connects those people to our murder?'

'Nothing. They died years ago.'

'Indeed they did,' said Quisty. 'But what I want to know is . . . why did Mrs Handibode mention the name Falk in her notes in connection with the words "ANDREW T – SECRET", and why was Millicent Falk's precious wedding ring on the finger of our murder victim, Miss Pomerance, yesterday?'

Upon hearing the news of Savidge's release, Helen Greeley had found herself in a world of doubt and uncertainty. She wanted to apologise to him for telling the police where he'd been hiding but she suspected that he probably wouldn't want to see her ever again. Therefore, she'd asked Nicola Banton to relay a message to him at Bowcester Police Station to meet her at the Gondolier Italian all-day restaurant at five o'clock. If he didn't show up, she would have her answer. In the meantime, she had agreed to a short and informal press junket at the village hall, now reopened to the public. Thankfully, in an effort to cover up the debacle on the houseboat, the police hadn't released the identity of the suspect they'd been looking to arrest, which meant that no one yet knew about Greeley's involvement. However, they had been keen to ask her about other events and, after a flurry of questions about the fire and the explosions at the hotel, the line of questioning had turned to her non-appearance on Saturday night and to romance.

'So who is this mystery man you were with?' asked a lady from the *Bowcester Mercury*. 'Anyone we'd know?'

'That's my business for now,' said Greeley. 'But I will tell you that he's not famous or rich or powerful. He's just a guy. And he's a lot like me in the way he looks at the world.'

'How did you meet?'

'Ah, now there's a story! And I may share it with you one day,' said Greeley, smiling. 'But not today.'

'Is it true he climbed up to your room on a rope?' asked the showbiz editor for the *South Herewardshire Bugle*.

'It all sounds frightfully romantic, doesn't it?' said Greeley with a wink. 'Had there been a rose-covered trellis I'm sure he'd have used that instead.'

'So just how serious is it, Miss Greeley?'

'I don't know yet,' she said enigmatically.

'And what do you say to the rumours that you were abducted and held prisoner?' asked a lady from the *Lady*.

'I say nonsense. But now I must go and get changed and have

something to eat before tonight's events. It's been a frightening and terrible experience for everybody and my heart goes out to those who were injured. Thank you.'

And now, as she sat in the Gondolier and waited to see if Savidge would turn up, she toyed with a new phone she'd obtained and wished that there was someone she could talk to other than reporters. Normally she'd have phoned her agent for advice and a girl-to-girl chat. But the court case wasn't yet finished and, as a member of the jury, Portia was unavailable. In fact, having been held incommunicado at a hotel for several nights, it was quite possible that she hadn't even heard about the events in Nasely yet. Greeley realised just how much she relied upon her agent for advice, help and reassurance. But, to her surprise, she realised that the person she most wished she could talk to was the man she knew as Stingray.

Savidge walked through the crowds of Millies in extreme discomfort. Partly, it was the constricting nature of his cocktail dress. But it was also because of sudden flashbacks and fuzzy memories of his experiences the day before when the very sight of a Cutter had filled him with horror. Even now, walking among them felt uncomfortable and he'd shuddered several times. Thankfully, a police doctor had prescribed him replacement pills and they were helping to take the edge off his distress.

There had been no point in going home as he'd left his keys and wallet in Greeley's suite at the hotel and had no way of getting into his house without breaking a window. He'd therefore gone back to the hotel where he'd been told by the police that his property had been seized and taken to Bowcester. He cursed his own stupidity for not realising, but he had no desire to go back to the police station. And, besides, there wasn't time now. He had a dinner date to keep.

He clomped through the hustle and bustle towards the Italian restaurant in Ormond Road and wished that he looked better for his reunion with Helen Greeley. Her message had come as something of a surprise, considering that she'd admitted shopping him to the police. But the invitation couldn't be ignored. He had suddenly realised how important it was for him to know that she was okay.

'Here's a good one, listen to this,' said Jaine. 'Andrew Tremens was going to reveal that Shirley Pomerance's Trupenie Prize-winning novel, *Dalí Plays Golf*, was ripped off from a previously unpublished Agnes Crabbe novel. He confronted her, there was a fight and he killed her.'

'But what about the knife with Tradescant's fingerprints on it?' asked Banton.

'Oh yeah. That's a good point,' said Jaine.

Jaine and Banton had been given the job of looking back through the many theories and explanations that had been put forward by festival attendees. All of them had been recorded as written statements and there were hundreds of them; every Milly was a wannabe lady detective after all. Quisty had suggested that there might possibly be some fact among them that the police investigation had overlooked; 'several hundred pairs of eyes is better than our five', as he'd put it. And there had been a whole new wave of theories following the identity of the victim being made public, some more sensible than others.

'I've got a better one, listen,' said Banton. 'It claims that aliens are abducting us for their experiments and that the murder was actually a botched matter transporter experiment.'

'These women are all lunatics,' said Jaine.

'Actually, this one is by a bloke,' said Banton. 'It's signed by someone called Ray Dalekcat (human). In case we thought he wasn't, I assume.'

'I don't see what Quisty hopes to achieve by going through this pile of rubbish.'

'It's a creative-thinking technique they use in business,' said Banton. 'You get a bunch of strangers, all people unconnected to your product or services, and you ask them for opinions and ideas. Like asking a plumber to tell you what he thinks about your breakfast cereal campaign, or asking a doctor about under-wear design. Quisty says that it provides fresh insights and new perspectives. One of the Millies might just have stumbled upon the truth.'

'No wonder the Chief Constable loves him, with all her modern policing nonsense,' said Jaine. 'Intelligence-led this and predictive, algorithm that. I don't hear hard graft and pounding the beat get much of a mention in her weekly podcasts.'

'She calls them Plodcasts,' said Banton.

'Bloody hell.'

'And anyway, I think the Chief is right. Bringing new ideas into policing is a good thing. Oh, here's a corker . . . It just says "Gypsies done it".'

'See what I mean? Fresh insights, my arse.' Jaine waved a piece of paper. 'This one says that Shirley Pomerance was blackmailing Andrew Tremens because he's gay.'

'But he's openly gay, isn't he?'

'Yes he is. Ha! This one mentions Jack the Ripper. These spin-sters are all loons.'

'You should stop using spinster like a term of abuse. I'm a spinster too, you know.'

'Yeah but I didn't mean you . . . I mean . . . well . . .'

'I bet you don't even know the origin of the word, do you? It described a woman who excelled at spinning wool and who, without the distractions of a husband and kids, could run her own successful and often lucrative business at a time when women were generally thought of as second-class citizens. It used to be something of a compliment.'

'Hey, I didn't mean anything by it. Consider me educated.'

'Sorry, I didn't mean to snap. It's just this case. And Blount. He brings out the worst in me.' There was a ping from Banton's laptop and she quickly scanned through her emails. 'Where's Quisty at the moment?'

'Him and Woon have gone over to the pub. He wanted to meet Shunter and I had his mobile number so I arranged it.'

'Bloody hell, does Blount know? He'll go spare if he finds out. Look, I'm just going to pop over there to deliver some news to him.'

'Good news?'

'Kind of. Tell you when I get back. I'll only be five minutes.'

'Where is the guv'nor anyway?' Jaine looked around the library. 'He's not in the crapper again, is he?'

'So you're Frank Shunter, eh?' said Quisty. 'I've heard a great deal about you.'

'From Blount, I presume,' said Shunter. 'I expect he's told you that I've been interfering and trampling all over his homicide, eh?'

'It is a very problematic investigation and people are naturally a bit edgy and irritable,' said Quisty. 'I wouldn't take things too personally. As far as I can see, you've done a great deal more good than harm.'

'Thanks,' said Shunter. 'So, what can I do for you?'

'I heard about what happened earlier at the boat sheds. I'd like to hear your side of the story.'

Shunter related the story of the tractor and the fire while Quisty took it all in. 'I suspect that Dallimore was following a trail. Maybe a trail that started here with the murder. You'll have to ask her when she's conscious. The fire investigators are going to contact your colleagues at Bowcester when the cause of the fire is known. I'm just hoping there was no one inside those sheds. They wouldn't have stood a chance.'

'Our kidnapped solicitor and the missing ladies perhaps?' said Quisty. 'Yes indeed, let's hope not. Ah, here's the redoubtable Nicola Banton. Have you two met?'

'We have. Hello again,' said Banton, shaking Shunter's proffered hand. 'I have some information for you, guv. Case-related stuff.'

'Ah,' said Shunter. 'Shall I disappear?'

'It's fine,' said Quisty. 'Go on, Nicola.'

'It's about the jam jars in Miss Nithercott's fridge. They only have her prints on them.'

'Jam jars?'

'I don't suppose this was included in your briefing as it's not directly connected to the murder,' said Banton. She quickly explained about the taxine poisoning and the mention of yew-berry jam in Esme Handibode's book. 'So, it looks like we can forget that avenue. The local officers found a recipe for yew-berry jam at her house. It looks like simple misadventure. And something of a red herring for us.'

'Not necessarily. All information is useful,' said Quisty. 'Tell me, in which of Agnes Crabbe's books did Mrs Handibode make the note about taxine? Was it *Swords into Ploughshares* perhaps?'

'It was, yes.'

'Interesting. Have you read the book?'

'Yes,' said Shunter.

'No,' said Banton.

'You really should, Nicola. Her best book by far,' said Quisty. 'Taxine poisoning is how Merryk Pengelly is murdered. And it was by way of yew-berry jam.'

'So Mrs Handibode's note is just a note about the plot?'

'Probably, but we'll add it to our web of facts,' said Quisty, with a smile. 'Now then, Frank, it seems to me that you know this area and you know a damned sight more than most about homicide. I'd just like you to know that I welcome any insights you may have regarding this investigation. My door is always open.'

'Thank you,' said Shunter. 'I'm not looking to get involved but if I see or hear anything I'll pass it on. I haven't figured out how to switch off my copper's hunch yet.'

'Perfect,' said Quisty. 'I can ask no more.'

'Good luck,' said Shunter.

Lurking around the corner of the bar and hidden from sight, Brian Blount stifled a yawn and greedily swallowed an energy drink. He had listened intently to the conversation between Shunter and Quisty and decided that there was only one thing he could do now to stand any chance of saving face and earning his long-sought-after promotion.

He would have to find and catch the murderer on his own, by fair means or foul.

26

The box van suddenly came to a halt and there was the sound of feet on gravel outside. The rear shutter was lifted and Mrs Handibode and Miss Tradescant squinted at the figure silhouetted against the light.

'Toilet break,' said Andrew Tremens.

Shunter nursed his pint and mulled over the events of the day. In particular, he found himself remembering the look on Mrs Dallimore's face. It had been one of absolute terror and almost certainly due to something more frightening than an out-of-control tractor. His instinct told him that she had been escaping from something. Or someone. He had to go back to the boat works and have a look for himself. Mrs Shunter had the car for the day so he phoned for a taxi.

Savidge arrived at the restaurant and had to run the gauntlet of a large group of fans and paparazzi who'd insisted on taking hundreds of photographs of him as he'd entered. He found Helen Greeley waiting for him at a table in a small private room.

'You came,' said Greeley, smiling.

'Yeah.'

'I wasn't sure you would. You must be so angry with me right now.'

'I'm not angry,' said Savidge. 'I got what I deserved.'

'Oh, but you didn't! None of it was your fault, was it?' said Greeley. 'Do sit down. It's hurting my neck looking up at you.'

'Sorry I look so terrible,' said Savidge, sitting. 'I've been wearing the same pair of underpants for two days. I did have a swim in the canal so they got a sort of wash but . . .'

'You look fine.'

'And I have no money for dinner.'

'It's on me. It's the least I can do after what I've put you through.'

'I put you through a lot worse,' said Savidge, gloomily.

'Can we call it quits then? Start again from scratch?' said Greeley. Her phone pinged and she glanced at it. 'I managed to get a new phone couriered to me and I've been reinstalling my contacts; they're all backed up on some cloud thing. Ah, lovely Dame Maggie wishing me well for the play tonight. I'll say this, Mr Stingray, yesterday's events haven't done my public profile any harm. Look, do I really have to call you Stingray?'

'Most people call me Savidge.'

'That's just as bad. What's your second name again? Troy? That sounds better, doesn't it?'

'I've never really thought about it.'

A waiter had appeared at their table. Helen Greeley quickly scanned the menu.

'I'll have the orata all'acqua pazza, please,' she said. 'What do you fancy, Troy?'

Savidge looked at the menu. 'Spaghetti carbonara maybe?'

'Is that the only one you know?' teased Greeley.

'I don't get to eat out much,' said Savidge. 'I run a burger van. Ran a burger van.'

'There's nothing wrong with a carbonara,' said Greeley. 'Delicious. Now, drinks.'

'I'll have a beer.'

'Nonsense. You need wine with good food.'

'Red then.'

'Really? Ah well, *chacun à son goût*.'

'I'm not keen on the French stuff.'

Greeley laughed. 'Oh you are priceless! It means "each to his own taste", and if you want red wine with your carbonara you go ahead. It's your stomach. I'm having white with my fish so we'll get one of each. I'll have a Verdicchio. Can I suggest you try an Amarone? It's not too bad with creamy or cheesy dishes.'

The waiter scurried away.

'So, do you feel happier now?' she asked.

'I guess,' said Savidge. 'It's just . . . this is a new sensation for me. People don't usually like me, especially if they've seen me when I've been . . . you know.'

'Maybe I have a dose of Stockholm syndrome, eh?'

'What's that?'

'It's when hostages or kidnap victims start to feel sympathy for their captors, and even start to defend their actions. Have you ever seen *Seven Brides for Seven Brothers*?'

'No. Why?'

'Sometimes they even fall in love.'

Shunter arrived at the boat works and paid the taxi driver. The site was still glowing and sputtering with small fires but it was safe enough for him to chat to the two uniformed police officers who were patrolling the perimeter and to the fire investigation team who were picking over the ashes. From them, he learned that fires had been deliberately started inside all three sheds. The good news was that there was no evidence that anyone had been inside.

Outside the cordoned-off area, Shunter wandered around to the crumbling older brick buildings. Inside the first there was nothing worth noting, but inside the second he found evidence of recent occupancy. There were chocolate-bar wrappers on the floor and he picked one up and saw that the sell-by date had yet to pass. Of course, it could be that kids from The Rushes hung out in the old buildings, just as he and his school friends had played around inside an old abandoned factory when he was younger. But maybe not. He decided not to risk the stairs to explore the upper floors – the whole building looked as if one strong gust of wind would topple it – and wandered out into the loading yard beyond instead. There were more wrappers here and fresh muddy tyre tracks on the concrete, which suggested that a vehicle had parked there since the rain on Friday. It had been a large vehicle too, like a van. Again, Shunter had to concede that there might be a perfectly innocent explanation for the tracks; perhaps they'd been made by one of the police or fire-brigade vehicles? They led away from the yard and on to a muddy lane that, presumably, fed out on to the main road between Nasely and Sherrinford. Shunter walked a short way along the lane and could see, in the near distance, that it passed by the canal community among the reed beds. And then his eye caught sight of something glinting in the sun in the mud ahead of him. He picked it up and looked at it closely. It was a single pierced opalescent pearl. With renewed enthusiasm, he set off towards The Rushes.

Blount had had an epiphany. When he had interviewed Helen Greeley earlier in the day, the subject of Savidge's medication had come up. She'd explained that he was prescribed some kind of mood-stabilising tablets, but that he wasn't terribly good at taking them. She had also mentioned, in passing, the fact that he apparently had a brother with similar issues who self-medicated with alcohol. Remembrance of this, plus his conversation with the custody officer, had given Blount an idea. What if the man in the van was Savidge's brother? He didn't know the brother's name but he did know, thanks to Greeley, that he was a vicar, so it hadn't taken him very long to whittle the list of Reverend Savidges down to three. And, as one was on the Isle of Man, one was in Totnes and the other was in nearby Spradbarrow, he was pretty sure which one it was. A quick visit to the website of St Cunigunde's Church had produced a photo of the Reverend T. Savidge and he was, to Blount's delight, a dead ringer for the Savidge he knew.

He carefully deleted his Internet history. He was damned if he would leave any clues for the infernal Quisty and Woon, or for his two turncoat Detective Sergeants, and then drove off towards Spradbarrow in his nondescript black Vauxhall. And as he drove, he mentally patted himself on the back. Quisty had no idea who the murderer was. And nor did Shunter. It would be good to rub their noses in it when he brought his prisoner in. Quisty could keep his bloody plates in space and his precious connections. He was going to nab the suspect with good old-fashioned police work, and Quisty would have to acknowledge him as at least an equal. And Shunter too would get his comeuppance for trying to make him look like some kind of bumpkin bobby. The more he thought about it, the more he realised just how much of his current misery was the ex-detective's fault. It was Shunter who had found the paperback belonging to Esme Handibode, which was why Blount had erroneously circulated her as wanted for the murder by jam of Gaynor Nithercott. And it was Shunter who had found the CCTV footage that had led Blount to arrest Savidge, resulting in the fiasco that had cost him his case and his promotion prospects. It was all very clear now. Shunter had been there right from the start, deliberately feeding duff information to the investigation team so that he could solve the case and claim all of the glory for himself. And now he was sucking up to Quisty.

But now Blount would show Shunter some real policing. And he'd prove to his divisional commander and to the Chief Constable that he could catch a murderer just as well as any Gavin bloody Quisty could.

'You've gone all quiet,' said Greeley as she ate her bream. 'Not that you're exactly a motormouth, but still. What's up?'

'I was just thinking about what you said, about doing wonders for your public profile,' said Savidge. 'Are you saying that we're having dinner together just to get you talked about in the papers? Is that what that crowd outside was all about?'

'Of course not!' snapped Greeley. 'Any accidental media coverage is great, but that's not the reason why I'm here. I wanted to see you.'

'But why? After what I did.'

'I've been horrible to you too.'

'Yeah, but I deserved that.'

'Shhhhh,' hissed Greeley. 'We're quits, remember? Listen, Troy, do you like me?'

'Depends if you insist on calling me Troy,' said Savidge.

'Seriously.'

'Yes, of course I do.'

'Why?'

'Why? Because you're nice and you're pretty and—'

'And you hardly know me,' said Greeley. 'You don't watch my TV shows and you don't read the gossip mags, so it's not some fanboy infatuation. I'm almost a stranger to you and yet you have decided you like me and you'd like to know more about me. Am I right?'

'Yes.'

'So why should things be any different for me just because I'm famous? Yes, we got off on the wrong foot. Well, a weird foot anyway. You weren't yourself and, after what you'd been through, I can't say I blame you. But once you had become the real you again, I liked what I saw.'

'Really?'

'Really. I spend my life being chatted up by men who want to get into my knickers because I'm off the telly or because I'm worth a few bob. Everyone I meet is either shallow, self-obsessed or desperate for a leg up in the industry. And a leg over with a celeb helps, especially if you sell the story afterwards. So where do I get to meet nice guys? I can't go to the pub or a club because I'm too recognisable. I can hardly join a dating website either. Why do you think celebs nearly always marry other celebs? But then you turned up, literally delivered to my room.'

Savidge frowned.

'Don't frown, you'll get wrinkles. And, okay, to begin with you weren't very nice. But that wasn't your fault and you got better. And do you know what the best thing was? No interest in my money. And no interest in my body.'

'That's not strictly true. I am only human, after all.'

'Yes, but you did nothing about it, did you? And you didn't take advantage of me on the boat either, even though I was three sheets to the wind. You were, despite your appearance and threats, a gentleman. And I like gentlemen.'

Shunter arrived at The Rushes. Decoratively painted houseboats lined both banks of the canal and, here and there, stands of tall bulrushes and assorted reeds had been planted to give this part of the Oxbow Deviation a more natural, river-like ambience. Coots and moorhens paddled about happily, and the air was filled with damselflies and the noise of a powerful outboard motor being revved as a big man in a dirty vest repaired a small motor cruiser. The hull had been painted in a swirl of vibrant colours, which made it look a little like John Lennon's famous psychedelic Rolls Royce. Someone somewhere was playing 'Smells Like Teen Spirit' on a ukulele. On the cabin roof of the narrowboat nearest to the road, a black cat soaked up the sun and washing waved lazily in the warm breeze. An older woman was sitting at the rear of the boat crocheting. She wore a hand-knitted beanie and her chin was covered with wispy hair that caught the sunlight.

'Excuse me,' said Shunter.

The woman turned slowly to face him and he could see that she was smoking – or vaping – an electronic pipe. As she drew on it, the fake embers glowed incongruously blue and a wisp of liquorice-scented vapour escaped her flaring nostrils.

'Yup?' she said.

'Did you happen to see a white van pass by here earlier?' asked Shunter. 'It would have come from the old boat works. Around the same time as that big fire started.'

The pipe lady sat back and contemplated a passenger jet making white lines across the sky. A buzzard soared high above on the warm spring thermals.

'You police?' she said.

'Ex-police. My name's Frank Shunter. I'm trying to track down some people who may have been kidnapped. Did you see a van pass by here?'

'Yup,' she said.

'Fantastic,' said Shunter. 'I don't suppose you remember any part of the registration number, do you?'

She cupped her pipe and gently removed it from her mouth. A thin bridge of spittle connected the mouthpiece to her lip. It snapped and fell as a droplet on to her rainbow-coloured fishing smock. She peered down and wiped it away with her crochet. 'Nope,' she said.

'Damn,' said Shunter.

'Can show you, though,' she said, passing over her smart-phone. 'Bugger killed a duck and didn't even stop. Took a photo of him. Already told the police an hour back. That's why I thought you was here. Don't know about no kidnappings, though.'

Shunter looked closely at the photo on the screen. As he'd expected, it was a white Transit-style box van.

'Dent in the front offside of the over-cab box. Probably hit a tree branch,' said Pipe Lady. 'Needs a good wash.'

'This is excellent,' said Shunter. He scribbled the registration number down in a notebook and then used the phone's zoom facility to focus in on the cab. It was impossible to see the driver but there was no mistaking the person in the passenger seat. He recognised him immediately from the festival brochure as Andrew Tremens.

'You goin' after him then?' said Pipe Lady.

'I don't have a car,' said Shunter.

'Borrow one of my brother's,' said Pipe Lady, throwing him a bunch of keys and pointing at a crowd of vintage vehicles. 'He does 'em up as a hobby. They all work. Oy! Merlin! Can this here copper borrow a car? He's after that duck killer.'

'Ex-copper,' said Shunter.

The man working on the cruiser engine raised a thumb in the air.

'The old Cortina GXL is the fastest,' said Pipe Lady.

As Shunter drove off she took a deep drag on her e-pipe. 'Go get that duck killin' bastard,' she growled and returned to her crochet.

Helen Greeley had insisted on taking Savidge by taxi to Bowcester Police Station to collect his belongings and then on to his little house so that he could get showered and changed. She had persuaded him to be her production guest at the 8 p.m. performance of *Evil Company Corrupts*.

As he showered upstairs, she looked around the lounge. The room was entirely anonymous and gave no clues to the identity of the person who lived there. His furniture was mismatched but it was all good quality; probably bought at auctions or car boot sales, she guessed. There were no framed certificates, no trophies and no family photographs. What ornaments there were had a charity-shop feel to them: plaster cats, china dogs and glass fish. These were not the kinds of things that people bought as presents for others, which meant that Savidge had probably bought them for himself. Even though she'd only known him a short time, Greeley could see that here was a man with a troubled past who found it difficult to make friends. The room seemed to be a sad testament to that fact.

Savidge picked out his best jeans, a lumberjack-style shirt and a pair of brown faux-leather shoes to wear to the play. They were,

he realised, his best clothes but they seemed to be wholly inadequate for someone that the glamorous Helen Greeley thought of
as . . . what? Their relationship was only a kind of friendship
born of shared adversity. He wondered if he dared to hope that it
might be something more one day. But why would an inter-
nationally famous TV star be even vaguely interested in a burger
van man? Or, more probably, an unemployed ex-burger van man.

He sprayed on some unbranded aftershave and went downstairs. Greeley was waiting for him with two glasses of Scotch.

'I hope you don't mind that I helped myself,' she said, handing
him a glass and downing her own in one. She walked to the fire-
place and examined her face in the mirror that hung over the
mantel. 'God, I look haggard. I have a tricky balancing act to pull
off tonight, Troy. I'm playing a vision of Miss Cutter's Aunt Pie,
so I have to look sort-of ghostly but still glam enough for the
fans.'

'You'll look fine,' said Savidge. 'You always do.'

'Ugh. I look half dead already, which will help. And every year
that passes, it gets harder to hide the wrinkles.'

'You don't need all that make-up. I could understand it if you
had something on your face like a scar or pockmarks or a birth-
mark or something to hide. But you don't. You're okay as you
are.'

Greeley smiled and put her arms around Savidge's neck.
'Anyone else would have told me that I look gorgeous or fabu-
lous. But you said that I look "fine", that I'm "okay" as I am.
You're the first honest man I think I've ever met, Troy.' She kissed
him on the lips and then inhaled deeply.

'Mmmm. You smell cheap,' she said. 'Totally unpretentious. I
love it.'

27

'So where are we?' asked Esme Handibode between bites. Andrew Tremens had removed her gag and was feeding her a chocolate bar.

'I don't know,' he said. 'He made me curl up in the footwell out of sight. I'm as stiff as a board.'

'You should try being in the back,' said Mrs Handibode. 'We're being thrown around on plywood floors and walls. I'm black and blue.'

'Is she any better?' asked Tremens, nodding his head towards Brenda Tradescant who seemed to be staring vacantly into space.

'Not a peep out of her for hours,' said Mrs Handibode. 'Anyway, why aren't you in the back with us? What's so special about you?'

'He says it's in case we get stopped by the police. Because I'm a solicitor they'll be less inclined to ask questions,' said Tremens. 'Plus, he says that, as a man, I'm less likely to be hysterical.'

'Sexist pig,' said Mrs Handibode.

'Yes, and he obviously doesn't know me very well,' said Tremens. 'It's all I can do not to burst into tears. Every time he puts that balaclava thing on I want to scream.'

'I don't see any obvious landmarks,' said Mrs Handibode, looking around. 'One bit of the canal looks much like the next without landmarks. Have you really no idea at all where we are?'

'None. After we left the boat works, we drove around for a while and I was in the footwell. You can't see out of the windows down there. We eventually stopped in a car park in some woods and he told me to get out because we were going for a walk. But then some cars turned up and he sort of panicked and pushed me back down on to the floor again. I've been scrunched up there ever since. We've stopped at a few other places but only briefly. I never got to see where.'

'I imagine that he's looking for somewhere nice and isolated where he can do us in,' said Mrs Handibode.

'Oh god, do you think so?'

'Is that what he's planning, Brenda?' asked Mrs Handibode.

Brenda Tradescant said nothing. A small trickle of drool escaped the corner of her mouth.

'I think we're somewhere near Sherrinford,' said Mrs Handibode. 'I heard a distant clock chime a few minutes ago. It sounded to me like the chimes of St Uncumber's. What's the time now?'

Andrew Tremens looked at his watch. 'Just after six. Dear god. That means we've been missing for more than a day. Why hasn't anyone found us yet? Surely Dallimore must have called the police by now?'

'You said it yourself, no one knows where we are,' said Handibode. 'And I have the most horrible premonition that, wherever we are, it will be our final resting place.'

'We really ought to be heading back to the village. You're onstage soon,' said Savidge.

Helen Greeley snuggled into his bare chest and sighed. 'I suppose so. I just want to stay here, though. In your bed. With you.'

'But the play . . .'

'Fuck the play,' said Greeley, biting him cheekily on the nipple.

'I thought this sort of thing only happened in films,' said Savidge.

Blount parked his car behind the Herewardshire Hog pub and walked out into the tiny main street. There was very little in Spradbarrow: just the pub, a scattering of cottages, a village store and a hairdressing salon. The church of St Cunigunde dominated the end of Chapel Street and seemed overly large for such a small hamlet, but it had been built to cater not only for the spiritual needs of the villagers, but also for the many pig farmers and their families who made up the larger proportion of the parish. Standing next to it was the smallest building in Spradbarrow, a tiny red-brick two-up–two-down cottage that served as the vicarage. It was towards this that Blount ambled as nonchalantly as any man who was one 'Uncle Brian' tall could be said to amble. As he walked he took photos on his phone and tried desperately to look like a tourist.

Shunter had come to a junction where the muddy track met the main road and looked for any clue – fresh mud or tyre marks – that might tell him whether the van had turned right towards Sherrinford or left towards Nasely. But there was nothing. He stepped out of the old Cortina and used the extra height this afforded him to peer over gates and hedges in search of farmers out in the fields who might have noted a white van pass them by. But the fat Herewardshire hogs were all alone and regarded him with indolent disinterest.

Shunter sighed. There was nothing more he could do. He checked his phone and, finding that he had a weak but operable signal, he dialled Bowcester Police Station to report that the van involved in a reported duck killing earlier was also the van sought in connection with the murder of Shirley Pomerance. The operator thanked him for his information and asked if he could attend the station to make a statement. Shunter gave the operator his details and assured them that he would.

He wondered whether to follow one more hunch before he went to the police station. There was more fresh mud on the road towards Sherrinford than towards Nasely. And, despite claims to the contrary in crime thrillers, not many murderers returned to the scene of the crime. Arsonists maybe, as many had an almost sexual obsession with fire. And burglars often did because they had the advantage of knowing the layout of the premises and just what pickings were on offer second time around. But not murderers. Not unless they got a kick out of seeing the chaos they'd caused. Shunter had dealt with a lot of homicides and this didn't feel like the work of such a person. It had been brutal, yes. Frenzied, even. But the killer had taken steps to cover their tracks and that smacked of sanity tinged with panic. Having convinced himself, he climbed back into the car, put it into first gear and turned right.

'Mr Savidge?' said Quisty.

Savidge and Greeley were about to call for a taxi when the doorbell rang. To their surprise, on the doorstep stood two plain-clothes police officers presenting their warrant cards as ID. One was tall and rather dapper; Savidge couldn't remember the last time he'd seen someone under forty wearing a cravat. The other was a slight woman, possibly of Chinese descent, with jet-black hair cut in a bob not dissimilar to that worn by Miss Cutter in the TV shows.

'What am I supposed to have done now?' said Savidge, frowning.

'Nothing at all, as far as I know,' said Quisty. 'We just wanted a brief chat. May we come in?'

'Actually, we were just about to book a cab,' said Greeley. 'We need to get to Nasely. I'm taking part in a play at eight and we're already later than we should be.'

'Then allow us to give you a lift,' said Quisty. 'We can chat on the way.'

Blount peered surreptitiously through the vicarage's front window. The room was dark but, as his eyes adjusted, he could see a man asleep in an armchair, his face sporadically illuminated by the light from a TV set. It was the Reverend Savidge; the likeness between him and his brother was striking. Perhaps they actually were twins? He looked unkempt, unshaven, and had no trousers on. He also appeared to have a spear lying across his lap but, more alarmingly, Blount saw that the wall beyond the sleeping clergyman was covered in primitive but deadly looking weapons: spears and pikes, cudgels and clubs, whips, longbows and swords.

'He has a bloody arsenal in there,' muttered Blount. He looked again at the assegai that lay across the man's lap. 'And the bugger looks like he's expecting us.'

He walked back towards his car, snapping a few photos of a pretty thatched cottage to satisfy the curiosity of an elderly man walking his dog, and called Sergeant Stough on his mobile. It was best to keep this kind of conversation private.

'Tell me about your maternal grandmother,' said Quisty.

Savidge stared at him. 'What?'

'Are you trying to solve a crime or psychoanalyse him?' asked Greeley.

'As surprising as it sounds, I believe the question is pertinent to our homicide investigation in Nasely,' said Quisty. 'Was your grandmother called Millicent?'

'No idea,' said Savidge. 'I was adopted. What's that got to do with anything?'

'If I'm right, everything,' said Quisty.

Shunter had driven barely half a mile along the Sherrinford road when suddenly, through a farm gate that afforded a gap in the tall country hedge, he caught a glimpse of something white. He stepped on the brakes and slowly reversed back to the gate. The view looked out on to the relentlessly flat countryside. And there, parked beside the meandering canal and bathed in the warm evening sun, was a white box van with a dent in the box above the cab. Shunter picked up his phone.

'A signal!' he said triumphantly.

'So you don't know who your biological mother was?' asked Quisty.

'No. And never wanted to,' said Savidge. 'She dumped us all at the first opportunity she could. She didn't want her boys. So I don't want her.'

'How sad,' said Quisty.

'My brother, the vicar, might know. But, if he does, he's never told me and I haven't asked. A few years back, he went through a phase of wanting to track her down. He said he wanted to forgive her. Personally, I think he was just after money.'

'He has money problems?'

'He's a vicar. And he drinks. Of course he's got money problems.'

Quisty's phone suddenly began to chirp and he answered it.

'It's HQ,' he explained, hanging up. 'Shunter's found the van near Sherrinford and the suspect is still with it.' He looked over his shoulder at his passengers. 'Do you mind if we take a detour?'

Before they could answer, Kim Woon had wrenched the steering wheel around hard and stamped on the accelerator.

Blount gathered Stough and his TRU officers around him in the pub car park. Two of them were looking very much the worse for wear with bloodshot and puffy eyes.

'I hope this isn't another wild goose chase,' said Stough. 'We were just about to knock off. My lads are tired and they've had a difficult day.'

'I imagine they have after that balls-up earlier,' said Blount. 'I thought you said they were highly trained?'

'They are,' said Stough, defensively. 'But it was their first live operation. There were bound to be teething troubles.'

'Teething troubles? It was a bloody fiasco.'

'No one warned us that the boat had been booby trapped.'

'Well, I hope they're better prepared this time. Because this, I promise you, is definitely not a wild goose chase and I do not want any more cock-ups. Firstly, I want radio silence in case the suspect has some form of scanner.'

'Is that likely?' asked Stough.

'He's been one step ahead of us all through this investigation. I'm taking no chances.' In truth, Blount had no reason at all to suspect that the Reverend Savidge could monitor police transmissions, but Quisty could. The man was not going to steal his thunder. Not now that he was so close to an arrest. 'Right, that building I pointed out to you just now is the vicarage. And inside is the person that I believe is responsible for the murder of Shirley Pomerance.'

'With all due respect, guv, that's what you said earlier at the boat,' said Stough.

'I was fed duff information by a malicious former police officer,' said Blount. 'Savidge wasn't our man. But his brother is.'

'You said vicarage. Is he a vicar then?' asked PC Tom Renny (TRU 2), a born-again Christian. 'I don't think I could shoot a vicar.'

'I don't want you to fucking shoot him!' said Blount. 'I want him captured alive and fit enough to stand trial for murder.'

'But you say that he's definitely armed?' asked Stough.

'He is. But just hand weapons from what I saw. Spears and clubs and that sort of thing. No guns.'

Stough's phone began to ring. He looked at the screen.

'It's DCI Quisty,' he said.

'Ignore it. This is more important.'

'But—'

'Ignore it. On my authority. Are you all set to go?'

'We are. We're going to use tactical option fourteen.'

'What's that?' asked Blount.

'I call it the Scorpion's Tail,' said Stough, grinning.

'There is definitely a person or persons being kept in the rear of the van and I've seen a man who I believe to be the missing solicitor Andrew Tremens moving about,' explained Shunter to the group of police officers who'd responded to his phone call. As requested, they'd arrived without sirens and blue lights so as not to alert the van driver.

'Is Tremens the murderer then?' asked an officer.

'Honestly, I have no idea,' said Shunter. 'I've seen him in the passenger seat rather than in the back of the van so he could possibly be an accomplice. There must be another suspect who was driving the van. I haven't sighted him or her yet. Just be aware that there is another person to watch out for. My advice is: don't take any silly risks.'

A car turned up with Quisty and Woon on board. And, to Shunter's surprise, Helen Greeley and Savidge.

'I'm just briefing the lads and lasses with what I know,' said Shunter. 'Which, to be honest, isn't much. You can't see a lot from here with the naked eye.'

'Let's try these then, shall we?' said Quisty, lifting a large pair of binoculars to his eyes. 'Two women in the back, by the looks of things. They're in deep shadow and I can only see their legs. Both have their ankles tied. I can see Andrew Tremens – it's definitely him – and he's chatting to someone in the driving seat.'

'What's the plan then?' asked Woon.

'We can't approach over land as it's completely flat and there are few hiding places, just a handful of isolated shrubs and trees,' said Quisty. 'And while there's been no suggestion that the suspect is armed, if he, or they, do have a gun they could pick us off far too easily. And, for some reason, I can't seem to raise the TRU on the radio or by phone.'

'So what do we do?' asked one of the officers.

Shunter's eyes followed the canal a short distance to where he could see the painted boats moored at The Rushes.

'I have an idea,' he said. 'How about this . . .'

'The boy is clearly unhinged,' said Mrs Handibode. 'You've seen what he is capable of.'

'I have. Which doesn't bode well for us,' said Andrew Tremens.

A man in a balaclava emerged from the van holding a baseball bat in his gloved hands. The business end of the bat was stained a disturbing reddish brown.

'You three,' said the figure, waving the bat menacingly. 'We're going for a walk.'

Thunderbirds Jeff Scott John Virgil Gordon Alan Parker Lady Penelope Savidge woke with a start. He reached for his glass of brandy and sipped at it to take away the unpleasant taste of sleep. He'd woken to the theme music of *Murder, She Wrote* and he smiled as Angela Lansbury's beaming face appeared on the TV screen. It was a show that he was very fond of, mainly because of his exceptional hit-rate in identifying who the killer was likely to be. He'd been a regular watcher of the show for thirty years and had seen so many episodes that he had started to see patterns emerging. For example, there were certain actors who, as he put it, 'always played the baddie', so if they turned up in the cast they were very likely to be the murderer. The same applied to the most famous guest star in any episode, or to anyone who drove a European car such as a Mercedes or BMW; the good guys always drove American marques like Chevrolet or Buick. He took another gulp of brandy. It was Sunday evening, the day of rest, and his work was done so what harm was there in relaxing with a bottle of the good stuff? Well, half a bottle now. It was a very fine brandy.

He got unsteadily to his feet and propped the spear that had been on his lap against the wall. He'd got into the habit of always sleeping with a weapon in his hands during his time as a missionary in South Africa in the early 1990s when a white man, even one who was doing God's work, wasn't always safe from the vigilantes that prowled the townships. He walked unsteadily into his kitchen to see what was available to nibble on. Finding a couple of cold sausages in the fridge, he smeared ketchup along their lengths and stood idly chomping them while looking out of the window at his untidy garden and pondering upon what had gone wrong with his life. He'd been an idealistic youth, if a troubled one. Unwanted at birth and adopted by a bully of a man with a foul temper and no qualms about dishing out a good beating, he'd looked forward to the day when he was old enough to move as far away as possible. And that was what he'd done, joining a Christian relief mission inspired by Live Aid the year before. For the next five years, he'd moved around Ethiopia and Somalia before settling in South Africa where he'd found his calling. Inducted as a minister of the Anglican Church of Southern Africa, he'd gone on to serve for ten years in various townships. They had not always been happy years. Revolution was in the air and it was difficult to source the medication he needed to cope with his panic attacks and anger issues. Over time he had, instead, taken to drink whenever it was available, and when it wasn't, he'd distilled his own. It was a brew of such strength and potency that it had rendered him next to useless as a minister. Eventually, the bishop had decided that perhaps he'd be better off back in the UK where medication and counselling were more readily available. The Reverend Savidge had returned home to South Herewardshire in 2001 and had been tending to the spiritual needs of the sleepy parish of Spradbarrow ever since. However, his need for alcohol had, if anything, increased now that it was more freely available.

He returned to his sitting room and saw, to his satisfaction, that an actor who always played the baddie was in the cast of this evening's episode. Secure in the knowledge that he now knew who the murderer was going to be, the Reverend Thunderbirds picked up his assegai and sat back down in his favourite armchair. An amusing thought struck him; what if the show's sleuthing heroine Jessica Fletcher was the murderer in every episode? After all, people seemed to get killed wherever she happened to be. He smiled as he considered how much fun it would be to make a final episode of *Murder, She Wrote* in which it was discovered that Fletcher had been one of America's most prolific serial killers all along. Perhaps, from now on, he'd watch each episode and try to figure out how she could have committed the crimes.

A sudden noise caught his ear. A decade of living with the constant threat of death had heightened his sensitivity to suspicious noises no matter how drunk he was and there had definitely been an unexpected squeak from the direction of the back garden. Clutching his spear in one hand, he reached down a knobkierie from the wall with the other. It was one of several dangerous-looking weapons that he'd brought back as souvenirs. He then decided that the club, as threatening as it looked, didn't have the range he might need. He therefore dropped both it and the spear and selected instead a hunting bow he'd been given by the San people of the Kalahari. He swigged directly from the bottle of brandy for Dutch courage and staggered to the kitchen. They'd find him a harder man to kill than most country vicars.

'I've just got another text from DCI Quisty saying that I should contact him urgently,' said Stough.

'Ignore it,' said Blount.

'But he might—'

'Ignore it. I take full responsibility.'

'Okay. If you say so,' said Stough. 'We're in position and ready to go.'

'Good. So, why do you call it the Scorpion's Tail?'

'Distract with the claws and the victim doesn't see the tail until it's too late. Watch.'

Two of Stough's officers were standing one each side of the vicarage front door. One of the officers rang the bell.

Inside the vicarage, the Reverend Savidge heard the doorbell but ignored it. Whoever it was could wait. He was more concerned with the person that was skulking around in his overgrown back garden. The noise he'd heard had been the rusting hinges on his back gate complaining. He'd since spotted a dark figure furtively lurking behind a bushy rhododendron. The movement of a nearby photinia, despite the lack of a breeze, made him suspect that a second intruder was also hiding in his garden. He fitted an arrow to the bowstring and crept towards his kitchen door. He lay down on the welcome mat and gingerly pushed open the cat flap with the tip of the arrow. He could now see two pairs of legs dressed in black trousers moving suspiciously from one over-grown shrub to another as they made their way towards the vicarage. Both of the trespassers, he noted from their hands, had dark skin. And both were carrying rifles. The Reverend's heart began hammering in his chest and he suddenly found it hard to breathe. His nose began to bleed as a wave of panic rolled over him and, suddenly, he was back in South Africa during some of the worst violence of the late eighties and early nineties. It was a time when he'd seen police officers firing indiscriminately into crowds and thrashing people with their long leather sjamboks; when people, black and white, had been hacked to death with axes and machetes and when Africa had given the world a new and hideous form of execution by way of 'necklacing' – putting a petrol-filled tyre over a person's torso, trapping their arms by their sides and then setting it alight. The Reverend would not let that happen to him. The Bible might tell him that it was a sin to kill another human but there was nothing to say he couldn't maim someone in self-defence.

'"And thine eye shall not pity; but life shall go for life, eye for eye, tooth for tooth, hand for hand, foot for foot",' he muttered to himself as he carefully took aim. 'Or a thigh for a thigh,' he added as he let the arrow fly before passing out.

As the arrow thudded into PC Oduwole's leg and embedded in the bone, he screamed once and involuntarily clenched his fists, pulling the trigger on his semi-automatic rifle and peppering the rear of the vicarage with bullets.

The man in the balaclava had bound Andrew Tremens's hands and hobbled his feet with just enough length of rope to allow him to walk with tiny steps. All three of his prisoners had been bound the same way.

'Let's go then,' he said.

'Please don't do anything hasty that you might regret,' said Tremens.

'Walk,' said the man. He prodded his three captives in their backs with the baseball bat for emphasis. Tremens took one step and fell over.

The two officers at the front of the vicarage heard the staccato sound of semi-automatic fire and ducked as the front windows of the building blew out in a hail of lead. One bullet grazed the arm of the officer closest to the window and he responded by immediately firing back into the house. One of his shots found the already injured PC Oduwole's shoulder. In response his colleague, PC Khalsa, returned fire under the assumption that the bullets were coming from inside the kitchen. His slugs tore up the room and two of them passed right through the building and slammed into the window of the Chapel Street hair salon opposite, setting off the burglar alarm. The officers at the front of the vicarage retaliated by firing into the Reverend's lounge and destroying his television.

Blount watched it all in horror from the safety of the TRV.

'Stop firing!' he yelled. 'Stop fucking firing! I want him alive!'

'He's shooting at my men!' shouted Stough. 'They have the right to retaliate with reasonable force!'

'Reasonable force?' spluttered Blount. 'They must have let off two hundred rounds already! Can't they gas the bastard?'

'They don't have gas with them.'

'Why not?'

'He's a vicar! We thought the threat of guns would be enough. But there's a case of gas grenades behind your seat. Grab a handful and get ready. They can't gas him but we bloody can.'

Stough turned the key in the ignition and the TRV roared from its position in the alleyway beside the Herewardshire Hog and drove menacingly towards the front of the vicarage at speed. As the vehicle screeched to a halt outside the building, the two officers who were pinned down by gunfire leapt into the back. Blount opened his window and pulled the pin on a CS gas grenade. He lobbed it towards the vicarage's broken front window but it bounced off the wooden frame with an annoying clunk and landed on the pavement, already spewing gas. Blount swore, pulled the pin on a second grenade and was about to try again when a fresh burst of machine-gun fire erupted from inside the house. As the bullets slapped into the side of the armoured vehicle, Stough swore loudly and stamped on the accelerator. The TRV jumped forward and so powerful was the movement that his two officers fell out of the open back doors and Blount dropped his primed grenade into the footwell. As the vehicle began to fill with gas, another hail of bullets hit the TRV, bursting a tyre. Coughing and spluttering and unable to see where he was going, Sergeant Stough drove through the front window of the village store.

The residents of Spradbarrow had started to emerge from their houses to see what the noise was all about. Many were now howling in anguish, as were the two TRU officers, as the billowing clouds of CS gas drifted across the street and caught them in the eyes. Burglar alarms clanged incessantly and police sirens could be heard in the distance.

The Reverend Thunderbirds Savidge was unperturbed. He'd been unconscious throughout the entire siege.

'Listen, I realise that you have some serious issues with this lady but that doesn't mean that you have to harm any of us,' said Mrs Handibode.

The man in the balaclava was beginning to regret his decision to hobble his captives. Their progress was tortuously slow, each step being no more than a few inches in length. All of the captives had fallen over several times and, for the entire length of the journey, Mrs Handibode had been bending his ear.

'Lord knows, there are times when I've wanted to kill Brenda myself,' said Mrs Handibode. 'But you won't feel any better for doing so, mark my words.'

'I don't want to feel better,' snapped Balaclava. 'I just want to be rid of her.'

'But why?' said Mrs Handibode.

'You really have no idea what she's done to me, do you?' said Balaclava. 'She's—'

He was interrupted by the thrum of a distant outboard motor. A small, curiously painted pleasure cruiser was approaching from the direction of The Rushes at some speed.

'Shit!' said Balaclava, replacing all three of his prisoners' gags. 'Back to the van! Now!'

They turned around and began shuffling away from the canal in a comically slow penguin waddle. Andrew Tremens fell over again.

'He's still breathing,' said Stough. 'In fact, I'd swear he's asleep.'

He was examining the recumbent and half-undressed form of the clergyman who had been dragged from the vicarage by the uninjured TRU officers and unceremoniously dumped on the pavement. Somewhere along the way, the vicar had lost his underpants and he was sporting a quite unnecessary erection. At first glance, he'd looked to be seriously injured but the copious amounts of blood around his head and upper body had turned out to be the result of a nosebleed. Otherwise, and quite remarkably, he had sustained no injuries at all. The same could not be said of the TRU officers. In their enthusiasm to take out the murder suspect, two of them had successfully shot each other and one of those also had an arrow in his leg. All were suffering the effects of CS gas exposure. And there had been no trace of a gun found in the house. Stough was looking shamefaced, a condition made infinitely worse by his reddened, weeping eyes and the facial injuries he'd sustained from crashing the TRV into the shop while not wearing a seatbelt.

'I don't understand,' said Stough. 'My men were sure that he—'

'Get him under lock and key at Bowcester nick and get your people some medical help,' said Blount. He had fared even worse than Stough; he'd had an allergic reaction to the gas and his face was bright red and swollen like a tomato. His eyes, already pink and painfully bloodshot, had been reduced to tiny slits. 'The important thing is that we've caught the bastard. We can work out what happened and why it happened later.'

'Where are you going?' asked Stough.

'I have a public announcement to make,' said Blount, walking towards his car and hoping he'd be able to see well enough to drive back to Nasely.

The cruiser, a zippy little thirty-footer decorated with psychedelic whorls and patterns, chugged up alongside the towpath and, to the man in the balaclava's horror, it appeared to be slowing down to stop. His prisoners were not even close to the van and so, in a desperate effort to conceal them, he pushed them bodily behind one of the few large shrubs nearby and forced them to lie down. Leaving them with the threat that he would kill them if they uttered a sound, he pulled off his headwear and ran to his van. He was pretending to be examining one of its tyres when the cruiser came to a stop and a man jumped to the bank with a rope and tied it to a mooring ring. The kidnapper cursed again. This meant that he'd have to find another location to do what he had to do.

'Hello there!' shouted the man from the boat. He was middle-aged, portly, with a clipped grey moustache. He was wearing a tie-dyed T-shirt, a dreamcatcher around his neck and a panama hat. He walked towards the van, smiling. 'Could you help us, please?'

'Actually, I'm just leaving,' said the kidnapper.

'I shan't keep you a moment,' said Shunter. 'It's just that we need a strong pair of hands to help us open the door to our cabin.

The wood has swollen and it's got stuck. I have a bad back and I'm afraid that my wife's arthritis is just too bad these days.' He waved to the stout lady behind the steering wheel of the boat. She puffed on an e-pipe and scowled.

'This nice strong young man is going to help us!' shouted Shunter.

Her scowl became slightly less of a scowl.

'Now wait . . . I didn't say that I—'

'It'll take just a minute of your time and we'd be ever so grateful,' said Shunter, taking the kidnapper by the elbow. 'Then we can be on our way.'

Begrudgingly, the kidnapper allowed the old hippy to lead him back to his boat. He could hardly kill him in cold blood in front of his formidable-looking wife. She looked to be quite a bit older than her husband and had a face like thunder. Her eyes never left him as he climbed aboard.

'That's the door there,' said Shunter. 'Can you see if you can open it?'

The kidnapper took hold of the handle and braced himself. As he prepared to pull, the man in the panama hat suddenly whistled and the cabin doors were flung open by someone inside. The kidnapper was planted firmly on his backside.

'What the fu—'

From inside the boat came a crowd of aggressive-looking canal folk armed with cricket bats, motorcycle chains, tyre irons and other assorted weapons. The kidnapper backed away, realising that he was hopelessly outnumbered and that escape was his only option. He turned and found himself suddenly face to face with Quisty, Woon and four uniformed police officers who had appeared on the towpath carrying long riot batons and handcuffs.

From somewhere in the distance came the sound of the police helicopter approaching at speed.

'Good afternoon,' said Quisty. 'You are, as they say, nicked.'

'Bloody duck murderer,' spat Pipe Lady.

Helen Greeley had watched the entire police operation through Quisty's binoculars. It had all been very exciting. But now she handed them to Savidge and checked her watch.

'Shit!' she exclaimed. 'Doors open in quarter of an hour and I haven't even done my make-up yet. Can one of you lovely boys take us back to Nasely?'

'No problem, Miss Greeley,' said a blushing young police officer. 'I'll just clear it with the guv'nor and I can have you there in ten minutes.'

'Thank you. You coming, Troy?'

Savidge dropped the binoculars and his face looked pale and drawn.

'What?' said Greeley, concerned.

'I just saw who they've arrested,' said Savidge.

A police van and several cars had now arrived by the canal side and the prisoners had been located. As she was helped to her feet, Miss Tradescant saw the kidnapper in handcuffs and began whimpering. It was the first noise that she had made in hours. A police officer worked at untying Esme Handibode's and Andrew Tremens's bonds.

'Are you all unharmed?' asked Quisty.

'Yes, I think so,' said Tremens. 'What a nightmare that was!'

'These officers will take you back to the Incident Room where we'll take your statements. If you're up to it, that is,' he said.

'I am,' said Mrs Handibode. 'I'm not sure I can say the same for Brenda, though.'

Brenda Tradescant had dropped to the ground once again and had curled herself into a ball. She was wailing like a fire siren.

Frank Shunter watched as the suspect was loaded into the police van.

'Like peas in a pod,' he said.

28

Blount emerged from his car and waved to the handful of Crabbe fans that were still lingering around outside Nasely Village Hall.

'I've caught the murderer,' he said simply. 'Press conference here in ten minutes. Spread the word.'

The Millies ran away in excitement to tell everyone they knew.

It was 7.30 p.m. and the doors had opened at the Masonic Hall for the evening's all-star performance of *Evil Company Corrupts*. The play and the subsequent Helen Greeley talk marked the end of the festival, and most of the Millies would be heading off home immediately afterwards, which was why most of them were now dressed in their everyday clothes. There were still a few camera crews and interviewers roaming about, recording vox pops and people's reactions, and caching some useful pieces for later inclusion in documentaries and tribute shows about Shirley Pomerance. But it was clear that the extraordinary events of the weekend were coming to a close.

The play's director looked at his watch. Where was Helen Greeley? And where, for that matter, was his audience? As the doors had opened, he'd expected a flood. Instead there was barely a trickle.

*

Blount smiled the widest smile his swollen face could manage as he walked into his Incident Room. Dangerously sleep-deprived, pumped full of coffee and energy drinks, and still suffering the after-effects of CS gas exposure, he sounded and acted like a man on some kind of drug trip.

'Press conference! Ten minutes!' he shouted.

'Jesus, what's up with your face?' said Jaine.

'We were starting to worry about you, guv,' said Banton. 'DCI Quisty has made some—'

'Sod Quisty,' said Blount. 'I have caught the murderer. Me. Not the twat in the cravat. Me.'

'You have? But I thought that—'

'I caught him! Me! Ha ha!' said Blount. 'You didn't think that I could do it, did you? You thought that I wasn't as smart as him.'

'I never said—'

'He's a genius, is he? Like some kind of Sherlock Holmes? Ha ha! Well, I'm sorry to disappoint you but I'm the better detective in this case, Nicola. I figured it out. Ha ha! And I made the arrest. Me!'

'Yes, but—'

'Press conference! In ten, no, nine minutes. Next door in the village hall. Inform the media, will you?'

'Listen, guv, I really think that—'

'That's an order, Banton.'

'Whatever you say, guv.'

'What's up with your face?' said Jaine again, but Blount was already out of the door.

Helen Greeley and Savidge arrived at the Masonic Hall to find the play's director in a very nervous state.

'Something terrible has happened,' he said, wringing his hands. 'They've arrested the man who killed Shirley Pomerance.'

'I know. We were there,' said Savidge morosely.

'How is that terrible?' said Greeley.

'Look!' said the director.

Helen Greeley looked out from behind the curtains and into the main hall. Row upon row of empty seats faced her, peppered every so often with fans who, somehow, hadn't heard yet of developments in the Pomerance murder case.

'Is it normally this bad?' asked radio actor Maggie Woodbead, emerging from a changing room. 'I've come all the way out from London for this.'

'We could have sold every ticket five times over,' said the director. 'It's this bloody murder business. It's stolen our audience.'

'They'll come back when the initial excitement passes,' said Greeley. 'What you do is hold off curtain-up until nine o'clock and you'll probably have a full house by then. It'll be fine. Now, where can we get a drink in this place? I'm not on until the second act so there's time for a snifter or two. Troy, you could do with one as well, I expect.'

She held on to Savidge's arm as the director led them all to the bar.

'Fictional murder is so much less stressful than the real thing,' said the director. 'At least you can schedule it.'

Inside the village hall, Blount was ensuring that everything was perfect for his press conference. This was his hour of glory at last, his defining moment, the single event that would see him elevated to Detective Chief Inspector at the next round of promotions. He alone had caught the murderer, despite his Chief Superintendent's lack of confidence in him and despite Quisty usurping him as lead investigator. He couldn't stop himself tittering with glee.

The news of the arrest had spread like wildfire and the hall was soon full to capacity. Those reporters who had decided to stay on until the bitter end of the festival were gloating among themselves and thanking their lucky stars for the opportunity of such a great scoop.

'Ladies and gentlemen, if you could all either take a seat or find somewhere to stand that doesn't obstruct anyone else's view, we will kick off in a few minutes,' said Blount.

Jaine's phone buzzed and he read the screen. 'Guv? It's a text from DCI Quisty. He says that he hasn't been able to get hold of you and that he's on his way here.'

'Oh no. Oh no no no. He's not going to take this away from me,' said Blount, suddenly very serious. He looked at his own phone and at the long list of missed calls and unread texts. 'We have to do this now.'

'But shouldn't we—'

'Ladies and gentlemen, thank you for coming,' said Blount as he stepped out in front of his surprised audience and took a seat behind a table. Camera flashes popped and an expectant hush fell upon the crowd. With the rampant boar of the South Herewardshire Constabulary helmet badge proudly rearing up on a display board behind him, Blount allowed a small smile of triumph to flicker across his horribly inflated face.

'Ladies and gentlemen. As you all know, yesterday the brutal murder of prize-winning author Shirley Pomerance took place here, in this very hall,' he began. 'It was an event that shocked not only us, but the entire literary world. However, in the past twenty-four hours, I have tracked down the perpetrator of this crime and he is now under arrest. Me. I did that. Ha ha!'

There was a round of applause and a few cheers. Blount smiled painfully and applauded himself.

'I am delighted to report that this evening I took into custody a male who I know to be responsible for this terrible crime,' said Blount. 'He is the Reverend Thunderbirds Savidge, Vicar of St Cunigunde's Church in Spradbarrow.'

The room was suddenly full of murmurs.

The arrival of another police car, this one containing DCI Quisty, DS Woon, Esme Handibode and Andrew Tremens, was greeted with excited cheers by the Millies in the street who hadn't been quick enough to get a spot inside the village hall. The officers shouldered their way through the crowd and into the building.

'So why did he kill her?' asked a reporter from the *South Here-wardshire Bugle*.

'That is something I'm still in the process of investigating,' said Blount, suddenly spotting Quisty coming in through the door. 'But this is my arrest – Detective Inspector Brian Blount, spelled B-L-O-U-N-T. I arrested him. Me. No one else. Just me.'

'What's up with your face?' said a reporter from the *Sun*.

Quisty indicated with his head for Blount to join him in the kitchen area.

'Two minutes, ladies and gents,' said Blount, rising to his feet. The room erupted in excited conversation.

'I messaged you to say that I was on my way,' said Quisty.

'I must have missed it,' lied Blount. 'And I didn't see any problem in pushing ahead with a press conference.'

'The problem, Brian,' said Quisty, 'is that you aren't in possession of all the facts. And without all of the facts, you can't know the whole story.'

'I don't need another lecture about gravity and plates!' snapped Blount. 'I know exactly what I'm doing!'

'Maybe you should listen to DCI Quisty,' said Banton.

'*Et tu*, Banton?' said Blount as, once more, he stepped out in front of the crowd. 'I will take a few more questions now,' he announced.

Quisty shook his head sadly. 'Will you tell him or shall I?'

29

'It's one of the golden rules of murder mystery that you never suddenly introduce an identical sibling as the murderer,' said Miss Wilderspin.

'Quite right, Molly. It's a cheap cop-out and it destroys the illusion of reality,' added Mrs Handibode. 'That's why it was one of the great Ronald Knox's "Ten Commandments for Detective Fiction", the bible for all crime writers.'

'Yes, but crime fiction operates to a set of rules. Real life doesn't,' said Shunter. 'I saw a lecturer make that exact point yesterday.'

'But triplets, for goodness' sake! Who'd have guessed?' said Miss Wilderspin.

'Truth is invariably stranger than fiction,' said Shunter.

The play, eventually staged at 9.15 p.m., had been a huge success and, following a series of curtain calls with Maggie Woodbead and a deliciously euphoric Helen Greeley, the coaches had started to arrive to take the faithful home. Frank Shunter, Miss Wilderspin, Mrs Handibode and Andrew Tremens had gathered in the Happy Onion for a drink together.

'I love the fact that you used a speedboat to catch him!' said a beaming Miss Wilderspin. 'A good story always ends with a thrilling chase.'

'Not so much a chase as a sneaky way to get close enough,' said Shunter. 'Thankfully, he'd parked the van just a few minutes' drive from The Rushes. I got over there as fast as I could and, as soon as I told the boat people what was happening, a chap called Merlin offered us the use of his cruiser and brought a few of his scariest friends along for the ride. We broke a few canal speed limits I can tell you. And I nearly blew it when I saw who the kidnapper was. So like his brother. The rest you know.'

'Not everything,' said Miss Wilderspin. 'Esme, will you please tell us what happened to you? I've heard all sorts of versions of events but you must tell us in your own words.'

'Andrew should start,' said Mrs Handibode. 'If you want the story in the right order, that is.'

'Well, it all began with the discovery earlier this year of the Gobbelin diaries,' began Tremens.

'Do you mean Iris Gobbelin? Agnes Crabbe's best friend?' said Shunter.

'Yes indeed,' said Tremens. 'Her diaries changed everything.'

At the library, the process of decommissioning the Incident Room had begun. But, first, the team was opening a few bottles of Prosecco; police budgets didn't run to Champagne. DI Blount was having to miss the celebrations as he'd been admitted to hospital with suspected anaphylactic shock. Once discharged, he was due at Divisional HQ for a serious debriefing with his Chief Superintendent.

'So how the hell did you make that leap?' asked Banton. 'I mean from some random historical marriage data to Agnes Crabbe having had a secret baby?'

'As I've always said, it all comes down to connections; finding the facts between the facts,' said Quisty. 'Once we'd added the

Welter/Falk/Tradescant family tree to our web of information, it simply jumped out at me. A child called Millicent who was adopted by the Falk family in 1916, almost eleven months to the day after Daniel Crabbe's last visit home from the war. It had to be Agnes and Daniel Crabbe's daughter.'

'But how could you be sure?' said Banton.

'I couldn't be totally sure but the probability was very high,' explained Quisty. 'Nasely is a small village – it was even smaller back then – and nearly all of the men were at the front. Babies were in short supply. And, as you know, Millicent wasn't a common name and I just happened to know, because I once foolishly read Pamela Dallimore's execrable biography of her, that Agnes Crabbe's mother was called Millicent. Connect those facts together and we have a strong likelihood that baby Millicent was Agnes's daughter. But even without those particular facts, the evidence of a secret child was there in front of us in Agnes Crabbe's own writing.'

'*Swords into Ploughshares*,' said Banton.

'Exactly,' said Quisty. 'As the title suggests, the book is about a group of soldiers returning to Little Hogley, a predominantly farming community, after being demobbed from the Great War. When someone starts to kill them off one by one, Miss Cutter finds herself embroiled in the investigation. It's Agnes Crabbe's best whodunnit by far but it is an unusually melancholic book for her. It dwells on personal tragedy much more than in any of her other books. But that makes sense if you imagine that you're Agnes at that time, a young woman suddenly left widowed, alone, scared and pregnant. The story becomes one giant allegory for how she must have felt. All of the soldiers' deaths are tragic and pointless, reflecting what she saw as the senseless loss of life in the trenches, particularly the loss of her own husband, father and brother. That's a lot of grief for a young woman to bear when she's already having to deal with the stress of being pregnant. And then there's that poignant moment with the empty crib on page 103 where the widowed Primrose Pengelly breaks down in tears because she knows that she cannot cope with her newborn baby alone and has to give it away. It's Agnes Crabbe exorcising her demons on paper. The clues were all there in the book.'

'So "Evidence of MC" was evidence of Millicent Crabbe, a secret daughter, and not Millicent Cutter,' said Banton.

'Exactly. The daughter that Agnes had to give away but whose name she took from her own mother and then immortalised with the creation of her great fictional detective. And the name Falk was there in black and white too, in Mrs Handibode's notes. The Falks were great friends of the Gobbelin family and Iris worked for them as a maid. She arranged the adoption.'

'It all makes sense,' said Banton. 'So when Mrs Handibode wrote "ANDREW T – SECRET", I guess she suspected that Andrew Tremens knew about the baby too. It was the big secret that he was going to reveal in his talk.'

'But I still don't see how all of this relates to the murder of Shirley Pomerance,' said Jaine.

'Bear with me. We'll get there,' said Quisty. 'We can't be sure what prompted Agnes to write *Swords into Ploughshares* nearly fifteen years after the end of the war, but I suspect it was something to do with the realisation that the daughter she'd never known would have been turning sixteen and becoming an adult. Maybe the enormity of what she'd done suddenly hit her. It's certainly true that she didn't write anything else for a while after *Swords*. And when she eventually did, her writing changed direction and she wrote those three dreadful Trayhorn Borwick books.

Perhaps she just found it too painful to write about anyone called Millicent.'

'That's some amazing detective work you've done,' said Banton.

'Just following the connections,' said Quisty, smiling. 'But, while I'm happy to take the credit, do remember that Mrs Handibode worked it out before I did. She's the smart one.'

'*Swords into Ploughshares* is such a curious book – so different in style and tone to the ones before and after it – and I knew there had to be a reason not accounted for in Agnes's diaries,' said Esme Handibode. 'There's so much focus on the futility of war and on the importance of children. And then it suddenly came to me . . . what if she'd had a child herself? Of course, I was sceptical. As I say, there's no mention of a child in her diaries which, otherwise, are very detailed. It would be an extraordinary omission, especially as a diary is, by nature, a very private and personal record. And, besides, how would she keep the child a secret from her mother? Did you know, by the way, that Agnes's mother was called Millicent?'

'I remember reading it in *The Secret Queen of Crime*,' said Molly Wilderspin.

'You read that terrible book?' scolded Mrs Handibode.

Miss Wilderspin nodded sheepishly.

'It actually wasn't that hard to keep it secret,' said Tremens, picking up the story. 'Her mother had already pretty much withdrawn from public life after she'd lost her husband and son to the war. She took to her bed and didn't get out of it until she died. It was Agnes's best friend Iris who helped her with the birth and who shared the duties of looking after the baby. It's all there in her diaries, even if it isn't in Agnes's. The woman was a saint.'

'So all of those stories of baby-snatching and cannibalism I heard as a lad might have had some basis in truth,' said Vic. 'If locals heard the baby crying, for example.'

'Quite possibly,' said Tremens. 'I suspect that Agnes was suffering with depression during her confinement and didn't leave the house, a behaviour she continued for the rest of her life. That's maybe why she couldn't write about the baby, at least not directly. She instead incorporated her grief into *Swords into Ploughshares*.'

'I became convinced that she'd had a child but not having access to Iris Gobbelin's diaries I didn't know whether the child had died or whether Agnes had perhaps given it away,' said Mrs Handibode. 'So that's when I started searching through the parish records.'

'Iris wrote in her diaries that it was obvious that Agnes wasn't suited for motherhood,' said Tremens. 'She wrote that she formed no bond with her baby and seemed indifferent to its fate. So Iris arranged for the baby to be adopted by a family in Bowcester. She worked for the Falks as a chambermaid and knew them to be a kind and generous family, though childless.'

'I had an inkling that I was on the right track after finding a Millicent Falk, born in 1916, mentioned in the 1931 census data,' added Mrs Handibode.

'So little Millicent Falk grew up just a few miles away from her real mother and wholly ignorant of the fact that she was adopted?' asked Shunter.

'Yes. And I'm not sure that she ever found out who she really was,' said Tremens. 'Maybe that was another reason why Agnes never mentioned her in her diaries – so that the child would never find out. But Millicent had a lovely childhood in every other way and she eventually married a jeweller called Henry Welter in 1939. They had their first child, a little girl, in 1945.'

'Who grew up to be Brenda Tradescant?' asked Miss Wilder-spin.

'No, who grew up to be Shirley Pomerance,' said Tremens. 'Oh!'

'Henry was killed in combat just a few weeks before Shirley was born, tragically near to the end of hostilities, and Millicent's life started to fall to pieces,' Tremens continued. 'All of a sudden it began to mirror that of her mother's, although she didn't know that, of course. But she didn't have an Iris Gobbelin to help her, and she couldn't cope as a single mum, especially as she had to keep the jewellery business going all by herself. She put Shirley up for adoption at ten months old but it did her no harm to be brought up by the Pomerance clan. They were academics and they brought out the best in her.'

'But Millicent did keep her second child,' said Miss Wilder-spin. 'After she remarried?'

'That was Brenda, yes,' said Tremens. 'She was born in 1947, two years after Shirley. By that time, Millicent – now known as Milly – had married Ivor Tradescant, a coal merchant.'

'You can just imagine how I felt when I completed assembling the family tree and the awful truth was revealed that one of my chief rivals and critics, and a writer of truly atrocious stories, is the granddaughter of Agnes Crabbe,' said Mrs Handibode. 'I could have wept. I had nightmares imagining what Brenda Trad-escant would do if she ever found out that she was the rightful heir to the Crabbe estate. I saw bookshelves filled with endless badly written new Miss Cutter novels, all carrying some kind of gravitas and authenticity because they'd been written by a blood relative. The thought was too dreadful to contemplate. Of course, I didn't know then that she had an older half-sister – one who can actually write – and that I needn't have worried. All I knew was that I had to keep my findings to myself and hope that no one else would find out the secret. But then Andrew did.'

'So the "S&B" in Mrs Handibode's notes was Shirley and Brenda,' said Banton.

'Quite so,' said Quisty. 'But she wasn't the only person to have figured things out. When Andrew Tremens found the Gobbelin diaries, he realised the magnitude of the story and decided to turn these revelations into a public event. You can see the appeal, can't you? Agnes Crabbe's secret baby is adopted and grows up with no knowledge of who her mother is. She then gets married, has two daughters of her own, one of whom gets put up for adoption, and neither child has any idea who their real grandmother was. Then Andrew discovered that Brenda Tradescant also had children who were put up for adoption. Triplets, in fact.'

'Three generations of adoptions. It's no wonder the trail was so cold,' said Banton. 'So Tremens had the idea to track down Brenda Tradescant's sons to involve them in planning a splendid jape for the festival?'

'Indeed,' said Quisty.

'Big mistake,' said Jaine.

'Very big mistake,' said Quisty.

'By sheer bad luck, the first triplet I tracked down turned out to be the bad penny of the family,' said Tremens. 'Well, the baddest penny.'

'Fireball,' said Mrs Handibode.

'Yes. Fireball XL5 Zodiac Venus Matic Robert Zoonie the Lazoon Savidge to be precise,' said Tremens. 'I asked him if he would get in touch with his brothers to ask if they would be part of the event. I had no idea that he'd had no contact with them in years and they'd pretty much written him out of the family. Nor did I realise how much he hated Brenda – his birth mother – for having put him and his brothers up for adoption. The Savidges were terrible parents, and Fireball, Thunderbirds and Stingray had a miserable childhood. In the meantime, as a cover, I spread about a rumour that a new Crabbe book called *Wallowing in the Mire* had been discovered, just to throw people off the scent.'

'Oh. So it's not true then?' said Miss Wilderspin, disappointedly.

'Well, it might be. There's plenty of evidence for it in both Crabbe's and Gobbelin's diaries. But I haven't found a manuscript yet. Anyhow, I knew that a rumour like that would sound authentic and bring the crowds in. So, the plan was to run the show in three phases: Phase One – I'd have Shirley Pomerance and the Savidge triplets hidden among the crowd in plain sight, all dressed as Miss Cutter. We'd pull Brenda out of the audience and do the whole family reunion thing with her three sons who she hasn't seen since they were put up for adoption as babies. Phase Two – we'd bring Shirley out of the audience and do the big reveal that she's Brenda's hitherto unsuspected and long-lost older half-sister and aunt to the triplets. And then, after Brenda had got to grips with that, we'd spring the Phase Three surprise on her *and* Shirley, i.e. the fact that they are both Agnes Crabbe's granddaughters. It would have been fantastic.'

'But Fireball spoiled it,' said Miss Wilderspin.

'That is the understatement of the year,' said Tremens.

'As I understand it, the young Brenda Tradescant was a bit of a tearaway,' said Quisty. 'Her parents both ran businesses and she was something of a latch-key child. And then she got pregnant at seventeen and decided not to have a termination.'

'Pregnant with triplets at seventeen,' said Banton. 'Wow.'

'They were all born prematurely and suffered oxygen starvation, which may be partly to blame for their behavioural issues,' said Quisty. 'And Brenda suffered crippling post-natal depression, which may explain why she chose to have no contact with them after they were adopted. Unfortunately, the Savidges were not the best choice of adoptive parents. Back in the early sixties, they didn't have the vetting mechanisms for adoption we have today I'm afraid. Mr Savidge senior was, and still is, a nasty piece of work.'

'It's extraordinary that the Savidges adopted all three,' said Banton. 'That's a hell of a lot to take on. But then again, I imagine that the boys would have hated to be separated. Twins and triplets have very close bonds.'

'They were mere babies at the time and probably hadn't formed those bonds yet,' said Quisty. 'And I'm afraid that Mr Savidge wouldn't have given two hoots about their feelings anyway. All he was interested in was the family allowance and all the other monetary benefits that came with adopting three identical baby boys. He drank it all, of course, and they had a wretched childhood.'

'No wonder they turned out the way they did,' said Banton. 'And Fireball was the worst of the three.'

'Certainly the least under control. As I understand it, Stingray manages to keep his anger at bay with tablets but has occasional lapses. And Thunderbirds is so drunk most of the time that he barely functions as a vicar.'

'I hear he's gone completely doolally since the siege and has had to be shipped off to a psychiatric hospital,' said Jaine.

'Poor bugger,' said Banton.

'But Fireball . . . well, he's a different kettle of fish altogether,' said Quisty. 'He's a manipulative, greedy, unrepentant narcissist and he cares about no one but himself. He embraces his bad behaviour; I think he sees it as a gift rather than as an affliction. He's spent his whole life fighting, whoring, gambling and drinking. He shouldn't be still alive, the amount of drugs he's injected or swallowed. And there's a long, long list of angry loan sharks and drug-dealers who would love to get their hands on him.'

'So when Mr Tremens told him who his great-grandmother was, all he saw was pound signs,' said Woon. 'You don't have to be an Agnes Crabbe fan to recognise that she's a gold mine.'

'And, presumably, this was when he also found out who his birth mother was,' said Banton.

'As I understand it, he already knew her name because Thunderbirds had found out years before and told him,' said Quisty. 'But he'd never met her. And why would he? She wasn't of any value to him. And Brenda Tradescant had made it clear that she didn't want to reconnect with her sons as it would upset her partner, an easily shockable bank manager. But Andrew Tremens didn't know any of this when he approached Fireball. And the first thing that Fireball did when reunited with his birth mother was try to emotionally blackmail her into paying off his gambling debts.'

'But Miss Tradescant refused, even after he showed her a threatening note he'd received from loan sharks,' said Banton. 'She was adamant that he must sort out his own mess.'

'Her refusal is why he then blurted out to her that she was Agnes Crabbe's granddaughter,' said Quisty. 'He told her that she could afford to clear his debts because she would soon inherit the estate.'

'Which is why she went to the village hall to get confirmation from Tremens,' said Woon.

'And we all know what happened then,' said Quisty.

'Fireball and Brenda turned up at the village hall in his van, just as I was rehearsing the event with Miss Pomerance,' said Tremens. 'This would have been around quarter past three. And of course, I hadn't told either woman about their Agnes Crabbe connection at this point. Then there was the most terrible fight. Fireball was accusing his mother of being some kind of uncaring martinet. And she was shouting at him that he was irresponsible and stupid. So then Fireball effectively scuppered the whole event by telling Brenda and Shirley that they were sisters and both heirs to the Agnes Crabbe estate.'

'How selfish,' said Miss Wilderspin.

'But then Shirley told him that he wouldn't get a penny because, as the older of the two sisters, she would most likely inherit the estate and, if she did, she would use the money to set up a charity to help new writers,' said Tremens. 'Well, talk about red rag to a bull. Something just seemed to snap inside him. He grabbed up a baseball bat and hit her with it full in the face. She staggered around for a second, pleading for someone to help. She tried to make a grab for Brenda who recoiled but not before Shirley got a grip on her pearls.'

'Ah! The pearls were hers!' said Shunter.

'But then Fireball hit her again,' said Tremens. 'I heard bones crack and she went down like a sack of spuds. I thought I was going to be sick.'

'And this is where you enter the story?' said Shunter.

'Indeed,' said Mrs Handibode. 'I'd mislaid my copy of *Swords into Ploughshares* and recalled that the last place I'd seen it was on a wall in Handcock's Alley. So I went back there in the hope of finding it, which I did, thankfully. There's five years' worth of research in those notes. Anyway, as I passed by the rear of the village hall I heard shouting. Naturally I was curious so I crept closer to take a look. The rear door was ajar so I popped my head inside and I saw what had happened within.'

'Oh, how awful for you,' said Miss Wilderspin.

'I can't pretend that it wasn't a shock. Miss Pomerance was clearly already dead and Fireball Savidge – I didn't know who he was then of course – was furiously stabbing her body with a knife.'

'Why did he do that?' asked Shunter. 'She was already dead, surely?'

'Brenda had grabbed a carving knife from the kitchen area with which to defend herself after seeing what he'd done to Shirley,' explained Tremens. 'But Fireball easily disarmed her.'

'Then he had a kind of fit,' said Mrs Handibode. 'He started stabbing Miss Pomerance's body repeatedly with the knife and shouting, "This is all your fault!" over and over again while looking at his mother. No one argued with him after that, mark my words.'

'And that's why her fingerprints were on the knife handle,' said Miss Wilderspin.

'But his weren't,' said Shunter.

'He had gloves on,' said Mrs Handibode. 'Anyway, I must have gasped or made a noise or something because he saw me at the window and dragged me inside.'

'So what about the business of disguising Shirley as his mother by leaving her bag by the body?' asked Miss Wilderspin.

'I'm not really sure why he did that,' said Tremens.

'I think that was simply a delaying tactic, putting the police off the scent by making them think it was Brenda who'd been killed,' said Shunter. 'I also think leaving the note with her body was intended to make us believe that she'd been killed by loan shark heavies.'

'Ah, the threatening note. It belonged to Fireball of course,' said Miss Wilderspin.

'Yes,' said Shunter. 'I think that, in his naivety, he assumed that we'd believe she was Miss Tradescant from the clothes and the handbag. Miss Pomerance was wearing an almost identical Miss Cutter outfit to Miss Tradescant's for the event.'

'Anyway, after the stabbing, Brenda went into a kind of stupor, like a walking daze. She just tuned herself out of reality. And I think that Fireball suddenly realised the gravity of what he'd done,' said Tremens. 'He tied our hands and frogmarched us to his van and locked us inside. I didn't dare argue, not with a man who could do such terrible things. Brenda went quietly too.'

'Leaving the trail of pearls,' added Miss Wilderspin.

'Yes, but not Esme. Definitely not Esme,' said Tremens. 'She fought and kicked all the way.'

'Hooray!' said Miss Wilderspin, clapping her hands with glee.

'Once we were outside, I thumped him in the tummy as hard as I could and made a break for it and started running up the canal towpath,' said Mrs Handibode. 'Sadly, I wasn't speedy enough and he caught me.'

'Which is when you dropped the book,' said Miss Wilderspin.

'Yes. I was so upset to lose it.'

'He tied our legs together to prevent another escape attempt and then, once we were all in the van, he took his mother's handbag and left it next to Shirley's body,' said Tremens. 'He threw our mobile phones in the canal and the rest you know. We were held in those boats overnight, Esme and Brenda in one, me in another, while Fireball drank and ranted and agonised over whether or not to kill us. Then, after Pamela Dallimore escaped on that tractor, he set a series of fires and loaded us into the van and drove off to find a good spot to do us in. I think he planned to bop us on the head and throw us in the canal unconscious to drown. Thank god we were found in time.'

'Thank god he didn't just knock us out and leave us there to burn in those sheds,' said Mrs Handibode.

'This is all so complicated,' said Molly Wilderspin. 'It's like a really bad murder-mystery novel.'

'Appalling,' agreed Esme Handibode. 'It doesn't follow the rules at all.'

'And that's why none of your amateur detective Millies would ever have solved this case,' said Shunter. 'Murder investigation isn't some romanticised game. Real life is nasty and vicious and cruel and maddeningly random. As I said before, there are no rules.'

'There isn't even a happy ending to this story,' said Mrs Handibode.

'There isn't?' said Molly Wilderspin. 'He got caught and no one else died.'

'Yes, but with Miss Pomerance dead, Tradescant not only inherits the Crabbe estate but the rights to the books too,' said Mrs Handibode. 'The wrong sister got killed and now Tradescant is a millionaire and the canon is doomed to become a slew of terrible pornography.'

'Oh dear,' said Miss Wilderspin.

Outside in the street, as the final few Millies climbed aboard their coaches and said their goodbyes, a busker serenaded them with a rowdy rendition of South Herewardshire's best-known folk song, 'Go to Hell!'

So when you feel the hand of fate and hear the deathly knell,
Remember good men go to Heav'n – but you might go to
Hell!

You might go to Hell! You might go to Hell!

Remember good men go to Heav'n – but you might go to
Hell!

The festival was over for another year.

And, in a modest little house on the outskirts of Bowcester,
Helen Greeley and Troy Savidge, as he'd now accepted that he
had to call himself, lay sleepily in each other's arms.

'I'm so sorry about your brothers. What an awful day you've
had,' said Greeley.

'It's been the weirdest weekend of my entire life,' said Savidge.
'But I'm very glad it happened.' He kissed her on the forehead.

'Do you know why I'm here, in this bed, right now?' said
Greeley.

'Not really, if I'm being honest.'

'It's because you accept me as I am and not as the person
everyone wants me to be.'

'You know I don't give a toss about all that stuff, don't you,
Helen?'

'I do and that's why I'm here. Do you believe in love at first
sight, Troy?'

'Is that what you're saying has happened?'

'I don't know,' said Greeley. 'But . . . this feels right. At least,
for the moment it feels right.'

'Good enough for me,' said Savidge. He kissed her gently on
the lips.

30

'They reckon the new hotel will be open in time for next year,' said Vic, looking out of the pub window at the busy building site opposite. A powerful bulldozer rumbled past. 'I'm not sad to see the old one being torn down. It was always a bloody eyesore. So, how's the job-hunting going?'

'To be honest, I'm not really trying,' said Shunter. A pint and a pie at lunchtime had become something of a regular habit in the three months that had passed since the festival. His waistline was evidence of the fact.

'I did happen to notice that they're after admin staff at Bowcester Police Station,' said Vic. 'That's the kind of job a lot of ex-cops do, isn't it?'

'It is. But not me,' said Shunter. 'I never tried for promotion because I wanted to avoid all the admin that came with it, so I'm damned if I'll do other coppers' admin in my retirement. I need something a little more challenging. Besides which, the pressure is off for a bit. I've earned a tidy little sum from the newspapers in the past few months. It means I've been able to get the builders in to make the cottage look a bit more like the house that Mrs Shunter deserves.'

'Very nice.'

'Oh, and did I tell you? I've been approached by a publisher.

Apparently, there's some interest in me writing a book about the Pomerance murder. Quisty put them on to me.'

'Now there is one very clever man.'

'And another reason why I'd never go back to police work. I'm an old-fashioned flatfoot and the villains I caught were old-fashioned villains. They threw a brick at a window, grabbed some jewellery and ran. These days, the bad guys click a mouse and steal ten million pounds from a bank on the other side of the world. The bad guys are super-smart and the coppers have to be even smarter. I'm a dinosaur, Vic. PC Plod. I had my time. The job needs people like Quisty now.'

'Don't put yourself down, Frank. Quisty may have figured out all the ins and outs of the case but it was you that found the bad guy and caught him. Don't forget that. So, are you going to do the book?'

'I'm not sure I have the skills to write a book.'

'Maybe you could get someone to ghost it? Brenda Tradescant, maybe?' said Vic. 'I hear she's changed her name to Brenda Crabbe now that she's recovered from her ordeal.'

'God help us, eh?' said Shunter. 'But I couldn't afford her now even if I wanted to. Her first "New Adventures of Miss Cutter" book has already notched up half a million in pre-orders. It's called *A Dagger in My Reticule*. The innuendo couldn't be any less clumsy if it was in a *Carry On* film.'

'There's always Pamela Dallimore.'

'She's busy writing a sequel to her biography of Agnes Crabbe. It'll probably be just as inaccurate. And sell just as well.'

'What about your friend Molly then? Didn't she want to write a book?'

'Ah Molly! She was something of a dark horse, wasn't she?'

'She was?'

'Didn't you hear? She's shacked up in some cottage in the Scottish borders with Esme Handibode's husband and is working on her first murder-mystery novel.'

'Really? But I thought she was . . . you know.'

'Gay? Me too. But it turns out that she and old man Handibode have been at it like knives for years. She just played up the whole dotty lesbian spinster thing to put Esme off the scent. Call myself a detective? I didn't see that one coming.'

'She had me fooled too,' agreed Vic.

'And the two of them have been enjoying their own private joke at Esme's expense. They wrote a series of terrible romance novels together under the name of Simone Bedhead. It's an anagram of Esme Handibode, you see.'

'Ha!' barked Vic.

'Once Esme figured it out she flipped her lid. That's why Molly and Mr H beat a hasty retreat. Mind you, Esme got her own back. Three years ago, she inherited a great deal of money from a dead uncle but didn't tell her husband about it because she suspected he was having an affair, although she didn't know with whom. She kept the money to herself and was using it to fund her obsessions. He'll never see a penny of it now.'

'Speaking of dark horses, what about Savidge and Helen Greeley?' said Vic.

'I saw them on TV the other night at the Golden Globes,' said Shunter. 'The media loves them. Calls them "Helen and Troy".'

'He is one jammy bastard. I don't suppose we'll ever see him back here in the Onion again.'

'I would have thought that would please you,' said Shunter. 'What did you call him? Kryptonite for publicans?'

'Yeah, but he'd have exactly the opposite effect on business now. He's Helen Greeley's fiancé. And he's Agnes Crabbe's great-grandson.'

'He grilled a good burger too.'

'Yeah, he did.'

'Hell of a festival, Vic,' said Shunter, smiling. He raised his glass. 'Here's to next year.'

'There are a few who would rather forget it, I think,' replied Vic. 'Blount for one.'

'He brought that all on himself. If he hadn't been so paranoid he'd have had a nice little case there. A real promotion booster.'

'He must have felt like a complete idiot after that press conference.'

'Announcing the wrong murderer is a bit of a *faux pas*,' agreed Shunter.

'And a vicar as well! I heard that he was transferred over to Morbridge and busted to Detective Sergeant. He only kept his job because, luckily for him, the armed response guys caught most of the flak.'

'It'll be interesting to see if the events of this year have an effect on festival attendee numbers,' mused Shunter. 'Maybe the Millies won't be quite so keen to play detective next year.'

'I wouldn't count on it,' said Vic. 'I bet you they'll be back in greater numbers and they'll be worse than ever. They've had a taste of it now.'

In the library of her house in Oxford, Esme Handibode finished boxing up her extensive Agnes Crabbe collection, all ready for the auctioneers to collect. The sale would generate a tidy sum, certainly enough with which to build upon her collection of Ngaio Marsh first editions. She loved Marsh's writing; in fact, there were times when she thought to herself that she could have been the

New Zealand author in a previous life. And, now that her enthusiasm for all things Miss Cutter had soured, she rather fancied forming an Inspector Alleyn Society.

And, of course, it would be the best of all the Inspector Alleyn societies.

Afterword

In 1990, my late father Michael began writing a murder-mystery novel called *The Chief Constable Regrets*. Under his pen-name of Myghal Colgan, he'd already had many articles published – mostly in country lifestyle and Cornish interest magazines – but what he really wanted to do was tell stories.

Set in 1931, the novel centred on the surviving members of a platoon from the Duke of Cornwall's Light Infantry who had fought together in the First World War. Dad had been research-ing the historical background for a number of years and was determined to get his facts right. He was the sort of person who needed to meticulously work out the plot and the background for his stories before he started writing them and, in those pre-Internet days, that meant a lot of letter-writing and book-reading and visits to libraries and museums. I can remember long tele-phone conversations with him (I'd left the family home in Cornwall in 1980 and was working as a police officer in London) when he would tell me all about some new fact he'd discovered and how he planned to incorporate it into the book. He was also very lucky to have known Dame Daphne du Maurier, who was living in Tywardreath near Fowey at the time, and his discussions with her always left him sounding childishly excited and inspired. However, I also recall his frustration over never seeming to have any time to devote to the book; a frustration that any author who isn't lucky enough to derive their main income from writing knows all about.

Dad was also a police officer, a career detective who specialised in homicide. And, because the Devon and Cornwall Constabulary covers a huge area, being called upon to work on an investigation in somewhere like Plymouth or Exeter would often see him working anything up to 150 miles from his beloved typewriter at the family home in Hayle. There were no affordable laptops back then, of course, and he would often spend weeks away on some serious investigation that took up all of his time.

But then in 1985, and despite good health and fitness, he suffered an unexpected and massive heart attack. He was forty-five, and very lucky to survive it. As he later wrote in an article: 'Vigorous external cardiac massage and three jolts of enough electricity to resurrect Frankenstein's monster had been needed to return me to the land of the living.' He was to endure several smaller but debilitating attacks over the next few years as his body tried to reject the damaged part of his heart. He also suffered painful arthritis of the spine and ribcage caused by the aforementioned cardiac massage, and this kept him from sitting for too long at a keyboard. But he remained cheerful and upbeat and continued his research whenever he felt strong enough.

By 1990, he was feeling stronger, he'd retired from the police, Mum had bought him an expensive newfangled word processor, and now, finally, he had the time and the energy to devote to his unwritten novel. But he was never to finish it. Dad suffered a final heart attack in 1991 and died at the age of just fifty-one.

It took a little while to sort out his affairs and part of that involved me going through the boxes of floppy discs on which he'd stored his work. I was able to convert his documents to a modern format, which means that I now have them safely backed up and preserved for posterity. Everything he'd ever written was there but, to my dismay, there was no trace of Dad's novel on any of the discs. Nor was it stored on his processor's onboard memory. I knew that he'd written some of it because he'd once read an extract to me over the phone. But now, it seemed, whatever he had written had somehow been tragically lost.

However, a couple of years later, while sorting through some box files of material that Dad had accumulated while researching our family tree, my brother Si found some notes relating to the novel and twenty-four printed pages of text comprising the first three chapters of the book. The notes seemed to suggest that maybe this was how far he'd got. In some ways, I hope that's true because I'd like to believe that everything he wrote has been saved.

In the quarter century since he died, people have suggested to me that I finish *The Chief Constable Regrets*. I love the idea of doing so but, sadly, I have no idea how. The only notes that Dad left behind relate solely to the characters, their backgrounds and their relationships; there are no clues as to the plot and I can't even be sure who commits the murders (although I can make an educated guess) or how. I wish I could remember details of the discussions we had back in the 1980s, but too much time has passed by. It might be possible to finish it one day, however. The one thing that no one in my family has found yet is Dad's notebook. He carried it with him everywhere and he was always jotting ideas down (I do the same thing myself). I assume that's where most of the historical details and his plot ideas were stored. If we ever do find it, who knows what might be in there? In the meantime, however, I thought it might be nice to incorporate some of his first murder mystery within the body of my first murder mystery as a kind of tribute to him.

The plot of *The Chief Constable Regrets* revolves around a group of demobbed soldiers who had all been part of a 'Pals and Chums Battalion' during the First World War. The War Office believed, and with some justification, that people from the same village, or cricket team, or college, would look out for each other during battle and make for a more cohesive fighting unit. Therefore, friends, colleagues and family members were often assigned to the same platoons. However, this also meant that, during the bloodiest engagements, the men who had enlisted together often died together. It was not uncommon for the entire male line of a family to be wiped out in a single push, the evidence of which can be seen on war memorials up and down the country. In Dad's novel, the survivors return home and settle back into civilian life, but then someone starts to systematically kill them off, one by one, presumably because of something that happened to them all during wartime. Maybe they left someone behind for dead? Maybe there's a German survivor with a personal grudge? Maybe it's a soldier suffering from post-traumatic stress disorder; what they called 'shell-shock' back then. The fact is, I just don't know. However, I thought it might be fun to use the general plot of *The Chief Constable Regrets* as the plot of a book called *Swords into Ploughshares* written by my fictional detective, Agnes Crabbe. By doing so, it meant that I could use Dad's novel, or part of it at least, as an important component of *A Murder to Die For*. You'll find Dad's writing in Chapters 5, 16 and 17 when Mrs Handibode and DI Blount are reading extracts from the book.

This year marks the twenty-sixth anniversary of Dad's tragically early death and I still miss his charm, his wit and his wisdom every day. But, by using extracts from *The Chief Constable Regrets* in this book, I'm making sure that he finally got his novel into print – or some of it, anyway – and I hope that this will, in some small way, commemorate a talented writer, a genuinely lovely man and a wonderful dad.

And I don't have to pay him any royalties!

He'd have laughed at that.

Stevyn Colgan
Somewhere near Nasely, South Herewardshire
March 2017

P.S. Do you fancy playing detective yourself?

In a sudden fit of mischievousness, I found myself hiding the titles of ten Agatha Christie novels throughout this book. They all take the form of anagrams and they're all proper names. So, for example, I might have hidden *The Pale Horse* as the name 'Peter Holeash', or *Absent in the Spring* as 'Tessa Perth-Binning', or I could have turned *Giant's Bread* into a place name like 'East Brading'. As it happens, I didn't use any of those in the book. But I did use ten others.

Good luck finding them all!

You can read more about this book and its characters at
amurdertodiefor.blogspot.co.uk

Acknowledgements

I have a lot of people to thank for helping me to make this book a reality. And I should start with the Queens of Crime.

The earliest origins of the detective fiction genre may lie with stories like Edgar Allan Poe's 'Murders in the Rue Morgue' (1841) or Wilkie Collins's *The Moonstone* (1868), but it is generally held that the era of the classic crime-fiction novel really began with Sir Arthur Conan Doyle's Sherlock Holmes stories, which entertained readers from 1887 to 1927 (and, indeed, still do to this day). But, as Holmes and Watson bowed out, the twenties and thirties ushered in the 'Golden Age of Detective Fiction', which was dominated by women writers and four in particular – Agatha Christie, Dorothy L. Sayers, Margery Allingham and Ngaio Marsh – the so-called 'Queens of Crime'.[1] Their books were immensely

---

[1] There are many other authors worthy of note including Josephine Tey, Anne Hocking, Anthony Berkeley (writing under several noms de plume including Francis Iles and A Monmouth Platts), J. Jefferson Farjeon, Freeman Wills Crofts, G. K. Chesterson, E. C. Bentley, R. Austin Freeman, Michael Innes, Philip MacDonald . . . but space precludes my listing them all. And, of course, for the purposes of this book, we must also add Agnes Crabbe to the list. Oh, and if you're interested in where Agnes Crabbe 'came from' (people are always asking authors where they get their ideas), she was inspired by the extraordinary story of photographer Vivian Maier whose work, like Crabbe's novels, only became known after her death. Do look her up. Her story is fascinating.

popular; Agatha Christie alone has sold over two billion books – a figure beaten only by Shakespeare and the Bible. Her stories have been translated into more than 600 languages and have spawned endless TV series and film adaptations.

But why is reading a classic British Golden Age 'whodunnit', with its often exaggerated snapshots of the English class system and bloody murder being done in the billiard rooms and libraries of great country houses, so much fun? I suspect that it's because it's rather like playing a game, and just like *Cluedo*, the board game based on the genre, there are rules.

In her excellent book *Talking about Detective Fiction* (Faber and Faber, 2010), the late crime queen P. D. James summed it up very succinctly:

> What we can expect is a central mysterious crime, usually murder; a closed circle of suspects, each with motive, means and opportunity for the crime; a detective, either amateur or professional, who comes in like an avenging deity to solve it; and, by the end of the book, a solution which the reader should be able to arrive at by logical deduction from clues inserted into the novel with deceptive cunning and fairness.

And, back in 1929, the British author and theologian Ronald Knox made an attempt to codify these rules by creating 'The Ten Commandments for Detective Fiction' (I mentioned them in passing in Chapter 29). They are that:

1. The criminal must be mentioned in the early part of the story, but must not be anyone whose thoughts the reader has been allowed to know.
2. All supernatural or preternatural agencies are ruled out as a matter of course.

3. Not more than one secret room or passage is allowable.
4. No hitherto undiscovered poisons may be used, nor any appliance which will need a long scientific explanation at the end.
5. No Chinaman must figure in the story.
6. No accident must ever help the detective, nor must he ever have an unaccountable intuition which proves to be right.
7. The detective himself must not commit the crime.
8. The detective is bound to declare any clues which he may discover.
9. The 'sidekick' of the detective – the 'Watson' – must not conceal from the reader any thoughts which pass through his mind: his intelligence must be slightly, but very slightly, below that of the average reader.
10. Twin brothers, and doubles generally, must not appear unless we have been duly prepared for them.

These rules were very much in my mind as I 'played the game' and, I happily confess, I broke as many of them as I could.[2]

Why?

Because, dear reader, real life doesn't have a rule book! That's something I learned very early on in my thirty-year career as a police officer. I hope you'll take my deviance in the satirical spirit in which it was intended.

And now, on to the twenty-first-century thanks.

---

[2] The year before, in 1928, American mystery writer S. S. Van Dine – real name Willard Huntington Wright – created a rather more wordy 'Twenty Rules for Writing Detective Stories'. They are easily found online and cover much the same ground as Knox's 'Ten Commandments'.

This book isn't the first novel I've ever written. But it is the first that I've felt was good enough to put forward for publication and I am deeply indebted to everyone at Unbound for believing in it. Particular thanks go to Mathew Clayton and Phil Connor, who got the ball rolling, to Anna Simpson and Imogen Denny for guiding the book through its production, to Mark Ecob, Neil Gower and Livi Gosling for the amazing cover illustrations and design, and to my stalwart editors Tamsin Shelton and Justine Taylor.

Big thanks also go to my agent Piers Blofeld and to my cadre of critical readers, sounding boards and drinking chums: Jason Arnopp, Terry Bergin QC, Dr Sue Black OBE, Ben Dupre, Jo Haseltine, Steve Hills, Andrew Hodge, Andrew Kerr, Dr Sarah K. Marr, Dr Erica McAlister, Stuart Peel, Justin Pollard, Phil Speechley, Janice Staines, Tammy Stone, Huw Williams, Stuart Witts and the ever-dapper Michael Dillon who often had to endure my enthusiasm across the bar at Gerry's Club, Soho. Thanks too to Mark Vent for suggesting the term 'Millies' and to Keith Sleight for the ACDC (Agnes Crabbe Detective Club). And additional thanks are due to Chris Addison, Jimmy Carr, Paul Cornell, Graham Linehan, Robert Llewellyn, Richard Osman and Holly Walsh for 'bigging me up', and to Neil, Sandi and Stephen for their generous cover quotes.

I must also mention Dawn, my long-suffering wife, who not only had to put up with me disappearing for days on end while I wrote this blighter, but who also had to endure me watching pretty much every episode of *Marple*, *Poirot*, *Jonathan Creek*, *Columbo*, *Murder, She Wrote*, *Midsomer Murders* and any other murder mystery that's been on the telly for the past eighteen months. She's a saint. And, annoyingly, she's much better than me at guessing whodunnit.

ACKNOWLEDGEMENTS

*

Lastly, my warmest thanks must go to the wonderful, generous people who made this book possible by putting their hands in their pockets (or in other people's pockets) to help fund its publication. In these sadly unenlightened times, when bookshops are as rare as ropes of tortoise hair, when publishers have become frustratingly risk-averse, and where the accountants have taken over the asylum, it's people like them that keep writers like me on the bookshelves. I thank them from the bottom of my heart and they're all listed on the following few pages.

If you've enjoyed this book, do consider helping to fund other new books at unbound.com.

Roll the credits . . .

Supporters

Unbound is a new kind of publishing house. Our books are funded directly by readers. This was a very popular idea during the late eighteenth and early nineteenth centuries. Now we have revived it for the internet age. It allows authors to write the books they really want to write and readers to support the books they would most like to see published.

The names listed below are of readers who have pledged their support and made this book happen. If you'd like to join them, visit www.unbound.com.

Alfie Adams
Lily Adams
Rosie Adams
Mark Adley
Andy Aliffe
Annie & Moo
Helen Arney
Jason Arnopp
Tim Atkinson
John Auckland
Ann Aucott
James Aylett

Corinne Bailey
Duncan Bailey
Olwyn Bailey
Linda Baker
Jack Baldwin
Jason Ballinger
Sally Banks
Tony Bannister
Damian Bannon
Stephen Mark Banton
Ruth Barlow
Helen Barrell

Paul Barrier

Bruce Barrow

Emma Bayliss

Paul Baynes

Andrew Beale

Naomi Beaumont

Bob Beaupré

Paul Beebee

Adrian Belcher

Sarah Bell

Justin Bellinger

Julie Benson

Julian Benton

Terry Bergin

Jonny Berliner

Kathy Bibby

Sue Black

Claire Bodanis

William Bonwitt

Ruth Bourne

Mark Bowsher

David Bradley

David Bramwell

Donal Brannigan

Jen Brant

Richard W H Bray

Sherry Brennan

Billy Bridgeman

David Briers

Tom Brown-Lowe

Lesley Bruce

Chris Budd

Joseph Burne

Alex Burnett

Pauline Burney

Ali Burns

Christine Burns

Marcus Butcher

Barbara Campbell

Andrew Campling

Phillipa Candy

Jill Cansell

John Carney

Jimmy Carr

Catherine Catherine

David Lars Chamberlain

Guy Chapman

Kenny Chapman

Laura Christie

Karen Christley

Meagan Cihlar

Elanor Clarke

Dane Cobain

Jonathan Coe

Martin Coleman

Liam Colgan

Gina R. Collia

Nick Collier

Debra Collis

Louis Constandinos

Andrea Cook

Paul Cornell

Jake Courage

John Crawford

Brian Crowe

Ruth Curtis

Lotte D.

Trisha D'hoker

Steven D'Souza

Steve Dabner

Michelle Dale

Margaret Danby

Ade Dann

Geoffrey Leonard Davey

Nick Davey

Suzanne Davidson

Matt Davies

E R Andrew Davis

Eta De Cicco

Amanda de Grey

JF Derry

John Dexter

Miranda Dickinson

Michael Dillon

Mar Dixon

Thomas Dommett

Michelle Donlan

Wendalynn Donnan

Pam Dormer

Winona and Matthew Doubrava

Jenny Doughty

Allan Douglas

Connor Doyle

Marjorie Drysdale

Jessica Duchen

Helen Ducker

Rachael Dunlop

John Dunn

Ben Dupre

Robert Eardley

Richard East

Dan Edwards

Scott Edwards

Brian Eggo

James Ellis

Sean Ellis

Dan Ellis-Jones

Ptolemy Elrington

Chris Emerson

Clare England

Jennie Ensor

Derek Erb

Tony Evans

Simon Everett

Kash Farooq

felion247 felion247

Charles Fernyhough

Lindsey Fitz

Joann Fletcher

Josh Fletcher

Piers Fletcher

Bevin Flynn

Lizzy Fone

Colin Forrest-Charde

Hilly Foster
Clare Fowler
Paula J. Francisco
Julia Frost
Paul Fulcher
William Gallagher
Natalie Galustian
Ash Gardner
Alison Garner
Craig Gay
Andrew George
Alex Gilbert
David Gilray
Darren Goldsmith
Elma Goncalves
John Goonan
Heather Govier
Jacinta Gregory
James Gregory
Zena Gregory
Paul Groom
Stephanie Grootenhuis
Johnny Guiliani
Laura Gustine
Geoff Haederle
Anita Hall
Dave Hall
Lyn Hamer
Richard and Ruth Hammond
Paul Hargrove
Jan Harkin

Pat Harkin
Wendy Harper
Christine Harris
Steve Harris
A.F. Harrold
Faye Hartley
Jacqueline Hartnett
Joanna Haseltine
Adam Hawkesford-Johnson
Liz & Mike Hayward
Di Heelas
Jean Henderson
Sandy Herbert
E O Higgins
Mike Higgins
Kathryn Hill
Matthew H. Hill
Catherine Hills
Steve Hills
Roger & Jayne Hinds
Peter Michael Hobbins
Andrew Hodge
Kitt Hodsden
Ivonne Hoeger
Paul Holbrook
Graham Holland
Sarah Hook
Stephen Hoppe
Spring Horton
Sheila Howes
Kaj-khan Hrynczenko

Rachael Hulbert
Julian Hynd
Johari Ismail
Kevin Jackson
Oli Jacobs
Crispian Jago
Clifford Jaine
Rosy James
Lisa Janda
Alexander Jegtnes
Paul S. Jenkins
Amanda Lloyd Jennings
Paul Jeorrett
Jacqueline John
Marjorie Johns
Kitty Johnson
Al Johnston
Joyce Jones
Peter Jones
Tim Lund Jørgensen
Juanjo
Elena Kaufman
Roger Keeling
Peter Kelly
Sian Kelly
Chloe Kembery
Andrew Keogh
Dan Kieran
Patrick Kincaid
Shona Kinsella
Doreen Knight

Ian Knight
Stefanie Kudla
Pete Lacey
George Ladds
Mit Lahiri
Terry Lander
Nick LaPointe
Anna Lawrence
Iszi Lawrence
Ewan Lawrie
Jimmy Leach
Sean Leahy
Samara Leibner
Graham Linehan
Gemma Lodge
Angela Lord
Ann Lowe
Ric Lumb
Betty Lumley
Cherise Lund
Mathew Lyons
Rhona Macfarlane
Tina Mackenzie
Alistair Mackie
Eva Maclean
Cait MacPhee
Gaynor Maher
Rebecca Major
Philippa Manasseh
Simon Manchester
Dave Mansfield

Sarah K. Marr

Melanie Martin

Natalie Martin

Vic Martindale

Dawn Mason

Victoria Mather

Trevor Mathers

Mike Matson

Pamela McCarthy

Iain McCulloch

Mo McFarland

Megan Mcgarrick

John A C McGowan

Alan McHenry

Anne McHenry

Aven McMaster

Jamie McNeil

Liane McNeil

John Melhuish

Steven Melvin

Andrew Merritt

Anne Miller

Ron Mills

Margo Milne

Janey Milner

John Minshall

John Mitchinson

Ken Monaghan

Cate Moore

David Moore

Rachel Elizabeth Moore

Gareth Morgan

Michael Mosbacher

Sami Mughal

Buck Mulligan

Lauren Mulville

Emma Murphy

Jessica Myles

Carlo Navato

Chris Neale

John New

Chris Nicholson

Marie-Jose Nieuwkoop

Jenny Noakes

Vaun Earl Norman

Laura North

Lewis Nyman

Jan O'Malley

Brendan O'Neill

Lisa Oldham

Matthew Oliphant

Ismail Omar

Lev Parikian

Marian Parkes

Samantha Parnell

Steve Parrington

Rebecca Pascoe

Jenette Passmore

Sarah Patmore

William Penman

David Perez

Rob Perks

Morgan Phillips

Jennifer Pierce

Kim Pike

Jane Pink

Justin Pollard

Mary-Anne Pontikis

Beki Pope

Daniel Pope

Matthew Porter

Niall Porter

Jackie Potter

Lee and Toni Tye Preisler

Lawrence Pretty

Rhian Heulwen Price

Trevor Prinn

Francis Pryor

Andy Randle

Paul Rawcliffe

Chris Rawlinson

Rebecca Read

Colette Reap

Simon Reap

Jenny Reaves

Karen Redman

Val Reid

Natalie Reis

Stephanie Ressort

Christopher Richardson

Deborah Rivers

Elizabeth Robson

David Roche

Alan and Angella Rodgers

Sid Rodrigues

Auriel Roe

Kenn W Roessler

Felicitas Rohder

Ricky Romain

Kalina Rose

Deb Ruddy

Andy Rudkin

Jenny Ryan

Bernie Sammon

Nat Saunders

Helen Saxton @Charaderie

Neil Sayer

Dan Schaffer

Danny Scheerlinck

Paddy Schoop

Shaun and Bethany Sellars

Richard Selwyn

Arsha Sharma

Sue Sharpe

Tracy Sherman

Keith Sherratt

Rebecca Sickinger

Silver Girl

Neil Simmons

Ian Skewis

Mark Skinner

Anne Skulicz

Niall Slater

Keith Sleight

Peter Sleight
Guy Smart
Toni Smerdon
Jennie Smith
Jenny Smith
Peter R Smith
Carolyn Soakell
Lili Soh
Fiona Sothcott
Emma Southon
Jenny Sparks
Angela Speechley
Philip Speechley
Liam Spinage
Elizabeth Stahlmann
Janice Staines
Karen Staines
Lauren Staines
Roy Staines
Ruth Staines
Terry Staines
Murray Steele
Bernie Stefan-Rasmus
Rosalind Stern
Kathryn Stevenson
Lucy Stewart
Tabatha Stirling
Tom Stone
Tanya Stratton
Tiffany Sullivan
James Sumnall

Mark Sundaram
Chris Swan
Mary Tao
Chris Taylor
Helen Taylor
Matthew Taylor
Andrew Tees
Sonia Tennant
Cheryl Thallon
Barbara Thomas
James Thomas
Mike Scott Thomson
Simon Tierney-Wigg
James Tobin
Stuart Todd
Sandi Toksvig
Kelly Townshend
Donna Tranter
Dan Trudgian
David G Tubby
Sarah Turnham
D@lekc@tus Tweeticus
Cara Usher
Shaun Usher
Vicky Vagg
Sue Vaughey
Mark Vent
Jose Vizcaino
Jenny Wade
Barry Wake
Damon L. Wakes

SUPPORTERS

Nick Walpole
Breda Walton
Julie Warren
Simon Watt
Andy VaultsOfExtoth Wears
Alan Webster
Rachel Wheeley
Colin White
Florence White
Jennifer Whitehead
Lindsay Whitehurst
Senga Whiteman
Carol Whitton
Heather Wilde
Suzie Wilde
Kitty Wilkinson
Geoff Williams
James Williams
John Williams
Julian Williams
Sean Williams
Alexa Wilson
Derek Wilson
Elizabeth Wilson
Gavin Wilson
Laurie Winkless
Magz Wiseman
Stuart Witts
Gretchen Woelfle
Rowena Wonnacott
Stacey Woods

Ray Woodward
Liz Wooldridge
Paul Woolgar
Colin & Rachel Wright
Jenna Marie Wright
Robert Wringham
Linda Youdelis